ACCLAIM FOR ALFREDO VÉA, JR'S
LA MARAVILLA

"Beautifully written, thematically vital. . . . I can't get it out of my mind."
—Carolyn See, *Los Angeles Times*

"Brilliant, rich, extravagant . . . a lustily told tale. . . . *La Maravilla* almost does it all!"
—*Washington Post*

"In search for the Great American Novel, it's time to start looking in this direction. . . . Unforgettable."
—*East Bay Express*

"A vibrant and colorful tale of magic, history, and human sorrow."
—*San Francisco Focus*

"A powerful and enchanting story. . . . From the very first sentence I was trapped and could not resist."
—Isabel Allende, author of
The House of the Spirits and *Paula*

ALFREDO VÉA, JR., was born in Arizona and lived the life of a migrant worker before being sent to Vietnam. After his discharge, he worked a series of jobs, ranging from truck driver to carnival mechanic, as he put himself through law school. A practicing criminal defense attorney in San Francisco, he published his first novel, *La Maravilla*, in 1993 to great acclaim. *The Silver Cloud Café* is his second novel.

The
Silver Cloud
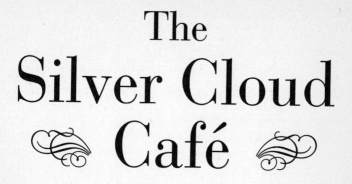 Café

Alfredo Véa, Jr.

A PLUME BOOK

., New York 10014, U.S.A.
TZ, England
Penguin Books Australia Ltd, Ringwood, Victoria, Australia
Penguin Books Canada Ltd, 10 Alcorn Avenue, Toronto, Ontario, Canada M4V 3B2
Penguin Books (N.Z.) Ltd, 182–190 Wairau Road, Auckland 10, New Zealand

Penguin Books Ltd, Registered Offices: Harmondsworth, Middlesex, England

Published by Plume, an imprint of Dutton Signet,
a member of Penguin Putnam Inc.
Previously published in a Dutton edition.

First Plume Printing, October, 1997
10 9 8 7 6 5 4 3 2

Grateful acknowledgment is made to the following for permission to reprint from
previously published material:

"Sin City" (Gram Parson) © 1973 Irving Music. All rights reserved. Used by permission
EMI. "Angel from Montgomery," words and music by John Prine © 1971 Walden Music,
Inc., and Sour Grapes Music. All rights reserved. Used by permission Warner Bros.
Publications U.S. Inc. "Tennessee Waltz," words and music by Pee Wee King and Redd
Stewart © 1946. All rights reserved. Used by permission Acuff-Rose productions.

Ⓟ REGISTERED TRADEMARK—MARCA REGISTRADA

The Library of Congress has catalogued the Dutton edition as follows:
Véa, Alfredo
    The Silver Cloud Café / Alfredo Véa, Jr.
        p.   cm.
    ISBN 0-525-94077-4 (hc.)
    ISBN 0-452-27664-0 (pbk.)
    1. City and town life—California—San Francisco—Fiction.   2. Mexican
Americans—California—San Francisco—Fiction.   3. San Francisco (Calif.)—
Fiction.   4. Supernatural—Fiction.   5. Revenge—Fiction.   I. Title.
PS3572.E2R43   1996
813'.54—dc20   96–6772
                                                                      CIP

Printed in the United States of America

*This book is dedicated to the immigrants,
whose vision of America is always the truest . . . and to
all migrant farmworkers past and present; above all, the
manong and the braceros—the gentle protectors and
messengers of my brown youth.*

Thank you,

Earl J. Waits, Stanley A. Read, Annette Oropeza, Miguel Govea, Prof. Roberto Cantu, Brendan Conroy, Dr. Boyd Stephens, Norma Paz Garcia and Bert Feuss, Allyn Stern, Charles Bourdon, Anita Minot, Barry Melton, Cynthia Marcopulos, Robin and Bob Mayer, Freddi Kirchner, Barbara Ulanoff, Stuart Kohler & Assoc. Investigations, Chris and Theresa Ordoñez-Gauger, Robert L. Allen, Janet Carter, Brother Timothy Mc-Daniel of the Ordinis Fratres Minorum, Cecelia Estes, Raj Inder Chabra, Vimal Kumar Dhanjibhai, Wally Bradley, Juana Paiste, Julia *y* Lupe Gomez, Lorraine Terry, Eugene *y* Dora Carbajal, Mary *y* George Avila, Mercedes *y* Cruz de Santiago, Dewitt Clinton Allen, Jr., Muriel Allen, Judith Beery, Edwin Brush, Ernest Dust, Jeanne Gerard Bartolini, Deborah England, Alfred and Jan Giannini, Elizabeth McCarthy, Lori Catlow, Trudi Fields, all the people of Morelia, and the wonderful women of Ocumicho.

A very special thank-you (*¡otra vez!*) to you: Rosemary Ahern, my editor, for your amazing insight and audacity; to you, Sandy Dijkstra, for your legendary persistence and energy; and to you, Susan Breall, for your support and your incredible patience.

And finally ... *mis hermanos del alma*: De and Eric, Dewitt Clinton Allen III and Eric Russell Caine, two brilliant misfit boys who were there to greet me when I left the fields of America for the streets of the United States.

We were such a moody tercet of young toughs, so loaded with weltschmerz; fully armed with Nabokov, Thelonius Monk, and García Lorca. We were vandals who defaced villanelles; brooding hoodlums who loitered on Pyrrhic feet, tagged in scansion, and so earnestly protected our stanzas of turf from the tyranny of the iamb.

Together, despite ourselves and despite the titanic allure of lesser options, we chose the word as the weapon. *Sigue igual.*

They are death-defying,
lofty and hazardous in their
handsome strength.
Yet you'll never see them,
you'll never track them down.
Still—they do leave behind
a faint earthbound trail:
scattered here and there are
broken men and broken women who,
like old Jacob, limp along,
injured by the burden of light.
But even these living signs
are far too few to follow.

"Only think rare thoughts,"
the chosen cripples say,
"and they will swoop down
here to grapple.
Remember well the past
—and laughing sweetly,
they will break your hip."

—A. V.

I

*I*N *the deep El Greco darkness between a small Mexican cantina and a drawbridge that straddled two worlds, there was the long stretch and uncurling and the slow, white unfurling of glowing wings as twin narcissus rose from the bramble. Los angeles se estaban yendo. The angels were leaving. Two world-weary beings of light were packing their bags and speaking softly in auras of glimmering glissando.*

The pair were perpetual brothers, or perhaps they were sisters, or perhaps both. But they were certainly unlike poor mortal siblings who are held together for those fleeting instants of childhood, then are forever separated by adulthood, reuniting now and again to glance backward at a common womb. These two would possess for all time the sexless breasts of fledglings, the secret language of twins, the murmurs of sleepless children gazing eternally at the same immutable wallpaper.

They had both been rank neophytes to the mundane riddle of this place, but now they were seasoned sojourners who had hidden behind Lot's door, posed for Leonardo's brush, stayed the hand of Abraham, and they had followed the very first braceros . . . heartsick Hebrews brought into Egypt to toil beneath the sun. These beings of light had seen so much, but this errand had somehow been different.

Each asked in levitating queries if they should confess their part in the strange story of Raphael's Silver Cloud to a surly god who works nights and is always tired, to a god who is still undecided on the exact shape of round. For isn't He a glacier-slow painter and isn't She a model who delights in movement? And hadn't the sweet mother of all things grown addled and unbalanced of late, given to sudden, violent outbursts of birth song and to a cold, orphaning cadence?

Dismayed by the presence of mortal emotion, the twins pulled away while struggling against a tugging twinge of regret. Having seen Orion from the backside, having rested on Rigel, how could this be? For wasn't this the place of all places in the universe where both poems and tumors were secretly planted in the forming minds of children? Wasn't it here that the mediocre walk was prized above the pirouette or the pas de Basque? But wasn't it also here, beneath their feet, that uncommon lives were lived and uncommon deaths were died?

San Francisco, May 15, 1993

The body looked as though it had been floating in the ocean for weeks and not for just a few hours. It was racked by water damage and had been subjected to severe insect predation, and an unusual wound ran from the man's chin down to his lower gullet, a ghastly combination of laceration and burning. It was as though the man had been gutted; then each side of the slit had been carefully cauterized, leaving the center of the wound closed, yet open. During the autopsy, the coroner was able to look down into the wound and see his own face reflected from the stainless-steel table beneath the body.

One of the rookie cops who had helped pull the body into the police boat had heaved his guts out for hours afterward, defiling the integrity of the crime scene with his late dinner. No one, not even the oldest cops, had ever seen anything like it. Not even the Chief Coroner knew what to make of it.

The Inspector looked out over the water toward the buildings at China Basin. He was a tall man and proud of it. He wore a light, plaid polyester suit that was too tight in the chest and cut too high above his new, hand-tooled cowboy boots. It was the popular "cop-reluctantly-in-a-suit" look, meant to show disdain for fashion in general and for high-priced, well-dressed defense lawyers in particular.

Other cops understood the important statement that such clothing made. They supported and respected it as a fraternal badge. Uniformed officers dreamed of the day when they too could reluctantly wear such a suit. The only problem was that sometimes the outfit was confused with the "old-jock" look.

Grown men who still lived on their high school football exploits always wore the same kind of suit. Also, the outfit bore an uncanny resemblance to the classic "hanger-on" look, the look of a man who has come to realize that he will never leave his hometown.

The Inspector squinted into the green, reflective water of the slough. Yesterday must've been a full moon, he thought. It seemed to the Inspector that every emergency vehicle in San Francisco had been on the road at the same instant. The jail ward and the psychiatric ward at San Francisco General Hospital had been filled to overflowing the evening before. But the two cases that everyone in the Homicide Detail was talking about were this murder on the Fourth Street Bridge and the weird fire that happened less than a half mile away.

There had been a report of arson at a Mexican bar over on Seventeenth and Shotwell. The fire had quickly gone to three alarms, and it was feared that the blaze would spread to several nearby warehouses, but when the trucks got there the fire was completely out and the alleged arsonist had committed suicide in dramatic fashion. Rumor had it that the deceased had mutilated himself before making his fatal leap from the rooftop. The Arson Inspector had found a strange silver tower up on the roof of the bar during his search for the fire's source. A poor, unfurnished shack perched on top of the tower had been the arsonist's home.

A second fire had been reported at a warehouse in the area south of Market. A Gypsy and an enormous transvestite had been detained as suspects, then released. Someone had set a small but bright fire on the top of a water tower. The Arson Inspector concluded that it was probably the work of some mischievous kids.

Calls about the fires had come in from as far away as Richmond and Berkeley. People in the Oakland hills, fifteen miles away, saw the flames, but the Arson Inspector's report indicated that there was almost no damage to the building or the water tower. He reported that the fire's measured footprint at the Mexican bar was just a couple of square yards. The silver tower had barely been scorched. Although he could not explain how so little structural damage could produce such enormous flames, he was able to confirm an arson, as unburned gasoline had been detected on the roof of the building.

The signed statement of an accomplice was included in the arson report. A naked woman clutching a hand mirror had been arrested and questioned at General Hospital. It had taken three cops to remove the mirror from her grasp. When the woman had begun screaming that she was blind without the mirror, one of the nurses had taken it from a sealed evidence envelope and returned it to her. The Inspector shook his head. What was this world coming to?

"The world would be a better place if every damn arsonist committed suicide," he muttered to himself. "It would be even better if they killed themselves before lighting the fires," he laughed.

He was a veteran officer who hated the computerized, talk-show world into which he would soon retire. He hated the new categories of crimes that had come into existence in the last few years: child abductors, disgruntled employees, and twelve-year-olds with machine guns. In the old days the world had been so much simpler. There had been real cops and real criminals, the good and the bad, and a hazy but visible line in between.

Now there were amateurs and civilians involved; stalkers, postal clerks, and kids who killed for designer shoes. The police force itself looked different now. There were female cops with degrees in sociology and gay cops who patrolled the Castro District and Noe Valley. The world even looked different. Now there were Guatemalans and Russian Jews everywhere you looked. Nowadays you needed an interpreter at every crime scene.

He spat his disgust onto the muddy bank, and as he did so he noticed that the man who raised and lowered the drawbridge was watching him through the window of his small control room. The Inspector laughed and spat again, a gesture calculated to prove to anyone watching that he didn't mind being seen laughing and talking to himself. Such actions were, after all, the prerogatives of a deep thinker.

The face in the window remained expressionless. The Inspector pulled out the sneer he reserved for any man who could be contented with raising and lowering a two-lane bridge. The sneer had no effect. The old man smiled in return. The Inspector exercised his final option.

"Damned immigrants. They're ruining the goddamn country."

He felt better now, not quite so exhausted. The incantation was soothing. "Damned immigrants."

For the first time, he noticed that a green cross had been crudely painted on the wall beneath the bridgeman's window. Had it been there last night? Yesterday's swing shift had certainly been a busy one. There had been this weird homicide on the bridge and the suicide at the bar, and the radios had been jammed all night long with crazy reports of unidentified flying objects, witches, and rockets.

The strange thing was that all of it had happened at the same time. It seemed like every soul in San Francisco had seen something last night at sunset and had tried to report it. But the only real eyewitness to the killing on the Fourth Street Bridge was the old man who was sitting up there in the control room. The man who was now grinning from ear to ear.

The Inspector walked from the edge of the slough and up to the bridge. After dodging a bicyclist and cursing at a motorist, he positioned himself at the exact center of a chalk circle that had been inscribed on the metal walkway. One of the lab technicians had drawn the circle. Most of the blood had been found there, within its circumference. A wide spray of blood led from the circle to the edge of the bridge and out onto the water. Debris ten yards from the bridge had been spattered with blood and with bits of viscera. The severed appendage had been found there, at the center of the circle.

He looked up toward the control room. The view was unobstructed, and the circle was directly beneath an overhead lamp that was situated just above the green cross. The light of the full moon combined with the light of the lamp would have made the bridge as bright as noon. There could be no doubt about it: Unless he had been asleep at the time, the old man in the booth had seen it all.

Next to the chalk circle was a pile of what seemed to be garbage. There were spatters of blood on some of the orange peels and paper cups, so it must have been dumped before the murder. The Inspector admired his own thought processes for a moment. He then picked through the pile carelessly with the toe of his boot, dismissing the garbage as irrelevant. As he did so, he admired his snakeskin boots, an early retirement present from his wife.

He walked to the stairway and began the climb up to the control room. He had made the same climb only hours before. The old man inside dutifully rose from his place at the window and opened the door for the police officer. He had done exactly the same thing last night.

"Buenas tardes," he said, bowing slightly and pointing toward an empty chair. Even as the old man bowed and smiled, he secretly cursed himself for doing it. He had inherited the bow from his father and from his father's father before him. What Indian in Mexico did not bow to authority?

"¿Quieres café y pan dulce?"

The old man offered both to the Inspector, who impatiently waved away the coffee and the tray of pastries. He was hungry but didn't trust any bread that came from one of those Mexican bakeries down on Twenty-fourth Street. The old man put the tray down, then took an *empanada de piña* for himself. His own cup of coffee was steaming on the window ledge.

"¿Quieres naranja?"

The old man pointed to a half-filled bag of oranges on a counter near his small cot. Next to the bag was a small can of green paint and a brush that was soaking in a jar of paint thinner.

"Can't you speak English? I know you can speak English," said the Inspector as he lowered himself into the chair. He then rose abruptly to look through the window and down at the chalk circle below.

"Totally unobstructed," he groaned as he resumed his place in the chair.

"Are you ready to tell me the truth?"

"I told you everything last night, señor," said Miguel. "I told you in Spanish and in my best English last night. I don't have anything more that I can tell you."

Miguel Govea, the man who raised the drawbridge, watched as the Inspector reached into his coat pocket and pulled out a notepad. It was the same notepad he had taken out the night before, and there were scribblings on the first page, perhaps one word for every ten that Miguel had spoken.

"You didn't make a statement, Mr. Govea," said the Inspector, "at least not something that I would call a statement. I've taken a whole lot of statements in my time, and believe me, I know a witness statement when I hear one. You sat in the same chair that you're sitting in now and you sang a song for me and my Spanish interpreter. Now, it was a nice-enough song, whatever the hell it meant, but not exactly what I expected from a man who had witnessed a grisly murder just hours before."

"There was no murder, señor," smiled Miguel. "How can God commit murder? Only men can make murder, that much I know about this life."

"Are you speaking from experience?" asked the Inspector. He raised his eyebrows in a practiced gesture that had once carried with it both menace and intimidation. But since his recent hair augmentation, it only served to raise those hairs that were strategically combed downward to hide his woven hairline. He remembered this fact and quickly went back to squinting.

"Have you ever killed someone?"

"Long, long ago . . . and *en mi Mexico*," answered Miguel. The *viejito* lowered his eyes in a reflexive, involuntary gesture of self-acknowledged guilt. His people, the Tarascans, had once fought the mighty Aztecs to a standoff, but they could not fight the allure of those Mexican army uniforms and the promise of a monthly paycheck. Dozens of boys from his own village had joined up. He had killed while wearing that uniform, but in reality the uniform had killed him.

"Just like you, I was following orders. I pulled a trigger, and I died along with my target. In the end, every uniform murders the one who wears it. The crime that I committed was legal at the time, and I have spent the rest of my life paying for that act of evil. I know now that the laws of men are not always lawful. *Sí*, señor, I have killed someone. And every night of my life, until last night, that someone has murdered my peaceful sleep."

The old man lost himself for an instant in the memory of his transgression. The memory was always hot and blinding in its brightness. It had burned a deep hole into the secret area just behind his forehead, and the old man kept all of his regrets stored in that hollow. Soft beads of sweat broke out now in an odd pattern just above the old man's eyebrows. Some of the sweat collected, then ran down past his left eye to form a laborer's tear. With a gnarled finger, Miguel lifted the tear from his skin, then held it up to look at it. "Are you going to arrest me, señor? I will go peacefully."

The old man used one hand to pull back some of his black hair where it had fallen forward and into his eyes. Most of his hair fell down the back of his neck, where it disappeared into his blue-and-gray Tarascan shirt and down between his shoulder blades. The action left a thin layer of Brylcreem on his gray palm. His face now clear, the *viejito* stared directly into the eyes of the policeman. The Inspector shifted uneasily in his chair, putting one boot up on the edge of a trash can. In doing so, he had successfully averted the Indian's piercing stare. This position felt much more authoritative, and it compensated for the envy he felt at the old man's abundance of hair. It just wasn't fair that a man who was over eighty should have so much hair.

The salesman who had sold the Inspector his expensive hairweave had taken great pains to explain that the appliance was 100-percent human hair: not hair that had been subjected to the debilitating effects of pollution and harsh shampoos, but hair purchased from Mixtec peasant women from southern Mexico. The Inspector had the uneasy feeling that his lovely new locks belonged on Miguel's head.

"You've got nothing to worry about. I've got no jurisdiction over anything that happens in Mexico. However, I do have jurisdiction over what happened last night not fifteen feet below your window." The Inspector was pointing down toward the deck of the bridge and raising his voice to compensate for a motorcycle passing below.

"Don't you understand, Mr. Govea? A man named Bambino Reyes was killed while you were on your shift, and his killer, some fellow named Cabiri, has been arrested and put in jail. The suspect had the murder weapon in his hand when he was apprehended. There was blood all over the blade. Cabiri has confessed to everything that happened, and you saw it all. We have in our hands what is commonly referred to as the smoking gun."

"If that were really true, you wouldn't need me," whispered the old man.

"We don't need you . . . not really."

His own lack of conviction annoyed the police officer. The Inspector was losing his patience, with the witness and with himself. Why on earth had he come back to the bridge to speak to this cryptic old anachronism? The officer considered putting the old man in custody overnight to loosen his tongue, but one look at Miguel told him differently. This crazy old fool would probably enjoy a night in the slammer.

"We can convict the suspect with what we have. We have the body and we have the confession by the perpetrator. Hell, Cabiri has made ten confessions. And they're all legal and Mirandized and signed."

"*Tienes nada, mi patrón.* You've got nothing. I can see it in your eyes right now, señor *fregado*. You didn't even listen to a word I said last night, did you?" Miguel was not bowing now. There was even a hint of anger in his voice.

The old man reached into a drawer located below the radio and bridge control panel and pulled out his Hohner Corona Mark II, a beautiful little accordion. It was the accordion of choice for *Norteños*. Flaco Jimenez had one just like it.

"Not again," sighed the Inspector, who rubbed his knit brow with his thumb and forefinger in a studied look of exasperation.

"There is no way that the knife you have seized and the man you have arrested could have made those injuries. No way."

The Inspector's face grew deathly serious. Without knowing it, he had raised his eyebrows again. He leaned toward the old man, unaware that the front edge of his hairpiece was now visible and suddenly unsure just who was controlling this interview.

"Then you have seen the injuries?" he asked gruffly.

"No, señor, but I saw him when the injury happened. It was no man that cut him open."

"Hate can make a man very powerful," answered the officer. "It can make a man do things he never thought possible. He wasn't just stabbed, you know. Hell, the guy who drives the coroner's wagon called it a desecration, and he's seen them all."

"*Escuchame,* he wasn't killed for hate," countered Miguel as he popped off the leather straps that secured the folded white

bellows of his instrument. The little accordion sang out grate-
fully as it inhaled its first breath of air in hours. Though Miguel
dearly loved his new accordion, he still missed his old one. That
one had been handmade in Mexico and was carried across the
border in December of 1939. It was still kept in a closet in his
small house in the Mission District. The old accordion maker at
Nineteenth and Shotwell had tried his best to repair it, but it was
too far gone. It was falling apart now, just like its owner. Both
Miguel and his old accordion had lung problems.

"You see," he continued as he ran his fingers over the keys, "it
was a *consagración*, not a desecration. There was a great gathering
to do a holy thing."

The Inspector leaned forward in his chair as he stared into
the ancient, lined face of the man who raised the bridge. Now he
was getting somewhere. A gathering was a conspiracy. A conspiracy meant a network, a web of frailties and foul appetites. It
meant a chain of intention and causation. And every chain had a
weak link.

A conspiracy meant more arrests and more self-serving statements. It meant retiring in a blaze of glory. Perhaps one of the
conspirators could even explain the bizarre injuries. The man
who had confessed could not . . . though he had tried again and
again.

"Who else was involved?" he asked.

"*Santos y espiritus y viejitos.* Saints and spirits and very old men
conspired with the heavens," said Miguel. "Believe me, there are
angelic powers here on earth, señor."

"Look," said the Inspector, "this was just another murder.
Two people—Cabiri and Reyes—met and one died at the hands
of the other. It happens every hour of every day in this city and
in every city in America." As he spoke he turned to look at the
skyline that loomed above the Fourth Street Bridge. "Hell, murder is one of our biggest industries and our fastest-growing ex-
port. It was just another murder, and we've got the evildoer in
custody, Mr. Govea."

"You don't even have the wrongdoer," answered the old In-
dio in a voice that was barely audible, "and the evildoer is dead.
All you have in your jail is a little hummingbird. Who on earth
can keep a *pájaro mosca* trapped in a cage?"

It was clear that the Inspector was losing his patience once more. His face was beginning to glow a deep red.

"Mr. Govea, I know all about you. I know you were once a junior officer in the *Federales*. I know that you resigned one day without giving any explanation whatsoever. Your superiors on the force attributed it to psychiatric problems. Your dossier indicates that you suffered from insomnia and that you were a gun-shy cop. You see, I had you checked out. You disappeared from your home in Guadalajara one day and never went back. You never told anyone in your family where you were going. You've never written to them in all of these years. You didn't even take your clothes with you. And before all of that you were in the Mexican army for years. You never rose above the rank of private. It seems you were an unhappy soldier, Miguel.

"You have never married. There are no children. You crossed the border at Juárez around nineteen forty. Your tax records show that you've been a migrant farmworker most of your life. It seems you've picked just about every damn crop there is. Cutting asparagus is quite a comedown from the *Federales*, don't you think? But you do know all about law enforcement, don't you?"

The old man shook his head and exhaled hard at the police officer. The blast of air hit the officer full in the face. It was a gesture of anger that all old Tarascan men eventually adopted. All of Miguel's brothers, wherever they were, living or dead, exhaled their anger in the same way.

"You were a cop and soldier," the Inspector continued. "You know there's no magic in killing, nothing to sing about. There's nothing mystical about any of this. It's the same old one-man-killed-the-other-man story. They fought over a woman or for money or drugs; it's that simple. It's always that simple. That's what every murder in this world is about! There's nothing else out there! It was either a cold, premeditated killing that you saw yesterday, or a heat-of-passion killing and nothing more. And you can forget self-defense. There is no evidence whatsoever that the deceased was armed. Now please, just tell me what happened here! What did you see?"

The old Mexicano pressed one of the keys on his Corona, then hummed softly to match the pitch. Realizing that he still had some of his *empanada de piña* in his mouth, he washed it down with a swig of steaming coffee. He cleared his throat, then hummed the note once more. He nodded to himself and began to squeeze out his beloved Tarascan waltz. As he played, the old man once again bore witness to another world even as the policeman's voice droned on and on. Looking westward, Miguel could see that the cherubim were leaving now, and their departure made him very sad.

"We know," persisted the Inspector, "that Bambino Reyes had been in town only two weeks when he was killed. The desk clerk at the Hotel Zee recognized the dead man's description in the newspaper and called my office. It seems that Reyes came up from L.A. on a Greyhound bus. We've tracked him through five or six flophouses in the Tenderloin. He's been picked up for vagrancy and public nuisance in almost every state in the Union. He had no identification on him and no possessions, just a few dollars and a lot of street maps. Did you know him? Do you know this guy Cabiri?"

Miguel resented being torn away from his vision by an unseeing policeman. He would say nothing now that was not called for by the tempo and key of his music. It was an ancient air from Michoacán. It was a timeless, unwritten song, once sung by hundreds, perhaps thousands of pilgrims who had been privileged to see the heavens touching earth. Though the tempo had been borrowed from the French, the melody and the lyrics were from the island of Janitzio, where the Tarascan people rose from the soil at the dawn of time.

"The things you ask about have happened before," he said over the music and his own flying fingers. "There are protectors on this earth. They've been here always. They live in places where people have forgotten to look, on the fringe of things. They are commanded by angels."

The Inspector closed his notepad, then angrily glanced at his watch. It had stopped. He took some comfort in knowing that the watch the department would give him at his retirement dinner would be more expensive.

"I have to go interview an arsonist now. It's a good thing that insane fool jumped last night or I'd have to interview two of them. When you have something to say to me that makes sense, give me a call." He pulled out his wallet, plucked out a business card. Rather than hand the card to Miguel, the Inspector let it flutter to the floor. He had wasted enough time. The Indian ignored the card and continued his explanation in song.

"I know what you think. You think that there are only men in this world, men and their desires. There is much more than that, so much more than that. I could guide you for just a moment, if you would let me. I could be your *gomecillo*, señor *ciego*. You see only your world and none of the thousands that surround you."

The Inspector had resumed his squinting as he walked to the door. All at once he was very glad that he would be retiring soon.

"I'm getting too old for this," he said to himself.

He stared coldly at the old man who was bent over his accordion, singing over the music. Every word was clear and understandable, but for the life of him the Inspector could not say what language he was hearing. And tonight there were new words to the old tune. Even the Inspector could tell that it was not quite the same song that he and his Spanish interpreter had heard the night before.

The officer opened the door while the old Tarascan Indian sang. He put his notepad away, and as he did so he felt beneath his left armpit for the comfort of his pistol. It was hanging there reassuringly between his arm and his chest, dangling from his second crotch. There would be a gaping hole in his side and in his self-image on the sad day that he took off his shoulder holster and his pistol for the last time. There was nothing in his life that could fill the emptiness.

He walked outside to the stairs and back down to the bridge. He was suddenly famished. He would go down to Donut Heaven on McAllister Street and order three glazed beauties and a cup of mud to go with them. Real food . . . and thanks to an easily impressed cashier, it was free.

"If it don't stink, don't stir it," he said to reassure himself about his case. It was a popular phrase around the Homicide Detail, where half-full cups of tepid coffee from Donut Heaven were abandoned on every shelf and desk. Still, something about this case wasn't right, didn't add up. But he had a body in the morgue and a suspect in custody who had confessed a dozen times. It was enough. It had always been enough. Let the jury figure it out. Twelve good citizens from the community would take one look at the suspect and convict him before the first witness was sworn.

"Señor!"

It was Miguel calling from up above. The old Indian had stuck his head out of the window. His shirt was open and his hair was flying behind him unrestrained. It was at least two feet long and black as a raven's feathers.

"The man on the rooftop . . . the old man who set the fire was not insane . . . he was chosen. His name was Humberto . . . Padre Humberto. He was pulled from right out of his grave, ripped away from his own death. His wounds were only temporarily covered over, and he was lured north to lead us. God sent out fliers and handbills; the sojourners read them, and we all came here. *Entiendes?* This army, this firing squad was handpicked! The little hummingbird was chosen!

"That was not a fire last night. It was *una pira.* It was a holy pyre that cleansed us all of our ancient sins! Last night many things were finally set right."

The old man was crying his words now. Tears were falling past his smiling lips. "I was there when he died, señor. I was standing right there when poor Humberto died! I saw him fall!"

The Inspector laughed, then continued walking. The old Indian was as insane as the arsonist who had jumped to his death! Now the old fool was claiming that he had witnessed both deaths. It was an impossibility. He had never left his control room, and the Mexican bar was not visible from up there. The arsonist and the corpse pulled out of the slough, Bambino Reyes, had died almost simultaneously, with about fifteen city blocks between them. There was absolutely no connection between the two deaths. He shook his head violently as if to clear it of foolishness. The Inspector then winced as he realized that something on top of his head had shifted as a result. The spirit gums were coming loose. The Inspector's dark aura was listing slightly to starboard.

"What's the story here? What really happened?" he whispered to himself for the last time as he walked past a small restaurant and toward his unmarked police car. The question died in his mind as he sat in the driver's seat and called in his next location to the dispatcher.

"Ninth and McAllister."

Even after all these years he could not say the words "Donut Heaven" into the microphone. He looked into the rearview mirror and carefully readjusted his hairline while imagining the dashing figure he would cut as he gave an accomplice arsonist the third degree in front of all those cute nurses. The thought made him smile. The crackle and static of the police radio was even more comforting. It seemed to pull him back into the present, the here and now, and far from the Indian in the control room.

He knew that he would soon miss the call signs and codes that were the official euphemisms for violence and human suffering. He pulled the car out onto Fourth Street and spun the tires as he hit the metal span of the bridge. He sighed with relief as he began to cross over the bridge and back into his own world of skyscrapers and panhandlers. Through his open window he heard the piercing sound of the accordion and the surprisingly strong voice of the old man, who was standing at his window singing to no one.

The old muezzin in his high minaret sang his sacred song to the cloying swarm of humbling memories that climbed his pant legs and shirt and covered his body and weeping face like mossy shoots from an invisible taproot.

He chanted in Tarascan words, in valiant verses of raisincake, milk, and maize to the hovering ancestral spirits that crowded his control booth. He sang to his beloved copper-faced brothers, wherever they were breathing and wherever they were interred. He intoned an auburn song of tamarind dyes and soft Tarascan cloth, of riven sash and epaulets—a Mexican plague of canticle and cordite. He sang a heartsome hymn of welcome forgiveness after so many blameworthy years in his own wilderness.

"Do you see them, Señor Inspector?" Using his face and eyes, the old man was pointing toward the sky. The Inspector slowed his car to look upward. He saw nothing but the rising moon.

"*Los angeles se van.* The angels are leaving. They've finished God's cutting. They've picked this field clean and they're leaving. They are going home to rest up and to wait for the next harvest."

The old Tarascan threw open the controls on his console. The green bridge began to rise as a signal to the heavens. A foghorn blared its warning, and colored lights flashed sequentially as the prostrate roadway rose groaning to its knees.

"There is great mystery here, but this is more than just a story of murder, señor." Miguel directed his words to the Inspector's vanishing car. "This is a story of braceros, both of this world and otherworldly, *de carne y hueso, y espectral.* Sometimes God sends His eternal workers down to do jobs on worlds where everything must grow old and pass away. And this is a story of harvests, both earthly *y sobrenatural,* not of this earth. They are asking a question right now. They are wondering if they should tell God that everywhere on this earth love dies on the vine."

Miguel turned his gaze downward to the currents that moved sluggishly below his bridge. He looked beyond the lapping scum and floating dregs and down into the lightless, nocturnal silt. For an instant, he thought he glimpsed a glowing fuse, a small point of blushing radium anchored deep in the rippling and melancholy abyss. He then raised his gaze; his eyes opened wide to see the angels as they climbed past the moon.

They were leaving now, and each was earnestly swearing the other to a solemn vow of secrecy, for they had tarried with mankind, and, upon seeing that the pain of life itself is holy, that sacrifice is the plate upon which celebration is served, they endeavored to keep the secret from God, for He is a sad, doddering old man and a sad, milky-eyed old woman who are forever destined to outlive their countless children. And She is rubbed barren with endless births and He is breathless and speechless, having built from nothing the first voice to utter the first word.

In a key two octaves above the spectrum of notions, their bloodless harmony as tight as the Everly Brothers', the departing duet sang an aria of couplets devoid of lyrics. They sang No—milky verses and honied refrains of No. They had decided in mute persiflage that they would return and report in as usual, that all the different worlds were one and harmonious.

They rose with the help of old Zephyrus, whose blue breath smelled of the mistral. Each impatiently brushed away the foxtails and burrs of living life that had collected in their hair, then dawdled a moment, breathing air akin to absinthe and hovering and giggling at a moon whose infatuation with earth has it trapped in a bad affair. They would return as always, return preening their primary remiges by mystic light, and they would return, keeping forever the secrets of Raphael's Silver Cloud.

II

San Francisco Civic Center, May 22, 1993

ON Polk Street the wide expanses of grass in front of City Hall were glutted with the colored bedding and the scattered litter of the homeless. Squads of squalid men gathered here and there, limping and groaning like lost detachments of a decimated regiment. Like living ghosts, they haunted the corners and curbs of the city, carving out cold cloisters and hidden catacombs in the full light of day.

Who could believe that each one of them had been born perfect and blameless and coated with the gleaming gloss of a mother's innermost hopes? It was as though they had all been thrown down from the sky, absorbing the impurities of the atmosphere while falling. They had been allowed to strike earth, where they now lay stunned and powerless to move in an alien world.

The homeless were being shunned by the city, as if an old Amish custom of punishment were suddenly revived. Inside City Hall, the City Attorney's Office had assigned Lex Dedwood, one of its lawyers, to do research on a possible ordinance that would clear the plaza of the wayward poor. In his latest official memo to the Mayor, the attorney presented a new statute that had incorporated whole paragraphs from Henry VIII's act for the punishments of vagabonds, rogues, and beggars. In his footnotes, he had included specific references to Elizabeth's act of 1562 against Gypsies, nomads, and counterfeit Egyptians, and the

1666 edict by Louis XIV providing for the punishment of Bo-
hemians and wanderers.

Each homeless man or woman held a cup or a hat for the
spare change that would be asked for that night. It is, a priori, a
basic rule of begging that no one will place money into the
naked flesh of an extended palm. The rule is spontaneously
understood in Byzantium, Bangladesh, and Berkeley. There
must be an inert, neutral entity between the mendicant and he
who deigns to give. Hats and cups lined Polk Street, Larkin, and
Van Ness . . . extended like the untouchable's broom to passing
sahibs.

Across McAllister the mass of dark, double-breasted suits was
pouring out of the state and federal buildings; white kids from
the front rows of a hundred untold grammar schools dutifully
raised their eager hands again, but this time for a taxi. En masse,
they had all recently turned away from sushi and after a small
bacchanalian flirtation with Cajun were on their way to Thai.
Above this lunchtime scene, the flagpole atop City Hall jutted up
over the trees; the blue sky behind it seemed open straight to the
sun, and cold.

Beneath it, Lex Dedwood, with an indignant new briefcase
slapping against his hip, walked toward the building. The lawyer
assigned to draft the ordinance against the homeless was anxious
to get back to his work. He had spent the entire weekend culling
usable language from a German tract called *Fremdrasse*, the alien
race, and from yellowed copies of California's old antimiscegenation laws.

A tall man walked past the attorney and in the opposite direction, past the main army of homeless that had made camp for
the past year in City Hall Plaza. He stepped carefully through the
tossed litter and rags and toward a bench where a brown-skinned
man had been sitting for an hour or so, enjoying the sun and
watching the mass of dispossessed. Behind him, a bored street-
sweeper had mistaken dog tags for gum wrappers.

Near the bench two ragged men, one black, one white, were
talking loudly to no one, neither facing the other; both were
guarding shopping carts that contained their life's inventory.
They could just as easily have addressed each other but never
would. Their words and the meanings behind them went out

and up, unheard, toward the heavens. It was as if they spoke separate languages, even though their alternating rages and soft soliloquies were somehow couched in English.

The tall man was Stuart Yentzer, a private investigator who specialized in criminal cases and who had the habit of changing his last name to fit his changing moods. The other man was named Zeferino Del Campo.

Not far from the bench, and away from the homeless, there were two groups of protesters carrying picket signs and standing on opposite sides of Polk Street. The group directly in front of City Hall carried anti-abortion signs stating emphatically that ALL LIFE IS PRECIOUS. This raucous group was obviously being antagonized by the unwanted presence of another group across the street, a group that carried signs imploring fellow citizens to ABOLISH THE DEATH PENALTY. One of their number had caused the antipathy by hastily drawing a new sign for himself: ALL LIFE IS PRECIOUS, BUT ONLY UNTIL AGE EIGHTEEN?

The tall man sat down on the bench next to Zeferino, stretched out his legs, and laced his fingers behind his head.

"Sorry about being so late, Zef," he laughed. "I didn't get your message until a few hours ago. I've just got to get a new answering service."

"The woman who answered the phone didn't even recognize your name at first," smiled Zeferino. "I tried two or three other names, but she was new on the job and it took a while for her to figure out just who you were. She said that you had an appointment this afternoon at the Lady in Waiting, but that she could have you meet me here beforehand. By the way, just what name are you using today?"

"Stuart Gontsermacher," he smiled, "because I like to make things happen. Would you look at this," he continued, looking around at all of the human refuse sprawled across the grass.

"Do you think somebody places ads in the rest of the country? 'Wanted: shadow boxers and toothless women, openings at the San Francisco Civic Center.' There must be sixty people talking to themselves within forty feet of this bench. Would you look at that, even a deaf-mute signing to himself! Christ Almighty!"

Both men laughed out loud. What did a man hear, who signed to himself?

"Yeah, the city that knows how has sure made homelessness criminal," said Stuart. "Some of these guys are younger than we are. Look at them. Women, kids . . . these people don't stand a chance against the cops and all those new ordinances that they're cooking up. Which angel of antiquity holds the key to this urban abyss? *Goldeneh Medina*," he sighed. The Golden Country.

"So, I hear you have work for me," said Stuart, awaking from his reflections.

"You probably knew about it before I did," smiled Zeferino. "It's been all over the front pages this week."

"I've read a little something about the case. Both newspapers misspelled your name. You picked up a weird one this time, my friend," said Stuart with a grin. "You've got a homicide case by special request of the client."

"Yeah, some strange old guy wants me to be his lawyer. Judge Garcia called and said the guy won't take anyone but me. They've appointed two lawyers to the case already, but he has refused to see either one of them. He even seems to know my name and something about my past. I don't know a thing about his case except what's been in the papers. David Garcia wouldn't give me many specifics over the phone. He did say that the prosecutor, Al Giannini, is going straight to the grand jury with it. I must admit that it sounds interesting. Do you know someone by the name of Miguel Govea?"

Stuart shook his head no.

"According to Judge Garcia, Miguel Govea is the guy that raises the drawbridge over on Fourth Street. Miguel found the body over by the Filipino restaurant there, between Berry and Channel streets. It seems that Señor Govea saw the body fall into the slough. He gave a statement to the police but refuses to talk to the press. The cops are very unhappy with what he's given them so far. He must have seen more than he's letting on."

"Carmen's restaurant?" asked Stuart Fresser, who was always hungry. His interest in the case had just taken a sudden leap forward.

"Yeah. But please interview Miguel Govea before you eat. You are worthless on a full stomach. Remember when we were there the last time? You had two full plates of adobo and *lechon* and over a dozen *lumpia.* Remember? That was the night when eight sailors from the Philippine navy sang 'The Impossible Dream' to the dinner crowd."

The two men laughed at the surreal memory. Every *f* in the song had been replaced with a *p.* The amplifiers had been set on full reverberation, and the sailors had been accompanied by an excessively loud electronic organ. The organist, a man named Placido Suave who billed himself as the Filipino Liberace, had been grinning weirdly above the keys. There were rhinestones set into his front teeth, and an electric candelabra had been glowing just above his keyboard.

"Yeah, some kind of weird mutilation," said Stuart, "the murder, not the singing. The *Chronicle* and the *Tribune* have been real quiet about it. They haven't even described the manner of death beyond the fact that it was brutal. It seems something very strange happened to that man. The *Examiner* says it was a ritual murder, but there's no description at all of how he died. They usually say whether it was a stabbing or a shooting. Nothing. Not a word. Just a gruesome ritual murder. Maybe it's like that crazy cult stuff down in Matamoros. There's been no statement from the Coroner's Office either. Not even a written statement from Dr. Stephens.

"The word on the street is that the victim was eviscerated. He was originally listed as John Doe number thirty-nine, but the suspect knew the full name of the deceased and where he was from. There was absolutely no form of identification on his body. The suspect even knew which village he was from back in the Philippines and every town the victim had been in since he left the Islands. He seemed to know everything about him. When you get hold of the autopsy report, call me and let me have a look at it. Promise me now?"

Zeferino nodded.

"I can't believe it," continued Stuart. "The papers say he confessed to everybody, even a traffic commissioner who was touring the jail. The suspect gives a full confession to every cellmate, to every inspector in the Hall of Justice, then he refuses to have a court-appointed lawyer. He even turns down Tony Tamburello, Doug Schmidt, and Stuart Hanlon to get your brown ass to defend him. He's got to be mentally incompetent!"

They both laughed out loud at his playful insult. Tamburello, Schmidt, and Hanlon were local attorneys whose proficiency in murder trials was well known in San Francisco and beyond.

"He's certainly not doing you any favors!"

As they walked along, Zeferino wondered why Teodoro Cabiri, the name of the suspect who had been arrested at the scene of the homicide, seemed to mean something to him when he was so positive that it shouldn't. There was a strange resonance to the two words, as though an unnamed and untapped memory had suddenly been given a location and a label. Teodoro Cabiri.

"Teodoro Cabiri—have you heard of him, Zef?" asked Stuart while turning a complete circle to smile at a woman with purple hair and black lipstick.

Zeferino wondered for a moment if the investigator had been hearing his thoughts.

"He was arrested at the scene of the homicide holding a big machete," continued Stuart. "The crime lab has confirmed that the victim's blood was on the blade."

"Never heard the name before in my life," said Zeferino, suddenly not so sure that what he was saying was true. "Such a strange name. Teodoro Cabiri. Is it a Greek name? Is he a Gypsy?"

"Are you going up to see him tonight?" asked Stuart.

"Yeah, we're both going to see him at the City Jail as soon as we're finished with this business of yours. Do we really have to go to the Lady in Waiting?" asked Zeferino with a feigned look of trepidation and distaste. "Remind me not to help you out anymore."

Stuart laughed. Both men secretly enjoyed the strange places that their jobs took them. Neither man had ever been seduced by the profound lie of social normalcy.

"Are you ready to go? Hey, where's the Kosher Cruiser?" asked Zeferino, his voice rising in volume to compensate for a noisy traffic jam in front of City Hall.

"It's in a white zone on Van Ness," smiled Stuart, with a gleam of pride in his eyes.

The Kosher Cruiser was a battered, one-eyed Toyota station wagon that had evolved an ecosystem all its own, the result of numberless meals consumed during countless uneventful stake-outs. The floor was a plush carpet of crushed fast-food contain-ers and the gray-green mold that springs spontaneously from mummified french fries and hamburger buns. A slick of relish and sweat glistened on the armrests and seats. The upholstery of the Kosher Cruiser was in constant ferment. Only Stuart could discern any semblance of order in his mobile chaos. He alone could read the glyphs in the rolling rubble.

Stuart kept a small ice chest in the backseat, hidden beneath a mound of manila files and candy-bar wrappers. It was his trea-sure, his secret ark. In the ice chest he kept a quart of milk, a bottle of seltzer, and a jar of Fox's U-Bet chocolate syrup. There was also a squeeze bottle of chicken fat, a half loaf of rye bread, and a butter knife, all lying on a bed of blue ice. He called it his Yiddish dowry.

The two rose from the bench simultaneously and began walk-ing across the park toward Larkin Street. In the skies overhead, in the lowest heavens, the Blue Angels, the navy's precision fly-ing team, was streaking by, practicing for their annual air show. The loud roar of their engines rattled windows and thrilled most onlookers. But it drove Vietnamese families indoors, where they hid in their Tenderloin apartments, shivering under beds and cowering beneath couches. It sent Cambodian monks flying pro-tectively toward their shrines. Zapotec mothers cursed the war-planes, then ran to hide their children.

Down below the green copper dome of City Hall, on Larkin Street, each controlled intersection had three chafing, careen-ing cars to run each red light. Each old lady in each crosswalk had two grave, middle-aged white men in leased Porsches to im-patiently curse her small steps. People who had consciously cho-sen their sculpted hairdos within the last thirty days were moving from restaurant to restaurant on Van Ness Avenue searching for the menu with the most adjectives. Clutches of leggy, profes-sional women with hair-oriented gestures tossed their tresses from the left shoulder to the right and back again with each look of concern, with each nod of conceited accord.

At the corner of Larkin and Golden Gate an imported car with an electronic voice was castigating a Laotian woman for standing too close to its seven coats of paint. When she turned away from the car, the child on her back no longer violated the vehicle's electronic airspace and the deathly metallic voice ceased.

The city had grown hard since the days when Hunter's Point was a shipyard bustling with workers and the long docks were dotted with lunch boxes. A mortal rigor had set in slowly, imperceptibly, as the number of office workers doubled and redoubled on the myth of a service economy. Workers had been replaced by investors, insurers, and market prognosticators. Men and women without calluses had come to town and sealed themselves into towering glass closets. Their disciples had followed closely behind, doing lunch and monotonously chanting the bottom line. New royalty had arrived, bringing their own priests with them.

They hid up there, wagering on work as if somewhere steel would still be smelted, as if somewhere in America dies were being cut and oxyacetylene was still being lit. As if human hands still spot-welded fenders. As if someone in America was still bending to cut the cauliflower, to caress the asparagus; as if black newborns down below weren't dying in their earliest sleep.

The city ossified as the corporations exported their jobs under the new rationalization of a "global economy," the old "free-trade" characterization having run its expedient course. When viewed from the thirty-first floor, the graffiti hastily scrawled on the tallest building's cornerstone was all but invisible.

"America is extinct in the wild."

When viewed from the thirty-first floor, the only thing that was clear was the price of things . . . not the cost.

Zeferino and Stuart stepped around the brooding, silent shaving-cream man, a black man who was never seen without his face and hair covered with a thick lather of Burma-Shave. Zeferino wondered aloud what mirror in the past the poor man might forever be staring into, a razor poised in his right hand. Only ethereal, vaporous creatures who maintained their heavenly memory could hear the sound echoing in his shaving ears, the sound of a pistol shot, deadened weakly by a desperate mouth fastened to a blue steel muzzle. His wife had killed herself one work morning, in a house long forgotten, in a nameless town in the Midwest. The new teapot in the kitchen had whistled as advertised, until the water evaporated and the pot turned black.

On their way out of the grassy plaza, Zeferino and Stuart greeted old friends of the sidewalks, the monkey man who had a pillowcase filled with photographs and drawings of monkeys, every kind of monkey known to man and a few marmosets and lemurs for good measure. His hands were warmed by two small monkey puppets. His last sane thought had been decades before in the Central Highlands of Vietnam. One morning, after discovering that the soldier he'd killed was a ten-year-old child, he heard whole families of spider monkeys screaming in the spreading, scorching tide of napalm.

They said hello to the marble man, Señor Canicas, an old Cuban who spent his time polishing his cat's-eyes and steelies before arranging them in the dust according to some unknown design and strategy. No one who ever walked by would recognize in the positions of the colored glass spheres the gun emplacements of the Playa Giron, the Bay of Pigs invasion.

Above the two men, the Wilon curtain of first heaven was shining seven times brighter than silver. Only high stratus clouds dared to mark its brilliant face. In those rare, radiant places where lowest heaven reached down to touch this world, the place that the prophets Enoch and Ezekiel called seventh earth, stunned half-men drifted along in a malaise, caught in a bright fog of forgetfulness and hearing distant sounds of another place and time. Some of these men, dolorous and silent, were the true descendants of banished Adam and fell here from the first man's earth of exile. Some were Cheyenne, some Romani; all were far from their own soil.

Other beings were living here who once walked on Adama, second earth, a fabled place of a dozen harvests a year and of gold lying wet and uncovered. Some were drunken *asparas*; some were passive watchers who clung to dank curbsides, angelic earthbound presences who have forgotten themselves. Before they were lost, kidnapped, or abused, they were golden children wrapped in a brief heyday of hope. Now they were confused, displaced, and forever doomed to a somnambulist's gait on Eddy Street and on Sutter. Now they were as lost as the ancient *grigori*, those angels whose fire had forever changed to flesh by mere contact with men of the lowest earths and with the daughters of those men.

Sixth earth was here, too, its edges having jutted upward into the cool air of the city. Hideous pieces of hell now poked out brazenly into the light of day. Its cozening denizens were everywhere, their hands in every till, their thumbs on every scale, their vile hearts' desire just a contract, an election, or a pistol grip away. Disoriented creatures from each sphere moved about among the fragments, the dust of their own worlds still clouding their eyes.

San Francisco always seems to be gleaming, glamorous, and babbling. It seems perfect to visitors and tourists, the way it looks on television and in travel ads. These people see only the canopy rising above the second floor and up to the fiftieth, and nothing beyond or beneath that. It is Adama, second earth, that they see, the name behind its name, the legendary land of melancholy toil. It is the realm above the mezzanine and below the flagpole.

Today a skyline obscured the sky, a skyline that was something the city had grown very fond of, the way a prisoner of war comes perversely to love his cell. And like the POW's dream-infested cell and those ubiquitous fawning pamphlets for tourists, San Francisco was full of insubstantial things: a metal-and-glass canopy sheltering imaginary labor; lease futures; productivity options; insurance-policy buyouts. Buildings that no one sleeps in, they are filled with manila files and actuarial charts, the mere shadows of lives.

"As above, so below," said Stuart, quoting the hoary maxim of the Hebrew sages and the ancient cabalists. "The tree of life has been left untended. Which one of us"—Stuart paused, surveying the sprawling city around him—"is going to be Virgil?"

"But here," answered Zeferino, whose gaze had turned upward, "the sinners are the ones closest to heaven."

The tall structures above their heads were climate-controlled, hermetic shells; there was no frozen music to be found in their form. If you listened with the ears of seraphim, placed your ear directly against the side of a building, you could hear the scuffling, the dutiful, officious rubbing and friction of flannel suits in staid, discrete combat over someone's money.

If you looked with the eyes of watchers, you would glimpse

Tziah, fourth earth, where Chinese, Mexicans, and Russians washed dishes and cooked in the kitchens of French restaurants. Pretending to be urbane Romans and suave Parisians while in the dining rooms, they smoked and laughed in their own languages at the back doors of every café and boutique.

On Dolores Street long-headed Mayans and tough, wiry Zapotecs stood on street corners, waiting for construction work, while locals used the same corners to ask for a handout. In the Tenderloin, you saw reclusive Hmong tribesmen learning to make change and to fry eggs over easy. You saw hundreds of huddling Asian seamstresses, their necks craned in concentration, piecing together miles of dry fabric, the pads and straps of an exclusive line of French swimwear.

The real city by the bay passed into history when San Francisco was envisioned as the new Geneva, when Montgomery Street went vertical and Fisherman's Wharf put in the Wax Museum and began importing crab from Oregon. The real city left with the shipyards, with the hulking longshoremen and the quiet, bending welders. The steelworkers who built the skyline never knew that they were busy erecting their own memorial monoliths.

They never knew that they would all vanish interstate, leaving behind powerless, jobless heirs who would someday divide up the Mission District and the Fillmore District into meaningless quadrants and then defend them to the death; penniless heirs who would fracture Double Rock and the Army Street projects into small warring nations. The steelworkers couldn't know that their children, retired in infancy, would live out their lives with live ammunition, hunting possessions in the unstable firmament.

Their sons, black boys, on night patrol and moving stealthily in platoons, were now stripped of every jazz, their sadness shed of blues; there was no 4-4 bass line to their modern walk. Their carved and woven African world, having crashed into a metal mercantile universe, left warriors fighting for shoes and jewelry.

Their Chicano sons were on their scarred, brown knees in short, impious pilgrimages from their homes to the street corner; their Mexican lyricism had been calcified around their cradled bones. As they closed thin apartment doors behind them to face a fierce land of easy monthly installments, there was the unforgotten yet unrecognized smell of the Yucatán at their backs. Their mothers' flashing hands, *como pájaritos en el aire*, had once ground golden maize into compliant *masa*, then browned the fresh tortillas in handmade ovens. Now they waited in line to buy Wonder bread.

Now their children were pulling triggers in the shadow of those same wealth-ridden high-rises, when once they defended the blue canals of Tenochtitlán to the death. Now they fought over nothing and lay claim to littered streets that were but a shadow of the deep chasm beneath their feet. Pandemonium called to them as nightly they teased at the apocalypse with dull, television-filled eyes.

"Spare change, man."

A middle-aged black man in filthy clothes held out an empty Dixie cup.

"All I have is four bits," said Zeferino, dropping two quarters into the cup.

"That's all right, man. We got a glass ceiling down here on the sidewalk, too. These days, nobody reaches for their wallets. They don't want the embarrassment of having to pick through big bills to find a buck. And no one carries a lot of change any-more, 'cause it ruins the pockets of their suits."

The man pulled one of the quarters out of the cup and dropped it into his pocket. One quarter at the bottom of a cup is somehow more pathetic than none.

"I'm a Vietnam vet, you know," said the black man, hoping for some paper money.

"What was your M.O.S.?" asked Zeferino, referring to Military Occupational Specialty.

Caught in a lie, the man grinned sheepishly.

"I guess you got me there, partner," he said.

"You ain't getting a red cent now, my man," said Stuart. "My friend Zef hates phony veterans more than he hates clerk-typists and motor-pool mechanics with delayed stress syndrome."

"Let's go," said Zeferino, looking back at the lawn where hundreds of combat veterans lay swaddled in nightmares. One of them, a skinny white man whose nightmares spilled over into the bright of day, was frantically calling in an airstrike aimed at the copper dome of City Hall. With Waterboy radio buzzing in his left ear and Arclight in his right, he watched the invisible B-52's releasing their loads from seven miles up and five miles down-range. He watched as a dark flock of gray bombs materialized below a high condensation trail, then slammed into the side of City Hall. He watched the dome shatter violently, and then he felt the ground quake with the deafening impact of five-hundred-pound bombs on American soil.

The drop pattern of bombs leveled City Hall, then cracked in red and black clusters of hot hell across Van Ness to envelop the Art Museum and the State Bar Building in huge, curling, rising balls of fire. Windows broke and eardrums bled within a three-mile radius of the target zone. The unearthly rumbling sounds of the explosions could be heard by homeless veterans in Oakland and in the faraway Napa Valley.

"They wouldn't vote for war so fast if they had to feel it!" the skinny man was screaming. By the time the last clusters of bombs had hit, the B-52's were halfway back to Guam, their radios switched to the World Series.

"Plant rice, and B-52's will come to feed!"

He called in the grid coordinates every day. He screamed out the instructions into an invisible radio and witnessed the same terrible results day after day. Behind him, descending ominously through the acrid, rolling smoke, air-mobile choppers filled with green-faced infantrymen were flipping off their safeties and preparing to move in. As they landed, their lead gunships strafed and raked one or two nearby restaurants with sustained bursts from their door-guns.

"Xin-Lôi," the grunts would scream as they descended. "Sorry about that!"

They would hit the bureaucrats and computer operators hard, killing them where they sat.

Zeferino turned his eyes from the carnage. It had taken him years to free himself from the horrid, otherworldly vision. He no longer envisioned it on his own, but he could still see it in the eyes of others. He shook his head until the whoop-whoop of weighted choppers and the muffled smack of small-arms fire disappeared. They were mopping up now. There were a few sporadic pops here and there. Probably mercy killings, he thought, mangled people reaching out for the muzzle, begging for the jacketed round.

For a moment, he considered getting his two quarters back from the mendicant who had no M.O.S. Instead, he turned toward Stuart, exhaling the cordite that had filled his lungs. As he looked away from City Hall Plaza, beehive rounds were pocking the trees and a pretty secretary, walking toward a cab, stepped on a landmine.

"Ah, life in Chelm," said Stuart, turning a full circle to view the city that surrounded him and referring to the mythical land of the foolish and confused.

"Bambino Reyes, whoever he was, found his death in our fair city," smiled Stuart, who slapped his friend on the back, then began walking up Larkin Street once more. "Just another day in Chelm. Well, the Lady in Waiting should be heating up right about now. It's the social cold spot of the season. Everyone who is no one will be there," grinned Stuart. Zeferino smiled, but images of machetes and mutilations were filling his mind. He was anxious to get to the jail.

"Now let's see. Got on my funky shoes that I'm gonna throw away the second we leave that place. I don't want to know what kind of shmutz they got on that shumtzik rug in there, but I think it must have been organic at one distant point in time. Their rug is stickier than those in the porno theaters down on Eddy Street."

"The rug is cleaner than the Kosher Cruiser," laughed a distracted Zeferino. The images in his mind that should have been the vague product of imagination were somehow becoming sharper, almost as though they were the product of memory.

Ignoring his impertinent friend, Stuart opened his black leather jacket and felt an inside pocket.

"Yeah, I got my pack of Handi Wipes just in case I gotta shake hands with somebody . . . heaven forbid. How do you do." He feigned a handshake. "My name is Stuart Shekinah, and I'm so enchanted to make your very androgynous acquaintance." He bowed gracefully to an invisible person.

"Every time I go in that place I get a pain in my groin," said Zeferino.

"Amen," said the tall man, pulling the front of his Levi's out to look down between his own legs at his testicles.

"Yeah, those two beauties are dangling right there."

Both men laughed uncomfortably. Neither liked the exotic pathos of the Lady in Waiting. Though the diminutive bar and social club was surrounded by tall buildings and by tens of thousands of people, its interior seemed like a lonely barracks in some far-flung legionnaires' outpost, all but forgotten by a distant, uncaring empire. The television that hung above the entrance to the bathrooms seemed more like a periscope that poked its turning eye into another world. The world outside.

They walked up noisy Larkin Street past the State and Federal buildings and up the slow incline. The prostitutes were out in force on Larkin and Leavenworth and all the way up to Broadway and Nob Hill. Each working girl was busy posing for the passing traffic or attempting to make eye contact with drivers stopped at red lights. The hierarchy was clearly visible to Zeferino and Stuart as they walked.

The lower streets were the exclusive domain of the underage male prostitutes, the methamphetamine-addicted transvestites, and some Cuban transsexuals from the Mariel boatlift who had developed an unquenchable lust for cocaine. Here was where cosmetics and eye pencils faced their sternest tests . . . and generally failed.

"¡Hola, guapos!" the Marielitos would scream out above the traffic.

"¿Quieren tocar mi culito lindo? Look at my sweet behind. ¿Quieres mammado?"

Some of them lifted their shirts for passing cars.

"Mira, tengo bustos! I could feed your children with these."

On the street above them were all of the other drag hookers, and on a street corner above these were the Christian transsexuals who plied Mary Magdalene's trade by night and attended twelve-step programs for drug abuse and various eating disorders during the day.

"Wanna date, mister? I'm better'n any woman in your memories. My sweet crack was sketched on a notepad, carefully planned out, then diagramed. I went to counseling for eight long months to get this indentation. For a mere pittance, you can ravage my emotional confusion!"

"No one is ever really fooled," remarked Stuart as he walked, smiling broadly at the prostitutes.

Cars were pulling over to the curbside, and drivers were busily conversing with the girls. There were gray-haired men from out of town and boys fresh from their first beer, their new tattoos still burning on the skin of their forearms.

"Those guys in the cars drive around until they spot the corner that is the mirror of their soul," explained Stuart.

Above these were the crack-cocaine and heroin whores; the old female prostitutes with missing teeth and flesh the texture of stucco mix, higher up only because they were white and possessed natural pudenda.

"Drain your lizard?" They spoke distractedly and without conviction.

"Taste your progeny?"

"Stuart Momzer's the name," grinned Stuart at one of the leaning streetwalkers, "and I am a veritable lover of all women. A devoted admirer of the female form. From senescent to prepubescent, from Rubenesque to wraith, each form has its own particular beauty."

High at the top, above Geary, were the young ones, the pretty ones who still bathed before sleeping the day away, still cared about the innocent allure of their clothing and sucked on breath mints between tricks. Their dreams reached as high as the gray buildings above their heads, where perfumed call girls rushed from beauty appointments to service foreign businessmen and politicians.

"You are almost the first, sir," they mimed coyly beneath streetlights and at the front doors of better hotels.

"Look at me. I am barely a child. I am probably from Iowa, lost here and confused. Someone should call my worried parents. Only months ago I was a tree-climbing nymph with scraped knees, an androgyne and the apple of my proud father's eye. Just last year I was hipless and had no breasts to speak of . . . none to speak of . . . but you can betray me."

They wore the face of a child above a hairless notch and a mile of leg in black heels, breasts just below the chin. The male's dream: nothing in between . . . no womb; no stomach; no personal needs.

"Instant sperm count, no waiting."

Puerile, practiced mouths, they still spoke of marriage and of formal weddings and still dreamed of home. They were still getting out of the life someday.

"You can betray my dreams. Yes, especially you, sir."

The Lady in Waiting on Eddy Street was a transvestite and transsexual bar that shared building space with Peniel Mission, a small soup kitchen and chapel. Both men had gone there before, looking for clients or witnesses. The walls there were covered with photographs of female impersonators and of mythical alumni who had gone under the knife and were presumed to be living normal female lives elsewhere . . . Paris, Luxembourg . . . dressed in lace, lounging on fur, and planning hubby's dinner. There were photographs of slender girls playing tennis and of smiling, demure women surrounded by family; photographs curled and yellowed by endless envious glances.

The building just to the right of the Lady in Waiting was an ostentatious edifice of glass, plastic, and plants. It was the home office of J. Mulciber and Sons, the architects who had designed many of the hard rectangles that clotted the skyline.

"When I asked you to meet me in the Civic Center Plaza, it was to talk about my new case, not to go investigating one of yours. This is the last time I go with you on one of these cases," Zeferino said while shaking his head. "I swear you must specialize in investigating transsexual assault cases."

"It's got to mean something," Stuart answered with a grin, "but it's not something I really want to think about. I've just got to remind Beatrice about her court appearance on Monday. She's being charged with aggravated assault and prostitution. The alleged victim in her case is a businessman from Seattle. He claims that he was being robbed, but Beatrice told me that the alleged victim had gone off with one Robin Daimon, a local transsexual prostitute and Beatrice's best friend. Robin and the alleged victim had mutually agreed to a price for some kind of sexual act and had gone behind a pickup truck on Eddy Street for a little action.

"Well, a few minutes later, Beatrice hears Robin screaming

and howling like the world is ending. Now, when I tell you that Robin is little, I mean little. She's under five feet tall and just about ninety-five pounds dripping wet if she's holding a five-pound bag of lox and cream cheese in her arms. Beatrice is very protective of her, to say the least."

"Since when have you ever said the least?" asked Zeferino.

"So, Beatrice went over behind the pickup and sees that this guy has beaten Robin's face in: broken jaw, broken eye socket, and two teeth missing. Beatrice grabs the guy and wrestles him off of poor Robin. Beatrice then tosses him over the truck. Right over the cab! An eyewitness said that he cleared the cab by two and a half feet. She tossed the lascivious bastard like he was a toy! Broken arm, broken clavicle, three broken fingers, and a broken hip. His ego is a quivering pile of mush.

"When the police arrived, they looked at the bloody white guy, then at the two transsexual whores, and, of course, they arrested Beatrice and Robin. We're going to trial on this one, no plea bargains. You've gotta hear the beauty part of this case. The alleged victim's wife is going to testify for the defense." He grinned broadly.

"On a hunch I sent her a copy of the preliminary hearing transcript, and when she read that her husband testified under oath that he came to San Francisco on business, she flew down from Seattle to talk to me. She got on a plane when a phone call would have sufficed. It seems our innocent victim is unemployed and it seems the man's been convicted of whipping two or three whores up there in Seattle. The girls up there had extended hospital stays. And what's more, all of those lovely working girls were transvestites or transsexuals! Seems our innocent victim has a penchant for the outré."

"Trouble in paradise?" said Zeferino.

"She's getting a divorce."

At the Peniel Mission, the line of penniless diners stretched down the sidewalk and around the corner. A small paper sign in the front window of the mission announced the day's bill of fare: shepherd's pie, green beans, and a scoop of tapioca pudding with a maraschino cherry at its peak.

Stuart drew a deep breath, then pushed open the front door. There was an overpowering smell of mildew as the door opened;

mildew and sweat and the sweetness of women's drinks being sipped—grasshoppers, mimosas, and gin fizzes—and the scent of a woman with unwashed hair. The rugs and the upholstery were tawdry. The harshness of daylight was not flattering to the interior of the Lady in Waiting. The faces inside that turned to see who was coming in were caught by the hard light, pinned like moths on display; square jaws under makeup, biceps embarrassingly large, and under the barstools and tables were those undeniable size 13 feet that no operation could shrink.

They all turned away from the light. The light that was as bright as Rembrandt's sleeve, as bright as the flash of an intrusive, unerring, unforgiving camera.

Zeferino saw that the two restroom doors at the back of the bar both had the word WOMEN on their brass push plates. As they had entered the bar, he had noticed a white stand-up urinal lying at the curbside next to the garbage can.

"There's Beatrice," said Stuart excitedly, pointing to an enormous Tongan wearing a huge velvet dress that Queen Elizabeth I might have worn if she had weighed three hundred pounds.

Beatrice the changeling looked exactly like the grand stairway at the Paramount Theater in Oakland. On her feet were a pair of size 16 quadruple-E high heels and the thinnest gold anklet placed strategically on the left ankle. It was a sign that Beatrice was unattached. She stood leaning against the jukebox, watching the two straights who were very carefully negotiating the rug, a double mai-tai in a plastic coconut swallowed up by her huge hand. She dropped two quarters into the jukebox, made a selection, then walked over to greet the two men.

"*Uli-uli,*" she grinned at Stuart, using the Tonganese phrase for a black man. Stuart appreciated the name. He'd earned it on the basketball courts of the Fillmore District and the Sunnydale.

"You afraid of the carpet?" asked Beatrice, smiling.

"God knows what's in it," answered Stuart, grabbing the edge of the bar and using it to steady himself.

"It's just gum and mixed drinks," cooed Beatrice.

"No way, man. That shmutz down there is organic. I know it!"

"I'm not a half-man anymore," said Beatrice proudly. "I got the operation and I'm on the hormones. I've been to Denver."

She lifted her huge skirt with a flourish to show her panty-hose and panties. Every face in the bar turned to look. There was a look on Beatrice's face that was a mixture of shyness and pride. Her crotch was smooth and flat. The aggression, the confusion, had been sliced off and thrown away. She suddenly dropped her skirt as excitement and pride gave way to feminine discretion.

"I've got a vagina now. And I don't beat up white men any-more—no more, and on top of that, I'm losing five pounds a week." She grinned at Stuart. "And I've got a new apartment with an old friend of yours, Mr. Del Campo. Do you know Angelica Cambio-Changé?"

Zeferino shook his head.

"Never heard of her."

"Do you remember Angel Lomismo?" Beatrice smiled.

"Yes," said Zeferino excitedly. "He used to stalk women. The police thought he was a rapist, but they could never prove it. He quit following women around just before the stalking statutes were enacted."

"He wasn't a rapist or a stalker," smiled Beatrice patiently. "He was just doing research. He was trying to find the look he wanted to have in his next life. You should see her now: calves like a gazelle and the waistline of a wasp. She's a redhead and we have become sisters, she and I. In honor of our new friendship, I have even taken her last name. It's all legal and documented. I am now Miss Beatrice Cambio-Changé."

Beatrice had once been Kafu, not her mother's only son, but the one that she loved the most. Probably because he was the only child that was missing from her warm, windowless home. Because there were too many sons in the family, Kafu had been brought up as a *fakaleiti*, a male trained to function in the family as a female.

Once he had daily awakened to the sound of waves and the call of a rooster. He could recite the generations of his family all the way back to the very day that the god, Tangaloa, pulled Tonga, like a verdant mass of seaweed, onto the surface of the endless sea. But after high school was done, Kafu slipped away to America, following an ambiguous ache in his groin and in his vision of the world.

Beatrice's selection began to play on the jukebox. It was a

tune by Gram Parsons and the Fallen Angels called "Sin City," her favorite song.

"Things are clearer now; things are better for me." Her eyes were smiling in her huge, round face. "You see, mister lawyer," she said, turning to address Zeferino, "despite my imposing body, my particular mind is a very gentle jungle; survival of the fittest thoughts is not the rule in here."

She touched a finger to her temple. She put her drink onto the bar, then reached into her purse. She pulled out a small book.

"Every little insecurity, every fear, all those evil glances that I get out there, in the world of men"—she nodded toward the street—"every insult has an equal place in my soul. I know it shouldn't be that way, but it is. This is my diary," she said, holding up the book. "This is my *fioretti*, as the girls here call it. On each page I still see hope and conflict and pieces of my old self. That's why I want probation."

Stuart started to protest, but Beatrice began again, placing a huge right hand on his shoulder.

"I know you think we will win, but you don't have to get up there and testify. You don't have to have twelve people from the other world staring at your shoes and your pantyhose and snickering at your matching accessories, hating you in their smug hearts. You know what all those jury studies say—they make up their minds in the first five minutes. What on earth will they think of me? Why, I barely live in their world."

Beatrice was hurting now and could barely restrain her tears. It was clear that she wanted the lawyer and his investigator to leave. They were holding her back, reminding her that she had the sickening strength to throw a two-hundred-pound man over the cab of a pickup truck. The whole case was holding her back, delaying her entry into the world she had chosen.

"You don't have to be on display for their stares. I just can't bear the thought of it right now. I haven't been a woman long enough; I'm not ready yet for that kind of toughness. I want probation. Besides, I have a job now. I've been gainfully employed for six or seven months. I'm a bartender and security person at this beautiful little bar in the Mission District. It's not a gay bar, but it's not straight either. I guess it's a Mexican bar and café. It's not like any place I've ever seen. Just working there these past few months has restored my hope for us all. I'm afraid I would lose the job if I had to take two weeks off for trial."

Even as she said it, Beatrice knew that it wasn't true. The bar was already closed down, its doors and windows locked and shuttered. The owner of the bar would never have fired her, under any circumstances. The place that she had come to love no longer existed.

"Come by sometime. I'll buy a round for the both of you," she lied. "It's over on Seventeenth Street and Shotwell, between Folsom and South Van Ness. There is a sign on the roof that is amazing to behold."

As Zeferino and Stuart left the Lady in Waiting, Beatrice's tune played on the jukebox for the third time in succession.

This old earthquake's gonna leave me in the poorhouse.
It seems like this whole town's insane.
On the thirty-first floor, a gold-plated door,
Won't keep out the Lord's burning rain.

No one in the bar seemed to mind. The only two songs that were ever played at the Lady in Waiting were "Sin City" and Edith Piaf's "Non, Je Ne Regret Rien." No one knew if there was even a third song available on the machine.

Beatrice watched the men leave, glancing through the door with the eyes of a woman. Where the men saw only hard sidewalks, she glimpsed hyssops growing, the legendary flowers of penitence. She saw cutting thorns and nagging thistles and the fragrant herbs of the field. With her softer ears she could just pick out the holy syllables from the torrent of words around her. But the torrent still frightened her.

The bar doors closed behind the lawyer and his investigator, snipping the shafts of sunlight that had flooded into the dark bar. The rays of light, cut off from their source, fell lifelessly onto the carpet.

III

The City Jail, May 22, 1993

Z EFERINO climbed the first few steps of the Hall of Justice
and paused for a moment before entering the cheerless
utilitarian edifice. The pause contained equal parts of pathos
and revulsion, and the smallest desire to turn and run away from
the problems of the pressurized world within the gray cinder-
block building.

The air within the walls was a stifling swirl of wide-eyed confusion, sweating addictions, benumbed ignorance, craven guilt,
and hopeless innocence. Behind the walls there were hundreds
upon hundreds of men who had been charged with acts of stupidity, abuse, and base cruelty. He had been going in and out of
these same doors now for a dozen years to intercede on their behalf.

Recently he had been noticing his own hesitation at the front
door. It had probably been happening for some time but had
somehow managed to remain submerged in his thoughts. Entering this building meant entering the turbulent lives of the men
and women upstairs, their constricted minds and their caged,
defensive hearts. It meant learning their languages, sometimes
inarticulate and sometimes foreign, and it meant seeing with
their narrowed eyes. It often entailed hours and hours of dissect-
ing the minutes and seconds before, during, and after an act of
violence. It meant effort and, sometimes, it meant pain.

Tonight the front of the gray building was covered with

scaffolding and tarps. It was an improvement. There were dormant pile drivers and cranes in the street and in the parking lot. The jail was being enlarged once again.

"The wickedness of man is great on the earth," said Stuart, quoting Genesis, chapter 6, as he put two quarters into a nearby newspaper vending machine.

Zeferino wondered if Stuart was referring to the men in the jails upstairs or to the rising cost of newspapers.

"Look at this glaring headline," said Stuart, holding up the paper. MUTILATION MURDER AT CHINA BASIN.

"There's a full interview of your new client on the front page. It quotes him as saying that he is absolutely remorseless and his conscience is perfectly clear. He gives another full confession and says there was no shame in anything that he did. What do you make of that?" smiled Stuart, clearly amused by the article.

"I think Teodoro Cabiri, whoever he is, is either very old or he is not an American."

"Why do you say that?"

"Because the words *conscience* and *shame* are no longer in the American lexicon. Those concepts have been wrung out of our language and our consciousness."

"Do you want me to read the confession to you?"

"Not unless he explains why he did it," answered Zeferino.

"No such luck," said Stuart, "but he does say that confession is not good for the soul. What do you think that means?"

The lawyer froze upon hearing the phrase. Someone long ago had said something very much like that. Where had he heard the phrase? Who had said it to him?

"Confession," said Zeferino, looking upward at a building that was filled with them, "was not developed by the ancient church to pardon sins or to maintain the moral health of the flock. There was a deeper, darker reason for the confessional. It was a device cleverly designed to detect heresies at an early stage. Sainthood is similar. Most people believe that the church canonized worthy martyrs in order to honor them. That was true to some small extent, but its main purpose was to absorb any cult whose power had grown to such a degree that its existence threatened the larger church. Someone told me that a long time ago, Stuart."

"Are you sure you don't know this guy?" asked Stuart.

"For all I know, he's from another world. Is there a photograph of him in the article?" asked Zeferino.

"It says that he has refused to speak to any reporter who had a camera or a photographer with him. He won't allow pictures. That's why there are no pictures of him in any of the papers. It quotes him as saying that only one photographer in the world could capture his true essence."

Stuart folded his newspaper, then placed it into his briefcase. There was a contemplative look on his face, a look that had recurred since leaving Beatrice at the Lady in Waiting.

"Have you read the Cabala?" Stuart had asked the strange question as he parked the Kosher Cruiser across from the Hall of Justice.

Zeferino had not answered the question for two reasons. First, Stuart would invariably answer his own questions, whether or not they were answered by his companion. Secondly, Zeferino was too busy picking disgusting pieces of french fry and crumbs from his pant legs to respond. Stuart began to answer his own question as soon as he folded the newspaper and they began the climb up the remaining steps to the entrance of the building.

"Speaking of another world, the Cabala contains some very interesting constructs. Among other things, there are seven parallel earths beneath seven domes of heaven. Enoch and Dante, among others, claim to have visited them all. The worlds are all held together by long, infinitely powerful rods of gossamer. We are on the seventh earth . . . or at least we think we are. It is the land of exiles. Hell is on the sixth earth, right next to us. But lately I've concluded that it's closer than that.

"Some sage Hebrew commentators, myself included, consider the Cabala to be more than a metaphorical system. It is a description of our condition, our gains and our losses, our assets and our deficits. If God naps for just a minute in third heaven, things are bound to fall apart down here. If God goes to sleep on the job, then Azrael, the dark angel of death, is free to leave the smoke and sulfur of Gehenna, and all the other worlds go insane with fear.

"In two parallel earths, third and fourth, Harabba and Tziah, a building like the Hall of Justice would never exist. Those other

earths are either too dry or too wet for the fabrication and cur-
ing of cement. Their halls are made of either sand or an exotic
kind of wood that grows in long, precut planks. One earth is like
the Gobi Desert, while the other is always flooded.

"On one of those earths, the inhabitants collect fragile glass
vials filled with arsenic, instead of collecting handguns as people
do here. On the other, the people collect hollow glass pistols
filled with sulfuric acid."

Before entering the dark building, Stuart looked back affectionately at his car, which was parked in front of Al Graf's Bail
Bonds. Stuart had parked the Kosher Cruiser with one wheel up
on the curb. One poor tire was pinned helplessly between the cement and the steel rim. But the Cruiser would never complain. It
was Stuart's loyal friend, his stallion and chariot, his *merkabah*
rider. Encased within the four doors of the Kosher Cruiser, Stuart, like wizened Jewish mystics of old, rose each evening and
penetrated the myriad and menacing veils of the city.

"On both earths it is a cherished constitutional right to carry
poison and acid. There are pickup trucks with arsenic racks in
the rear window and specialty stores that sell beakers and ban-
doliers of high and low molarity acid. There are magazines and
periodicals for arsenic buffs; national conventions and local
clubs. Huge numbers of people derive a substantial portion of
their identity from the corrosive strength of their acids.

"Article six, paragraph thirty-three, of the Harabba constitution specifically states that there is a right to bear acid. Most say
it's for target spraying or for protection. 'It's not the acid that
burns,' they say on fourth earth. 'It's the creature behind it.' The
people of third earth aim their vials of arsenic at targets and toss
them just like darts in a pub. Of course, poisonings and disfig-
urements are epidemic on both of those worlds, but no one ever
seems to know why."

Before opening the front door, Zeferino looked above the
doorway to the building for the squatting pigeons that were forever assailing those below with droppings of white and off-green
disdain. Sure of their absence, he entered confidently, then
walked past the screeching metal detector toward the jail elevator. Stuart walked behind him, spewing an unbroken chain of
words.

"The sons of Adam and Eve are on the first earth, where they work in a bored, unhappy state. Second earth is a place of malaise and forgetfulness. There are no communities there. It's a lot like America."

"From which world is Teodoro Cabiri?" asked Zeferino. Stuart did not answer.

In the evenings there was no security. The cops at Southern Station would be working elsewhere, somewhere out in the dark streets. The darkened halls were empty of lawyers, defendants, bondsmen, and family members.

Marble walls, impervious to water, wind, and earthquake, had been eroded by posturing, worn away by words, by distracted conferences above open briefcases, by the frenzied intimacies of disoriented families, the splenetic bitterness of subpoenaed victims, the impatient whine of waiting cops, their crumpled subpoenas in hand.

He pushed the UP button and waited while the noisy, slow elevator groaned upward from the basement to stop at the first floor. The two men entered. The elevator slowed at the second floor, groaned once more, then dropped a foot or so before ascending again. Zeferino hated this elevator, having been stuck between floors in it on more than one uncomfortable occasion.

The second floor was the municipal court. There were one or two judges on this floor who, as lawyers, had never tried a criminal case before a jury. One had tried a single misdemeanor case in order to claim extensive trial experience during the campaign for the position. Another had run for every position on the city ballot until a judgeship came through. Yet there they were on Monday morning, screeching at the inexperience of the young lawyers in their courtrooms. It was the magic of the robe—put it on and revise your own history.

The third floor was the Superior Court. Zeferino felt more comfortable on this floor. This floor was old school, to be sure, but at least some trial lawyers had become judges.

There were defense attorneys in this building who had never tried a serious case, and yet they were busily supervising young lawyers, assailing them with apocryphal tales of their own prowess. There were prosperous lawyers who were deathly afraid of juries. For some, Zeferino mused, this was more than just a building. This was the universe; the pecking order, the back-stabbing, the personal mythologies, and the ego battles were the be-all and the end-all of their lives. To some, this gray place supplied a complete identity, a full persona. So many seemed to forget the dark faces crowded and caged upstairs . . . the point of this profession.

At the seventh floor he showed the deputy his Bar card and driver's license. Stuart produced his lapsed investigator's license. The deputy looked quickly at all three though he knew Zeferino and Stuart very well. After their briefcases were searched, an electric lock snapped open inside a metal door that led down a long hallway to the main line of cellblocks. On the right, just inside the door, was a bank of interview rooms, each with a small table and a few chairs, none of which matched.

The jail was dark and silent. Nothing like the din, the pandemonium at noon with ten blaring televisions set to different stations; books and cigarettes flying across the aisles in frenzied fits of trading; trustees mopping and chatting and chained groups of prisoners going to court or just coming back.

"Cabiri, Teodoro," Zeferino told the deputy at post 8, who turned to the first page of his day list, then called the name over an intercom to a listener located somewhere deep within the painted metal and cement walls.

"Lucky man," smiled the bailiff, sarcastically. "I wondered who was gonna get this guy. We haven't had a celebrity in here for some time. You're the first guy I've seen today that didn't have a press badge."

"Did he confess again?" asked Zeferino dejectedly.

"Confess?" answered the deputy. "You'd think he'd just won an Academy Award. He even had a prepared speech. He thanked the police who arrested him and the officers who booked him. He thanked his wife for standing by him. He confessed to everybody in here, including some pimple-faced folksingers from a drug rehabilitation center.

"It seems like everyone in the city knows his name and the name of his victim, Bambino Reyes. He is one strange hombre," said the deputy, shaking his head. "Did you know that every night, without fail, a huge raven comes to the window above his bunk? The prisoner keeps feeding it newly baked bread, and we can't figure out where he gets it from. We'd shoot the damn bird, but the sight of that raven at the window every night scares the shit out of the Mexicans and the Nigerians."

The deputy laughed at his own mental image of frightened Zapotecs crossing themselves and religious Nigerians cowering under their bedsheets.

Zeferino sat down in the third interview room, the one with the paintings that he enjoyed, one of a fire escape in Brooklyn and the other of the strange yet pleasing face of a man. The faced was grizzled and hardened but had eyes that declared that adversity had been transformed into wisdom. Stuart got an extra chair from another room, then sat at the same table. A man who was seldom silent, the investigator found the jail at night disquieting. Across from the interview room there was an even larger painting entitled *The Ghost of the Moulin Rouge*. In the painting were festive, masquerading spirits in parti-colored finery. They were masked even further by an unnerving sense of gaiety in death. One elegant spirit at the ball was walking a leopard who strained at a leash.

The lawyer and the investigator sat silently together as they had done so many times before. Each felt the familiar tension that arises when a defendant who is charged with a terrible crime meets his defense team for the very first time. Even Stuart had no words for these moments. It was a meeting of two distinct worlds that never touched, never communicated except at the courtrooms and holding cells that had been designated as frontier checkpoints.

Each wondered if the suspect would be cooperative. Would he be able to testify? Would he be smelly and belligerent? Could he assist in the preparation of his own defense? Would the jury hate him? Could he cross at the checkpoint and, for a few hours on the witness stand, withstand a heated interrogation by the inquisitor and speak to twelve strangers in their own language?

Just when Zeferino decided to concentrate on the Moulin Rouge painting in order to pass the time, the heavy door churned open in the hallway. There would be no waiting at this hour. The hard clank of metal announced the fact that the defendant had been awakened and was coming through post 8, where he would be given a full-body search, then searched again after the interview.

Zeferino wondered what he looked like, this man accused of some sort of mutilation killing. Teodoro Cabiri. He imagined a tall man, a San Quentin *pinto* with a rap sheet a yard long and faded tattoos at the corner of his eyes and covering both muscular arms. Zeferino was comforted by the thought. He preferred experienced clients, old-timers who sat down and said, "I fucked up. Now what can you do for me?"

They were a pleasure compared to the whiners and criers and the ones who kept repeating, "There must be some sort of mistake," in a voice that always sounded like Blanche DuBois.

Pimps were the worst. They closed their eyes every time they lied to their lawyers. It was as though a genetic mutation took place whenever a skinny, fast-talking man put on a white leather jumpsuit and failed to bathe for a week. It was a strangely selective malady. The mutation affected only the eyelids during prevarication. It probably came from years of avoiding the eyes of women.

Career child molesters were next in line. They were the princes of insidious rationalization, and it never stopped, not with their families, not with their lawyers, and not with themselves.

"It's the system's fault! Don't you understand? Love can't be limited by statute! You can't legislate the heart. It's this form of government! It's those damned suburbanites out there who don't have an understanding of true love."

Young white rapists whose families had money were third worst. "Look at me. I made the dean's list three semesters in a row. I used to model for extra money. Can I show my portfolio to the judge? I can have any girl I want. Do I look as though I need to rape a woman to get between her sheets?"

Transvestites from the Cuban boat lift were the fourth worse.

"Señor *licenciado*, I have proof of my innocence. Mr. Lawyer, they said a man did this awful thing and . . . just look at these bosoms," they said while lifting their shirts.

"As you can see, I sure ain't no man . . . oh, did I touch your knee? Are you offended? Can you get me my hormones in here? I need my 'mones."

Zeferino reconsidered his hierarchy and decided to downgrade the pimps to second place. Everyone below them would have to move down a notch. The absolute worst clients were the ones who confessed to the police and anyone else who would listen, then lied to their lawyers in the all-too-common belief that defense attorneys must believe in their client's absolute innocence before they can aggressively attack the prosecutor's case.

"Get all my confessions thrown out!" they would scream. "If you don't, you dump-truck shyster, I'll give them a real statement to work with! I'll videotape a confession! I'll put it on laser disc!"

Zeferino shook his head without knowing it. Beliefs were the defense attorney's worst enemy. What would Mr. Cabiri say about all of his confessions? Across the table, Stuart was busy cleaning his teeth with a business card.

"Cabiri, the room with the light on."

It was the deputy directing the defendant to the interview room. Zeferino could hear chains rattling and the scrape and tapping of a strange shackled walk.

The door opened. The new client shuffled in. He had silvery leg chains on and black handcuffs on his wrists. At his midriff was a huge waist chain that was connected by even more chain to the handcuffs. Stuart stopped picking his teeth to stare in amazement.

The suspect was brown-skinned and gray-haired with a bald spot on top. The jailer had indicated that the prisoner was at least seventy years old, but the man who stood before them had a face that seemed ageless. There were no jail clothes to fit him, so he had been spared most of the orange jumpsuit. Over his own clothing, he was swaddled in an orange-and-black shirt, denoting his lockdown status. He had a small hunched back and tiny fingers, and he was wearing special shoes; one had a sole that was at least five inches thick. In his right hand he had a small cane.

The man who was charged with a mutilation homicide on the Fourth Street Bridge stood just over three and a half feet tall. His tiny, bent body was wedged uncomfortably between two perpetually shrugging, parenthetical arms. He walked in, then stopped just beyond the doorway, his eyes riveted on his lawyer's.

"Zefe," he said softly.

*   *   *

Zeferino remembered him instantaneously, the moment his childhood name was uttered. The single memory pushed upward through a deep submergence and tried to carry with it a thousand others, pushing up simultaneously, painfully, opening layer upon layer of sleeping thoughts, sequestered bygones. His mind went almost white for an instant as the blood left his brown face.

The small man stood quietly while the deputy pulled a ring of keys from his belt to remove the chains and the *esposas*, as the inmates called handcuffs. They were a special pair of handcuffs made for a small juvenile. But before the deputy could insert the key, the little man, with a flourish, stepped from the leg chains and dramatically presented the opened cuffs to an amazed and frustrated jailer. The waist chains dropped noisily to the cement floor. The little man extended both arms to his sides, palms up, and bowed his head slightly as if acknowledging a rousing round of applause.

"The last thing that freedom is," exhaled the little man in puffs of cigarette smoke, ". . . is physical. I swear I could do this escape suspended upside down in a vat of pineapple juice. I did just that, once, in a floor show in Honolulu."

"I don't know where you're getting your cigarettes and matches from," said the flustered deputy, "but there's no smoking up here. Do you understand? And if we find any more bread on you or near your bunk, you're going on isolation."

The suspect did not answer. He was smiling as the deputy searched him once again for tobacco and matches. Each time he exhaled, a haze of blue smoke curled around the deputy's red face. Stuart had gotten up from his chair and, tooth for tooth, was returning the little man's smile. As soon as the bailiff had gone, a smoking cigarette appeared in the prisoner's grinning mouth.

"Teodoro Teofilo Cabiri, lover of God, lover of God and protector of shipwrecked men," said Zeferino, pulling the phrase up, culling it up from a memory he had seemingly lost long ago.

Before this instant he had only barely remembered the little man—some small details about his amazing appearance and nothing else. He had been a small boy when this man came into his life, and that had been for just a few months . . . over thirty years ago.

"But you can call me Ted For Short," smiled the old man, who managed a stiff bow toward his lawyer.

The jail was fully darkened now, except for the light in the interview room and the small spotlights that ran down the center of the main line. In a few hours, even these lights would be extinguished. The two men, for a long moment, stared closely, one at the other. A deep, timeless stare that was unfettered by halting, polite self-consciousness.

"I can't believe it," Zeferino said in a voice that was only barely audible.

"I can't believe it. Oh," he added suddenly as his investigator politely cleared his throat, "I forgot to introduce you two. This is my investigator, Stuart . . ."

"Mazuma," interjected Stuart. "Stuart Mazuma."

He reached out and shook the little man's hand.

"I'll be the defense investigator on your case."

"There's really nothing to investigate," said Teodoro. "I'd do it all over again."

"Yes," said Zeferino patiently. "How on earth did you find me?"

"I found your name in the phone book," smiled the little man, proudly. "I looked up your name long before this happened. I'd heard sometime back that you were *mananangol, un abogado.* All the boys in the fields say proudly that one of us has become a lawyer."

"I have a lot of questions for you," said Zeferino, who had suddenly become aware again of the reason for this interview.

Ted For Short reached for the cigarette that had died on the edge of his lips, then relit it with a flourish.

"If you say this'll stunt my growth I'll kill you," he smiled. "I'm a murderer, you know."

He jumped down from the chair, the cigarette pinned between two stubby fingers. He put his left hand on the bald spot on top of his head.

"Pretend that the cops haven't taken my beautiful toupee. You should see it. I bought it in Beverly Hills. I tell you, it's top of the line."

There was something different in his voice now as he spoke.

"Close your eyes," he said, "both of you."

Zeferino did not comply. He could not comply. It was one thing to recollect a vague memory; it was another thing altogether to see memories suddenly forming where none had existed before. He tried to close his eyes and to staunch the flow, but he could not. He walked to the window and stared out into the dark hallway. It would have to do.

"Teodoro Teofilo Cabiri, lover of God and protector of shipwrecked men, welcomes you," he said, holding his crooked cane up to his face like a microphone. He had deepened his voice to a smooth disc-jockey baritone.

"Tonight, we have a special treat for you. Direct from Manila, it's old Brown Eyes himself! This first tune, a real golden oldie, and one of my favorites, was penned by Harburg and Lane."

He turned his small, contorted, curved back toward an invisible audience, then grinned.

"I have a hunch you'll like it."

Ted For Short began to belt out "That Old Devil Moon." Zeferino, near the window, could not believe his ears. Stuart Klezmer raised his head from a notepad, blinking his unbelieving eyes at the scene before him. The deputy, who had returned to his station, came closer to hear what was going on. After two steps he was frozen in midstep, incredulous.

The voice, strong without being loud, resonated melodiously down the long corridor of the main line, curving around brass locks and sliding mellifluously between iron bars. There it jostled defendants' dreams, turning their soured reveries into innocent visions of childhood and moments of sweet, forgotten civility.

The small man behind the lawyer, whose eyes were now closed to listen, was lit by a single intimate spotlight, the sequins on his jacket and pants glinting red and green. His bow tie was studded with rhinestones, and there were heavy gold rings on his fingers. A cigarette was perched daringly behind his left ear. There was the unmistakable sound of musical accompaniment, a guitar, a drum, and an electric piano.

Wanna cry, wanna croon. Wanna laugh like a loon. . . .

He moved to his left with his arm extended as he sang, asking the audience to show its appreciation for a small three-piece band behind him on an elevated stage.

The song ended with a shattering smash of the cymbals. There was a timeless pause in the instant it takes a final note to die, in the time it takes for the tide of mundane to sweep back in and sunder the finery of the figment. Zeferino, his ears still ringing and stunned with the silence, turned back toward his client as the mesmerized deputy retreated meekly to his post. He found himself faintly surprised to see that his client was still wearing his dull prison garb. Slowly, he gathered his thoughts again and remarked to himself that there is a thing about reality that plunders romance.

"Thank you, thank you," said Teodoro Teofilo Cabiri to an appreciative applause, his baritone still operational.

"If you liked that tune, there's more where that came from, but first we have a fifteen-minute pause for the cause. In other words, me and the band here have got to get some refreshments and make a visit to the sandbox."

He laughed.

"But seriously, folks, it's all venereal . . . it's all ethereal."

A smiling Teodoro walked over to Zeferino, then motioned for him to bend down. The little man pulled back the shirtsleeve of his short right arm, then spread the fingers of his hand. He then reached behind his lawyer's left ear and with a wide grin pulled back a golden wedding band.

"Did you know that I got married just a few days ago?" he asked without caring if Zeferino answered. "After all these years alone, I am a married man. Her name is Radiant Ruby."

The defendant then put a pudgy index finger to his lips, signifying both silence and secrecy. After checking the hallway to make sure the deputy was gone, Teodoro climbed into a chair, then placed his cigarette on the edge of the table. "They are such gullible fools here at this jail . . . so easily misled," Teodoro laughed mockingly as he gestured over his shoulder at the departed deputy. "It is the bird who is feeding me."

IV

DRESSED in airless sheen, the shining moon, unable to arouse her distant lover, tugged and pulled coyly at its tight blue girdle of oceans. The fulsome moon, the lesser luminary, incapable of turning her face from the heartless, spinning earth that she so adored, sent a shaft of limpid light downward to touch her lover's side. The bright beam, brimming with conciliatory lumens, fell downward through the heavens to strike a poor shanty that rested atop a tall tower that had been carefully erected upon a building. A frenzied man moved beneath that ray of moonlight. And so it was that lunar glow fell full upon a lunatic.

The frantic old man on the moonlit rooftop was a prisoner of memory, serving out the last long day of a life sentence. He was an old, unpardoned murderer who had once, in passing, embraced the body of a dying saint. And on occasion, Humberto the arsonist had gone so far as to rudely censure the sweet gossip of angels from the discomfort and convenience of his own high home. And now, in the final hours of his life, he turned his scathing gaze downward to the bedlamites who lived below him, in the somber houses and on the haunted sidewalks.

"Each morning when I am exhumed from my bedsheets, I see that my dark tossing sleep is a poor redundancy, that the shut door of my room is but a wooden lid lined with word-muffling silk." Like the ancient baptist, he shouted his crazed words, pushing them out on tides of stale breath past his blue cracked lips and out onto the rooftops below.

"Mañana, in my next life, if I must have one, I want to come back as a blue satin high-heel shoe."

He preached at the top of his lungs to the earthlings below.

"I'll pass on humanity . . . *no gracias, no mas.* You can have it. I've already had seconds, a heaping serving of eunuch years, a solitary interlude of toxins and tortures and tawdry peep-show dreams. Until tonight I had wasted both of my lives."

The man who spoke the words had existed far too long for so short a life, and the very thought of it made him weak and weary.

"*Zapatos azules de tacos altos.* Blue high-heel shoes." He had loved but once in his lives, and then for only a fleeting instant . . . a woman who had watched him die. He had seen her just once. He had spotted her sitting in shade with a small palette of soft colors poised in her upraised hand. Her shoes were blue points at the end of long brown legs. They had almost blinded him.

He climbed down the ladder from his silver home above the roof. It was his home next to the very dome of heaven. The novice pyromaniac had once been a voyeur in his own kneeling lives, seeking love, as though it were a rolling coin, moving just beyond his reach in the cracked floorboards of brothels and dance halls.

"*El amor me ha astillado.*" A lunate smile appeared on his lips whenever he spoke Spanish. "Love has splintered me."

He had lived for two souls, in a life not good enough for one. Now, he was an earnest man in the moonlight who wished to end it all; to die a second and final time, a death more perfect than the first . . . and with infinitely better execution. An incurable disease, contracted at his first death, had rendered him immortal and doomed him to perish his whole life through, in a hundred incompetent suicides; to live out his demise again and again in mangled stanzas of bad verse. Now, at last, he could taste it. He finally had lived too long. There was a tincture of laudanum in his tongue's memory, the remains of an ancient remedy.

He was a sinuous, aged man, a lifelong traveler who was about to be released from years of spiritual entailment, from hard and fast rules of flight that had, long ago, fixed the manner of his descent.

El viejo con la rabia, the rabid stranger began to scream again at the top of his lungs that he is unrequited in this land, that the land down below him is a fickle lover—abusive and brutal in one moment and so adoring in the next. First wooed then jilted, he flinches now with every kind and fractured thought.

Moving about quickly, he was joined by a second person, a black woman who was without a stitch of clothing. In her right hand was a small mirror with a blue frame and handle. The two sprayed a wide trail of gasoline on various objects on the rooftop, then tossed the gas cans over the edge, where they clattered to the gutter below.

The feverish man called out, as he tossed burning matchsticks and furiously set his surroundings alight, that this country is a flowing river. And like a river she is defined by what she has swept away.

"And so . . . I am part of her definition."

The man and the black woman by his side stopped moving for a moment and stared intently at the eastern horizon. They were waiting for a signal.

"There it is!" cried the woman, who pointed into her hand mirror at the horizon.

The male form on the roof bent intently to his mysterious task, then retreated quickly as something on the roof exploded violently, sending a flaming object high into the air and out toward the East Bay. The blast from the explosion knocked the man and his accomplice flat on their backs.

He stood up slowly and watched, squinting with awe as the apparition slashed across the evening sky, leaving in its wake a carpet of drifting embers as red as Fra Angelico's vestments or Orozco's pit of fire.

"My ex-voto!" he cried as he watched the object rise.

"It is as crimson as Greek fire flung from a catapult."

He was joyous at the sight and bounded across the roof, arms upraised in victory. His cries wafted upward from his smoking, rooftop censer, his pulpit and pyre.

Those who saw it did not believe it, and so they only stared upward in disbelief. Those who would have believed—who had

waited the entirety of their lives to believe in just such a thing—
were not looking at it when it passed overhead in the lowest
heaven. Their numbed gazes had been averted by years—
centuries—of uncaring skies; their heads were bowed by the weight
of inherited, inbred disappointments. Those who would have believed did not join the legion of frantic callers who flooded the
switchboards at Mission Police Station and at the Hall of Justice.

Had they lifted their heads, just one or two of the believers as
they moved here and there along the earth—had they raised
their downcast eyes to see the glowing body, spanning air, spraying hot rivulets of solder, they might have rejoiced with the rare
mystery of it. They might have turned it over on their tongues
and passed it on to their children; they might have embellished
it a bit, lied about its height and power, given it the weight of
myth and written it down.

Those who saw it turned away, mumbling numbly in mundane words of ballistics, conjectures of stray comets or of falling
airplanes. Some even spoke of auroras, while others saw an arc
welder splicing a fractured sky. Such is the fate of miracles in
modern times, and in modern lands; no one looks to the heavens any longer. The heavens that were once so full.

Nowadays they say that there are only tinsel satellites to spin
lonely ellipses up there, when once above an age, they spoke of
angels, they told of handservants to the airy spheres, who rushed
breathlessly from horizon to horizon to be of fawning assistance
at the skirts of waning dusk.

On these modern evenings there are only new rifts torn in
the ageless ozone when once the skies were crowded with dare-
devil gnostics, laughing madly and gyrating between pointed
minarets; the many-eyed seraphim with numberless wings—and
filled, too, with the hopes of mortal men.

Those who saw it watched it arch across the Mission District,
gaining in velocity and raining a trail of gilt-edged fire as it flew. It
trailed a cloud of smoke behind it that was draped in the sky like
newly hung laundry. Beneath it all, furious, aproned shopkeepers
rushed up to their roofs to hose down their smoking shingles.

Even those who failed to see did not fail to hear the piercing
voice of the man on the rooftop. A voice that seemed to send the
blazing specter on its way.

"*Para ti, mi hermano;* for you, my dear brother," he shouted. "For you ... a victory for saints and for poor sinners like me! Even now one of the beasts is clawing vainly at his mortal wound! At last I can tell you in which faraway land I am to die."

His thin screaming, rather than blending into the screeching tires and the rude, blaring horns of the crowded Mission District, seemed instead to silence them. For the first time in almost anyone's memory, lowered cars manned by black-jacketed pubescents moved silently, courteously through controlled intersections, and graffiti-blighted municipal buses, at each corner, started and stopped gently, in rare deference to passengers.

It was as though a deep, placid layer of invisible snow had fallen on the Mission District and the area south of Market. A serene blanket of quiet that had existed only once before in times long past, when the Coast Miwok and the Ohlone walked the sloping, verdant hills of the peninsula, their fish baskets filled to brimming and their laughter softened by rich foliage.

"Listen to me, all of you! *¡Escuchame!* I'm dying again—for the second time in my life. This is my very last day of suffering on this embittered earth!"

Posing whores shivered on their street corners when his deranged voice reached them. For an instant, the pathos secreted in their trite come-ons and tight costumes showed through, became permeable to insight. Prostitutes fell into a contrite, childish shame as they listened, suddenly chilled by a lack of clothing. His crazed screaming seemed to frighten them into coyness. It seemed to numb those who heard, to sedate them. No one who heard it felt at ease.

"*Compadres.* Remember how, back home in Mexico, we always used to place the body of a little dead hummingbird into our pockets, to help us find love—a lover? *Hijos de los angelitos,* they were called. *Picaflores.* A dead hummingbird that died and fell to earth of natural causes. Remember? *Pedaso de cielo?* Couched there in our pockets, buried beneath pesos and keys, a tiny feathered piece of heaven."

Those who looked for the source of the voice lifted their eyes to the top of the distant building. There they saw him framed in flame.

"The Tarascans say that hearts are drawn to the children of angels."

He raised his arms to address the sunset. The intense red of it joined with the flames to paint his sooty face with an eerie brush.

"They say that the angels who are closest to God have no minds, and those who are farthest from Him have no souls, and all those in between—all those who are stuck doing business in this mad interchange of spirit and substance—they are all migrant workers, lovesick migrants like those cherubim."

He pointed to the burning object beside him on the roof. The old loco was no stranger. Everyone in the Mission District had seen him at one time or another, squatting on the roof or posturing like a griffin high above the street. Each evening he could be seen gesticulating wildly on the west wall, but no one had ever heard his words before. He was different from all the lollards, beghards, and beguines who roamed endlessly over the sidewalks of San Francisco . . . he asked for nothing, and his demeanor was like no panhandler or crazy the city had ever seen.

He was thin and bronze with twisted, black-veined limbs that seemed to cry out in agony. No one who saw him ever failed to ask themselves just how he had been tortured. In which war? In which obscure revolution? Had he been whipped or suffocated to the point of collapse or beaten senseless by rifle butts? Had his wife and children been murdered for a cause?

It was his eyes. His eyes held close to the memory of torture. There was a constant rippling of the iris that kept the visible foundations of his earth as unstable as the fault lines deep below his feet.

He had a shock of burned white hair above those eyes. Wild and unkempt, it flared around his stern and raving face. His thin body was wrapped in loose linen. He seemed like an image plucked from an ancient fresco.

But no one had ever heard his words before. His voice—yes, but never his words. Such babbling was not unusual in the city of a hundred known languages and a thousand dialects never to be deciphered; personal dialects of private, muttering pain; mendicant and homeless words; ancient tongues that sprouted spontaneously within modern mouths. The extinct language of Manx. Lonely Aramaic words that find no welcoming ears. Macedonian slang from the time of Alexander, preserved nowhere but in the muddled mind of a homeless woman, her hands holding fast to a tear in her mangled dress.

In a land where strangers never speak, where monologues prevail, nameless languages live, forgotten tongues abound.

Those who listened to the old man on this night found his tempestuous speech disquieting, yet somehow mesmerizing.

"Women make a separate world inside them!" he screamed into the crisp *aire de noche*, "a womb in the heart to match the one in their thighs! Hombres, you and I, we are only men. All we can have are words curled up in our poor heads. And we are Mexicanos. Our lives are spread across the front of a church like a chiseled frieze. Look around yourselves. Do you know what this is? This is the single place of all places where the best things happen and the worst things happen.

"This is the land like a river that hates living heroes, raises them from the same dust and seed that spawns their very assassins! *Esta tierra se resaca, sola* . . . This land washes itself away!"

The old man's voice was growing hoarse. He continued to preach his sermon to the whole neighborhood. The fire at his back swelled up to match his oratory. The nearby Chapel of Engine Additives idled down its evening services to hear his wailing voice. A long line of young Mexican novitiates, car deodorizers pinned to their chests and their heads swaddled in strips of muffler bandage, turned their rapt eyes toward the sound. The anointment of cheap cars with golden motor-honey and liquid tune-up could wait.

"Those of you *pendejos* who are still able to hear with the ears of the virtues and dominions, hear that tonight—this very night, the enemy has been annihilated. The devil himself has finally lost a round!"

The old man's voice shook nearby branches and leaves, sending flocks of pigeons and swallows scurrying upward toward the last fading light of day. In the broken calm of sunset, a complaining flock of parrots and parakeets circled impatiently for a fifth time, banking against neon glare and diving between billboards for their home in exile in Dolores Park.

They were blush rouge, albino, and jealous green as they flashed in and out of sight. They were feathered, unwilling expatriates, thousands of miles from their jungle homes. They were escapees from elaborate metal cages hung in the lofty chambers of Pacific Heights matrons and Russian Hill pensioners.

Their beautiful wings were flashing almost beyond color as they neared the turning ebb of substance and darted in noisily among the candescent, fluorescent embers that glided and swooped with the wind. Roof tiles buckled, and stubborn steel members swelled and glazed blue with the inferno. Behind a blaze of popping gases, a tall pillar began to discolor and blister.

The prophet and his disciple stumbled here and there, bumping blindly between scald and scorch; each alternately followed, then led the other, between ventilation vents and over turnbuckles to the edge of the building, where they stood swaying breathlessly two stories above an asphalt street.

Dizzy with vertigo and asphyxiation, the old man paused in his soliloquy, then turned and solemnly handed a greasy crescent wrench to the woman. There was a deep sense of ritual as he passed the tool to her waiting hand. She accepted it, then enfolded it ceremoniously within the cleft of her breast.

"I don't want to hear your prayers, my dear houri," the old man said softly. "No more prayers. You see, I climbed up on this rooftop to die. It was part of the plan. I see it so clearly now. It was always part of the plan."

The woman adjusted the mirror she always held in her hand to catch the reflection of the madman's face. Below him, the Mission District resumed its customary clamor and racket, and the flock of birds, finally united, descended for the night. A small squadron of indigenous birds still circled faithfully overhead—they were Ruby's birds. Radiant Ruby, the feathered dancer, must be somewhere nearby.

Slowly he pulled a long-bladed knife from beneath his linen wrap. He had used the knife to cut through wires and turnbuckles on the roof. Reaching behind and across his back he drew the tip of the shining machete downward with relentless force—then changed hands and, grimacing, drew it down again. To the eyes of mortals, the cuts had reopened ancient bullet wounds that years ago had been covered over by mounds of scar tissue. In truth, the cuts had merely broken a spell and exposed unhealed wounds that had been sterilized by incantation and bandaged by woven layers of wraith.

"Only my dense eyes have kept me from seeing that they have never healed," groaned Humberto. "For all these years God has kept me spellbound."

The knife edge was slick rubescent, having fed, and twin cuts were razored down his latissimus dorsi, parallel and layered cuts from the white of epiderm to the deep rose of crying, mourning muscle. The two long cuts downward were deep enough to touch the scapula—to involve the teres and the external oblique in the outrage of screaming nerves—one slice below each shoulder blade.

"Ah . . . at last," he breathed as though the cuts were opened louvers, relieving an age-old suffocation.

The woman at his side stepped backward and turned her mirror to stare dolefully at the wounds.

"Your poor back is all so twisted up. But I see moving clouds of muscle." She reached out suddenly to touch the wound on the left with her fingers and with the cold metal of the crescent wrench.

"Did wings once go here?" she asked quietly.

"Don't be silly, woman," he interrupted impatiently. "*¡Que locura!* You might be as crazy as me."

She touched the quick of the wound, and the old man grimaced in response.

"Did wings once go right here? Did you ever fly? Can you flex your back like no man living on this earth?"

She asked the questions with profound intensity and fervor.

"Did you lose them down in old Mexico, or when you crossed over the border? I betcha God pulled them out, didn't he, like my crazy brother who took and pulled wings off of poor flies and moths. He used to save them. Had a box filled to the brim with wings. Then he would set all the wingless insects free; it was worse than death. The poor things would crawl around with wet, aching shoulders. They became just like my brother, spooked with dreams of flying. I betcha God went and plucked you. It made me so damn sick to see that box. So sad to have a lid shut down tight on so much flight."

The old man did not respond to her questions. He looked at

the mirror in order to meet her gaze. Over time he had given up trying to look directly into her face.

"Have I told you how I originally received these wounds?"

The woman did not answer. She knew the story by heart.

"Years ago I stood exactly like this, wrapped in a sulfurous mist, but it was my body that was on fire."

He went quiet for a moment.

"Do you know how a mother loves her child?" he asked in a feverish and desperate tone.

The childless woman sadly shook her head no. Their relative positions were such that the man's face eclipsed the moon in her looking glass.

"Well, a mother loves almost completely. Almost—but not quite all the way, you see. She loves the child suckling at her breast with a love beyond husband; a love beyond self . . . perhaps even beyond the love of God . . . please forgive me for saying it. Yet even this seemingly total love is tempered. The mother will hold something back just to keep her own sanity. She will keep a small distance just for herself. A distance that will allow her to survive should the child be lost or die or be snatched up, as so many children are these days. She reserves just enough distance to survive, you see.

"Well, when my poor brother died there was no such distance between us. Not an atom of distance, not a molecule. You see, I had no choice but to go insane"—he shrugged—". . . no choice at all. Oh, God, I fell onto my brother's body, in a trench, and I watched him die. Face to face and eye to eye. In a trench I watched him die."

He closed his eyes with the pain of the ancient memory, his bleeding back forgotten. The red of the fire deepened the wrinkles on his face. There were carved river deltas in the corners of his tired eyes.

"I am exactly like a plucked gypsy moth," he said aloud to himself. "Exiled to the ground and yet I am still drawn to flame. *Soy una luciérnaga* . . . a firefly."

He shrugged his shoulders in resignation. He knew now that his second life had never been his own. It had been lived for someone else's sake. Every act of free will that he had exercised since his brother's death had been preordained. He had not been pulled from his own grave to live, but to serve.

"Sing words into your past," he mumbled quietly, "and the echo that bounces back to you will be the sound of your own future. My past is such a poor sounding board," he sighed. "*Luciérnaga.*"

Those who know of the fabled war in heaven believe that it happened long ago, in an age before time, and imagine a battle between weightless titans and shapeless forms. There are those who say that the darkest warrior cast down from heaven was once the twin of the Redeemer, that he was expelled for the sin of love. Sworn to bow down only to God the Beloved, he was asked one day to show fealty to mankind. Lucifer's refusal to divide his love became a jealous stone-hearted vow to love neither God nor mankind.

Some say that it was vainglorious pride that caused the damnation of the bringer of light. It is told that he was created second only in beauty to the master of all things. One day, while craving some measure of evidence of his own exalted worth, he dared to sit upon the heavenly throne. It was this original act of free will that sealed his doom.

Most believe that the echoes of that choice and the stupendous battle that followed it, the war between the very hosts of heaven, live on only in metaphor and allusion, in the verses of poets, in the lyrics of modern minstrels and in the hands of sculptors. But, even now, the conflict persists in full force in the feeble hearts of men. The proof is there in clandestine gatherings of cross-burning buffoons who, in the name of God, demonize others who are different in language or in color. The proof is there in the legion of hair-sprayed and bewigged televangelists who insist through perfect teeth that personal wealth and a full head of hair are a true measure of heaven's favor. The proof is in the constantly recurring fall of man's wisdom, from far-reaching vision and personal enlightenment down to institutionalized teachings, and from there downward to close-minded dogma.

Few know that one small but deadly military engagement of that heavenly war actually took place here—not in the distant Hesperides, not in faraway Eden, but here, south of the Rio

Grande in the land of Mexico. It happened, not in iambic pentameter and English, but in Spanish, Uto-Aztecan, and Nahuatl. Instead of a timeless engagement of towering symbols and sublime and deathless carnage, the war in Mexico was lowly and rude and blemished by rash acts and their grievous human results. It was fought by *hombres y mujeres*, by men and women whose wounds were cursed by the infernal poverty of mortal blood, mortals whose cause was blighted by the plenitude of human pain and by the ungodly prospect of cold, everlasting night.

There are no grand, sprawling ruins of this war, no epic poems or flowing, white statuary. There are no tall monuments and few if any headstones. Few remember the so-called Christero War and the deaths of tens of thousands. But there is one small landmark to that war and to its countless dead, and it can be found in each and every cathedral, church, and chapel in Mexico. The marker is a room, not a dignified chamber or silent cloister or reverent alcove. It is simply a room lined with shelves and coat hooks that is not a part of the church, nor is it part of the secular world outside. It is, in all truth, a way station on the frontier between the two.

Visit any church in Mexico. Stroll through the tall front portals made of weathered, handcarved wood. Walk quietly down the aisle, rubbed concave over the years by countless brown knees. Move past the pews—notice the brightly colored paintings and icons overhead as you walk; there is a gold-and-red aureole; there is a mandorla in white and deep blue, a halo, a nimbus, a vision of glories. Go past the altar and toward the chancel. Someone may be there sitting silently in the glow of candles. Ask a pious priest or a gentle nun to come take a walk outside with you to enjoy the sun and air of Morelia or Cuernavaca or Guadalajara. They may very well agree to walk with you, but first they must visit that special room. It is not a tradition that they must follow. Nor is it a mandate of the church. It was once the law of the land, a law preserved even now in the Mexican heart.

Habits, cassocks, and birettas must first be removed, then carefully hung there; they are not to be seen in public. Cinctures must be loosened there, albs and maniples folded away. Brooches must be unpinned there, and scapulars are hung up with the surplice and stole. Nowhere in Mexico may these vest-ments be seen on the street. It is the last and only reminder of the Christero War.

In 1914 the Mexican Catholic Church owned more pesos than the Mexican government, half the arable land, and one of every three buildings in the country. In the face of horrible star-vation and pestilence and the growing fury of the Mexican Revo-lution, the church continued to preach to the campesinos and the peones its age-old doctrine of resignation and submission. The sermons had changed little in four centuries.

When the revolutionary cry for land reform was the loudest, the church hierarchy issued an anathema against all agrarian re-formers, thereby alienating all but the most conservative ele-ments within the country. Intellectuals, teachers, students, even the poorest of all and the foundation upon which the church was built, the Indians, turned against the priests.

In 1917, all temples and churches were seized by the state; their naves, confessionals, and poor boxes were nationalized. Priests, brothers, and nuns were suddenly given the lowly status of tenants at suffrage. Ultimately, all religious processions were banned from the streets of Mexico and the wearing of clerical garb was made a crime punishable by imprisonment.

But the final blow to the church was a clause that was added to the Mexican constitution requiring that six years of socialist education be given to every Mexican child. A new program of mandatory secular education was initiated, flooding the country-side with enthusiastic and impatient young teachers. Angered bishops and priests believed that this would surely mean the end of religion in Mexico . . . and the coming of the antichrist.

The Christero War began right here, between the school-teachers and the parish priests—in minor backwater skirmishes over the souls of peasant children. The church conspired to blame every sickness, every miscarriage, every drought on the new teachers, while the teachers exposed and publicly con-demned nuns who had taken secret spouses and priests who had sired illegitimate children.

For the first and only time in the long history of the church, the papacy in Rome ordered a religious walkout, a strike that would leave the common people without Mass, without baptism, and without the Eucharist for a full three years. The angry Vatican branded President Plutarco Calles as the true antichrist and confidently predicted that the campesinos would raise a woeful clamor and cry for the return of their cherished priests. Even the president believed that the prediction might be right.

Both were wrong. The churches continued to be filled with penitents and worshippers each Sunday morning. The smoking censer swung in Indian hands, the votive candles still burned, and the long pilgrimages to sacred shrines continued. Centuries of strict ritual and rigid formalism had created a flock of silent penitents who did not require a subdeacon at the pulpit or a robed priest at the confessional. The Indians had never paid attention to the Latin Mass; their Bible was in the icons and in the paintings on the walls of the church. The absence of the church hierarchy was barely noticed. But this indifference did not put an end to the conflict. It was only the beginning.

In the years that followed the Vatican's order, the army paid local informants for the names of devout worshippers who were seen praying in their homes or anyone who inadvertently made the sign of the cross. Bounties were placed on the heads of priests, and anyone caught harboring a priest was shot. The military hung Catholics from every telegraph pole and tree. They dynamited churches and machine-gunned pilgrims as they walked to their shrines. They forced priests to marry or be killed in the town square. It is recorded that on several occasions priests were forced to consummate their new marriages in public.

The priests and their militant sisters superior led squads of infantry against schoolteachers and administrators, butchering them at their blackboards and behind their desks. Monks, altar boys, and nuns became experts in the manufacture of firebombs and in the use of explosives. They terrorized farmers who had moved their families onto church land, and they massacred both soldiers and civilians on passenger trains. Finally, in 1928, at a state banquet celebrating the election of a new president of Mexico, Álvaro Obregón, two Christero soldiers, a portrait artist named José Toral and a nun, Sister Concepción de la Llata, known to history as Madre Conchita, succeeded in assassinating the new president as he ate his dinner.

Some claim that this strange war did, in fact, have one

solitary formal monument dedicated to its memory: the bullet-ridden bodies of a martyr and his brother. In 1952, despite no formal normalization of its relations with Mexico after the end of the Christero War, the Vatican's Congregation for the Causes of Saints accepted the petition for sainthood of a young Jesuit priest named Miguel Augustine Pro, an alleged member of the National League for the Defense of Religious Liberty. Condemned as a conspirator, he was put before a firing squad, and it was said that he died with the cry of the Christeros on his lips: "*¡Vivo Christo Rey!*"

In 1986 Pope John Paul II approved a decree of Beatification of Miguel Augustine Pro. Documents unearthed decades later proved that it was his brother who had actually shouted those fateful words with his final breath, that it was his brother who had plotted against the government. Miguel Augustine and his brother were both put before a firing squad and were killed by a single salvo of bullets. History tells us that the executions took place on the hottest day of the year 1927. Witnesses to the event recalled that Miguel never spoke a word, but that his brother never stopped speaking until the moment that the bullets silenced him. His brother was a man named Humberto.

There are those who believe that history skulks and broods in the shadows just out of sight of the living, that the past is merely the running hunt and the agile quarry of crippled memory. Such men do not see with the eyes of watchers. There are those who look back in time and see only cold, unwilling wedlock between our abridged lives and the countless dead. Such men do not share the long gaze of messengers. Some even hold that the moment dies with the man, that love and hate can only be suspended in protoplasm. These men are unable to witness with the eyes of angels. To those mortals who yearn to see, Humberto's tale flutters—along with all of man's remembrances—in the airless wind above the worlds.

In 1927, it was burning and dusty as only the state of Michoacán can be. It seemed that even the insects were going crazy in the heat. It was so stifling and airless that they could not possibly fly. Humberto could see them there and over there, crowded together in the shade of trees and on windowsills. He realized that the absence of their buzzing and chirping had created a heavy and hopeless silence. He had hoped to live so much longer than this. He had hoped to end his life far away from here.

"Have you ever seen such a thing?" he asked his brother, but Miguel was deep in prayer and did not answer.

The two condemned men were escorted by four poor soldiers who wore military surplus uniforms. They were mere boys dressed in those French abominations that Santa Anna and Díaz made all the rage—those lavender-and-white uniforms with the enormous epaulets.

"You see, *mi hermano*," said Humberto to his unhearing brother, "ours is to be a fashionable demise. From the look of the Mexican army you would think that Maximilian and Carlotta were still alive! No wonder the *Federales* are always so demoralized— they are forced to wear bedroom drapes and kitchen curtains. *Dios mío*, our firing squad looks like a clutch of hairdressers!"

Miguel Augustine only rolled his eyes with a look of sublime disgust as his brother attempted to make light of their condition. Miguel nodded solemnly toward his brother, then slipped back into his prayers. Humberto did not have the strength to pray; he never did.

"Such a stylish firing squad," Humberto continued, with a feigned air of bravery and the sound of disgust in his voice. "We are to be assassinated by fops and jackanapes. I know those boys, *hermano*!" he shouted into his brother's endless stream of prayers. "They are boys from your flock! They are Tarascan boys who have confessed their lewd little sins into your ear. They are altar boys who have lit the candles, then slept through your sermons."

They were local Indian and mestizo boys who had found the military more exciting than the Mass. He cursed their uniforms as he walked, pointing out *pantalones* that were too short, sleeves that were too long, and one shirt that was inside out. He wondered aloud that they didn't have the good sense to trade *pantalones y camisas* back and forth between them until they at least looked presentable. And none of them had ever worn boots before—that much was obvious to Humberto. He could see the pain in their pathetic marching, and he shouted the fact to the spectators who watched their progress.

"So, it will be those *payasos* who will be the death of us," cried

Humberto. "It will be these bumbling, untrained ragtags on this simmering day, and that *gordo* from Quiroga." He nodded toward the scowling figure that walked to one side of the procession, an obese corporal who had managed to transform his self-consciousness about his great girth into a personality of unmitigated cruelty. There was sweat raining down from beneath his hat, and wasps were hovering at his hairline for a taste of pomade.

"I am sure that birds will always go miles out of their way to shit on him," sneered Humberto.

The corporal's uniform was streaked with the disdain of the skies. He was the one who shouted the dreadful orders that morning. And pursuant to those orders, the four *soldados* led the condemned men out to the field where they were to die.

The seven men made a curious parade for the calm perusal of the townspeople; those vile lavender uniforms, a Jesuit priest's black-and-white vestments, and Humberto's tan dustcoat were all draped on the rising heat like a moving clothesline. It was a soundless, two-dimensional walk, a walk of length and a walk of breadth, but it was a walk without time.

The procession moved up the path to the south of the *zócalo* and passed by a large, open doorway that looked onto the *plaza de los muertos*. Its double doors were opened and tied back with leather cords. There was a woman seated in the doorway, intently putting on her makeup. Her pad of rouge stopped for an instant. Did she sense Humberto's thoughts swirling frantically about her face?

I think that she is so very beautiful! ¡Que linda! *She is mestiza. Her cheekbones speak of Lake Janitzio, and her sad eyes tell of Catalonia. All this heat and there is not a bead of sweat on her brow. I cannot believe the length of her slender brown legs . . . endless legs! Yet they are somehow punctuated by the bluest of high heels. One satin shoe is off her heel and swaying gently on her toes, the other has edged over on its side to tenderly kiss the dust. I pray that we will walk slower as we pass her. I intend to remember forever the smoothness of her lithe, elegant fingers; it is as though all of the peasant stock has been carefully wrung from her bearing but has somehow been left behind in her soul.*

God, the things one wishes to remember! Our eyes will soon meet, mine and hers. Every man knows when that happens, even a man like me—who is about to die. Imagine—her beautiful city is burning, her church is about to be razed to the ground by the army, and her padre is about to be assassinated along with me, his foolish brother, and there is holy war raging between families and friends . . . and here she is carefully lining her lovely, languid eyes and her full lips.

He looked deeply into her eyes, and all at once he began to believe that it was a fierce care, a raging care, that he saw there. Each wisp of the light hair of her lashes seemed to be leaping imperceptibly. He could not admit this to his brother, but his last clear thought would be just how much he loved women . . . how much he loved this one in particular . . . this woman who would soon watch him perish. Now that her eyes had caught his own he could see her hurriedly, desperately reaching for a color . . . any color.

I am there, hovering eternally there, frozen above her small palette of hues. I am as red as a felt dress; green as youth; blue as the sky in Oaxaca. Do her slender fingers hover near me, somewhere over the color of musk? There are colors like scents, flashes of another world in the tints, the musk of my moldering memories. I choose to remember her, not my brother's prayers, not the three wooden, bullet-ridden silhouettes or the logs stacked up behind them to prevent ricochet. I must remember her and not the end of me, the pain that waits for me.

The walking suddenly ended. Their feet would never move again. Some faceless man shoved them up against the silhouettes and began to lash their bodies to the riddled wood, but the fat corporal grunted an order and the ropes were dropped. Humberto smelled the breath of the faceless man. It smelled of fear. It smelled of kerosene. The brothers began to weaken within; their souls were closing up and their bowels were losing their grip. Humberto felt humiliated by his own quivering. He knew in that moment that there was no place in the entire world where he could sit or lie down in peace. There was no cool drink or savory food for him in all the universe. Others would have his.

He could hear his brother praying. He heard his brother refusing the blindfold out of bravery and then his own voice refusing it out of anger. They could not acknowledge each other; they could not say good-bye. Neither man had the will to validate or even countenance this horror. The brothers began to breathe quick, shallow breaths that soon merged into a single synchronized wind. Death was coming; it was squinting at them down a long, dark barrel. Fingers that just months ago had lifted the blood of Christ to their lips were squeezing triggers.

Humberto had been watching the beautiful woman's eyes, and all at once he saw them shiver and close. He heard nothing of the world now because his heart was louder. He did not hear the commands or the cocking of the weapons, but her blue eyelids were measuring with great precision the few moments left of his life. He turned away from her and from the firing squad and caught a last glimpse of his living brother, eyes wide open, facing the oncoming missiles. His face was as handsome as some holy immortal's.

Suddenly Humberto screamed something at the top of his lungs. His mind no longer commanded his voice and he began to sob just as the *balas* blew his backside open.

For a moment . . . perhaps an instant, I am flying above it all. Vuelo sin callerme, I am flying without falling. I see the plaza of death, the town, the world. I see the bodies of my brother and me. We are linked by stillness, embracing each other and eternity. The moment ends as quickly as it began, and I am falling back to earth, suddenly saddened and hounded by the demands of solid things. Numbness and heat clutch at my edges, then invade me. Cell after cell of a twisted body lays claim to a piece of my soul and, finally, I am occupied. My moment of flight is over.

All was quiet but not silent. There was no silence, merely the unsteady hush of the town groping for its usual patterns of life after some piece of it had been cut away. At the far edge of the square the soldiers were sitting in the shade and smoking cigarettes. The fat corporal and three others were laughing. One of them had moved away from the others. Was there sadness on his face? The cloud of sulfur that had enveloped the bodies was giving way to the smallest of breezes.

A farmer's wagon creaked loudly through the streets. From somewhere in the distance there were the rustle and thump of sugarcane being loaded. The sound of children playing penetrated Humberto's ears, and dozens of insects were making their way into his wounds and his eyes. A motionless Humberto wondered if it were possible that dead men could hear and see for a time. He mused that if he was no longer alive then there must be a level of death beyond this, and his poor brother had found it— for he was far more immobile. Death had settled onto Miguel's face like dusk on a far horizon; the edges of Miguel's skin were becoming vague and indiscernible from the dry dust. If I am alive, thought Humberto, then I dare not move. I must copy Miguel—I must mimic his stillness.

When the soldiers had gone, Humberto heard the gossip of curious passersby as they came to stare at the bodies. Some mothers whispered softly to their daughters that the priest had been shielded from the bullets by his brother, that he had deliberately thrown himself into their path. Some veiled crones with rosaries hidden in their girdles declared under their breaths that Miguel was a martyr. One toothless old man came over to where they lay and made the sign of the cross before tearing a button from Miguel's tunic. The same old man returned an hour later and, with a razor, removed Miguel's ring finger.

That beautiful woman in the blue high-heel shoes, whoever she is, she alone knows that I acted out of rank cowardice. I feel her gaze bearing down on me, even as my brother and I lie outstretched in this trench. I can see her through half-closed, motionless eyes. She has finished her makeup. Now she lifts a mirror to her face for a fleeting moment . . . and now she is leaving, going somewhere inside. First she divides the universe in two; then she walks away . . . just like God.

All around the bodies, nervous but polite village parishioners were standing and whispering, staring . . . washing clothes and preparing themselves for bed. They had watched as two men moved into memory. They had seen the sky brushed thick with the black pigments of woe, and they had seen the sudden blaze of crimson and white infused with strokes of burnt sienna as shots were fired. But each would return quietly to his own life. There had been a photographer there, a tiny man with an enormous tripod and field camera. There had also been an impatient mortician to take some quick measurements, then leave for the night. But there was no Francisco Goya among them.

The fire on the rooftop reached upward to lick at the trails of smoke that were curling into the ink-black sky above San Francisco. Without warning, the old arsonist removed his trousers, then tossed them over his back and into the waning fire. The pants would feed the flame. In the distance, the faint sound of the ambulance and the firetrucks could be heard.

"Miguel Augustine!" Humberto screamed into the cold streets below. "I have not said my brother's name aloud in over sixty years. I can say it now. Miguel Augustine!" He screeched the name into the night air of the Mission District.

"*Nos abrazamos hasta el amanecer.* We embraced until dusk. I enveloped him with my arms, and my soul held close to the memory of that lovely, distant woman. I think that it is the flux, the confusion between the two embraces, that has kept me alive so long. Then, when the town was lost in fitful sleep, I rose from our common grave to begin what very few would call a new life. And he . . . he became dust, and the dust became land, and the land became a landmark for a pilgrim's journey's end. My brother, Miguel, became a martyr."

His hands moved to his eyes, and he pressed his palms against his eye sockets as if to purge the vision.

"I saw her blue high heels flashing into the dark as she left my dying world for the solace of her kitchen. Her lovely shoes were the last things I saw in my first life."

"You see"—he looked over his own shoulder at the two wounds in his back—"they have never really healed. I have merely reopened them."

The woman at his side said nothing. She merely stared into her looking glass at his wounds. Humberto's agony had been pressed like runes into his clay. Lovingly she swabbed his back with his tunic and watched as the light of the fire blazing behind them played across his face and danced wildly in his quaking irises. For a moment, she was tempted to look directly at him, but changed her mind. The very thought of it made her shake with fear.

He put an arthritic finger to his temple and tapped the skin and hair there for a few silent moments. He was hearing again the diminishing tap-tap of heels on tile.

The old man stopped moving as his ears caught the sound of the approaching sirens.

"*Las sirenas,* the sirens are not what they once were. We were once powerless to resist their haunting call, yet these days we can only shudder at their high, cutting voices. We turn away from their chrome pectorals and brass lungs. These days their melodious singing has gone monotone, and they've stooped to warning men of a doom that has already transpired."

The thin, faraway note at first seemed directionless, everywhere, just a painful wheeze in the breath of the city. Then, as the breeze shifted, worried heads began to turn in unison and animated gestures slowed for an instant as human souls measured distance, direction, and proximity of the siren's call.

On Twenty-fourth Street, turgid green mangoes waited on stainless-steel scales while customers triangulated the alarming sound. A sad gray fish in a Chinese restaurant lived a moment longer while a fry cook measured the song. The sirens could be going to only one particular place, and the city was made up of so many millions of places.

The fire's glow transformed blown cinders into a red as deep as drifts of purgatory. At the roof's edge there was blue flame licking upward from an electric throat, and at its base the two long-shadowed arsonists embraced in simple complicity.

"Some people shunned me as I ran from rancho to pueblo to *ciudad*." Humberto continued to rave his tale to no one in particular and to everyone. "Some tried to sell my location to the *Federales*. Some hid me and brought me food from their tables. I remember that someone pushed my wounds shut with her fingers while a praying crone poured a derivative of opium onto my teeth. I seem to remember the taste of wine.

"I had a trinity of wounds: two in the back and one in my abdomen. They were huge wounds, yet there was so little blood. I remember some faceless old man dripped dollops of hot wax onto my painful punctures while a quivering voice nearby recited the extreme unction. And I've outlived them all—every man and woman who was present at my first death! All of them but one," he laughed. Even as he laughed he wondered if there were two people still living. Could she still be alive . . . the woman with the endless legs and the blue high-heel shoes?

"I know now that I was recruited by God from right out of my cooling grave to come north and work in this furrow."

He pointed to the roof beneath his feet.

"And tonight I have fought alongside the angels. My brother would be so proud of me," the old man smiled.

Slowly, without losing his smile, he drew the knife across his abdomen. A deep red began to unfurl beneath a perfect line.

"This was my third wound. It has never healed anyway. Over sixty years now."

The fire at his back began to grow once again. It had changed from the blue of electricity to the bright orange that signals the involvement of newfound wood beneath the tarpaper and paint.

"Miguel, can you hear me?" he cried out into the night sky. "Do you remember Morelia and the towering cathedral across from all the coffee shops? Do you think it's changed in all this time? Can you see it from where you are? Do you recall that evening when there was a melancholy cavatina flowing from within the enormous cathedral in Morelia? Oh, *mi Miguel*, the years before our death were so naive and beautiful! I recall wondering at the time how something so tremulous, so tender as that melody, could flow from an edifice so huge, so imposing. It seemed to me that each precise note was bathed in a profound, desperate solitude and could only hope against hope that another note would follow. Such lonely notes.

"I remember that the music came forth at the very moment in the evening when the stifling heat of the day had just given way to the nightly, magical breeze that always seemed to sweep the crumbs from the tablecloths and blow paying patrons into the cafés across the street. It blew them in from their mundane chores and concerns to sit and savor the end of day. Ah, Miguel, *mi hermano*, the night sky in Mexico can be like a weightless ocean suspended above your head, wet with black and glowing with phosphorescent stars!"

The old man's eyes looked upward and backward, never seeing the glare of streetlights and the ceaselessly flashing lights of Sutro tower. He squatted down on his hams to rest. The soot and smoke had turned his face and hair to a dull gray. He looked like a thin gargoyle.

"You asked me the question that I have been so afraid to answer for all of these years. 'Will we be far from one another when we die?' What a thing it would be if every friend, every lover could tell those who care, at the very instant of their death, 'I am pinned beneath a beer truck in Belize. I am dying here in my sleep on a dark street in Tegucigalpa. I am gripped by palsy and falling forward into one of the lovely fountains in Paris.' "

Humberto spun around slowly as he spoke, casting his words into each of the four corners of the compass.

"We were on the plaza just outside the huge front door of the cathedral. There was sound of the cavatina . . . a single guitar. Have I said all of this before? My madness grows! Each note seemed to blossom from between the iron portals like the flowers of a cusp magnolia. I remember the guitarist's head falling slightly each time he plucked a string.

"There were votive candles in the doorway, hundreds of tiny red suns puddling their wax and gutting at their own roots. From where we sat they looked like blazing jacaranda. Some glasses even cracked violently as we listened and as I pondered your disturbing question.

" 'Will we be far away from one another when one of us dies?' I pictured Guadalajara. Back then, that seemed so distant. I even went so far as to imagine Mexico City. How could I have known that fate would give me two answers to that sad question?

"I turned to you to see whether the question was in earnest, and I saw your hand disappear into the blouse of your young female companion. Was her name Alyda? And to think, in just a few years you would be a priest and, a few years after that, a murdered martyr. I admit that I was jealous when I saw your fingers touching her bosom. She was a girl that I myself had eyed lustfully more than once. 'America,' I announced, with some anger. Do you remember? I said America to hurt you, to place a great distance between us at the moment of your death or mine. But you didn't seem to be listening. You were looking into the cow eyes of Alyda *quien sabe*, whatever her name was.

"It was a different time then, Miguel. It was before all our blessings began to singe us, before God's inscrutable whirl of wind blew my poor chrysalis this way and that. Our brows were embossed with youth; we had violet veins, and frail summer moths rode our thoughts. God, we spoke in cluttered voices with leather lungs! The intellectuals flocked to sit with us: young, poetic, suicidal Russians; Swedish girls whose anger verged on nymphomania. Knowledge was a silver portal. We were so young. We had so many answers!

" 'I have often thought of going to the city of the angels,' you said finally, in exchange for my angry statement about America. 'I will go to Los Angeles. I wish to hear the angels' gossip,' you said. 'More than the endless trisagion, I want to hear their gossip.'

"I scoffed at your frivolous dream. But I can hear the angels' gossip now. Now I know that your dream is not frivolous."

The old man on the roof looked toward the sky and the moon above his head and strained as if to hear something, some faint secret. Below him, on the street, a crowd had begun to gather to watch as he moved carelessly along the precipice. One or two people were standing in a nearby phone booth, trying desperately to get through to the police. At Mission Police Station, all of the phone lines at the dispatchers' desks were flashing.

"Angels burning?" the police dispatcher at the Hall of Justice asked incredulously.

"¡Angelitos ardientes?" asked another.

"A possible suicide? A naked prostitute and an unidentified flying object? A burning chariot that crossed the sky? And now we've got over a dozen reports of a homicide at the Fourth Street drawbridge! Jesus, I should've called in sick!"

Above his head, Humberto watched as the metal and glass pieces of a neon sign popped and cracked within the tides of intense heat.

"Do you hear it? Do you hear their palabras, the words of the angels as they depart?"

Shards of glass and burned wire were dropping into the street and onto the sidewalk.

"They can set meteors aflame with their harmonies. Their voices are as close as the twin prongs of a tuning fork. They can speak Tagalog one moment, Spanish the next."

Tenderly, he placed his hand on the woman's head. Her mirror was upturned to see the angels.

"From their slipstream vantage we are but a single refrain among so many."

He closed his eyes now to improve his vision of confusion.

"The shellac domes that once separated all the worlds have cracked and split, and strangers from every level leak into adjacent earths. They are falling everywhere around us, drifting down like dazed parachutists. At first they are stunned by their abrupt landing, but then they move on. They are all alien to one another. They wander from here to there not realizing that it's vertigo and loneliness that stun them. They mingle with the sons and daughters of man and forget altogether who they once were." He pointed downward to the people gathered in the street.

"Can you hear those loudmouthed angels speaking?" the old man asked them. "Can't you hear them? You'd better listen. They won't be here much longer. They're leaving us. The flames mean nothing to them. Nothing at all. *La verdad*, I can hear them."

The old man laughed. A strange little cackle. The black woman standing on the roof beside him stared into his eyes through her mirror, as if waiting for something else to appear there.

"They say that even my old world in Morelia has collapsed inward and commingles with all the others, high and low."

He suddenly moaned with the pain of his three wounds. Then, without a word of warning, he stepped to the very edge of the building, perching his toes just over the drainage gutter as though it were a diving board. He spread his arms, the knife extending from his right hand. He smiled at the woman by his side, then stepped suddenly into the night air, plummeting the two stories to earth. Flapping his arms did nothing to slow the fall. The crowd below, like Romans of old, fully expected the singular man to lift off and soar into the skies. They groaned when he smacked the pavement hard; then they rushed forward to where he lay writhing in agony.

The woman, now alone on the roof, stood stunned for a moment. She hurriedly removed her high heels, then ran for the fire escape and began her own descent to the street.

"Humberto, Humberto!" she screamed. "I'm coming, padre. Stay away from him! He can't fly anymore. His poor wings are flapping in a box somewhere. Get away from him!"

The old one was shivering on the sidewalk. The new pain of an arm broken in three places from the fall meant nothing when there was so much old pain. The sight of skewed limbs and the deep cuts on his body kept the curious but cautious crowd at a distance. The knife in his hand frightened many away. The few who remained took up a vantage point across the street to wait for either the arrival of the authorities or the alluring sight of death.

Slowly, the fingers of his right hand released their hold on the knife, and it fell to the sidewalk, where it rolled noisily, whetting itself on the concrete until it reached the gutter. It rolled over the edge and cooled in a yellow pool of transmission fluid. The knife would lie there for three days until it was discovered by a young, anonymous sociopath who would treasure it and nightly sharpen its edge with coarse fantasies.

The old man had begun to crawl, tentatively, yet with a look of expectation, his eyes locked onto the heavens above the stucco building to his right. He stared as though he expected his vision to be cleared, his line of sight to be unobstructed now by the abrasive, lifelong rub of ardor and the accursed power to live. His face showed the weariness of a man long lost in time and space. A man who has just fallen from the roof of a building and from the plane of seventh earth. A man far from the things that made him.

The woman completed her climb downward and ran to join the man. The sight of a naked woman who was bloodstained and carrying a crescent wrench and mirror drove the fearful onlookers even farther back into the night.

"*Lo estoy sintiendo. Lo estoy sintiendo.* I am feeling it."

He smiled weakly . . . a smile of genuine gratification. The old wound paths were alive again and pulsing with pain, and with the deep throb of holy revolution. Three undoctored, unsutured wounds had been clumsily closed decades ago, leaving behind hard crustifications of skin and karsts of senseless tissue. His wounds all resembled hastily covered graves; they had been filled in as quickly as they were made.

Humberto tried vainly to rise to his feet. The woman held her hands out to steady him as he dropped back down to both knees and then, finally, to a sitting position.

"The ambulance is coming," she said quietly. "I can hear it."

The old man smiled now and turned his head slowly to survey the streets and buildings around him. The bystanders, unable to understand the things they were seeing, and too scared to intercede, were slowly drifting away. The sound of the approaching sirens hastened their departure. None of them wanted to be witnesses.

"Tonight was a great battle, my sweet houri, my dear, gentle Aspara."

Humberto loved the very idea of the dark-eyed Moslem and Hindu consort angels who regained their virginity in paradise by losing it over and over again, by giving pleasure as a heavenly reward. He considered it to be such a pleasant conundrum, to prevail through continual surrender. It seemed so much more civilized than the sexless angels of Christian lore.

"A great battle indeed," he said, suddenly raising his left hand above his head in a gesture of celebration, a sign of victory.

"Today our small army has joined with heavenly troops, and together we have beaten the dark one. We've set him back a good month or two. Today we have won a decisive engagement against the son of the morning star."

He reached out and took the crescent wrench from the woman. He began to wave it back and forth violently until he lost his enfeebled grip and let it fly far out into the dark street. He tried to focus his eyes on the place where it landed, but he was too light-headed from the loss of blood.

"My relic. My sacred weapon in God's name," he muttered. "It was adjustable, you know. It could even fit nuts like me."

The puddle of rubicund liquid beneath his naked soles had spread out to cover the entire sidewalk for thirty feet. He felt its sticky warmth between his toes. There were more sirens wailing in the distance as he reached down once again to feel his opened scars.

His hand moved across his back from one rough, bleeding crater to the next. Core samples, he thought, as he plumbed the familiar holes again. The pads of his fingers stumbled from one to the other, measuring the rings of years. His weakening voice was barely audible now. His words were meant for a world long gone and for a dear brother long dead.

The woman by his side reached out again to touch the old man.

"You've gone and carried your guilt with you all these years," she whispered. "You've gone and bled another man's blood."

"And you, Queenie," answered Humberto, "are honored among women."

Above the bar, the remnants of the conflagration were smoldering and spitting. The fire had somehow burned itself out. Below the ashes and inside the bar, it was business as usual. Music was still spilling from the front door. The ambulance crew that finally arrived on the scene was shocked to see a sidewalk covered with shining blood for yards on either side of a thin gray man wearing only a piece of linen. A naked woman was seated adoringly at his side. At the edges of the enormous bloodstain there were people dipping pieces of cloth into the dark liquid, then hurrying off into the night.

As the doctor and the paramedic exited the ambulance, the driver proceeded to inform radio dispatch of his location.

"We're at Seventeenth and Shotwell. Looks like a war zone."

"Status?" demanded the dispatcher's dispassionate and disembodied voice. It was the paramedic who answered, speaking into a handheld radio.

"The male subject has three deep incisions, nonpunctate; they appear to be self-inflicted. It's very strange. There seem to be remote wounds beneath these. He's cut into scar tissue. He appears disoriented and he's losing pressure real fast. Looks like excessive blood loss to me. He's ninety over sixty."

"Normal saline is going to run right through him as fast as we put it in," added the doctor. "He's got too damn many leaks. Forget the morphine—he's feeling no pain. Besides, I don't think he could handle it."

The paramedic nodded. The enfeebled old man couldn't handle adrenaline either. He needed plasma or whole blood, but that was ten long minutes away, at the emergency room.

"Psych evaluation if he survives," said the doctor with a note of helplessness in his voice. "He keeps saying his brother's a saint."

"Whose isn't?" interjected the paramedic, who had just returned from a quick inspection of Queenie. "The woman with the mirror over there swears she's got her virginity back. She demands to see a gynecologist as soon as we get to San Francisco General! She claims that she can feel the maidenhead growing back right now! Where in God's name do these people come from? Where the hell do they come from? Why can't we close the borders and keep them out? What we need is a fifty-foot fence clear around this country."

Back in his seat, the driver looked through the windshield at the bloody man on the sidewalk as he was being placed onto a gurney. A cop had arrived and was giving the doctor and the paramedic a hand with the old man. In the rear of the vehicle, the black woman was mumbling something about her mound of Venus. The driver shook his head, but for an uncomfortable instant, her mirrored eyes caught his in the rearview mirror. It caused a simmering heat and sharp tension inside him that made him so uncomfortable that he turned away with a jerk of his head.

Struggling against the restraints of the gurney, the old man pulled off the oxygen mask that had been placed over his mouth, then reached up to grab the white lapels of the doctor's smock. The violent action ripped the IV needle from his right arm. In desperation, he pulled the young man's face toward his own. The intern, having seen death before, did not resist.

"What's he saying?" asked the paramedic from the front seat.

"He's delirious," said the doctor, "and there's almost no blood pressure."

"I'll bet the son of a bitch is always delirious. Crazy is probably more like it."

He turned in his seat, then lifted his right foot and rested it on the dashboard. He grabbed a clipboard and began to log in the time of pickup, the description of the patients, the cause of the injuries, and the prognosis.

"Do we have a name for this guy? What the hell do I put down as the cause of the injuries?"

"Evil," said the old man, suddenly straining to look at the paramedic.

"Put evil."

"Let's call this one in to emergency," said the doctor. "We'll need a gallon of plasma if he's not DOA, and a fourteen-day psych evaluation if he makes it. They'll probably put him in ward 7D, the security cells. We can dump the woman at the psych ward later, but I don't think she has any physical damage. I don't think any of the blood is hers. Shit, she even claims her hymen is healing. Someone else is going to have to check that out."

The ambulance pulled slowly away from the scene. Only a late-arriving fire truck remained behind. Its crew was loitering on the sidewalk and up on the roof. They could not understand why the fire had gone out by itself and why their water hoses, at their highest pressure, could not wash the bloodstains into the street.

"What's he mumbling about?" the ambulance driver called back to the intern as he reactivated the siren.

"He's saying something about angels. I really can't make it out."

There was a large compress at each cut that did little to stem the flow of blood. The saline was useless. It had soaked through the white sheets to the gurney pad and down onto the floor.

"These cuts just aren't that deep," the doctor screamed over the wail of the siren.

"He wants to die," said Queenie. "The last time he was killed, it didn't take."

The young doctor's eyes were almost trapped by those in the mirror when the old man began to speak once more.

"*Vuelo sin callerme.* I am flying without falling."

The paramedic in the front seat looked back to see the doctor, who was face to face with the crazy arsonist. The doctor looked up for a moment, and his eyes met those of the paramedic. The doctor then returned his gaze toward his raving patient.

"Kill the siren," the paramedic said to the driver. "He's almost gone."

In back, the doctor leaned closer to listen, out of decency. What else could he do?

"I am not me. Do you hear me? Never me."

There was desperation in the old man's voice now. He could feel a rope around his chest that was suddenly dropped to his feet, and he could sense his cavalier hand waving away the blindfold. He could see the carbines swaying now with nervous breath, the gunsights dancing maddeningly from thigh to heart to face.

"I always realize it at the same time and place in the reverie. A young woman in a doorway, about to turn her face from the hard sun, stops to gaze at me. I am not what you see. The one who soars is not me though I somehow rise on the winds. That much I do know.

"I am floating. I am unctuous with blue arms like a river. I am poised the way that windows and doors are poised in the openings of walls. I am hollow-winged, palsied, and armless between worlds, and I feel like a threshold. There is no other word. A threshold from which to salute those who suffer below."

The ambulance turned down Potrero Street and slowly moved through traffic toward the hospital.

"Now it happens. This is the place in my dream where something always happens. I try but I can't run from the stares of onlookers standing over my first grave. They see me ... right through me. My ribbons of rib bones, my canvas skin, and my broken eyes. I feel myself dying from their penetrating glances.

"Then I see it all from outside. I see that the body that is dying is not mine but yours. It is you, my sainted brother. I see it is you who is dying. You with the frost splitting you the way it splits stone, your skin curling like the gray leaves in a stagnant pond. Your legs are as limp as a spun bag of spider's eggs, and your feet are like paper. I am terrified. A fawn could step through you. Then all is still. My fear is gone.

"And from the tossing and turbulence of my nightly bedsheets I arose each day of my second life in false awakenings. I awoke to a life without landmarks. We are all lost and adrift on this land, so now I, too, drift away, a pilgrim in a land I cannot grasp."

The doctor felt the man's grip on his lapels weakening. Death was near. Suddenly, the dying man's eyes opened wide. Humberto pulled the doctor's face to his own.

"What does it mean, Miguel Augustine? Where is this place of freedom, this trap? What does it mean ... this snaring dream, this place on earth where children kill and postmen rampage? Where is it, this land of deep violence, beloved hatred, and soaring invention; of serial killers and armed cults; of grinding self-colonization and precious principle?"

The fat corporal's lips were moving. The woman's eyelids were dropping. The trigger fingers were bloodless now with the sudden pressure of exertion.

"How far away am I from you, my brother?"

There is the burn and soft severance of tissue ripped.

"I am dying here. *Me estoy muriendo aquí.*"

A failed voice exhaled with finality.

"America."

V

BOTH sides of the frontier were ominous and silent and as dark as pitch. Only the small enclosed outpost that marked the crossing point was illuminated, lit by a single beam aimed downward, barely striking the cement floor.

"You back already, counsel?" said the sleepy deputy, who yawned loudly and stretched before rising from his chair. "You just left here four hours ago."

"I know," said Zeferino, "but I couldn't sleep and I wasn't very happy with the first interview."

Teodoro had ended the first interview almost as abruptly as it had begun, citing old age as an excuse and bad bowels that offered almost no obstruction to foodstuffs.

"Didn't tell you a thing, did he? He's sure a piece of work," laughed the deputy. "Well, he talked to the press again right after you left. He says he needs to share his joy. I'll call him up for you. They're probably going to have to wake him. Did you catch him tonight on the late news?" Zeferino nodded, scowling at the memory of his client on the local news.

Beyond the meek light, deep in the realms of darkness, tethered men lay immobilized by their own living nightmares; only their poor and flightless dreams remained unfettered; the reveries of prisoners were failed alchemy, gibberish dreams of leaden lives never turned to almandine. Their dreams were as senseless and muddled as their crimes. The sleep of thieves was soaked with want, that of killers was turbid and boggling, encased within a sheath of sharpened lies. Rapists in their cots rubbed an abrasive nightmarish salve of calumny on their chafing thighs. Among these, innocent dreams hung from padlocks and door hinges like yellowed, forgotten bunting.

Then the guttural and hard sounds of barked commands could be dimly heard, their origins indiscernible in the black innards of the place. There was the sorrowful groan of roused men suddenly reminded of their circumstances and diving, once more, into the soporific arms of death's twin. There was the muffled clink and shuffle of chains on linoleum and concrete, which ceased for a moment as an interior door slammed shut.

Zeferino waited in the hallway, peering vainly through the bars of the heavy door that marked the border. As the sound of the scraping chains grew closer, the huge locking mechanism buried within the heavy door slid back reluctantly; its tightly wound relay and case-hardened bolt buzzed rudely, angrily, as though loathing every traitorous instant that they remained out of character, groaning in the knowledge that an opened lock is no longer a lock at all.

Suddenly an overhead light came on, illuminating the area just in front of the metal door. Zeferino could see that the bars of the door were fat and uneven, the result of countless layerings of paint by trustees beyond number. He stepped forward and ran his fingers over the paint. The last layer was a light coffee brown. A chip near an imperfect weld revealed that two previous layers had been blue and pink.

"They have to keep painting it," a voice said from the darkness behind the bars.

"It is a little-known fact that unresolved regrets, like salt air, will oxidize the hardest metal. The guilty and the innocent toss and turn. Only those here who have no remorse sleep well."

"Keep it down," another voice warned. It was the deputy who led the prisoner. Their voices grew less resonant as they came closer. Finally the forms of Ted For Short and the night deputy appeared at the bars. As before, the prisoner was full-body searched and stepped laughing from his chains just before the baffled officer could unlock them. As before, he entered the interview room with a cigarette burning between his bemused lips.

"You couldn't sleep, could you?" said Teodoro with a knowing laugh.

"I have heard, Teodoro, that you've confessed to just about everyone in this building and to anyone wearing a press badge. When are you going to confess to me?"

"Confession?" grinned Teodoro. "I guess it's very pious of me, isn't it? But I've never believed that it's good for the soul."

"Do you know what a Miranda warning is?" asked the lawyer. "Did any of the police officers advise you—"

The small man interrupted his lawyer by standing up abruptly and walking over to the small window. He looked out at the Ghost of the Moulin Rouge, thinking to himself that he would have preferred a Lautrec . . . a self-portrait of the artist.

"I don't want you talking to the press anymore. This is serious business, Teodoro; you've been charged with murder. Now, there are some preliminary matters that we have to get out of the way."

The smile seemed to disappear from the little man's face as he took his seat once again in the interview room. In truth the smile had only moved from his mouth to his eyes.

"I've spoken with the coroner, but I still don't have any of the police reports yet or the autopsy. I really don't know a thing about the prosecutor's case, except for what I've seen in the papers. Who is Bambino Reyes, Teodoro, and how do you know him?"

The suspect, without answering, looked closely at his attorney, confident that their meeting again, after so many years, had been preordained. It must've been. The last time the two had been together, the lawyer and the client had seen eye to eye, the two had been almost the very same height. What a horrible night that had been . . . the beginning of years of pain and hiding, the night that saw the first of three senseless killings. In truth, it had all begun decades before then.

"The newspapers say that Bambino Reyes had been moving from city to city for years," said Zeferino to an old man whose mind was elsewhere. "He's been chasing you, hasn't he? He's been hunting you."

"If we are gonna talk, Zefe, we have to start from the beginning. The very beginning of it all. I will tell you everything, even more than you want to know. Then all that has happened will make sense to you. You are involved in all of this. Didn't you know that?"

Zeferino could not answer. Nor could he respond to the uncanny sensation that everything that had happened to him since the moment he had heard of this case was all part of an elusive memory. In a dream, statements like Ted For Short's made sense. But dream or not, something kept the lawyer from affirming or denying the possibility of his own involvement. As he stared at Ted For Short, Zeferino Del Campo, for the first time, began to realize consciously that there had always been a mystery in his life, a locked room sealed off since childhood. He had always been aware of that forbidden room, but something had kept him from focusing on it, from prying that door open and peering inside.

"When you were a boy, Zefe, many people said many prayers asking that you be given the gift of forgetfulness, that you be allowed to forget all of the terrible things you saw. The price we paid for those prayers was that you forgot all the good things, too. You forgot us, Zefe. Well, it wasn't your fault. But that time has passed now. The angels will soon give you back your memories."

Teodoro turned his gaze away from the eyes of his lawyer, toward the window of the interview room and away from the haunting memories that he, himself, had never been allowed to forget.

"I will tell you everything . . . then I will do whatever you say. Is that okay with you, Zefe?"

His lawyer nodded, then stood up. Somehow he knew that, once again, Teodoro was ending the interview.

"You must do something for me, Zefe. Go to the café at Seventeenth and Shotwell streets . . . go to Raphael's Silver Cloud Café. There is a sign above it that will be irresistible to you. You must go now. Get some sleep. I have one last floor show to do in my cellblock. It's the midnight show." He shrugged impishly.

"Will it help the case?" asked Zeferino as he moved to the doorway and signaled the deputy that the interview was over.

"Just go there and see."

Zeferino fixed his client with one last questioning glance.

"I did it, you know," Ted For Short grinned sheepishly."I killed that . . . man."

Zeferino drove down Folsom Street wondering why he had never noticed Raphael's Silver Cloud Café and Bar. He had driven down Folsom Street, down Seventeenth, and even down Shotwell on hundreds of occasions, investigating scores of cases. He conjured up a mental picture of the area as he waited at a stoplight—the Rite Spot restaurant was there, a transmission repair shop, and an empty field surrounded by Cyclone fencing. How could he miss seeing something that Teodoro had insisted would be irresistible? He passed under the freeway at Division Street, then turned right onto Seventeenth. As he did so, a large advertising sign above the street suddenly came to life.

The instant he saw it he pulled over. He slammed one wheel into the curb, killed the engine, and slumped back violently in his seat like a man who has just had a fatal seizure. His lungs were heaving, his eyes were opened wide, and he seemed to be staring at the huge sign above the building to his right. In fact, he was pushing through the locked door of a room that had been sealed shut for over thirty years.

He reached up to place the heels of both hands over both eyes. He pressed hard against this inner sight, his wrists quaking uncontrollably as unfamiliar thoughts stepped tenuously out from a darkened corner of his soul; long-forgotten faces came forward into half shadow; lost names were almost audible; vanished places were cast in low light. Blinded by the palms of his own hands, he saw reincarnated lines of brown men laboring in their prime, bending in the hard, curving heat of the lettuce fields, their taut, salty bodies cupping soft, cool ideas within their sweating skulls.

Within his parked car, his thoughts flew with the speed of light back to Fat City: Sam Fao—Stockton in 1959. Back to noisy El Dorado Street, the Chinese-owned whorehouses, the noisy gambling rooms, the taxi dance halls. He smelled once more the foul, dank scent of opium dens in downtown Stockton, the musk of newly cut soil, and the alkaline odor of working men who have stopped sweating salt water and have started sweating their own life essence.

Before the lawyer emerged—before the ordered thoughts came forward, tied to the present by circumstances and by the constraints of linear time—Zeferino spent an instant inside a Quonset hut full of farmworkers somewhere in the Central Valley, a younger Ted For Short pulling silver dollars from behind an astonished boy's ear.

Stockton had once teemed with sojourners. It had been the world's capital of manual labor in those days. Beings from every world had gathered there to find work, to gamble, to love, and to learn to dance. Young men came from every place under heaven to spend themselves, to languish and grow old in anonymity.

So many things in his mind were crying out to be remembered, scurrying for a place on the tip of his speechless tongue. He seemed to recall a bench in a small park somewhere in downtown Stockton. It was a bench full of old men. From a feeding pigeons' level he looked upward at the oldest campesinos, sitting quietly on their bench in the park, any hopes of ever seeing Mexico or the Philippines again long gone. The bench had a name, a hard-earned name. What was it called?

Even as he asked himself the question, another memory pushed itself upward from his subconscious. He was a boy again, bending in the wilting heat of the Imperial Valley or the Central Valley and hearing once again the long-forgotten words of his Tia Juanita as she dipped dark green jalapeños into an egg-and-flour batter.

"Zefe, if you should ever get a toothache, pray to St. Apollonia. If you should ever see a leper, *mijo*, immediately say a prayer to St. Giles. And if you should happen to see a leper with a blonde, be sure to say a prayer also to Mary Magdalene, the patron saint of hairdressers. A prayer to those two should just about cover the situation."

It had been one of his Tia Juanita's ways of welcoming him to the camps, of preparing him for the hard life with the migratory farmworkers.

"St. Anthony watches over all of the workers, but *angelitos* will watch over you personally, *mijo*. You have my personal guarantee on that. They are always there," his aunt had assured him, "and they always will be there. I can see them now. There's one there and one over there." She had pointed about the room without using her hands and without looking up from her work.

The boy had not seen any angels when he labored in the sweltering heat of the Imperial Valley. Where were they? They were surely not there in the heat and the drudgery. Not even angels could stand that place; it was too much like hell.

At the edge of the hot, shadeless fields, Zeferino the boy silently worked the furrow closest to the highway. He was only dimly aware of the cars and trucks that passed in the distance, their shapes bent by snaking waves of heat. The squash he pulled from beneath the wide leaves were wet, and the stiff white hairs on the skin of the plants were working their way through his soaked leather gloves. Squash were as hard to pick as cotton, he thought. Both plants fought back ferociously; with all their fiber, they resisted being taken forcibly from their homes.

His hands were getting raw again, almost as raw as his back, which was now covered with a layer of white salt. The petroleum jelly that one of his *tios* had applied there to prevent sweat rash had been completely washed away by midmorning.

Zefe the boy paused to look to his right. What he saw there soothed and comforted him. Señor Chávez was out there as usual, passing out handbills that protested the miserable working conditions and the slave wages. He was young and unknown and picketing all by himself, stooping now and again to carefully smell the leaves for the telltale scent of insecticides.

Every fifth furrow from the boy's own to the far horizon held one of his uncles, Mexican *tios*, Pinoy *tiyos*, all of their arms flying from the plant rows to the wooden hampers that they dragged beside them. The ranks of workers were his family now, a male tribe of wanderers.

He could see their private reveries hovering above their bobbing heads like swarms of brown gnats. They would all sleep like death tonight, thought the boy. They always did. Now was when they did their dreaming. The boy could hear their dreams flitting in and out of his own like dolorous waves of radio interference. They were transmitting visions of windy corners and wet corridors and prisms of colored rain; of monsoon-drenched skies rushing down to batter banyan and of the flooded streets of Quiroga, the vendors scurrying to cover their wares with sheets of blue plastic. The dreams seeped like forlorn sweat through their skin and into their mouths and tasted like *halo-halo* and *agua de tamarindo*.

On so many cold mornings—far, far from this one, all of his *tios*, every one of his uncles grown old—their gray heads combed and motionless on silk pillows—would be lowered into the same dirt they had so lovingly tended with their lives. Even Señor Chávez.

As he gazed across the field, he saw that the *manong* and the braceros were racing each other again, having their usual friendly but intense competition. The boy found himself falling far behind once more. He wiped his eyes with the sleeve of his shirt and began to move with even more speed, the ache in his arms making him grimace. To ease the pain, he imagined that he was a foot soldier in Hannibal's army, laboring heroically across the snow-covered Alps. He imagined the cool lip of the enameled dipper and the dripping condensation on the sides of the water jug that waited for him at the end of the row.

He did not notice when the school bus pulled off the highway and turned down the dirt road toward the field. He did not hear the brakes being set or the door opening. He looked up from his work only when something told him to, urged him to in a small, directionless voice. He saw two shining black shoes perched together pertly at the edge of the field, not ten feet to his left. Above the shoes were white stockings and above those stood a little red-haired girl his own age, smiling with her whole face and wearing a flowered dress.

"Hi," she said, "I'm Tina."

Before the boy could answer her, a woman who had been busily lining up a row of children alongside the yellow bus called out frantically, then ran over to where Tina was standing. She knelt down and with a firm hand on each shoulder turned Tina to face her.

"Now, Tina," she said sternly but with obvious restraint, "didn't I tell you before we left the classroom not to get too close to them or speak to them? See, he doesn't understand a solitary word you're saying."

Tina, despite the restraints, turned her head to look at the boy, who had already moved down the furrow in silence.

"They're not from here, Tina."

The teacher had lowered her voice and found that she enjoyed hearing the heroic tenor of her own patience.

"Who are those people with him," asked Tina, "the shiny ones?"

"What shiny ones?" asked the teacher, who dismissed the nonsense with an impatient shake of the head. "They're all from another world. They're wetbacks. They're not like us."

Shading her eyes with her hand, she looked out at the brown men in the far furrows. Prideless men wearing ridiculous clothing, she thought. Straw hats tied down around their cheeks with red bandannas. And baseball hats under those! And why on earth did they wear three shirts? Then she turned her head toward the boy, to see what it was that Tina found so fascinating. All the teacher saw was a young boy working alone.

She shook her head, then tried to gather herself for her lecture on how vegetables got from God, to the fields, then to market, and finally to our dinner tables. She took Tina's hand and dutifully led her away from the dark furrows.

"From another world altogether."

Above Raphael's Silver Cloud Café and Bar, high above the entrance and in front of a strange ten-foot-tall shining pillar, was a sign. It was a sign from God. Two of His myriad, heavenly minions had been ordered to stay put. They were sensual lovers or doting siblings or laboring *compañeros*, sent by the builder of all heavens to work here and to remain laboring in this shabby world of men for a short season of a hundred mortal lifetimes.

The two were downed flyers, commanded to turn their ears from the synagogue of quarks, from the faraway, solemnizing rafters, and to listen from their feeble mast of lifeless metal and glass to the words of lowly man.

It was a two-sided neon sign, a brilliant, flashing display that could be seen from miles away. Twin Rubenesque cherubim were painted onto a metal form that had the dull-speckled, titian buff of a faded tapestry. Both had the burning red hair of a Pre-Raphaelite painting. Pink, crimson, and yellow neon tubes and lightbulbs were set off from the daubed metal surface by brackets and flashed brightly to mimic the image in paint.

The large-headed cherub closer to the street faced the northeast. He held a bow and arrow and fired it over and over at the other. The bowstring flashed yellow, dividing time into three distinct parts, from the draw of the string to the reverberating release, to the reloading and back, once again, to the draw. The red arrow flew between them. It was a pointed metal shaft on the greased metal track. Its bright neon profile plowed the atoms across the space between the cherubs, flashing three times before it struck home with a dull thud.

The arrow then darkened and returned slowly to its point of origin, where the bowstring was reloaded and a huge metal spring was recompressed. Each strike of the flying arrow caused a red heart on the eternally wounded cherub to glow brightly.

It was seemingly love that was shot so indelicately from one to the other: being sent, arriving, yet never, ever staying. It was seemingly blithe eros buzzing in concert with the loud, persistent hum of the transformers, clacking with the old mechanical relays and sparking with the motor, its worn carbon brushes glazed and crystallizing. It was agape that powered it all, the need for ideas to dive into form, for electrons to move like lemmings from negative to positive. When the glorious sign was alive and flashing, it was equal parts light and dark.

When Zeferino was finally able to open his eyes, he had been in his parked car for over an hour. It was another half hour before he was able to tear his rapt eyes away from the sign of the angels. He stepped from his car and began to walk slowly toward the entrance of the building. Beneath his feet, on the sidewalk near the front door, there were dark bloodstains that still seemed fresh, even wet. Wherever Zeferino stepped within the stain, the dull crimson seemed to ripple with depth.

Near the edge of the roof where it met the front wall were telltale signs of fire and water damage. Now he was sure of it—this was the site of the arson fire that had gone to three alarms at the same time as the murder of Bambino Reyes. Near the bloodstains and up against the wall of the bar, Zeferino saw hundreds of items, some hastily left, some placed with great care and deep feeling. There were crutches and prosthetic limbs, vials and hundreds of bottles of *medicina*. There were neck braces, syringes, and colostomy bags, a wheelchair, bottles of Vicks VapoRub and a single silicon breast implant.

"What happened here?" Zeferino asked himself as he stared down at the blood and the strange relics lining the sidewalk. He walked closer to the wall and began to read the small ex-votos glued and taped up here and there. One read "*Gracias*, Santo Humberto, for saving my son's life; his epilepsy is gone forever. For this great act of kindness, I will give up cocaine and I will kill all the *cucarachas* in my home."

There were thirty or forty similar ex-votos on the wall, some written in Russian and Portuguese.

Another read "Thank you forever, St. Humberto. I was a drug addict and a whore. When I witnessed your arching leap from the roof, I was down below rock bottom. Some guy on the sidewalk was taking bets that you wouldn't jump. There weren't many takers because, as you know, this here is a cynical world. He was giving eleven to one, so I bet everything I had. Well, to make a long story short, I cleaned him out. Now I am going home to Hayward with money in my pocket and nothing but a glow in the vein. I will pray to you each night for the rest of my life."

Below her ex-voto was a heroin kit. Next to it were condoms, some makeup, a small vial of breath freshener, and a tiny locket adorned with the face of Sophia, the angel protector of whores.

Zeferino tried the door but found it securely locked. He walked around the west side of the building, testing the windows as he walked, but each one was boarded up with plywood and ten-penny nails. There was a FOR SALE sign in each of the windows. He walked past the north side of the building, then turned to inspect the back of the bar.

Behind Raphael's Silver Cloud was a tiny twenty-five-cents-a-ride carousel that had spent its useful years in front of a Walgreen's store. Behind the sailor duck, the cowboy giraffe, and the zebra in a tuxedo forever following one another, there was an old yellow-and-black Checker cab body with all of its windows missing, its tires flat, and the engine and transmission long gone.

Zeferino walked cautiously to the cab, but not without a last, longing look at the tiny carousel. The childhood memories that were percolating in his soul had brought with them just as many childhood desires. Realizing with some sadness that the little machine was unplugged, he turned his attention back to the cab and noticed that the interior had been gutted except for the horn, the radio, and the trip meter. The ragged seats inside had been covered with blankets.

An old metal and neon sign that proclaimed EL CLUB MICHOACAN leaned unprotected from the elements against the trunk of the taxicab. So this was the bar's previous name. Beside the sign was a red tamale cart on wheels. It was covered with a tarp and protected from the rain. A sign on the cart declared it to be the property of the Queen of Tamales. Near the back door of the bar, the lawyer noticed a most unusual contraption. It was a rig made of ropes, a pulley, and a small platform that would allow for the transportation of things up to or down from the roof. To the right of the back door was a ladder.

Without knowing why, Zeferino walked to the ladder and began to climb to the roof of the Silver Cloud. As an adult he suffered from acrophobia but, for some reason, this two-story climb seemed no higher than stepping into his car. Halfway up he noticed, for the first time, that a small tent was pitched in the field next door to the bar. A fire burned in a pit in front of the tent and a pot hung over the fire. Why hadn't he seen the tent from the road?

Once on the roof, Zeferino noticed that a huge man was pushing a yellow cart on the sidewalk near the front door of Raphael's Silver Cloud. As he watched, the man and his cart came to a stop at the west side of the bar. Except for its color, the cart was identical to the one parked behind the bar. This cart was painted yellow and declared the proprietor to be the King of Tamales. Zefe smiled at the thought of royalty walking the streets of the Mission District.

Deciding that it was best to avoid being seen, he quietly backed away from the edge of the building. It was then that he noticed that there was a wooden tower on the roof. It was situated about ten feet behind the neon angels. On top of that tower was a small windowless shack. Both were newly painted a bright silver color, but it was obvious that some attempts had been made to repair the damage done by fire. Zeferino noticed that the angelic sign had also been repaired. On the roof next to an exhaust fan were old parts, burned and melted and covered with soot. There was an enormous motor covered with a tarp and a huge spring that had been burned off with a cutting torch. They were much larger than the replacement parts. The new track that guided the moving arrow looked like a toy when compared with the old one.

Next to the brilliant and noisy sign, the lawyer found a small bucket of grease and a screwdriver, someone's tool kit. Near the front edge of the building were two blue high-heel shoes. At the base of the pillar was an extra-large sleeping bag, rolled up and tied with a small rope. He climbed the short ladder that had been attached to the side of the tower, then stuck his head through a little hatchway and into the silver shack. Inside, there were two flat stones on a barren floor. Two small blankets were folded neatly and placed in a corner.

There were pieces of electrical wire that had been woven into a cat-o'-nine-tails. In a pile in the far corner of the shack were five or six bottles of rat, roach, and ant poison. Though there was no evidence of any sort of infestation, each bottle had been drained dry.

Zeferino reached in and softly touched the walls near the stone pillows. Instead of feeling the grain of the wood or the cold heads of the nails, he felt contrition in the walls; he felt the endless sorrow of a man who had suffered through a slow and lingering life; he felt the power of madness. He felt but as yet did not understand the feelings. Suddenly there was a noise behind him, the sound of spinning, squeaking metal and the banging of wood on wood. He turned quickly to see that the platform at the end of the metal and pulley rigging had been sent up to the roof by someone below. On the platform were a small white paper plate and two steaming tamales.

"Go on and try one," a deep baritone voice called up. "They is the best tamales you'll ever put in your mouth." It was the King of Tamales, grinning upward from the base of the ladder. He was a huge man. Zeferino noticed an old pair of boxing gloves that had been tied to the umbrella that shaded his cart. There was a half-full bottle of Wild Irish Rose in the man's hand.

"Lower the platform," shouted Zeferino. "I'll eat my food on the ground."

He climbed down the ladder, graciously accepting the plate of food when he reached the bottom.

"Zeferino Del Campo," he said as he extended his hand.

"King Pete, but you can call me King," answered the giant.

Zeferino walked to the fender of the Checker, where he husked the tamales and began to eat. He had noticed when taking the plate that the King of Tamales was very drunk, his brow was wet and feverish, and his eyes were bright red.

"You're right," he mumbled through a mouthful of corn-meal. "I can't remember having a better tamale. By the way, do you know someone by the name of Teodoro Teofilo Cabiri?"

"Maybe I does, maybe I don't."

"Do you know a man by the name of Bambino Reyes? Do you know what happened to him, why he was killed?"

"Man, you sure got a lot of questions, but you is moving too fast for old King. I'm a puncher, you know, not no boxer."

Emerging from a four-cornered, resin-dusted dream, he flinched hard to his left as a quick flurry of painful images jolted and stung him. As he did so, a soft halo of perspiration flew from his face and hair. He squared his broad shoulders to face the conscious present, then buckled down and to his right as if a hard left jab had landed upon his good intentions to be sociable.

King pulled out an old dented bucket from somewhere near the ladder and inverted it on the ground. He then lowered his body onto the bucket. His knees were not what they once had been. Zeferino moved away from the cab and closer to King in order to gain eye contact with the immense intoxicated man.

"Mr. King, I am Teodoro Cabiri's lawyer, and I would like to ask you a few questions about the circumstances surrounding the death of Bambino Reyes."

King's eyes were dull red slits in his shining face as he stared at the stranger. He bobbed his head almost imperceptibly from side to side, then blew gusts of wind from his nose. It was his defensive posture, not against a lawyer and his questions, but against the conspiring heavens that spread out haughtily above his life. His own personal god was a southpaw, and the black man who fought with his own bitter melancholy while sitting on a battered bucket had never figured out the southpaws. It was all he could do to cover up and hold on.

"Ray Arcelli done gloved me up once. I swear to God. Ray Arcelli, the world's best trainer and manager."

The black man extended his huge hands out in front of his barrel chest.

"So you is Ted For Short's lawyer, huh? Well, you should know he's innocent. He wouldn't steal a fly off'n a dead man's eye. What did you say your name was again?"

"Zeferino Del Campo," said the lawyer, stepping forward and extending his hand once more.

King shook the hand, then turned his bleary gaze from Zeferino and back down to his own two hands.

"Ted For Short didn't do nothing wrong, I'll guarantee that. You know, Mr. Arcelli done gloved these hands right here, and that's no lie. It was before my fight with Pepper Rojas. I wasn't his fighter or nothin'; he just wanted to help me out. It was good of him. I sure could have used a trainer like him. He could have looked out for me. It would have changed everything . . . everything. A fighter needs a good lookout. Now I ain't no atheist, but from where I sit, there ain't no management anywhere in this world."

He clenched his teeth and both fists in a gesture of regret.

"I could've had me a career. It was surely something though, the way he tore the tape with his teeth—every solitary piece was exactly three inches long, no more, no less. I measured them. I swear I did."

He shook his head in a demonstration of awe and sincerity.

"Then he'd take and lay them on the heel of the hand, across the crown of each knuckle and on the inside of the thumb like a sweet grandmother lays out them pieces of quilt. He'd stack the tape on, crisscrossing and overlaying so that none of his work would separate when them blows landed. Lordy, these here hands felt like snoozing papooses when he was done. Just like a couple of sleeping papooses, all snug and secure."

He smiled at the image in his mind. His wide face was a maze of cuts, and his ears were little more than twin mounds of layered scar tissue. There was a shallow trough behind his left ear where his skull had been caved in by a man wielding a pipe. Out of habit, King would lay an index finger into the trough as he asked a question or made an assertion. It was his most common gesture. It summoned up all of the complexities of both delivering and receiving pain, of wanting endlessly for some kind referee—just once—to lift King Pete's gloved hand into the air above the canvas.

"Happened in nineteen fifty-eight," he said, rubbing the trough once more with his left index finger. "I was sucker punched real good." He shook his head as he relived the pain. "I was working as a bouncer at a dance hall down in Stockton. I can't recollect the name of that place right now. But I shoulda seen it coming. I heard that the man who busted my head open got his comeuppance the very next year. No lie! Someone cut him up, sliced his throat from ear to ear. But still, I shoulda seen it coming."

As soon as his left index finger left the trough, a finger of the right hand replaced it there.

"Folks considered me a fighter, not a boxer, you see. I was a punching bag on legs that could hit back real good. A guy like me could always find work back then. My problem was, I could never see anything that wasn't right in front of me. Guys that could never pound with me could counterpunch me real good. When the word got out that I was blind at the sides, they all started to uppercut me and hook my liver."

He looked downward to a spot on his body just below his elbow, a spot that still gave him pain. Beneath his shirt and his skin, his organ, once liver maroon, had gone as gray as a dying fish.

"It sent me down to the nickel-and-dime shows real quick. I'd been climbing up the cards pretty good until word of my weakness got out. Pretty soon, I couldn't make the undercard at a dog fight. Then this happened." He pointed to the furrow in his head.

"The guy that did this come at me in a low stance, just like Jimmy the Sailor Melendez. Remember Jimmy the Sailor?"

The lawyer shook his head. As a boy, the braceros and Pinoys had taken him to the fights in Stockton, but he remembered no names or faces. He did recall that there seemed to be a lot of black and Mexican fighters.

"Jimmy the Sailor was killed in the ring about twenty years ago. It was down in El Centro, I think, or Calexico. They tried to tank him and got real careless. The coroner found some kind of drain cleaner in his system. Yeah," said King, "he fought that last fight in his sleep. He wouldn't go in the tank for them or nobody. He died standin' up. Anyway"—he returned his thoughts to 1958—"this guy outside the Rose Room . . . that's the name of the place!" He seemed pleased that his punch-drunk mind had actually generated a memory.

"This one guy outside the Rose Room pretended he was going to fight me straight up; then another guy up and smashed my head from the blind side. It's funny how things work"—his voice was cracking with emotion—"here I was working for a man over thirty years ago; then all these years later he comes out of nowhere and steals my woman away from me." King glanced mournfully toward the idle cart of the Queen of Tamales. "Then the old man goes and jumps off the roof."

"Humberto . . . the arsonist stole the Queen from you? You knew him thirty years ago?" asked Zeferino in obvious disbelief and understanding for the first time that the Queen of Tamales was one of the arsonists referred to in the newspapers. King Pete did not seem to hear the questions.

"Tell the truth, it wasn't much of a boxing career. But I stood in there with the best of them. Don't never doubt that for a minute. On my worst days I got paid ham and eggs and a cup of coffee if I was lucky. On my best days, my name was up there on the card and my mug was on picture posters that were almost as big as life itself.

"Willie Cooks remembers my hands, and so does Johnny the Longshoreman Bastille and the Irish kid, Battlin' Brendan Conroy. They all remember my hands, especially the right one." He held up a huge right hand.

"I've got a truckload of knuckles on this here fist. As soon as you get inside this here bar, Mr. Zeferino, you gonna have a lot of answers, and a lot more questions."

The old boxer wrapped a tamale with a napkin and extended it to the impatient lawyer, who wanted more answers, not more food. Zeferino accepted it and immediately began to unwrap it.

"A little girl named Annette Oropeza over in Oakland cooks these up for me every day. She makes the sauce, too. Buy a tamale from me and it's like they is so fresh you can taste Annette's fingers. I see you been up to the top." King gestured with a toss of his head at the tower and shack on the roof of the Silver Cloud.

"You know I built them things—the tower and the shack both—with these hands. You see, I loved Queenie, even when she was selling her body in the streets. I adored her when she was servicing them limousine drivers over at the hotels and blowin' the chauffeurs outside them Jewish ceremonies. I still loves her, them big legs and that high yella skin. I built it for her and for that crazy preacher man who finally went and killed himself. He'd been trying for years, you know."

King Pete paused for a moment to let his emotions subside. Every man in the Mission District had slept with Queenie, but he had never had the chance to consummate his marriage with her. He lifted his bottle of Wild Irish Rose to his lips and took a long, loving draw. No one prayed for King Pete's forgetfulness, thought Zeferino. It was homemade.

"Queenie was an eastern girl, you know . . . east Oakland."

The big man's thoughts were rambling now.

"My pappy named me after the patron saint of black men and slaves, that's a fact. I am King Pete Claver from Atlanta, Georgia, and a child of the Great Depression. Mr. Lawyer, just how is you fixin' to get into the Silver Cloud?"

Before Zeferino could answer, the huge man set his bottle down next to the bucket, then walked to the trunk of the Checker cab. He signaled with a nod for the lawyer to follow. After shoving aside the old neon sign, King lifted the trunk door. Inside, there was a large wooden box wedged between the spare tire and a case of Richfield motor oil. The box was made of hand-carved oak, painted in bright colors. King carefully lifted the lid of the box.

"Anatoly always says that Gypsies was given the right to steal by Jesus Christ himself."

Under the lid of the box were coins from every country in the world, eyeglasses, pens and pencils, wristwatches, billfolds, and cameras.

"But all this stuff was left in his cab," added King with a smile. "He tells me all the time to look and see that sometimes them artists paints Jesus with four nails in him when he's up there on the cross and sometimes there's just three. He says that out of all the people there, only the Gypsies tried to take him down from that cross. But they was caught after they had pulled out just one nail. It was then they was given the right to steal. You see, it was a gift."

After rummaging through the box for a moment, King held up a brass ring with a set of keys on it.

"I can let you in. No one tells me much, but I know you is supposed to go inside."

"What about the owner?" asked Zeferino.

King Pete Claver lifted a massive right hand into the air and pointed at the hotel next door to the Silver Cloud. There was a man sitting at a window on the fourth floor of the hotel. The man was staring down at King Pete and his guest. There was a smile on his face.

"The owner told me to let you in."

Raphael Viajero leaned out the window of his hotel room; the transparent white curtain rubbed against his forehead and nose as he looked downward to the roof of his beloved bar. A wave of sadness swept through him once more as he recalled the events of the past week. Such monumental things had happened on that roof and in the rooms below, events over a half-century in unfolding. Now he was packing his things and going home. He sighed aloud and was about to turn away from the window when he saw a car turn violently into the curb about a half block away.

He had watched as the driver sat behind the wheel staring at the sign of the angels and smiled as he stood incredulously in the center of the bloodstain that covered the sidewalk. Though Raphael had never met Zeferino Del Campo, he knew that he would be coming by sooner or later.

"None of us had any choice," he whispered to Zeferino through the curtains.

Behind Raphael, in his tiny room, were four large cardboard boxes and three suitcases all secured by rope, a traditional set of matched Mexican luggage. He was packing his things now that the business was put up for sale and the bar's purpose had been fulfilled—now that his own purpose had been fulfilled.

There was no cantina on earth like mine, mused Raphael. It was like an ark, like a *communidad de culturas*, a rest stop from all the selfishness and cruelty out there. Raphael looked down once again at his beloved bar. He would be taking the angelic sign with him when he moved. Raphael was among the few mortals in the world who could hear their conversations. Once after he had first installed the sign he had casually inquired about the situation up in heaven.

"¿*Como estan las cosas en el paraiso?*"

To his astonishment, he had been informed, almost matter of factly, that it was gloomy there because men on the various earths still did not understand that an act of kindness would always rise above the supposed glories and hobgoblins of all of their religions and all of their laws.

The answer from the seemingly lifeless sign had so shaken Raphael that he had only gone up to the roof once since that time. He had gone up to bring blankets and two large, flat stones to the mad priest Humberto and to Queenie, his reflective disciple. Like ancient anchorites, they had both wanted to use the stones as their pillows. On that occasion, the disembodied voice of the angels had asked him about the servitude to lies that was rampant on this world, about the bewitching luster of violence. The voice that Raphael Viajero had heard twice now was much too sweet for him to hear again.

The small billowing cloud that the twin angels stand upon is painted bright silver. "Lunar Agapeic" is the name on the gallon can that Raphael kept under the cash register, just in case the sign needed some touching up. When he had first opened his bar, Raphael called it the Club Michoacán, after his homeland, and it did a marginal business. Well, to tell the truth, it just barely made the overhead, month after month. The old sign is still out back. She's *la India bonita* with an earthen pot balanced on her head. She stands next to a bright green nopal cactus. He always served free *tacos y frijoles* at *la hora feliz*, the happy hour. He put up pictures of beautiful naked women on all the walls. Raphael recalls with a smile that one of his favorites had been a picture of a tall *Zapoteca con bustos como gotas de miel.*

But, aside from a few local customers, barflies *y borrachones*, there was never much of a crowd. He tried everything to make

Club Michoacán a success. He put in pinball games and staged a wet T-shirt contest every other week.

"We sprayed tequila gold on the girls. It works better than water. But I could tell there was something not quite right."

It was then that Raphael first met ravishing, resplendent Ruby. She just wandered in off the street one day, looked around at all the empty seats, and asked if he needed a floor show. She did a strip revue using stuffed turtledoves with real feathers. She told Raphael that she only used the bodies and feathers of her winged protectors after they died.

"I tell you, she was good!" Raphael sighed at the window as he watched the lawyer walk to the back of the Silver Cloud.

Radiant Ruby was so good at teasing that no one who saw her act could tell you if he ever saw any of her flesh. But even with her stripping, Raphael couldn't fill the room with paying customers. But Ruby had certainly filled the roof with her birds: sparrows, ravens, and parakeets. *¡Que milagro!* thought Raphael. Wherever she goes, they follow her, every kind of bird under the sun!

In any other place, Ruby would've packed them in. Raphael had heard that she did just that in Reno and Carson City. Things at his establishment were just not right.

"This whole place was not right . . . like something was out of balance; the toe-in or the caster and camber were all screwed up. I could feel it in the walls and in the air whenever I was alone or busy sweeping up. My business just crabbed along like a car whose frame had been bent in a collision. Something had to be done, but I sure didn't know what it was. I almost sold this place way back then."

He shook his head, then pulled a chair from beneath a nearby table and sat down. One day, a strange man named Simon from the old sign and paint company across the street came in and told Raphael that he had a special sign to sell that some fellow over in Daly City had contracted for; then his business, unexpectedly, had gone belly up. Simon insisted that Raphael come over and look at it. He told Raphael that he would sell the sign for his cost and throw in two or three gallons of paint.

It was mine as soon as I laid eyes on it, thought Raphael as he watched Zeferino climb to the top of the Silver Cloud. I put the sign of the angels up seven years ago and nothing has been the same since. *Nada*. Raphael gave in to the flood of memories for a moment.

"As you can see, Zeferino," he whispered to the man on the roof, "I've had it rebuilt since that day . . . since the fire. They repainted it and replaced the glass and the motor. The workman who restored the sign said that he'd never seen anything like it. The motor and springs were the largest he had ever seen on a kinetic sign, far more powerful than was necessary for a simple display. It seems that my Renaissance angels once had a medieval engine, *como una catapulta llena de luz*. It looks exactly the same as it was, but not really. Nothing here is the same. All I could restore was the sign and the roof, not the spirits that were once there."

He looked across the street as he spoke. Simon was no longer there. The Menander Paint Company went out of business less than a week after he bought the sign. Raphael watched as the lawyer climbed the second ladder into the silver shack atop the tower. The pillar went up a couple of months after the sign was installed. King Pete built the tower and the little shack there at the top with his own two hands. His only tools were a saw, a hammer, and endless grief. It was a hermitage, a mausoleum, a monument to his ruined marriage.

"No one asked my permission to build the pillar," he mused aloud, "and I really didn't care about it. I'm sure the city building inspector has seen it, but he never said anything to me and it never showed up on any of his reports. King built it for his wife. *Que triste*."

Then Queenie and that crazy Mexicano priest Humberto moved in. They had begun camping up there next to the sign after she abandoned King. It was Raphael's guess that he just wanted to put a roof over his wife's head, even if she didn't want him anymore. King always explained that it was his duty as a husband. It was the priest Humberto that drew up the plans.

In truth Raphael didn't know if he was really a priest or not. He had never had a real conversation with the man. But Humberto had once told Raphael that an old act of cowardice was the only thing that kept him from being ordained.

If Zeferino Del Campo can read Spanish, thought Raphael,

he will soon learn about Humberto's amazing story. There had never been a stick of furniture up there in the pillar. Raphael had given them some bedding and some candles, but aside from that, there was nothing else. Ruby got them some old clothes from the Salvation Army once. Otherwise, the two would walk around up there as naked as on the day of their birth. King Pete used a couple of gallons of the Lunar Agapeic paint to make the pillar and the shack the same color as the cloud beneath the angels.

Raphael watched as King Pete pushed his yellow cart down the street. The steam and smoke rising from his portable burners made his progress visible from miles away. Without fail, he stopped the cart for a moment of silence at Seventeenth and Folsom, the corner that Queenie used to work when she was a prostitute. She had also worked the same corner as a full partner in King's tamale business.

But King Pete was only truly happy when he was near the pillar and shack. Since the fire Raphael had rebuilt that, too, without really knowing why. The new owner would probably tear them down. He had done it for King. The old fighter still climbed up there almost every day and slept up there at night . . . even now.

"*Pobrecito* has nothing to live for since his wife Queenie went over the edge," Raphael spoke aloud to himself. "Padre Humberto is dead and she's over at Stanford Medical Center. They took her there from General Hospital." He twirled his index finger in a small circle near his ear to emphasize the insanity, without specifying just who was insane.

Experts had been flown in from all over the world to peer and poke under her pubic bone. Doctors came from the Hesperides, Zanzibar, and from Luxembourg to examine Queenie. The *National Enquirer* even ran a story about her. They reported that aliens landed on the roof of the Silver Cloud and abducted her. She was supposedly taken up to Venus, and when she was returned, she was a virgin again. There was even a picture of her on the cover. It showed poor Queenie with her feet strapped into metal stirrups, still clutching her mirror in her hand. She is surrounded by an army of men in lab coats.

Raphael shook his head to clear the yawning gynecological imagery from his mind.

"*¡Que amor lamento, que locura de amor!* Such crazy love!" exclaimed Raphael as he watched the platform rise to the roof with a steaming plate of tamales on it. Padre Humberto performed the marriage ceremony for King and Queenie and then he convinced her that, as his disciple, she could regain her virginity and her lost honor. Now King has nothing to live for but his work and his pigeons. There are so many pigeons in this city with deformed feet. Cruel people keep setting out traps and poisoned feed."

Each night, on the roof of the Silver Cloud, King fashioned tiny braces and splints for the birds so they could at least stand comfortably. He used matchsticks and the spirit gum that was used to secure hairpieces and wigs. He tore at rolls of tape with his teeth, then wrapped their little feet. He called it gloving, for a reason that most cannot understand. He gloved his crippled birds; then after a period of healing, he tossed his little healed friends headlong into the air above the streets. He buried the pigeons that died up there, too. First, he counted them out, then he prayed for them.

Rumor had it that King Pete Claver was once a renowned heavyweight fighter. The *viejitos*, the old ones, say he's fought all the good ones. Few people are old enough these days to verify the story, but no one on the street dares tangle with him, even at his age.

"He has huge hands, have you seen them, Zeferino? He shadowboxes at midnight, round after round, *episodios perdidos*. He uses the light from the angels. I used to let him clean up the bar after hours. He said the smell of ammonia wakes him up, helps him think."

Raphael walked over to one of the small tables, picked up a cup of coffee, then sat down once again. He seemed tired and a bit perplexed by his own need to relive the history of the Silver Cloud. He felt his coat pocket and was assured once again that the papers were there. He had rented a truck for the move and had gone to City Hall and the Hall of Justice to secure a coroner's release. He would take the body of Humberto with him.

When the sign went up, reflected Raphael, things really

started to happen around here. *Ay mierda*, business went clear through the roof. That was about the time everybody started wandering in—Anatoly, Ted For Short, King Pete, Miguel Govea over at the Fourth Street Bridge, and all the rest. All of them came at around the same time, even Humberto and Queenie. It was like they all had personal invitations. When Ted For Short and Ruby came here, the floor show got to be better than anything they've got in Las Vegas.

Down below the hotel window, Zeferino was unlocking the rear door of Raphael's Silver Cloud. It was pitch-black inside except for the eerie light that came from a jukebox in the far corner. King reached in and flicked on the lights.

Although there was no one in the bar, and no one had approached the jukebox, it suddenly decided to noisily flex its mechanical arm and fingers to extract a disc from a rotating, circular stack. Then, from the corner of the uninhabited building, the voice of John Prine broke into "Angel from Montgomery."

If dreams were thunder and lightning was desire,
This old house would've burned down a long time ago.

"Ignore her," said King Pete, nodding toward the corner, "Uriel always wants to put in her two cents."

There was a mover's tag on the jukebox.

"Raphael can't never sell her," said King in a low, respectful voice.

"I bought Uriel at a fire sale," said Raphael in his hotel room as the music reached his ears. "I plugged her in and the first night she played right through a power outage. *Está embrujada*, she's bewitched, that one."

Zeferino walked over to the bar. There was bright crepe paper hung above the bar and the floor beneath his feet was covered with sawdust and flower petals. There was a hand-painted sign over the entrance to the bathroom that said, COLLECT SMALL HERESIES AND YOU WILL FIND GOD. The initials TFS were written at the bottom. "Ted For Short," said Zeferino aloud.

The building itself was fairly plain. Like most Mission District bars, the front windows were darkened, and in the cavelike entranceway hung heavy red curtains as thick and as silencing as ancient tapestries. Walking into Raphael's was like walking into a darkened movie theater or into the confessional of an old Mexican church. The ceiling was fathomless and painted jet-black.

The ground-level interior was like most; there were small tables arranged on a rectangular dance floor. Each table had two or three chairs, an ashtray, and a candleholder. There was a pool table between the tables and the barstools. To the right of the entrance was a small raised platform, a stage. There was a microphone standing in the center of the stage that listened to everything that went on in the room and longed to repeat it to everyone. And at the foot of the stage were the microphone's two loud-mouthed cronies: twin, black Electro-Voice speakers. There was a silent drum set in the corner.

Filling the corner to the left of the entrance to the bar was a Wurlitzer jukebox named Uriel. Her beaming face was filled with gleaming red-and-yellow lights that shone into a kinetic display of moving bubbles pumped endlessly in a circle about her perimeter. There was no legend on her front, no listing of song titles or pushbuttons. Uriel played whenever and whatever she pleased, from Leadbelly to Mercedes Sosa; Thelonius Monk to Nadia Salerno-Sonnenberg.

Above eye level, there was a high shelf on the three walls not taken up by the bar itself. A hundred pieces of Ocumicho ceramics were displayed there, magnificent pieces made in Raphael's hometown in Mexico. Among them were ceramic buses filled with humble tallow-eared saints and pious bearded prophets. But the autobuses were always driven by a phantasm, a laughing, flint-skinned demon who cavorted at the gearshift and wheel. Capricious devils, formed of fuming webs and blooms of sulfur, children of cudgel and cinder were stalking the buses, riding on twisted tricycles, contorted ice-cream carts, and even in knotted airplanes.

There were four huge pieces depicting *La Ultima Sena*, the Last Supper. The first was the usual reverent, sandaled scene but, in the place of bread, the thirteen were eating slices of bright red and green watermelon. Black seeds pocked the grace and swirl of the tablecloth and the littered floor. In the second, only grinning, desiccated skeletons sat at the table, each group of six leaning, clavicle to collarbone, toward the center.

"This is my body."

In the third piece, the solemn supper was chaperoned by exaltations of blond angels, each with either a saxophone or a trumpet to its lips. And in the fourth, there were ranks of consorting demons resplendent in black tuxedos and top hats. But the obvious looming centerpiece of them all was The Fall, a huge piece whose blazing hues contrasted perfectly with the black paint of the high ceiling.

In ceramic, the peace of Paradise, *la paz del Paraiso*, was failing. Beyond the garden, drawn in rueful paint, sad air gathered itself into a killing wind. Sweet, supple mouths, built for praise and adoration, were transmuting into senseless beaks, and the shameful, unsheltered lovers screeched as though their contrite, desperate noises were words . . . understood somewhere, by insects, by weeds. There was verdant and crimson effusion, the leakage of sorrow, and the wreckage of perfection that was presided over by the white-robed Almighty Himself.

Zeferino walked around the room, carefully inspecting each piece of ceramic. Each work was stunning in its fragile power, its pious yet primal portrayal of heavenly love and heavenly wrath. King Pete watched him as he walked. He explained to Zeferino that Raphael's wife and daughter were the artists.

Inside his hotel room, Raphael paused from his packing for a moment, unable to imagine what his life would have been like without the Silver Cloud. He wondered what he was going to do with himself now—where he would go. At the same time he knew the answers to both questions. He had shared the directions with so many friends and customers.

In Raphael's mind, deep in his brain, there was a map. It was the road from Zamora to Tangancicuaro, bumpy and dusty, filled with cows and lined with *birria* stands. When Raphael dreamed of home he tasted the goat and the *sopa Tarasca*, his favorite tortilla soup.

"Take the right-hand turn at the yellow garage," he had told his customers in moments of nostalgia. "Ask directions from five Mexicanos. Four of them will point somewhere in the general direction of the town, the fifth will point in the opposite direction.

Throw out the fifth, then average out the other four and go that way. After you go about a mile, ask for directions again. Eventually you will get there. Mexicanos may not know where you're going, but every one of them will tell you how to get there.

"Follow the road until you reach the *llantera,* then turn left at the pile of old tires and go until the road ends. Go past San José de Gracia, past the fields of corn and cane, past the graveyard where long hoes are lifted and dropped by the hands of women. Past the squawking, darting chickens that poke at corn flung from the handwoven aprons of women. Go up the hill on the cracking, bounding cobblestone to the first house on the left— the one wedded to a small cliff, the one that is the shape and size of *una memoria.* You will find yourself on Guatemala Street. They say that electricity has come to Guatemala Street, that the little store in the center of town has an ice machine."

He never said to his customers that dearest Apollonia was there, waxing the wooden floor with the oils of her ankles, her single bed lined with Raphael's letters, uncashed money orders, and the scent of her own solitude. He wouldn't say that Apollonia was there, her teeth throbbing for his tongue, her skin cold with his absence.

She was Raphael's wife. She lived where there was a famine of friends. Around her bed were ceramic sculptures of men and women and malicious, colicky demons. She lived where clouds hung as heavy as lactating breasts and the land demanded to be fed once a day, where ghosts and humans slept by the same darting candlelight. She dreamed of the *creatio ex nihilo* and created from nothing the blaze of pottery at her feet. Yet she could not imagine San Francisco.

Jesusita, his daughter, was there, squinting, considering clay like a minor goddess about to breathe herself into it. Her works were covered with marigolds, the flower of the Tarascan past, the pre-Christian past. She was Catholic, like all Tarascans, but really, she knew nothing at all of the new religion. A gentle assailant of the clay, she shaped heaven's edge from gray earth while she unfolded a sweet song with her lips.

Neither woman knew that their village was famous in Berlin and Paris, that the agony of their Amazon dreams was coveted by connoisseurs, that Marin County matrons separated the pieces that crowded Apollonia's hovel into solitary displays on white pedestals marked with sums that Jesusita could not count. Neither woman fully knew how the quotidian landscape bloomed the instant they stepped forward from their dreary, dark huts into the light, a dazzling sculpture in hand. Neither woman knew why it was, in their tangled dreams, that angular demons played with stilted, stuttering monks and red serpents hissed painted heresies.

Ocumicho, Raphael's town, was a town of women. All of the men, like Raphael, had gone north, looking for work in the other world. Neither woman truly knew where he was or the places he had been. Neither knew why Raphael had not come home in ten years or what they would do if he did. They supposed they would love him because love is the feminine side of God. They did know of Raphael's power. They knew of it long before Raphael did.

"*Lo que Dios mande,*" they'd say, "as God demands," as they daubed bright paint onto a fiddling devil and his ill-mannered children.

Raphael had worked for years as a migratory farmworker in the Imperial Valley and the San Joaquin. He had even been as far north as Seattle to work in the packing sheds. Like so many other workers, his imagination had run wild while his rented body stood still, shoving stunned red salmon into gray machines. He had gone to Chicago, where he shined shoes in the basement of a high-rise, looking up at men who needed to look down. And he had been to Detroit, where he worked on the automotive assembly line while a man with a stopwatch and a degree in robotics watched his every move.

It was in Detroit that he discovered his singular power to see the future of metals. While working as a quality-control inspector, he suddenly came to realize that he knew which of the cars coming off the line would be involved in fatal collisions. He could sense in the metals the surprise, the terror, and the silence of immured children.

He could see the nascent stress of knotted fissures in a rolling urn, the fatal ooze past O-rings in the power rack and pinion. Sickened with his lonely knowledge, he had demanded that these cars be removed from the assembly line as rejects, to be rebuilt and repainted until the sorrowful canticle no longer sounded in his ears or the dark aura no longer shone.

He had been fired for his obstruction of the line, for his presentiments. At first he had been tolerated at the plant as a nuisance, until the day came when his warnings began to come true. He was let go when workers filtered into the plant carrying stories and newspaper articles of entire families killed, of a prom queen pulled violently from her newly dyed shoes and a young mother thrown from her car with her children and onto the hood of an oncoming truck.

The plant had gone mad for a day. The workers, following Raphael, had dragged three cars from the shipping yard and one from the line. They had dismantled the cars on the spot, cutting them to pieces with gas torches and diamond saws.

Raphael was fired that day in Detroit. A week later, in Selma, Alabama, a young girl purchased a car that she had not been destined to buy, and would live to be a great-grandmother.

He moved westward, driving slowly and pulling over whenever he spotted cars with the radiant onus. At first he had tried to warn the other drivers, but all it got him were psychiatric evaluations in Philadelphia and Kansas City. He seldom drove now, and he never allowed himself to be driven. He had grown tired of seeing future death wherever he went.

Zeferino walked to the back wall of the bar. On a small bulletin board below the Ocumicho ceramics, there were notices and notes placed there by the customers: lost dogs, cars for sale, and apartments for rent. There were photographs tacked up everywhere: tiny yellowed Polaroids, a page of contact prints, and a pair of eight-by-tens in haunting black and white. A three-hundred-pound Tongan male smiled uncomfortably in the first, while a large, happy woman played to the camera in the second.

"Beatrice," whispered a contemplative Zeferino. "So this is where Stuart's client found such happy employment."

In the lower left-hand corner of the bulletin board was a yellowed sign advertising King and Queenie's Famous Tamales, on sale every day at the Silver Cloud. The name of Queenie seemed to have been penciled out violently. Her name was crossed out with markings that looked like the flailing printout of a polygraph machine sensing a terrible lie.

"Did you want to see the album?" asked King Pete, who nodded anxiously to a large photo album lying next to the huge jars
of Polish sausages and pickled eggs at the end of the bar. The
lawyer walked over to the bar, grabbed the album, then walked
to one of the tables and sat down. Before opening the album,
Zeferino breathed deeply, then said quietly, "Mr. King, is there
anything to drink?"

King smiled. Now the lawyer was talking. He reached across
the bar and grabbed a bottle of Herradura and two water glasses.
He then poured the deep gold tequila into the large glasses. He
drank his drink down, then refilled his own glass before taking
the bottle and the second glass to the lawyer's table. He knew
that the lawyer would not want to speak to anybody for the next
hour, so he walked back to the bar intending to sit on one of the
barstools. Instead, he walked to a shelf, then returned, handing
the lawyer a pair of heavily worn Bibles and a folder filled with
old newspaper clippings. Before sitting down he apologized to
Uriel, then pulled her electrical cord from the wall socket.

Zeferino opened the first Bible. It had last belonged to the
man named Humberto. It had been given to him just days ago by
its previous owner, whose name was written just above that of
Humberto. In beautiful script was the single name *Faustino*. Zeferino closed his eyes and lifted his head for a moment. Did he
know Faustino? The other Bible first belonged to someone
named Miguel A. Pro and was dated 1919. The name of Humberto Pro was written below it.

"That's the full name of the priest who was up there? The
one who set the fire and jumped to his death?"

It was not really a question but King Pete Claver nodded, yes.

"The other name must've been a relative," said Zeferino,
"perhaps a son."

He then opened the folder and found the ancient front page
of a Mexican newspaper, dated 1927. The page had been sealed
in plastic. The entire page was shredded and decomposing except for a single column of print.

"Miguel Augustine was Humberto's brother," said Zeferino
as he translated the Spanish aloud. His voice trembled as he
read. "His brother was a priest in a small parish in Michoacán.
Both were accused by the government of belonging to the Na-

tional League for the Defense of Religious Liberty, the army of the cloth. He was executed by firing squad along with his brother . . . Humberto." A second and newer page noted the formal beatification of Miguel Augustine.

Zeferino had been to the morgue. He had gone there to see the victim in Teodoro's case but had been drawn, out of curiosity, to the mummified body of the arsonist. The entire office had been buzzing over the condition of the body. The tag on the man's toe had not indicated a last name. The perplexed medical examiner said that Humberto had done the impossible. When he was pronounced dead at San Francisco General Hospital, there had not been a molecule of blood left in his body. His arteries and veins had been as dry as a bone.

Dr. Stephens, the chief medical examiner, had taken a dozen photographs of the body and scratched his head endlessly over what he would write in the necropsy. The toxicology report showed traces of every poison under the sun.

"The man, at the time of his death, had the musculature and organs of a twenty-year-old," the doctor had explained. "He had an unusually large chest cavity; you could almost describe it as a keel. The outer skin was already thoroughly desiccated when I received him, and the process is continuing now, even under refrigerated conditions. I've never seen anything like it, counselor. It's like some sort of spontaneous self-embalming. It's as though he died years ago and we've only now exhumed him."

Bambino Reyes's body had been there in the morgue next to Humberto's. It was obvious that the mutilated man had spent much of his own life mutilating himself. Most of his wounds were remote and self-inflicted. At the morgue, the lawyer had never wondered if the two deaths were somehow connected.

Zeferino took a long drink of the tequila. A look of foolishness mixed with joy moved across his face as he drank. He felt foolish because he realized that he, like so many others, had succumbed to the smug belief that his own cynical view of the world was accurate. He felt joyful because memories to the contrary were now sprouting in his soul.

As he leafed through the first Bible, he noticed that there was a scrap of paper interleaved between the second and third pages of Exodus. The scrap contained two separate sets of stanzas of free verse in two different hands.

"Wedding vows," said Zeferino, though they were unlike any he had ever read or heard. The name of Radiant Ruby was written above the first stanza and Teodoro Cabiri's was above the second. All at once, from nowhere, the image of a man filled his mind's eye. Now he remembered Faustino; a thin man with a remarkable head of white hair was emerging from the mists of amnesia. "Faustino, Faustino," he said aloud as he returned his eyes to the vows. Ruby's were written in beautiful script, Teodoro wrote his in shorthand. The past was becoming clearer for Zeferino. Something horrible had happened in the asparagus field outside of Stockton, in a place called French Camp. He looked back down to the wedding vows. Ruby and Ted had both worked here. They had been married here. All of them had been here. Every path from the old, seemingly forgotten tragedy in French Camp to the strange killing at the Fourth Street Bridge had crossed right here at Raphael's Silver Cloud!

In the corner, Uriel lit up without electricity, the colored bubbles beginning their lazy circuit around her face. Zeferino opened the photo album, then spread the enlarged pictures across the table. He stared down into the photographs on the table in front of him. They were large, sixteen by twenty inches. They were all black-and-white with a haunting, almost tactile quality conveying depth. They seemed less like photographs and more like soundings into unknown lives, bills of human lading, inventories of every vulnerability and every power. Each was titled, then signed with the name Nemerov.

He looked even closer, peering down into the photos as though he were poking his head into a hidden room. Here, in this shadow, there is a buried infidelity. There, in the contrast between the eyes and the skin, there is the leaden, fossilized wish for a long-lost love. Each person had given the photographer just a sixtieth of a second, but the photographer had taken so much more.

The first photograph was of a woman in a wedding dress covered with ten- and twenty- and even fifty-dollar bills. There was a single five-dollar bill pinned to her shoulder. THE MONEY DANCE was written in pencil on the border just beneath the photo.

The sound of "Quando M'en Vo," "Musetta's Waltz," began to fill the room as Zeferino looked closely at the pictures, one by one. A woman who was no longer young seemed to push the years aside and danced in a long, exquisite gown. She seemed to be dressed in leaf-covered snow. There was a photo of a tiny car, a 1958 BMW Isetta two-seater with tin cans tied to its bumper and the words JUST MARRIED printed in soap on its rear window. The legend below it read A SMALL WEDDING. The photos were all candid, frozen moments possessed of an eerie, captivating beauty.

"Aristocrats," said Zeferino out loud.

There they were up on the stage, smiling, frozen midtoast in silver gelatin. White-haired and wrinkled now, there were his *tios* and his *tiyos*, all the angels of his childhood in the vegetable fields and fruit orchards of California.

"Who is this man?" asked Zeferino while pointing to one of the faces.

"Oh, that's Miguel who raises the drawbridge," answered King.

There was Humberto holding the Bibles and performing the ceremony. There was Beatrice again, in an enormous Victorian gown. There were many beautiful but aged women that Zeferino had never before seen, and in the corner of one photo, there was Faustino standing with a shy and smiling César Chávez.

THE TOAST, A FILIPINO MIDGET AND HIS NEW BRIDE, read a handwritten inscription. LOVE FOR THE DISCARDED, read another.

"Who are these women?" Zeferino asked himself. They were beautiful women, even in their old age. Each had a bearing and a carriage that Zeferino had never seen except in oil paintings by the Renaissance masters.

The last photograph was a group shot of the entire wedding party. There they were again, Roberto, Vicente, Mariano, Manny—all of them—caught in the aperture. So many people from the past, people who had been forever buried in his memories. Zeferino sat stunned by the faces in the photograph. They had been drawn here, inexorably, from separate and distant worlds; pulled here by desperation, by eros and eris; drawn here by . . . something. They had wandered in and staggered in from beneath the rain, still reeling from that night so long ago when misery came to the asparagus fields. Zeferino was remembering now . . . the night that death came to French Camp.

They had all been reunited here. He found the photo of Ruby and placed it on top of the stack of photographs. It was the incredible picture of a woman wearing dollar bills as though they were feathers. How old was she? She seemed ageless and endless in her beauty. All at once he noticed a face just visible through a corner of Ruby's veil. He had been behind her, applauding as she lifted the veil away from her face. It was a second shot of Faustino, Zeferino was sure of it.

Zeferino absentmindedly flipped the pages of Humberto's first Bible, the one that had belonged to Faustino. He noticed that a small piece of paper was stuck in the Book of Revelations, chapter 11. It was a small piece of frail, yellowed rice paper. On the paper were Japanese characters that were barely legible and a translation of the words written just below them. Something about it seemed familiar. He lifted the paper and pressed it to his forehead as if contact could help divine its meaning. He then replaced it in the Bible, more convinced than ever that he had seen this shred of paper once before . . . somewhere.

Suddenly, from the vacant lot behind the bar, a loud voice began screaming obscenities and there was the barely audible sound of a strangled car horn.

"What is that noise?" asked a stunned Zeferino.

"Oh, that's just Anatoly," answered King.

Zeferino rose from his seat and walked to the open back door of the bar. There, behind the wheel of the cab, was a man who was looking first over his left shoulder, then into the rearview mirror. He was merging into traffic, his leaden foot pressing the unresponsive accelerator to the floor.

Each day, without fail, Anatoly Bogomil, an old man in a brown canvas jacket and corduroy pants shining with age, walked from his small tent in the enclosed field to the gutted Checker taxi. He would exchange his threadbare Oakland A's cap for a Citycab hat with a plastic visor that he kept under the dashboard and out of the rain. There was a huge golden earring hanging from his left ear. It was rumored that in his youth he had been a genuine Duke of Little Egypt.

Then the meter would be turned on, the OCCUPIED sign

would flash yellow, and the horn that had been carefully muffled with rags by Raphael's patrons and neighbors would begin to sound. Everyone in the Mission District neighborhood knew by the dull noise that the cab was currently flashing down Fifth Avenue past Sixty-eighth Street and that Anatoly had picked up a fare at the museum.

"What's he gonna do now that the Silver Cloud is no more?" asked Raphael out loud as he emptied his closet of clothing.

"He's what folks call a Romani," said King, "a wandering man if there ever was one, but he is getting old. I hear tell he was married once, back in New York City. I hear tell that someone he loved is dead and that a car crash was involved."

"Sheeet, foooock! Gahdahm you!" Anatoly screamed out of the cab window. *"Layna! Ebané!"* he shrieked in Bulgarian. Anatoly removed his hat and wiped his sweating brow with the salt- and oil-stained arm of his coat.

"You know what's wrong with this country, why everybody is so fooocking crazy?" He turned his head to the rearview mirror to speak to an invisible young passenger who was obviously on leave from the navy.

"Because it's a free country, that's why. Me? I'm from Bulgaria. That's right, Bulgaria. Don't laugh at my country now, I'll leave you right here, foooock the fare! It's not a free country and everybody there is in their right mind! No, I know that the communists are gone, but it's still not free. I tell you, every gahdahm person from infant to old fogey, in my country, is sound as a dollar bill."

He extended his middle finger to a phantom cab from a rival company that was going in the opposite direction.

"Not like here! You see, freedom may be what you hand to the people on a silver platter, but freedom is not what they receive."

He turned for a moment to look at the imaginary young couple seated in the backseat. Neither of them could have been over twenty years old.

"Think about it while you're still young." He wagged his finger at the rearview mirror, then pointed toward the small carousel. "A zebra, a giraffe can break down a fence and be free, but only a man can have liberty. What is the difference?"

He turned his eyes back to the steering wheel and the windshield as the traffic ahead began to move.

"What is the difference? You know as well as I do," he said to the Hasidic Jew sitting silently in the backseat with his eyes closed.

"Freedom that is shared becomes liberty. Sure, we were an Axis country, but did you know that Bulgaria did not deport the Jews and the Romani—the Gypsies—to the death camps? We refused at a time when refusal carried a heavy price. Those bastards in the Vichy government deported everybody: homosexuals, Algerians, poets, magicians . . . everybody."

Anatoly had left his native land when the campaigns of assimilation had begun, when the Romani tongue was prohibited in the schools and Gypsies were not allowed to travel about. The government had called for a census of Romani and for identification cards to be carried by all legal citizens of Bulgaria.

Anatoly had to move. It was as much in his blood to be peripatetic as it was to be musical. The drum set up on the raised platform was his *cimbalom,* and his beautiful Checker taxicab had become his horse and *vardo.* America had always been his dream. Now foolish Americans, too, were constantly calling for a census of immigrants and their families, and for identification cards. Now they were restricting languages, closing schools, and sealing borders.

"If you despise difference, then difference will tear you apart."

Raphael watched Anatoly driving down below. Recently, the cab had acquired the glow, subtle at first, like a blush of amber, starting at the brake lines, then moving up through the frame and the suspension. Raphael knew that Anatoly would soon die in the cab. But this time, there would be no violent crash, only a peaceable death in his sleep.

"He's the drummer in our band, you know," said King Pete, who nodded toward the bandstand. "His name is Anatoly Bogomil. That tent is his home. All I really know about him is that he come from the Bronx. He just fell out of the sky a couple of years back. He showed up one morning looking for work. A lot of folks come to work here. Me and Anatoly keeps the place clean."

"You over there," said Anatoly, suddenly addressing the lawyer. "Is speech free if we are allowed to say what we want?"

Zeferino thought for a moment before answering.

"If there is a government or church that wishes to preserve itself from criticism, it can do one of two things, Señor Bogomil. It can either limit speech directly, or it can limit the people's ability to speak."

Anatoly was grinning now. He knew he had a live one.

"So," said Anatoly, "a populace that is losing more and more of its literacy and its vocabulary with each generation . . ."

"Can speak freely . . . ," interjected the lawyer, "because it has less to say and, therefore, presents less danger."

"Yes," said Anatoly, speaking more to himself now. "Yes. Words are the pockets that ideas go into. And you have to think better and better thoughts to be truly free. *Mislete polozhitelano za da badete svoboden.*" He repeated the phrase to himself in his native language. He then turned toward Zeferino to ask what was not really a question.

"Have you learned about the blood feud? What happened here"—he looked around the back of the bar and toward the tower on the roof—"was the end of a feud between the living and the dead, between sips of reason and a flood of hatred. The thing that died at the Fourth Street Bridge was a *mulo*, a ghost . . . not a man. And he was not killed by a man. Therefore, your laws don't apply to this case. They have no place here at all."

Anatoly turned away from Zeferino and King. He needed to start his second shift. The airport traffic from Kennedy was especially heavy in the late afternoon. He could make some good money today. He would buy flowers tonight, his wife, the Duchess, loved flowers. Some geraniums perhaps.

He smiled as her face formed in his mind. Maybe he would do the cooking tonight. They could eat dinner and watch the moon landing on television. After all, she would be very tired after driving all the way back from Albany, where she had gone to care for her bedridden mother.

Anatoly had always worried about his wife's driving, especially when she was tired. Anatoly's memories always stopped here, just before his whole world fell asleep at the wheel.

"Queenie didn't even come down for Ted For Short's

wedding," King suddenly sobbed. "The old priest come down, but not her! She didn't see fit to just come pass the time of day with me. I'm a stranger to her now and Queenie always said you could die from strangers. I can't be so misprized."

Zeferino could see that King Pete was disappearing now, calling it a day—allowing the alcoholic stupor to envelop him completely. Anatoly, suddenly aware of the here and now, called to his friend.

"King, come on and get in, I'll take you for a ride. I tell you Queenie is coming back." He gestured toward the backseat of the cab. King Pete staggered over, opened the back door, then slumped into the passenger seat. Up in his hotel room, Raphael returned to the window once again to look down on his two old friends. "How about you, Zeferino?" he wondered out loud. "Where on earth can Anatoly take you?"

Zeferino stood in the yard near King's inverted bucket. The remarkable images he had seen inside the bar were running faster than ever through his mind. As he stood silently, the strangeness of the bar and the odd people he had found there were slowly transformed into something deeply familiar. Now he understood why he had driven by this street corner for so many years without ever seeing Raphael's Silver Cloud.

This bar, like so many other places of refuge, had been buried deep in his memories. Now he recognized these people—King, Anatoly, Raphael, Teodoro, and all of the rest. People like these had always been in his life, hovering there at the edge of his existence. Somehow the ability to see them in the present and to remember them in the past had been taken away from him. Here, at Raphael's Silver Cloud, the power was slowly being given back.

"I was the one in a stupor," he said to an unhearing King. He smiled, then began to laugh out loud as one particular forgotten memory broke free from forgetfulness and leaped fully formed into his mind.

Long ago, a young welfare worker came out to the asparagus fields where Zeferino the boy had been working. She looked totally out of place in her suit and heels. Someone had told her that there was a boy laboring out there who should've been in school. Zeferino remembered that she had asked where his mother was and that he had told her that he didn't know, that she never spent much time in the camps. When she asked him about his father he told her that he had no idea who he was and that he had never seen him.

"But I have lots of uncles, señora. In fact, I have over thirty of them," the boy had explained. The welfare worker didn't seem very impressed by what he had said, so she dragged the boy—kicking and screaming—out of the fields. His *tios* had protested, but they all knew that she was right. They knew that a childhood should not be spent laboring in the furrows. Though the boy hated her at the time, he understood that the woman's heart was in the right place.

"I remember that she bought me some brand-new school clothes and made me take off all of my muddy gear," Zeferino said excitedly to an unconscious King and to Anatoly, who was parked in front of Radio City Music Hall. "Then she placed me into a classroom in some town that I can no longer recall. I can still see the faces of those children staring at my battered work-boots. I do remember clearly that the teacher in that classroom ended the first day of class by reminding the children that in three days the school would be having their yearly Father's Day celebration. All of the children were expected to bring their fathers to school on that day."

"*Pobrecito,*" said Raphael from above.

"I remember how miserable I felt as I walked back to the camp. I imagined myself at Father's Day, the only kid there without a father." It bothered the boy so much that he couldn't eat and even the sweet music from the Mexican Quonset couldn't cheer him up. He told one of his *tios* that night that he wanted to run away, that he just couldn't go back to that school on Father's Day.

"Well, I must have told my *tio* the wrong day, because, on the day before Father's Day, thirty farmworkers dressed in their work clothes walked slowly, single file into the classroom. Each one had carefully combed his hair and put on his cleanest dirty work-shirt. The entire classroom smelled of pomade and brilliantine and sweat.

"How could I ever have forgotten that morning?" Zeferino said, exhaling his emotions out onto the rusted hood of the cab and onto the windshield. Anatoly suddenly ceased his incessant chatter as Zeferino's voice dropped to a whisper.

"There they were, forming a circle around the class, all of them shifting nervously and smiling shyly at the teacher and so proudly at me. They had their sharpened paring knives and long machetes hanging from their belts. They had taken the time to brush the mud from their knee pads and each man had carefully folded his bandanna into his shirt pocket. Each of my uncles held his straw hat respectfully in his hands.

"They were Mexicans, Pinoys, and Hindus, all missing a day's pay . . . for me." Zeferino paused while the power of the memory washed over him. Anatoly said nothing and King moaned inconsolably in the backseat. Above them all, a silent Raphael watched and listened. Zeferino's eyes glistened with emotion.

"These were strangers in America, men who had been told again and again that their own lives were a poor imitation of the lives around them. But that morning, they all braved the other world for my sake. I remember that, finally, one of them stepped forward and with a heavy accent spoke a single sentence to the class: 'We are Zeferino's father.' "

Anatoly leaned toward the passenger door and opened it with a grunt and a jerk of his right hand. He motioned for Zeferino to get in beside him.

"Get into the cab," whispered Raphael Viajero from his window.

Zeferino took a few slow steps, then stood next to the open door.

"Go ahead," urged Raphael silently. *"Andale."*

Zeferino then stepped in and sat down on the blankets covering the torn seat. He closed the door just as Anatoly began to speak and just as Uriel began to play. From within the Silver Cloud came the strains of the "Rondine Al Nido."

"Where can I take you, pal?" asked Anatoly as he turned on the trip meter. "The East Side, Canal Street, you name it."

After a moment of consideration, Zeferino answered, "Stockton. Take me to Stockton, nineteen fifty-nine."

Smiling, Raphael watched from above as the immobile Checker cab carried them all away.

VI

Stockton in 1959

STOP the spinning moon, and despite her complaints, bid her reverse her course and go the other way. Coax the sun backward if you wish to remember; shove it west to east, again and again, until all the years lift away.

Call back the time and a dozen cut lilies, once dying in a florist's window, will climb back to their mothering stems; their petals will spread full, then clench back into the greening buds of infancy. Look back in time, and a willful, wanton flame, in its diminishment, will gradually rebuild the wood.

You must seek out remembrance, for ours is a land of amnesiacs who pretend that there is no past; that America is a multicultural land when, in truth, it is an anticultural place that has ever been blessed with persistent and enduring cultures that have survived never-ending efforts to drag them out of sight; push them out of mind; to imprison them in the past.

Gaze homeward with the eyes of memory, and an old woman's face will once again be fetching, the lost tempo in her hips renewed. Return to yesterday and a Filipino singer's deathbed will fill with songs; the old man's carcass will be swollen with life, the collected years tossed off like sea water from his youthful mane; and his clouded eyes will be brimming clearly with a long-lost vision of America.

* * *

The Oldsmobile crossed the California desert at night. It sped past Needles and Boron, up old Highway 50 past Atwater and Turlock in the unbearable heat of day. The road was different then. Every driver's headlights lit up whenever a funeral procession went past, and submarine-shaped Studebakers still cruised past Burma Shave billboards. There were Giant Orange stands along the route and railroad cars converted into shining diners.

Zeferino's mother, Lilly, sat in the front passenger seat, smoking Kool Menthols and impatiently punching the buttons on the radio. There was a look of contentment in her face. She was a long way now from that trailer camp in Yuma.

"I need to hear the Platters," she said impatiently. " 'Only You,' or 'The Great Pretender.' They're the best singing group of nineteen fifty-nine, don't you think? God, I hate that Okie music!" she sneered, not knowing that her next boyfriend, a man who was just about to be released from the Ohio State Penitentiary, would inspire in her a passion for Buck Owens and Merle Haggard.

Perfecto Lopez, her latest soon-to-be-ex-boyfriend, was driving and splitting his attention between the long road before him and his own image in the rearview mirror. The two side mirrors of the car were also aimed directly at his face and hairdo. When changing lanes to either side, he was treated to a view of himself.

Zeferino, the boy, slept most of the way through the Central Valley and into the San Joaquin. Each time he was awakened during the trip, he realized where he was and saw no reason at all to stay awake. But he was finally awakened fully when the speeding car abruptly slowed down and pulled into the long dirt road that ran alongside a slow-moving, green water slough. It was the entrance to French Camp.

From his passenger window, Zeferino saw an old metal sign that read NO TRESPASSING! PRIVATE PROPERTY OF THE DITTO BROTHERS. It was nailed to a tall wooden water tower that loomed high above a sky-blue, elephantine Buick sedan jacked up on wooden blocks. Next to the car was a rusting Caterpillar D-8 and its wheeled companion, an ancient two-banger John Deere. Zeferino could see faint Japanese lettering on the side of the water tank. Someone had made a cursory attempt to paint over it. Behind the tractors was a large rectangular building that the boy would come to know as the packing shed.

The long reflection of a fire burned on the green water near the Buick and a man and his inverted opposite in the universe cooked food over the flames. The man above the slough looked exactly the way the boy imagined a learned college professor would look, a brown college professor, if there were such things.

He was a small, frail-looking man with a thick mustache and turbulent white hair that contrasted sharply with his dark skin. The boy sensed a gentleness in this strange-looking man. The man in the water below was too obscure to see clearly.

"*Bakla*," sneered Perfecto Lopez upon catching sight of the man. He spat through his window to emphasize the point. The word burst from his mouth along with the spittle.

"Stay away from him, boy," ordered Lilly, from behind a thick blue haze of cigarette smoke.

The bunkhouses stood in the distance, far from the Buick and too far from the slough to have a reflection there. They were three long Quonset huts running parallel to each other and about twenty feet apart. Each hut had flimsy curtains in the front windows, and harsh unshaded lights glared rudely behind those curtains. Zeferino noticed that the curtains were made of old shirts or stained tablecloths and had been nailed or stapled over the windows. No woman had put them up.

Perpendicular to the Quonset huts, and on the other side of the road, were two small buildings. One was the communal outhouse and showers. The other was a small furnished cottage complete with an all-electric kitchenette and inside plumbing. Between the two buildings was a smaller water tower.

Behind the small tower a group of animated, gesticulating men was gathered in a circle around two frenzied, desperate roosters that lashed and kicked at each other with metal spurs. Beneath the dusty canopy of beating wings, one of the roosters was bleeding heavily, his comb and top feathers matted with opaque blood. The boy closed his eyes to the sight and turned toward the Quonsets.

Zeferino did not hear the music and laughter coming from the bunkhouses until the moment the car door opened and he was led inside; then human sounds rolled over him in waves. Once inside the rounded hut, he felt suddenly uneasy about the smiles he witnessed there. It seemed to him that the laughter from those brown faces was somehow tinged with pain, that their smiles were just shadows of real happiness to be found elsewhere under the sun.

He had sensed their feelings as he walked past the screen door and into the long room: our laughter is an imitation of joy; we will all be somewhere else next month and next year, perhaps even back home where we belong. But for now, this food will do, this bed will do.

Inside the Quonset, the boy felt as if he had been transported to another earth, an empty, arid land that had imported its inhabitants and trucked water in to wet it down and keep it living. In his short life he had never before seen a hard, womanless world of lifelong temporary workers. A world of bachelors.

They were among the first group to leave the Philippine Islands and to come to America, the oldest *manong*. They were easy to spot. Easy to differentiate from all the waves of Pinoys that came later. There was always the easily roused hope and naive enthusiasm in the Pinoys that followed, but only the first had embraced these shores with that particular ardor now turned to bitterness. Wooed by wartime intimacy in the mountains and foothills of Corregidor, seduced by MacArthur's words of love into leaving home, the *manong* would be jilted beyond words, beyond consolation.

Set apart by the thrift and invention that come from isolation, the oldest *manong* survived alone with only the braceros as brothers, only to be deserted by them once a year. Each winter the braceros went home to nearby Mexico or to Los Angeles, back to their homes and their families.

The *manong* used Cat's Paw shoe polish and edge-dye and a pile of old toothbrushes for cleaning between the lace holes and over the tongues of their wingtips. The first wave made a quiet flap-flap-flap of homemade slippers down the center aisle of the Quonset huts to the outdoor showers. These exiles polished their shoes, made them last two decades, and when the shoes were beyond polishing, they cut off the heel-tops and converted them to slippers. These old and worn-out men possessed immortal shoes.

The *manong* always lived in sequestered camps just outside of town, outside of Brawley and on the outskirts of Stockton and Manteca, and even Livermore, in the shadow of the Radiation Laboratory. Everything about their lives was worn smooth and held the patina of oxblood.

Their lives were Pacific theater, jerry-built; the cold showers and the corrugated tin fences. Everything was makeshift; the handmade pedal-powered sharpeners for the gray steel machetes and paring knives; the cold, outdoor showers. For them, the Second World War went on and on.

Only their old age would give them homes in town. The Bataan death march would continue down Kearny Street in San Francisco into the collapsing brick-walled rooms of the International Hotel and a hundred places just like it.

The first *manong* became a trapped inland sea of men surrounded by hostile soil in a silent thirty-year siege. A landlocked, irrigated sea of wet fields and their small brown lovers. They were dark men who were unable by law to marry any but their own kind, though women of their kind would not be allowed entry into the United States in any significant numbers for years to come. They could not vote in America. They could not own land, though they lowered their bodies to caress and tend the soil every day.

The first wave was a weary, dog-eared stack of dated marriage catalogues passed from man to lonely man. The catalogues were hand-rubbed, fading inventories of young women's happy faces above a two-paragraph biography in Tagalog. The photos were images of smiling entropy; energy no longer available; the true mark of time's inexorable direction.

Whole platoons from the Pacific theater had come over; whole fire teams and sapper squads with the smell of cordite still in their young, black hair. Long before the harvests were mechanized, these men, like squads of infantry, assaulted the fields of the Imperial Valley and the San Joaquin; carnal machines the equal of the braceros at pushing the knee pads and hampers just once more down the row, just one more back-breaking time. Like sweating grunts, they humped the furrows with gleaming knives and slung sacks, the salt sea pouring from their faces. They had once humped the savage boondocks in the highlands of misty Corregidor.

Zeferino stood at the entrance to the Quonset hut. He saw that it was about sixty feet long with small windows at either end. There was a string of naked lightbulbs hanging down the center of the room. Two-bunk cubicles lined both sides of the building. Near the front door and to the left was the cook's area, where stacks of enameled metal plates were arranged alongside buckets filled with navy surplus forks, knives, and spoons. In the boy's ears there was the splatter of falling dice, the clink of small change, and the forceful slam of a full house revealed.

There were three fifty-pound bags of rice on the floor next to the stove, a five-gallon can of soy sauce, and two bottles of *bagoon*, the favorite fish sauce of the Pinoys. There were small bottles filled with chiles suspended in vinegar, a huge jar of purplish shrimp sauce, and a dozen toothpick dispensers made of empty bottles of Louisiana Hot Sauce. The kitchen was spartan and strictly utilitarian.

There were cans of Pet Milk arranged down the center of the table, one can every three feet. Each can had two holes poked into the lid, one for pouring and the other to allow air in for a smooth flow. Each hole had a harmless yellow encrustation around it. Zeferino would notice the same arrangement of cans in the Mexican Quonset. Farmworkers loved Pet Milk in their coffee. It was clear that men did the cooking here.

The men who greeted the boy had to stop their noisy card games and look up from their piles of small change and poker chips. Someone rushed to turn down the volume on "The Ed Sullivan Show." The men were seated on both sides of a long table that almost spanned the entire length of the hut. There were no chairs, only long, handmade benches. Some of the men chose to stay in their cubicles, and even these rose to their feet when the boy was brought in by his mother. Women were rare in this world. Children were rarer still.

Each shy man then extended his hand to the boy and greeted him warmly, ten, twenty roughened and knobby hands. Zeferino would have a place in the Quonset hut with the Pinoys. If his mother had come into camp in a bracero's car, he would've stayed in the Mexicanos' Quonset.

His mother, Lilly, had been given the small cottage to herself. Privacy and distance were the universal prerogatives of beauty. Her current boyfriend had driven the Oldsmobile across the state and triumphantly into camp with the prettiest woman in the valley at his side. Now he was publicly humiliated when she informed him in front of the other men that she intended to reside in the cottage alone.

"Perfecto," said Lilly coldly, "you stay here. You can come and see me on payday."

Lilly blew him a smoke-filled kiss, then turned on her heel and headed for her private quarters, slamming the door on the derisive laughter of Perfecto Lopez's *compadres.* Ignoring a despondent Perfecto, the campesinos resumed their introductions. Each one announced his own name with a smile.

Bob was a short, balding man with a large growth on the side of his leathery face that made him look as though he were trying to swallow an orange. He was an old farmworker, bent now like a bonsai by the bindings of a hard life that had always conspired to stunt him. He wore only khaki, including a khaki belt with a brass buckle that he shined daily with Brasso. His shoes were army-issue class-A's. He had two pairs of them spit-shined and lined up beneath his bunk and ready for duty. He had worn those shoes every weekend since the war. Both pairs would be placed in his casket.

Tony had a noncontagious form of dry leprosy. While the others were busy playing cards or singing, Zefe had seen him sitting calmly in his cubicle where his girlfriend, a local outcast white girl named Jeanine, was spreading Vaseline on his legs, then covering them carefully, meticulously with long strips of white gauze. The boy watched as she patiently pressed the layers of gauze onto the petroleum jelly. He noticed that his legs looked like dark Swiss cheese.

"St. Giles and Mary Magdalene," Zeferino said aloud without realizing that almost everyone in the building had heard him.

Jeanine glanced up at the boy and smiled. "Not quite," she said.

Tony's feet were already completely covered with gauze. The

boy thought he looked like a half-wrapped, anointed mummy. Jeanine was good at her work.

"Hello, Zeferino," she said softly.

Tony placed one hand lovingly on her shoulder and extended the other to the boy, who took it without hesitation. Above the waist, he was a good-looking man with clear skin and a large pompadour. Tony, like most Pinoys, fancied himself a singer. "Hello, I am the Filipino Johnny Ray," he said, smiling broadly. Jeanine grinned with him, only mildly bored with the grand assertion.

Manny was a singer, too. He had a fascination with Italian tenors and Enrico Caruso in particular. But he fancied himself more of a Tony Bennett.

"I left my heart in Quezon City."

Whenever it was his turn to cook, he would pour canned marinara sauce over boiled bean threads or long-grain rice. The other Pinoys worked it out so that it was almost never his turn to cook.

When not in his work clothes, Manny was a dapper man who always wore his double-breasted suit on weekends, even if he seldom left the camps anymore. Somehow he always seemed to have a fresh flower in his lapel, even in winter. He dutifully wore his only double-breasted to dusty cock fights and kneeling dice games. He had long eyelashes and a crescent mole on his left cheek that he was very proud of. He sang at every Pinoy function from Livingston to Livermore. Most of his songs were aimed directly at the hearts of Lilly or her younger sister, Julia, who had only recently joined the migratory circuit down in El Centro.

The three Garcia brothers, Roberto, Vicente, and Mariano, came forward together to shake Zeferino's hand. They were tall, good-looking men with straight hair and white teeth, obviously lady-killers. They always smelled of Wildroot Hair Oil and William's Lectric Shave and steadfastly refused to use razor blades on their tender faces.

Tacquio was a field boss. After forty years in the furrows, he had been entrusted with the task of keeping the workers' piece-work tallies. He was the first nonwhite to have the job on a Ditto brothers farm. He was also the liaison man between the workers and the Ditto brothers, Pietro and Simon, the owners of the fields. In the chain of command, he was below the foreman, who was a white man and related by marriage to the field owners. Tacquio was far below the foreman. At the Ditto farm, no worker was allowed to speak directly to the bosses or to the foreman. If a worker had a grievance, he had to speak to Tacquio, who was torn between the privilege of his position and the futility of it. He was paid to keep his own people compliant and silent, and he knew it.

At the San Jose bean strike of 1952, he had begged the Pinoys and Mexicans to accept the owner's offer of fifteen cents per hamper. In the end, the workers had gotten thirty cents a hamper, but found themselves locked out the next season. Tacquio hated working the Ditto farm. The men were paid next to nothing, and lately there had been talk in the fields of a workers' union. It was a dangerous idea, thought Tacquio.

"If you persist in your grievance, they'll bring Hindus or Koreans in to do the work. Then where will we be?" Tacquio had pleaded. "You know what they did to us over in Watsonville."

His job had been easy at first. The docile farmworkers had always been battered and bullied into submission by the field owners and their henchmen. There had been occasional minor resistance, a few general meetings, and even one small, militant newspaper that had demanded equal treatment and a decent wage. It had protested the arrests and beatings across the state of Pinoys who had the audacity to gather in public parks. It had called attention to the abuse of brown men who had chosen to court white women. The newspaper had been burned to the ground by masked burglars after just a few editions.

Some workers had even taken their grievances into court. In 1931 a state law prohibiting "Mongolians" from marrying within the state was challenged. In the case of Roldan v. Los Angeles County it was held that Filipinos were not Mongolians. The state law was promptly changed to include "Malays." In 1934 the Supreme Court limited most constitutional rights to whites only . . . the right to own property, the right to apply for citizenship. The ruling specifically excluded Filipinos.

In Stockton as well as in many other places in California, antimiscegenation laws were translated into hundreds of local ordinances that prohibited everything from mixed marriages to

interracial dancing. Filipinos, Mexicans, and Chinese were prohibited from using public parks and recreational facilities as well
as public toilets. Though the antimiscegenation laws were struck
down in 1948 by the State Supreme Court in the case of Perez v.
Sharp, the local ordinances—now based on color rather than
national origin—lived on, both on paper and in the hearts
of landowners and the police, until the end of the civil rights
movement.

By using isolation and scab workers, the landowners had
managed to keep the various racial groups angry at one another
and alienated from American society. This tactic guaranteed low
wages and a ready supply of laborers. Most of the men had been
too afraid to complain. But recently, a young Mexican American
farmworker from somewhere outside of Phoenix had begun to
talk about a union that would represent all of the workers, one
that crossed all racial lines. And that man, Señor Chávez, was
working right here in French Camp.

For the first time in years, Tacquio was worried about his job.
Señor Chávez's latest pamphlet was the most audacious and im-
pudent of all. He was daring to call for a caravan of farmworkers
to get dressed in their best McIntosh suits and to drive into
Stockton together for an evening of dance lessons. Together,
they would challenge the illegal local ordinance that prohibited
social activities, specifically ballroom dancing between Asian or
Latin men and female members of the Caucasian race. Though
prostitution and white slavery had always been illegal in Stockton, the city fathers and the police didn't seem to be very concerned about recreational sex. It was the prospect of romance
that bothered them.

Tacquio shook his head at the very thought of brown men
dancing in downtown Stockton. Why couldn't they be satisfied
with the Chinese dance halls? Ordinance or no ordinance, the
police and the local thugs were going to do what they wanted to
do. They always had. What was the world coming to? Even the
Pinoy Tony Bennett and the Pinoy Johnny Ray had agreed to go
along.

"Don't you understand?" said Tacquio. "We may sing like
Americans, but we can't live like them."

In total, there were perhaps twenty-five or thirty Pinoys in the bunkhouse, playing cards or talking or watching the "color" TV up on the wall. It was not really a color television. Someone had sold the Pinoys a cheap black-and-white television with a multi-colored piece of plastic glued over the screen. The same man had sold an identical color television to the Mexicans in the Quonset next door. It gave everything on the screen a slightly yellow cast. After seeing the yellow picture for the first time, none of the Pinoys thought color TV amounted to much.

In the noisy melee of exclamations and curses at the card tables, one person in particular caught Zeferino's attention. He had been lying on the very last bunk on the right side of the Quonset. With his forehead knotted in concentration, he was busy attempting to roll a silver dollar across the tops of his tiny knuckles. Despite his efforts, the dollar kept falling down onto the bedspread, but still the man had persisted. Above the man's head, a rank of plastic angels hung down from strings tied to the rafters. Where the other men had tacked up pinup calendars and photographs of naked women, this strange man had nailed up a large street map of Venice.

He wore a small black-and-white-checked vest over a dark shirt and brown corduroy pants. On his head was an Irish tweed cap, cocked at a rakish angle. One of his tiny shoes had an enormous sole. There was a small black cane on the bed beside him. Zeferino could not take his eyes from the man. He was a midget and he had a small hunched back. As the boy approached, the little man suddenly sat upright on his bed, then made a graceful, sweeping bow, his hat in his right hand, his left hand behind his back and beneath his hump.

"Teodoro Teofilo Cabiri, at your service," he smiled. "My name was given to me by a vagrant band of transient angels. It literally means lover of God, lover of God and protector of ship-wrecked men . . . and there are a lot of them here."

In a grand circular motion, he gestured around the entire perimeter of the Quonset hut with his hat.

"But you can call me Ted For Short," the midget laughed.

It was an old joke, but he still enjoyed its impact.

"And you are Zeferino, eh? I shall call you Zefe. I've heard about you, my boy, and I believe that you, too, are a reluctant traveler. Well, you are among gracious wayfarers and fellow pilgrims here. Welcome to beautiful, exotic French Camp, Zefe, the asparagus capital of the western world!"

The boy stood staring and listening, as though transfixed by the seemingly misplaced beauty of Teodoro's language. Ted For Short swung his tiny legs over the bunk, jumped down and extended his hand. Zeferino shook it enthusiastically. Ted For Short was just a bit shorter than the boy.

"Did you know," said the midget, a mischievous look on his brown face, "that if you showed an Alaskan Eskimo the entire line of Studebaker cars from the very first model made to the very last, he could not know, just by looking, which designs are more modern and which are antique? He could not put an arrow on the line and say that time goes this way, or this way is progress."

Ted For Short and the boy stood face to face; both were intensely serious about the proposition at hand.

"We know which way the arrow goes only because we saw last year's model, not because there is any improvement."

"You know, you're right," mused a smiling Zeferino.

"Many times, change is only change, and nothing more. Looks can be deceiving," he smiled. "Look at me."

The midget removed his cap and bowed regally once again.

"My Tia Juanita always says that it's good luck to see an *enanito*," said Zeferino, smiling.

"Then this is certainly a fortuitous happenstance, wouldn't you say? Do you want a soda?"

Ted For Short gestured for the boy to follow and led Zeferino to the storage area behind the sleeping quarters. At the rear wall that separated the sleeping quarters from the storage area, the boy noticed a large cluttered altar depicting the Crucifixion. In the same spot in the Mexican Quonset he would see an altar depicting the Adoration. Behind the wall, there were three old iceboxes, the first of which had a handwritten sign taped to it marked PERSONAL. Inside were various bottles and bags each meticulously labeled by its owner. One bag had the letters TFS printed on the side. From this bag Ted For Short pulled two small bottles.

"This," he said, savoring the moment, "is a Yoo-Hoo chocolate soda, no ordinary liquid confection. It's pure ambrosia, my boy. The food of the gods. It's as brown as me and almost as sweet."

He shook the bottles, then popped both tops off on a nearby bottle opener; then, with a flourish, he handed one to the boy.

"Democracy and capitalism are not the same thing," he winked. "Just two years ago I had six or seven chocolate sodas to choose from. Now there is only one. Take the bunk next to mine, it's open."

As they walked back to the bunks, the little man busied himself by removing the cork from one of the Yoo-Hoo lids. He put the lid on the boy's shirt and pressed the cork into it from the other side of the shirt.

"Now you have a badge," he smiled. "Now you are an official sojourner."

Ted For Short raised his voice in a prideful shout to the preoccupied men around him.

"The boy is one of us!" he shouted.

There was no applause, no cheering. A few men groaned, then returned to what they were doing. One or two prayed silently to themselves that the boy would be spared this life.

"Now, I want to show you something," said Ted, beckoning to the boy. "Come over here and look deep into my ear."

The boy seemed surprised by the strange request, so the little man repeated it, then removed his cap and turned his head to one side.

"Don't be afraid. Come here and look way down into my ear. Imagine that you have the fingers of a prophet, the knuckles of a saint. Force those fingers in there and spread my skull open."

The boy cautiously complied, a tense smile of curiosity growing on his face.

"What do you see?"

"It's dark," answered the boy.

"No." Ted For Short smiled, wagging a stubby finger at his newfound friend. "Look carefully and you will see a horizon in there. God put it there and it's the same size in every man and woman . . . and boy. It's infinite. When you are critical of humans . . . and these days you have to be . . . you must say that they can't see their own horizons. It is a terrible sin, my boy, to have a little mind."

Zeferino went to his cot just before lights out. On a work night, that was ten o'clock. From his cloth bag he had removed a toothbrush and a comb. He pushed his bag underneath the cot, then reached into his pocket for a small photo of his brothers. He tacked the photograph to the divider that stood between his bunk and that of a dark little man from Zamboanga. Earlier, Teodoro had explained to the boy that the dark man was a sea gypsy, a sailor by blood who was now trapped in the doldrums.

On the boy's cot, someone had placed a pink handbill announcing another general meeting of all farmworkers, to be held on the weekend in the grape field over in Ripon.

"Chávez is dreaming," Tacquio muttered on seeing the boy with the offensive flyer in his hand.

It was only after he had made his bed and lain down for the night that the boy had the chance to study Teodoro's cubicle. In semidarkness he counted a dozen toy angels levitating on strings over Ted For Short's pillow. Each angel bobbed and twisted slowly on any breeze. The strings were tied to the rafters. Teodoro, like every other campesino, had a Bible near his pillow.

That first night in the darkened Quonset hut would be etched into the boy's mind forever, if not in retrievable, perfect images, in a moment of grief at the epicenter of every night's sleep. The sound of thirty drained, snoring men reverberated off the curved metal walls of the Quonset. Grown men whimpered out of loneliness into a corrugated metal parabola that collected it all and sent it back to them concentrated, undiminished.

Even Teodoro Cabiri whimpered as he slept. Sleep was their surcease and they all embraced that small void as a lover. Some men spoke in their sleep, fragmented, childish cries. Some wept unknowingly; others cried out in desperate outbursts like a castaway's marooned words. In his bunk, the boy shivered in hundred-degree heat. His teeth chattered as the sheer, wintry loneliness of it rolled over him in rasping, spitting, guttural waves of snores and murmurs. Finally, hours later, the dimming angels and the monotony of the loud din of solitude lulled him to sleep.

In the weeks that followed his first night in the Quonset, the boy went out daily into the hot, shadeless fields with the men.

Each workday, the metal martinet—the heartless alarm clock at the end of each Quonset hut—rang at precisely four in the morning. Each workday morning began hours before daybreak with a cup of hot coffee and a bowl of shredded wheat, both enhanced immeasurably by a splash of thick Pet Milk.

No one ever spoke over breakfast; no pensive eyes made contact with any others. When the boy tired of the Pinoy breakfast of cereal or pork chop suey, he went to the Mexican Quonset for *huevos revueltos y chicharones con salsa.* The Mexicanos seldom ate breakfast, but when they did the food was heavenly. The only thing he had ever seen a Hindu have for breakfast was a thick white tea and some dried bread. These early mornings in silence were the sojourners' only waking peace, the only moments of the day that were truly their own.

The workers scattered for this time, alone with their individual thoughts and their separated memories. This was not a time to daydream as when they were working, nor was it a time to suffer as when they slept. This was the time when things were far too clear, when men put their futures on the scales and found them to be weightless. The best thought they could have at this time was that they were still alive and breathing and still sending money to their families. It was this thought that sent them out, gloves in hand, to face another bending day.

Lunch was completely different; lunch was inhuman, mechanical, timed by the foreman's watch. It was a time not to eat, but to refuel. The farmworkers ate lunch like heaving, light-bellied trains, taking on water, taking on coal.

Sitting on cold stumps and wooden boxes and on the fenders of tractors, they used the early morning to conjure up visions of their families in scenes of Quintana Roo, Ilocos Sur, and the endless lapping and heave of the Ganges. Each man knew that the remainder of the day would be spent spending himself. It was said that a farmworker aged two days for each day in the fields.

In the evenings, the laborers would play cards or sing, but the energy of the weekends would not be there. Half-alive, on workday nights, they would wager hours of sweat on the cavalier turn of a card, casually tossing bills into the pot as though the work they did each day was not slavery but chivalry.

Zeferino went to work on the irrigation gang with Tacquio and Ted For Short, setting the shiny aluminum elbows into black furrows edged with fog, then placing the thin metal dams into the main canals before the pumps were turned on. Fields that were not being picked that day had to be watered. The boy soon learned to read the speed of the dark water and could tell if the flow was too fast for the depth of the furrows. Ted For Short always drew up an irrigation map the night before and all the hardware had to be in place by five in the morning when the flow began.

"Check the furrows for any nests!" Ted For Short yelled from across the field to the boy on the first day of work.

The two of them ran from furrow to furrow, searching for the telltale signs of a fragile ground nest. Zeferino found no birds, but a small, empty can of deviled ham had been used by a mother mouse to protect her tiny newborns. The little mice were squirming pink and blind inside the can. The boy lifted it carefully and placed it at the top of the furrow where the water would never reach.

"You gonna make that boy crazy, just like you," Tacquio said to Ted For Short, his voice filled with disgust.

One morning, while irrigating and scouring the furrows for life, Zeferino caught a glimpse of his mother in a bathing suit, swimming in the main slough and sunning herself in full view of a field of stooping men. It was then that he saw the Ditto brothers for the first time, loitering near the water pump. They looked like a strange pair.

"It's not polite to stare, Zefe," said Ted For Short, who knew what he was talking about. But Zeferino could not take his eyes from the two men.

The boy had been told that the bosses were twins, but he had not been prepared for what he saw. His stare could not settle on a single gesture or feature that might help in telling the two men apart. They wore identical clothing, striped engineer's coveralls and straw hats with unstained sweatbands. They had identical pigskin gloves and steel-toed shoes. Their clothing was spotless and spoiled by heavy starch and ironed creases.

They had come to the slough to supervise the critical irrigation process and to stare at the woman swimming there. There was a rumor in the furrows that one of the Dittos had been to the Philippine Islands a long time ago, that he'd left a woman behind . . . maybe even a kid or two. The men smirked when they whispered that he still had "brown fever."

Zeferino learned to work in the blessed cool of the packing shed where the asparagus shoots were trimmed, then placed onto a conveyor belt to be washed. Rows of moving boxes at the end of the belt caught the wet shoots as they fell. Once each hour he went into the cutting rows with Ted For Short on the John Deere tractor, pulling the filled boxes out of the fields and into the shed.

It was on one of these trips that Zeferino saw the man he had seen cooking by the slough that first evening when Perfecto's Oldsmobile had brought him to French Camp. In the daylight he noticed the wild white hair and thick mustache bending over and over again cutting carefully at the base of the asparagus plants and tossing the shoots into a box.

"Who is that man?"

"Oh, that is my friend, Faustino," answered Ted For Short with a warm smile on his face.

"Stay away from him!" shouted Tacquio, suddenly very angry. "He's a crazy man. He likes boys," he said, nodding toward Faustino. "He is not like regular people! He is unnatural."

As Tacquio turned to tally a man's load, Ted For Short put one of his short fingers to his lips.

"Faustino is my very best friend in all the world," he whispered to the boy. "I've known him since I was a little boy, back in the Islands. When I first met him, I was about as old as you are now. I'll take you out to meet him sometime, but you can't tell anybody," he warned. "Nobody. It has to be our secret."

"Nadie," answered the boy. *"Claro."*

"And he was a lousy soldier!" added Tacquio, who was speaking to no one in particular. "No good in the army," he spat, "no good in America."

Ted For Short smiled patiently.

"Tonight I'm cooking for the Mexicans, Zefe," he announced to the boy. "They're gonna send one of their boys over to cook for all of the Pinoys. We did it last week and it worked out pretty good. Once the Mexicans got past the vinegar and the

Pinoys got past all that chile, everybody had a real good time. Do you want to help me cook tonight? I'm going to make pork adobo, garlic fried rice, and bitter melon."

The boy nodded, yes. He had come to love Pinoy food almost as much as Mexican food.

"The Mexicans won't like the bitter melon," Zeferino said apologetically. He had tasted it recently and knew it would take some getting used to. There was nothing like bitter melon in Mexico.

"Then we'll make mongo bean soup, instead," said Teodoro, thankful for the warning. One of the deep green jalapeños he had eaten last week had sent him to the outhouse four times in one hour. He'd had enough time to read completely through two comic books, a catalogue of picture brides, and an issue of *Mechanic's Illustrated*.

On a warm Friday evening, sometime between the second and third cutting, when the older workers had gone into Stockton to spend their hard-earned wages at the boxing exhibitions, and the younger ones had run off to the Chinese-run whorehouses that dotted El Dorado Street, Teodoro decided that it was time for the boy to meet Faustino.

The camp was half empty and the Mexican braceros from the other Quonset were noisily playing cards or singing *corridos*. Ted For Short took Zeferino's hand and led him quietly to the front of the Quonset hut, where he stood dramatically surveying the length of the camp road before signaling with an assured nod. "The coast is clear," he said in a whisper.

"Where did everyone go?" asked the boy.

"Downtown," said Teodoro.

"There are no old men here," said the boy. "Did all the old ones go back to the Islands?"

"No," said Teodoro. "There's this park bench down on El Dorado Street . . . well, I'll tell you about it when you're a little older."

A shiver ran down his spine as he thought of the bench in the small park on El Dorado Street. He could never explain that bench to the boy, and he swore silently to himself that he would never sit on that bench. He and the boy tiptoed past the Hindu Quonset and out toward the dirt road that led to the highway.

Ted For Short took Zeferino to the turnaround behind the packing shed where the huge blue Buick sat on its blocks. The fire that Zeferino had seen the first evening was burning there again. There was a can of beef stew bubbling on the fire and strips of Spam were laid near the edge of the grill where they could cook more slowly on the heat. The oil that dripped into the fire hissed and spat and the night air above the slough was filled with the perfume of ground pork shoulder and with the sound of countless crickets and frogs.

Faustino rose from his haunches as the two approached. The two men hugged each other; then Teodoro announced, "Faustino, this is my friend Zeferino Del Campo." Faustino bowed, then shook the boy's hand.

Faustino was among the first Pinoys to come to America. His two older brothers had come here shortly after his own arrival. Unlike most, the three brothers had found work right away as porters for the Northern Pacific Railroad. But the pay had been terrible and the black and Filipino porters were not given a place to eat and sleep on the train.

This year Faustino had come to French Camp for the asparagus season just as he and his brothers had come for the last few years. But this season his two brothers had stayed on in Chicago. They had found jobs serving mixed drinks in the observation cars of silver passenger trains. They thought that stealing food from the dining car and sleeping standing up in the luggage car was preferable to working in the fields. No more stoop labor for them. Wearing red waistcoats with gold buttons and shining patent-leather shoes, they flashed past the fields, a coast-to-coast view of America on metal ribbons.

Once a week, while in the camp, Faustino would start the blue Buick's engine to charge the batteries so that he could read at night, and to keep Mahalia Jackson singing into the air above his car radio. Each morning at French Camp he would rise at four in the morning to work from four-thirty until sunset, when he would walk alone to his Buick to eat again in solitude and read by firelight. At night he would sleep in the backseat. On his first day off he had jacked the car up and put it on blocks in order to save the tread on his new bias-ply tires.

He had been sitting there alone, reading and sharpening his

machete, when Perfecto's car first drove by and into camp. He had smiled at Lilly, who had been smoking as usual and directing Perfecto's every move. Lilly had not smiled back. Faustino had heard that she was bringing her oldest son to French Camp, and he had caught a glimpse of the boy staring back at him from across the slough.

"You can borrow any of my books," said Faustino, who spoke in a low, soft voice while pointing at the crates filled with books in his trunk and passenger seat.

The boy saw that the man's hair was prematurely white; his face was youthful and gentle and the firelight gave the man's skin a color that was somewhere between orange and bronze.

"I have mostly scientific reading in the trunk. I keep the literary fiction in the backseat. Carson McCullers is my favorite storyteller. Actually, I can't decide between Harper Lee and Carson McCullers. Both are so good at dialogue. How I would love to have a life where there was so much talking, so much conversation! Have you read *The Member of the Wedding*?"

The boy shook his head, no.

"I just love little John Henry and Frankie. Is it possible that children can have so much to say? My own life is always so painfully quiet. My childhood back in the Islands had such a cruel, contemplative dreariness to it. Nothing at all like John Henry's. If it weren't for Teodoro, there would've been no kind voice at all in my childhood."

Faustino looked out over the green slough. The light green foam of the slow-moving water was barely visible now. The voices of a million frogs rose up from the reeds and cattails.

"I keep my poetry books under the front seat, beneath the angels," said Faustino, pointing to three small plastic angels that hung from his rearview mirror. They were exactly like the ones the boy had seen flying above Teodoro's bunk.

"I have Wallace Stevens, Ezra Pound, and Theodore Roethke, but I especially love the Greek poet Constantine Cavafy. He seems to speak directly to me. Two of my favorite poems are "When the Watchman Saw the Light" and "Waiting for the Barbarians." *There are pains that will not stay in the heart. . . .*

"I only wish I could've met the man," sighed Faustino. "I wish he were still alive or I were alive in his time. We could be such friends."

"Faustino writes poetry, too," said Ted For Short upon finally realizing that two lines of Cavafy was all that would be forthcoming.

"No," said Faustino curtly. He shook his white mane as he answered. "No. I only have the burning desire to write poetry, not the skill, certainly not the discipline or the understanding. God knows, I have the ache! I suppose it's only natural for someone who is as alone as I am, and as fettered with limitations, to turn to art."

"Faustino," Teodoro said softly, nodding toward the boy. With a nod of understanding, Faustino deftly turned the subject away from himself.

"Ted For Short told me that you like to read about science."

Zeferino nodded with a smile. He had just become aware of the fact that he liked Faustino, that the fields had given him another friend.

"Did Ethel and Julius Rosenberg really steal the secret of the atomic bomb?" the boy asked, seeing a picture of the two on a book cover in the trunk.

"Many would say that the answer to that question is different depending on who you are, and where and when you live. I know that subjectivity has its place, but I suspect that there is a truth somewhere out there that doesn't depend on the perspectives of man."

Faustino lifted the book to inspect its cover.

"You see," said Faustino, "the government needed to drop the bomb and it wasn't because of the Japanese. They knew that the Japanese would be suing for a peace settlement within weeks, so it was ordered that construction of the bombs be speeded up."

He paused for a bite of Spam and continued.

"It was the Russians that President Truman was worried about. The Russians had to be convinced that common knowledge was uncommon, that simple technology was complicated. But, most of all, he wanted to prove to Stalin and his successors that America had sole possession of the bomb and, even more importantly, was crazy enough to use it on human beings. So the Rosenbergs had to pay, whether they stole the secret or not. And the people in Hiroshima had to pay, whether they wanted to call it quits or not. That incredible heat over Hiroshima was the beginning of the cold war."

Faustino returned the book to its crate.

"The Japanese paid the price over here, too. This land here"—he gestured around him—"this used to belong to a Japanese farmer and his family. Have you seen the writing on the large water tank?"

The boy nodded, recalling the faint script that had been hastily painted over.

"The California Growers Association coveted the land around here. Even that paranoid J. Edgar Hoover agreed that the Japanese were loyal citizens, but the big farmers won out. Then there were those idiotic Ditto brothers, Simon and Pietro, both members in good standing of the growers association, and, coincidentally, first in line to claim this land.

"Now the Dittos own the fields and the store that sold me my Spam. The growers association owns a couple of cops and half the city council, so they came one day and took that Japanese farmer and his family away."

Faustino leaned over the fire to stir the stew. The night above his head was beginning to fill with stars.

"I wonder about this country sometimes. You don't trust people here; you can only trust their motives, their investments. It is the morality of the marketplace. Yet, beneath the store window, it is so beautiful and there is such a diversity of people. But, in the end, the very things that should be positive are perverted here. If people in this country see a beautiful landscape, they immediately want to sell it. They rush to put a hotel on it. Then they get angry if someone else puts a hotel in front of theirs. If they see a beautiful heritage, they exclude it until it's watered down enough to be acceptable."

"Not acceptable," interjected the midget, "marketable."

"I went back home to the Islands to fight in the war," continued Faustino. "I killed a Japanese boy a long time ago, back in the Islands. Many of the men here still hate them because of the war. I don't feel that way, not at all."

He shook his head back and forth. It was a gesture of regret over the death he had caused.

"Perhaps someday I won't see that boy's face in my sleep. Someday—somewhere—I'll meet him again, face to face, and apologize to him for what I did."

Faustino paused for a moment. He could still see the fear in the face of that Japanese boy. He saw the face every day of his life and made no effort now to forget it. The boy's parents in Tokyo could only imagine the death. The least Faustino could do was to preserve the reality somewhere on this earth . . . even if within his own tortured mind.

Faustino had fired a rusted, single-action .22 rifle at the boy, half hoping to miss. But the bullet struck the soldier at his temple and the glancing blow had knocked him unconscious. The other guerrillas from his village had surrounded the boy and proceeded to draw lots for the privilege of beheading him.

It was the policy of the guerrillas that any Japanese soldier captured alive would be beheaded and his severed head displayed on a pole. It was the only way to fight an enemy of superior size and weaponry: terror. And it was an effective way. First, cut off his testicles, then shove them into his horrified face just before the machete falls across his throat. Let his comrades find him that way . . . cut in spirit, cut in flesh. The Khmer Rouge would some-day do the same, as would the Viet Minh, the Viet Cong, the Pathet Lao, and young soldiers from Oakland and Pittsburgh.

"Let the *bakla* do it!" someone had shouted. "Let Faustino kill the man he wounded!"

After the shaking Japanese boy was allowed to clean his own running wound, he was given ten minutes to write his own death-poem. Faustino was led to a position just to the boy's left and just behind him. The boy was kneeling in a small clearing, his eyes darting back and forth behind his half-closed eyelids. He was an inexperienced child—attempting to focus on eternity.

"Forget his testicles," someone shouted. "A *bakla* would enjoy that too much!" There was laughter all around. Only Faustino and the young boy did not join in the laughter.

Faustino had raised his machete, and the boy, his poem in his trembling hand, had turned to see the face of death. Faustino had lifted the machete even higher, and after seemingly hours upraised, it would not fall. Another man had rushed forward at last to slice the throat from the front. The dead boy never saw him. His head fell forward onto his poem and into his own wet lap.

Faustino left the Philippines for the second and final time, a failure once more. He had snatched up the dead boy's poem and run away to the sound of cruel laughter and ridicule; his uplifted machete had become the grim symbol of one life not taken and another not lived. He had left the Islands as a truly homeless man.

"Shit," said Ted For Short to a friend whose mind was clearly somewhere else. "Before the war these white people here treated the Pinoy like shit; then during the war, just like magic, we are brothers in arms, fighting side by side in the boondocks. And now that the war is over, we're less than shit again."

Faustino, back in the present, reached behind himself and picked up his machete. The Pinoys used the long knives in the packing sheds. Many carried them in canvas scabbards as a remembrance of World War II. Faustino's was U.S. Army issue and many years old. Besides the poem on rice paper, it was the only thing he had brought from the Islands after the war. He absent-mindedly began to stroke it across a moistened whetstone.

The small scrap of stained paper with the young soldier's last words was pressed carefully between the pages of Faustino's Bible and locked in the glove compartment of his Buick. He had carried the death-poem with him for many years before he had gathered together enough courage to ask a Japanese farm-worker for a translation. And when the beheaded boy in the jungle finally spoke, it was with a clarity of vision, a simplicity, and a gentleness that sliced through Faustino's guilt-ridden soul.

> *all my seasons end.*
> *crimson stain on white blossoms—*
> *see . . . I ruin buds!*
>
> *kazuo*

"A crimson circle on white," whispered Faustino, who would wonder each morning and each evening of his life how a bleeding, quivering boy named Kazuo, about to die, could see the folly of his flag from so high above it all. How could he have written such a poem in ten minutes, an instant before his death? It was years before Faustino realized that the boy must have composed the death-poem long before the terrible moment when the blade fell. He had written the poem on some quiet, contemplative morning in his parents' garden just days after the Emperor demanded his presence in the great army of the Rising Sun.

Had his writings foreseen the last moment? wondered Faustino, or had the last moment written the past? Did the boy carefully count out the requisite syllables? How could such penetratingly sharp words survive so long on a crumpled, fragile piece of paper?

"Will you go back to the Philippines, Faustino?"

The question brought Faustino out of his thoughts, and he glanced momentarily at Ted For Short before answering the boy's question.

"Did you know that in medieval times if a family could not afford to keep a newborn child they simply placed it outside in the elements where it eventually died?"

Zeferino shook his head.

"Well, it's true. In some places they did this only to female newborns. Exposure, that's what it's called. We, here . . ."—he looked again toward his small, hunchbacked friend—". . . are exposed. We are placed outside the Islands so that our families in the Philippines can live. We are everywhere.

"Some of us have been out here for our entire youth, our entire manhood and into our old age. In our homeland we are already dead men."

He held the machete up so that the light from the fire struck its gleaming edge. A somber Ted For Short carefully shoved another small log into the fire. The three faces of the two men and the boy were glowing amber with the heat and color of the flames. Far above their heads the moon was full.

"I send money home to people I would no longer recognize and they would never know me if they saw me. When I went home to fight in the war, my whole family pretended that I was not related to them. After all that money I sent them, after what they did to me in Baguio!" Faustino shook his head, then began again to draw the whetstone over the edge of the blade.

Ted For Short had nodded solemnly in agreement. There

were beads of sweat forming on his forehead from the heat of the fire. As a child, he had been taken to Baguio, too. It was a small town just north of Manila, a town filled with psychic surgeons, quacks, and shattered dreams.

"We belong nowhere," he said sadly.

"Our time has passed," said Faustino. "The Philippines I left behind no longer exists and the America I came here for never did."

Faustino laughed a sardonic laugh with his small friend.

"Do you know about grass?" said Ted For Short, finally able to change the subject for the boy's sake. He pointed toward the damp fields beyond the packing shed.

"Waving wet grass over acres and acres of black, soaking soil? You know that when we say grass, we mean asparagus, don't you?"

The boy nodded; he had heard it in the fields.

"Asparagus officianalis," interjected Faustino, "sparrow grass. There are two varieties that grow here. Some refer to them as Mary and Martha Washington, but I call them the sisters of Lazarus."

"You've seen how we all tend that grass, Vicente and Roberto and Mariano, all the rest of us?" continued Ted For Short. "You've seen us feeding it, irrigating the paddies in the early morning when all of America is asleep. Is it only the *manong* and the bracero who can see that those plants are really cousins to the lilies? But, to our eyes, they are even more beautiful than lilies."

Faustino nodded in agreement. "All of your uncles love the grass."

During the time that Zeferino spent in the camp, he had come to refer to the *manongs* as *tiyos*, uncles, in the same way that many of the braceros had come to be his *tios*. All of them would be the father that the boy had never met, and would never meet. They would teach Zeferino and his brothers how to build and fly exotic Asian kites. Mexicanos would teach them how to drop a transmission without using a jack and how to rebuild an engine and have parts left over. Hindus would show them how to air-graft the branches of citrus trees so that each tree blossomed as on that first day when the earth put forth vegetation.

"The machines they have nowadays don't love the grass," continued Ted For Short. "When it comes time to cut we are like surgeons with our long grass-knives, slicing the shoots away without killing the crown, separating the children without endangering the mother. The first cutting has to be done perfectly or there will be no second or third cutting, and that would be bad for everyone. Then those fools the Ditto brothers would go crazy over the shortfall and all the markets would scream and our pay would dwindle. No, the first cutting has to be done very carefully, as if by a lover."

Teodoro removed his hat and, using it as a potholder, lifted one of the cans of beef stew to his lips. Using a small knife, he shoveled some of the broth into his open mouth.

"Everybody can pick stringbeans or squash," he said while blowing at the open can to cool its contents.

"Even the gringos can pick stringbeans and squash. Only your *tiyos* know how to carve the grass. Do you know that asparagus has to be eaten alive? If it's dead, it's stringy and hard, even the tip. No, asparagus has to be kept wet and dreaming; even when it's cut away and shipped, it has to be dreaming. That's why women are better workers in the packing sheds. Those shoots love the feel of a woman's hands, it keeps them green and stiff." He winked.

"When it's refrigerated, it has reveries. Do you know what the asparagus dreams?" Teodoro was grinning widely. "It dreams it is being cut by the hands of brown men. Asparagus, shafted with a kind jab of the blade, slit with affection, cleaned of earth and rock by lovers standing in wet earth up to their ankles. We are giants in a small sea. We are suitors who sing a backwater refrain. Even the asparagus in those new mechanized packing plants, hacked at and insulted by metal, still talks of the days when there were Mexicans and Pinoys in all of the fields. Shit. I'll tell you something else."

Tears came to Teodoro's eyes. Faustino pretended not to see, while Zeferino listened with rapt attention.

"When I worked the barley fields and the wheat . . . and I've worked them all . . . I used to run out in front of the cutters and harvesters just to warn the rabbits. People see those big machines cutting fields clean, what do they think happens to all the little things that live out there? Well, I found out one morning in the hayfields up in Altamont when I discovered a whole family of rabbits that had been picked up from the windrows and mangled by one of the mechanical bailers. Run away, little rabbit, I would scream. Run away, little mouse! This thing will tear you up and no one will know of your fear and your pain.

"People always laughed at me for that. They'd stand watching the big red harvesters, and all of them would be pointing and laughing at me. But I saw the rabbits that got away—five, six, seven tender spines that would not be twisted and snapped."

The stew was cooler now. He spoke around carrots and potatoes.

"The field is my island now. When I left the seven thousand islands of my first home, I came here to live on another island. I came here only to be marooned in plain view like every other dark man who bends in these fields. But I like to think that somehow I'm special, that I am like a diviner at ground level; I can find small life where it hides. It's what happens when you stare at kneecaps and below all of your life."

He removed his cap and used the sleeve of his right arm to wipe the moisture from his hair. The fire was hot, but he was a tribal man and so stayed close to the flames. The black of the jungle was to his back.

"All we've ever had over here was the work that no one wanted, the things no one else wants to do. Those things, the braceros and us, we do better than anybody. We are the ones who can put a pinch of dirt on our tongues and know if the soil needs more lime or more sand."

He held up his hands to look at them.

"You take away the work of the hands and everyone goes crazy. Everyone loses their memory."

Zeferino decided then to ask the questions that had been on his mind since he first saw Faustino.

"Why do you live out here all alone? Why do you live in your car and so far from the bunkhouses? Why is Tacquio so mad at you?"

Faustino looked at the boy, inhaled, then exhaled deeply before answering.

"I am *bakla,* I am a homosexual."

He waited after speaking to see the boy's reaction. It was something he had grown used to. Surprisingly, there was no visible reaction.

"The camps are all men, battalions of displaced men without any sort of leadership, without any rank. They are treated like lepers here, yet even they have ostracized me. They hate me. They always have. I am the lowest of the low: cast off by the castaways. Even in places like Brawley and Watsonville, where the white men have killed Pinoys just for existing, my own people will not allow me to live in their camp. So I work the fields alone," sighed Faustino.

"When I put one of my filled boxes on a pallet, no other man will put his box there. The pallet becomes mine alone. When I go to the water jug I can't use the dipper. I must drink from my own cup. So I live alone. I eat and I read out here on the outskirts. People in the Islands are very religious, you see, and the church calls people like me an abomination. This solitude is my life."

He looked around himself at his home on wheels and at the green slough beyond.

"And this year is far worse than all the others because my brothers are not here with me. They are flying along on the California Zephyr, in a shining silver car that is cutting through Colorado or Utah right now. They are making Bloody Marys and Margaritas for laughing, happy people. I should have gone with them this season, when I had the chance. We had many a good time working on that train. Perhaps we will again.

"Ted For Short has always been my friend. It's such a pity that you have to sneak over here just to see me." Faustino sighed again, then ran his brown fingers through his white mane. "Even Tony, with his leprosy, is treated better."

"My mother doesn't like either one of you very much," said Zeferino apologetically. "She says you are deviants."

"What in heaven's name would a woman like Lilly want with a fag and a midget?" laughed Ted For Short. "She's the belle of the camps, from here to Seattle! Even the Ditto brothers won't dare bother her, and they would both certainly love to get her attention. When she was taxi dancing last year over on El Dorado Street, the Dittos and their white friends trashed every club but the one she worked in. They wrecked every club but the Crystal Slipper. Your mother has those Ditto brothers eating right out of her hand."

Teodoro reached down and carefully lifted a slice of browned Spam to his mouth. Farmworkers' ham.

"They own the cops over in Stockton, you know. The police almost beat one old Pinoy to death a couple of years ago, just because he was dancing with some peroxide blonde that Pietro had his eye on. He's the one that had the City Council draft that illegal ordinance against brown dancing. Did you know that Pietro Ditto hangs out every day at the packing shed just to stare at your mother?"

"I've seen it, too," said Faustino. "It's the only time he's civil. Last season he and his mob hurt a lot of Pinoys over in Lodi just because they dress so well and they danced with Lilly. Every man who danced with her got a lead pipe across the knees. He's a jealous bastard, that one. Last year it was your mother's youngest sister, Cecelia, who shunned him. She let him have it over the head with a wine bottle."

Ted For Short laughed at the memory of Cecelia's rebuff.

"Did you see what Ruby did to him at the Rose Room last year?" he asked, referring to one of the dance halls in downtown Stockton. "She told that Pietro Ditto that no woman in her right mind would allow him between her legs. He wouldn't dare touch Ruby."

Teodoro smiled in a strange way that Faustino understood to be affection. Ted For Short had not seen Ruby in a year. Those brief moments with her on the dance floor of the Rose Room had been his last sight of her.

"I'd never let him touch Ruby," continued Teodoro. "Almost one year ago today, on the last day of the harvest of 'fifty-eight, when the Pinoys were so drunk that none of them cared that Faustino was *bakla*, I convinced him to go into town with us. We went down Charter Way together in our perfect McIntosh suits, inside my beautiful Pontiac that was all waxed and cleaned. All our suits were pressed and our hats were perfectly raked. Everyone knows that Americans are the clothes they wear and the cars they drive, and on that Saturday night, for a few fleeting hours, we Pinoys were Americans . . . brilliantined, gold-toothed Americans.

"We rode into town, our pockets crammed with wads of bills rolled especially for the women at the Rose Room. It was heat-rash and backache money saved for an hour's dream, a moment of grace and lyricism on a sawdust floor, a moment of blessed eye-to-eye contact with a woman. It was an illusion of riches."

Teodoro smiled broadly.

"And I, Ted For Short, daydreamed as I drove. My oversized shoes came complete with dancing taps, you know. That night I was Bogart and Chevalier rolled into one," he grinned. "Even Faustino, sitting in the backseat between the handsome Garcia brothers, dreamed on the way to El Dorado Street."

Faustino smiled. But it was a smile tempered by the painful memory of how that evening had ended. Teodoro had fallen silent now, unwilling to tell the rest of the tale. A boy should not have to hear such things. They had already said too much.

The Rose Room had "the most beautiful women in America," or so the sign outside had proclaimed. There was a small four-piece band and a ticket booth. The women waiting inside the dance hall that night had seemed as perfect as living statuettes.

On that evening a year ago, Faustino had only watched the dancers. He had waited quietly outside the front door, tapping his foot to the music and staring into the cold and wet street. Above his head, the trees and power lines were crowded with noisy birds. He noticed that across the street in the park, a bench full of old men was beginning to empty for the night.

A huge black security guard kept him company as he waited and watched. Mare Island shipyard was close by. The lowing foghorns of the port seemed as gray as the sky. His *compadres* dancing inside the Rose Room had purchased their illusions. Faustino's own illusion was formless, anonymous, guilt-ridden.

One of the matrons of the taxi-dance hall had graciously asked him if he wanted to come in, but Faustino had politely declined. Then Ruby, the woman of Teodoro's dreams, had come outside for a moment to rest from her labors. Faustino had even declined her sweet invitation to dance, though he had considered it for a fleeting second. He knew how Ted For Short felt about her. He had not wished to hurt him, no matter how impossible that might have been. He couldn't have known that her reasons for asking had been selfish. Teodoro's idea of dancing had been killing her poor bare feet.

Above his head he had heard the sounds of rehearsed, stylized lust drifting from the open windows of the whorehouse upstairs. Above those sounds, for an instant, he thought he had glimpsed a strange, moribund face staring down at him from a third-story window. Faustino had been standing there outside the Rose Room when the gang of men came to curse the audacity of dark men dancing, and to cause him great harm. Before he went unconscious from uncounted savage blows to his face and shoulders, Faustino heard the hollow sound of the metal pipe striking the security guard's head and he saw the eyes of blind hatred focused on him—just as the peaceful music stopped.

Faustino and Teodoro stood quietly by the fire. Zeferino could see that both men were caught in the grip of a memory. He could not know that they were trapped in the thrall of last year's savagery at the beautiful Rose Room. In the last few moments the sun had set and a full moon dominated the sky above them. Zeferino stood between them, watching pain move across their moonlit faces, his own mind burning, not with fear but with curiosity.

"Tell me more," he said to men who were unable to hear him. As a cloud obscured the moon, the boy began to realize that it was not strains of waltz music or the memorized sounds of some past agony that the men were hearing, but the growing, immediate sounds of a present danger. The boy saw that his two friends were petrified with fear. They had heard something—seen something.

As an ominous cloud obscured the moon, the chirping of crickets and the croaking of frogs stopped suddenly, leaving a cold, foreboding layer of silence on the waters. As the face of the moon disappeared entirely, the lives of two men and a boy were changed forever.

VII

Down on El Dorado Street there is a small park, dark and sullen beneath a canopy of black, brooding elms. Under the elms, there is a bench that fills daily with stoic, ripened men, old Filipino *manong* and old Mexicans whose seared, thickened blood can no longer bend in the sweating fields. They are *viejitos* who have given up their gray, bearded dream of ever going home. There is a similar bench in Portsmouth Square in San Francisco, where old Chinese men see a cloudy city through the dimness of cataracts. Like elephants, they go there to die.

The men, wrapped in their spun years, their hearts winding down, sat short-legged astride the Dead Pecker Bench. They no longer spoke words meant for the outside world, but ministered and muttered among themselves.

"How's your liver, *compadre*?"

"Fine, fine, *compañero*. I can have a drink now and again, but these days my blood looks just like soy sauce. How are your kidneys?"

"They're okay, but I pissed a stream of jagged crystals again today. It felt like someone was pulling a sisal rope right through my pisshole. But I can't complain, one of Fulgencio's eyes has turned to milk and Octavio has a growth on his ass that looks like Mount Rushmore."

Crossing the grass for a short, halting walk, they limped dangerously near the edge of the yawning portal that leads to the next world, explaining its looming dimensions to one another by being so careful to never speak of it.

"Here is one edge of it," they did not say.

"Here is where the darkness begins. Here, right below all of us, is a crater, a cold ravine that is the mouth of a bottomless gorge. I stand at the very edge," they never heard each other say, even as dreams of falling invaded their waking hours, even as their limbs and bones turned to waxen twigs as they sat. They were the next batch of kindling for the eternal flame.

With sparse words, they only spat out the bitter taste of ashen ennui and mumbled among themselves that Guadalupe Lopez's fish-belly legs were white as ever. Still white as youth.

"Remember in nineteen forty, her breasts always wanted to float skyward, away from her puffing chest? Like buoyant, adoring clouds they were. Twin honors pinned proudly to her heaving diaphragm. She had to wear a special weighted brassiere just to hold them down."

The old men laughed together, though none of them had ever seen Guadalupe's breasts, and none of them was sure anymore why Guadalupe's veined mounds were ever of such moment.

Their sap falling, each man secretly suspected that the bench itself might be at the seat of the problem, that constant physical contact with it had led to an insidious exchange of molecules. Their vitality, gone by osmosis, had oozed through their Ben Davis trousers and had stiffened the weathered oak beneath them, while the lead in the green paint of the bench had migrated upward, into their pants and into the congealed cartilage of their knees.

"All that genuflecting sure didn't help. If I had been a Protestant, I could still walk today."

The lead found its way into their walk: the Dead Pecker Shuffle, a step that involves hugging the slick handrail at the top of a staircase or taking an hour to navigate a crosswalk.

"Is this nineteen fifty-eight?" they wondered aloud. "*Qué lástima*, did the time pass by so fast? Is this really nineteen fifty-eight?"

Nine men one day, eight the next, in diminishment they remembered America, their adopted country, the way a limp remembers the ancient fracture. Some still recalled the Watsonville riots of 1930 when their brother Fimon Tobera was killed and the long bunkhouses were set afire. Some remembered when the rampant whites dynamited the bunkhouse in Gilroy. The two old ones at the very end of the bench, Raj and Vimal, remembered the Hindu controversy.

"After much consideration, the courts finally decided that we weren't white," they laughed toothlessly.

"Remember the Great Nasal Question?" Raj asked Vimal.

"There were people running around here in lab coats sticking calipers into every Hindu nostril. Our noses didn't have enough internal diameter to be African, but they just couldn't get past our dark skin. One of those fools over at the Superior Court even proposed a melanin index. He had prepared a color chart like they have at a paint store."

"I remember the chart," laughed Vimal. "They wanted me to run my finger down the row of colors until I found the shade that matched the color of my skin. They had a name for each color. If you were darker than Winter Wheat, you were subhuman. I knew I was in trouble when I got down past Burnt Mocha."

The entire bench roared with soft laughter. No one of color had ever been left alone for long in America. Color was all important in a country that was trying so hard to rid itself of its cultures. Without culture, color is all that is left.

Shoes gleaming, hats set perfectly, each man deftly tossed dried bread to scurrying, fluttering pigeons; gray children, so responsive in a world unmoved by the loneliness of old men. Pigeons who, each morning, greeted their benefactors like ambitious, needy sons.

After passing the day in the park, each old *manong* and bracero returned each night to his own small quarters somewhere in one of the cheap hotels that surrounded the park. Each meager apartment had a windowless bathroom complete with matching bath towels, all of which were free with each giant box of Oxydol laundry detergent. Each table boasted plates and bowls from Texaco gas stations and coffee cups given free of charge with an eight-gallon purchase of Richfield gasoline.

Each lonely efficiency room had one green formica table and two chairs. There were red plastic shakers labeled Salt and Pepper, deformed by the heat from a nearby electric hot plate. There was a bed that was coffin-small and smelled of mentholatum. The decor was an echo of the Quonset huts and shacks at the farm labor camps, complete with pinup calendars and jars of hair oil. Each old farmworker slept surrounded by the fruits of his labors.

Those who had managed to leave the bunkhouse or the cheap hotels for the narrow comforts of a rest home lived in rooms painted convalescent yellow . . . the last shade before hospital white.

Every morning, after carefully counting his Blue Chip stamps, the old *manong* slicked his head with his favorite brilliantine, shaped his hairdo with a comb dipped in William's Barbacide, then splashed Lilac Floral eau de toilette onto a wrinkled chin. In the bathroom mirror the ethereal glistened in his matted hair and anointed face. It was death that was splashed onto his head and chin each day. It was the spirit unfurling as the body, grisly with cellular chagrin, balked and tottered, ambushed slowly by loneliness and time.

The stillness of the sojourners on the bench belied the flurry of activity each early morning when brushes and rags raised a blinding cordovan shine on ancient wingtips. Hats were brushed and mustaches trimmed. No vision of the *manong* is complete without the gleam of old shoes embalmed with Shinola.

Old Mexican braceros spent the last years of their lives choosing their final hat. When breath and heartbeat abandoned them, they wanted to be found stiff as an erection, but well dressed, wearing the perfect brim and sweatband and a clean polyester shirt. Like clockwork, the very oldest farmworkers dutifully manned the Dead Pecker Bench until the day came when one leg or the other would not move and a bedpan stored somewhere was dusted off. Older Pinoys and Mexicans gambled their money away at cockfights, boxing exhibitions, or in Chinese poker houses until a spot on the bench opened up for them. The younger ones got dressed up on weekends only to get undressed. To these youngsters, the Dead Pecker Bench was as distant as the Sea of Tranquility.

The old men were regular anomalies, timeless anachronisms: nomadic anchorites, lifelong hermits against their will. Prejudice had renounced for them the pleasures of home and the vows of marriage. The old men, hardened merely on the outside by dreary toil, were one by one finally slain by shyness.

Across from their park and the Dead Pecker Bench there is a three-story building. The first two stories are business while the top floor is a residence. The street floor is the Rose Room, an elegant taxi-dance hall famous for the beauty of its dancing girls. Unlike the Chinese dance factories uptown, the proprietors of the Rose Room cherished both gentility and good manners.

Above the Rose Room, there is a filthy hotel called the Flip-Flop where no one has ever slept. Eyes are closed, dreams are dreamed, other faces and an occasional ballgame are imagined, but no one sleeps there. No one, that is, but the old Chinese desk clerk who has a navy surplus cot unfolded behind the front desk and below a wall of cubbyholes, one for each room. He usually sleeps sitting up, dreaming numbered and compartmentalized dreams. When he lies down to sleep, it is because the sun has risen and the last guest has located his pants and gone.

No one ever strikes the bell at the front desk and no one ever phones the Flip-Flop for a reservation. It is a whorehouse that caters mainly to migrants and fieldhands. The lobby and the front desk of the original hotel have been moved to the second floor. The wall above the mail slots and key hooks is covered with boxing posters, some old, some new. Local heroes pose in the same aggressive, repetitive stances from one poster to the next. All that ever seems to change in the posters is the color of the man and the hand he jabbed with.

At least half of the flyers and posters carry the face of the same fighter. It is clear that the Chinese desk clerk has a favorite.

"King Pete Claver coulda beat Joe Louis, no sweat," the desk clerk grinned as he collected the hotel's cut from a john who was being led upstairs by one of the girls.

"He work here, you know. He the bouncer and my good friend. He protect me and the girls from all the jerks that come in here."

He pointed to the missing key on hook number 3.

"There a jerk in there now with Amanda. Some fat low-fon named Lou. Not many white guys come in here. If I hear too much noise up there, if he start to be mean to her, I send up King Pete. He take care of things. He my friend," he grinned, then flipped a switch situated just below the third hook.

The voice of a breathless male could be heard over the intercom, promising to take Amanda to dinner if she'd pretend to be his sister.

"King coulda beat Max Baer, Two Ton Tony Galento, and all of them."

Satisfied that things were under control, he switched the intercom off.

"I see him one time a year ago on the undercard at the fairgrounds, going against Willie Pepper. Willie got real desperate in the ninth round and start using his head for weapon. He head-butt King real good."

The desk clerk used his index finger to indicate an area over the right eye.

"He bleed so much they have to stop the fight. Otherwise, King, he win."

He shook his head.

"If there a real cut-man in his corner, King, he win."

Above the entrance to the hotel was nailed a green cross, the old, frightening symbol of the Mexican inquisition. Such crosses were once seen all over Mexico, on street corners, above the doorways of barbershops. In every pueblo, innocent people had been dragged from their beds in the dark of night and were brought to stand below crosses just like this one. Within full view of God himself, they would be questioned by some local, holy inquisitor.

Below the green cross, in the shade of the front awning, King Pete Claver, the security guard and bouncer for both the Flip-Flop and the Rose Room, strutted in that particular way that men always strut whose past lives were defined by their arm strength and their wind. His skin was ebony black and his face was battered beyond speculation, beyond conjecture as to its original hue and form. Ridges of scar tissue had taken the place of eyebrows, and skin that had been insulted over and over again seemed as thin as wet paper. No one who saw King could say what he looked like beyond the fact that he was huge and that larger men must've beaten him down. Yet only the craven needed to fear him.

Decades earlier, the building that housed both the Flip-Flop and the Rose Room had once been described as a warm Victorian charmer, with brass pineapple sconces, gas lamps, and floral carpet motifs. It had once boasted textured wallpaper handmade in Persia and an intercom system taken from the innards of a wrecked Portuguese passenger ship that had been salvaged off Macao. When the Great Depression came, the hotel had been sold at public auction to the present owner, who bought the building through a white purchasing agent who had created a lucrative niche for himself by buying property for "ghosts," people who could not legally own property in America.

The owner of the building, a man who lived in a small dwelling built on top of the hotel, was named Humberto, an older man who was said to have fled Mexico in the twenties, when the Mexican government was busy hanging nuns and shooting priests. The green cross was his doing. It was rumored by all that he had once owned businesses similar to the Rose Room in Mexico City and in Los Angeles. The word on the street was that Humberto was a living ghost forever doomed to repeat the past.

It was said that he had stolen money from church coffers in Mexico in order to finance his many enterprises. In truth, he had used only family money in escaping Michoacán for the Distrito Federal. The taxi-dance hall he had opened in Mexico City had been called El Infierno. The previous owner of that building had been a glass blower who considered his own fiery vocation hellish. Humberto had decided to keep the name of the old glass factory. So he commissioned a local artist to cover the facade of the building with dancing, leaping flames in keeping with the name.

That taxi-dance business had been run in a similar fashion as the Rose Room. The men bought *ficheras* when they came in, then gave the girl of their choice one *fichera*, one ticket for each dance. At the end of the evening, the girls were paid according to the number of tickets they had collected.

El Infierno in Los Angeles had been the same as the one in Mexico City. But the Rose Room in Stockton was unlike either Infierno. Here, there was no communal makeup parlor, no powder room packed with hundreds of foundations, creams, and lotions crowded around a single plate where a peso or a penny was left whenever a girl freshened up. There was no battery of perfumes here to sweetly foul the air.

Los Infiernos had a tension about them, the electrical tension of sexuality confused with romance. The Rose Room had the illusion of love itself, of ardor tempered by manners, of passion softened by the dance of strangers and eased by the sweet salve of ordered and prescribed steps. All prurient sexuality was the purview of the Flip-Flop, upstairs. Despairing of confusion, Humberto had divided his world cleanly in two.

Los Infiernos had been dismal failures, both in Mexico City and later in Los Angeles. People in those cities were simply not lonely enough or had somehow grown accustomed to their special brand of bright, noisy loneliness. The migratory workers of the Central Valley, on the other hand, were afflicted with the kind of profound, muted loneliness upon which a profit could turn.

Guadalupe, of the buoyant bosom, proprietress and madame of the Flip-Flop, claimed that Humberto was himself a disgraced priest. She told everyone that he was a man who had suffered the humiliations of the flesh rather than perish before a firing squad.

"It was get married or die," Guadalupe would say, rolling her eyes toward the mysterious room above the hotel. "He had to renounce his holy vows. I see how he looks at me when I'm bending over a dustpan."

The brutal Christero Wars had reached even Guadalupe's small village of Jalisco.

"*Qué locura,* how perverse it had been, a shooting war between *monjas y maestros de escuela!* People renounced their precious baptisms, and meek choirboys hunted down anyone who wore bifocals or who read those Darwin books."

She is old enough to remember the rumors of baptisms in chicken coops and confessions whispered through a hole in an outhouse door. Her own brother had been baptized in an oil drum set up in the pigsty. She remembered overhearing discussions, late at night, between her mother and father. They could certainly use the money the soldiers were offering. The priest hiding in the village silo was a dead man anyway.

"Hadn't the Catholics ravaged us enough," her father had said, "first with their *encomiendas* and their missions, then with their green crosses? Now they own the entire *pinche* country. We all know that God never sees the money His priests collect. Where does it go? Ay, Jesus Maria, some of that money should come to us!"

It had been a strange time, a painful time when villagers had angrily taken down their precious Catholic icons, dragged them out to the fields and buried them amid curses and taunts, all the while taking special care to mark the place, to wrap each statue in cloth and to break nothing.

"This one didn't die," Guadalupe would say, nodding toward the priest's quarters atop the old hotel, "but he sure as shit ain't really living up there, either. We almost never see him."

Guadalupe would plumb the subject with anyone who would listen. Each morning as she swept the sidewalk in front of the Rose Room, she would conjecture aloud about the landlord who spoke with her only twice each year, at Easter services and at the Christ Mass.

"I can't complain"—she would shake her head—"rent's real cheap and he never bothers me. I just can't help but wonder why he has a house of pleasure and a dance hall full of stuck-up virgins, all in the same building. I think he needs them all. Somehow, I think he needs both halves of it, whatever those halves are. Only the Lord knows."

Ultimately, she would shrug her shoulders and speak to herself as she finished her chores and prepared the Flip-Flop for the evening's clientele.

"All I have to do is cook for him and place the tray in front of his door. I knock; sometimes I hear a movement *adentro*, inside. Sometimes he eats, sometimes he don't touch a thing. He don't ask for much, all he ever wants is Mexican food. I bring his business papers up to him and deliver them to the post office when he needs things to be mailed. I buy his poisons for him. Oh, yes. I almost forgot. I wear these for him."

She looked toward her feet, then lifted her right leg out from under her dress so it could be seen.

"I wear these blue heels for him. I have six pairs, all the exact same style and color. He had them delivered, don't ask me why. It does make it kind of tough to wash the floors, but otherwise, it's *muy elegante*, don't you think?"

The landlord above never failed to overhear her daily conjectures and speculations and was well aware of the gossip that circulated in the streets below. He had learned not to discount the twisted accuracy of gossip.

"Back in Mexico, during the holy war," Humberto would say to the four walls of his room, "there was gossip circulating in the streets of Morelia that federal soldiers were coming for me and for my sainted brother. I should have listened to it," he repeated to himself as he lowered his body to the floor.

Each day he knelt in his room above the hotel, peering at the working girls below as they arrived for the evening. In tawdry, breathless genuflection he watched them through cracks in the floor as they undressed for work and led their johns demurely down the hall. He spied on both groups of girls, the hardened prostitutes who smelled of tobacco and dumbly washed the walls of their own vaginal vaults by rote, and the supple dancers, the magnetic mistresses of the coy glance and the certain step. He knew when the dancing girls were arriving because a swarm of chirping birds always followed one of them. It was such an amazing sight to see. The birds filled the trees in front of the hotel, bending the boughs with their chatter until she left to go home.

As he listened to the girls and watched them practice their respective crafts, he rubbed his wounds the way another man would rub his crotch. They were three wounds that were thirty years old now. The bullets had passed completely through his body and, exiting unsatisfied, had screamed into the body of his brother, the true priest. His brother had died without a single shot being fired at him.

"Was I the first target?"

Humberto, ventilated and feigning death, had survived the firing squad.

"Had I been transparent? Am I still transparent? Had I been nothing—insubstantial, even to spinning bullets?"

His body had seemingly offered no resistance to the bullets, yet they struck his brother with full impact.

"When the firing squad took aim, did they even see me? Did they ever set their sights on me?"

Three altar boys and the young man who cleaned the church had been the men who fired at the place where he and his brother stood, elbow to elbow, within sight of the shallow graves they had been forced to dig for themselves.

Dimly, Humberto could still hear the fat corporal from Quiroga laughing as each novice soldier claimed to have fired the blank round.

"There was no blank round, you *pendejos*! One of you *idiotas* missed." The fat corporal had laughed like that for hours.

"It was as though time was reversed and ran backward," whispered Humberto. "We were born separate and we died as Siamese twins joined at our wounds, sharing a single demise. God reached down and chose to save Miguel. Me, He doomed to eternal failure. So long ago, back *en mi pais* . . . back in Mexico, there was once a great experiment."

The women working on their backs in the rooms below looked upward whenever he spoke. Sometimes they even saw his lips moving just above his splintered floorboards, their ceiling.

Humberto looked down to the woman who was now removing her clothing for the third time this night, in the room directly below his kitchen. Her long breasts and thin, spare shoulders seemed as smooth as Florentine marble. He knew as he watched her undressing that the mystery in his mind, trapped between his early and his belated death, trapped within the floor that separated the dancers from the whores, would finally be explained to him one incandescent day.

"Why am I alive?" he cried.

He rose from his sore knees, then walked to the window and looked up and down the dark street, his breath becoming more and more labored as the woman below lay down to her work. Humberto had run by night and hidden by day in villages from Morelia to Mexico City, then from San Miguel de Allende to Ensenada. There was a long trail of invalid baptisms and botched marriages that ran from this room backward in time and place to the death of himself and his brother. All of those fraudulent confessionals had converted him into an unabashed voyeur. Now he turned his gaze and his attention to the old men sitting in the park.

"*Como los banditos del norte,*" he said aloud. He could see the old men on the Dead Pecker Bench. "*Como los desperados* in the state of Sonora, they will lie in wait and ambush God right there in the park, kidnap Him right out there." He shook his head. He, too, would see God someday. But he knew that he would have to wait a much longer time than the *viejitos* on the bench. He didn't know how he knew, but he knew it was true.

In anger he kicked at a bottle of rat poison that lay on his kitchen floor. It rattled into the hallway where it shattered against another empty bottle that had once held fifty sleeping pills. Neither had worked. The rat poison had caused him to sleep for three days and had turned his skin a pale green. The sleeping pills had no discernible effect at all.

The woman below him moaned her usual moan and bedsprings were creaking now in two or three other rooms. The oscillating bedsprings beat frequencies with one another, generating second- and third-order harmonics that caused neighborhood dogs to howl in unison. From street level, beneath the metallic complaints, the elevated sound of a waltz wound its way up through the floorboards. The old building was awash with tones and overtones, conflicts, tensions, and resolutions.

"What a glorious victory it was to be for the church, for God Himself! My dearest brother and I waited, longing to hear confession once more; to hear again of the philandering of husbands; to hear of young men hunting the soft thighs of blossoming girls; and to probe again the sinful thoughts of young housewives. You see, the government thought the people would turn away from the church and to the Presidente. The church believed that the peasants would reject Calles and all of his empty promises of land reform and smooth roads. Well, the worst of all possible things happened. Nothing happened."

The same profound chagrin was there in those two words as when he had first uttered them to his brother in another time and another world: nothing happened.

"*Nada.* The same doleful Indias bloodied their short knees

on the same church thresholds as before. The same farmers brought adobe to patch the walls of the refectory and the same Tarascan builders repaired the roof and the water tower just as their forefathers had."

Humberto walked to the small stove in the corner of his kitchen. He reached inside and grabbed a pair of wire-rimmed spectacles. He had left them in the oven the last time he tried to use gas as an avenue to heaven. Guadalupe, upon detecting the telltale odor, had turned off the building's gas. She installed a new electric stove in her own quarters. Following the advice of the local General Electric dealership, she had decided to live better electrically.

"The fools didn't even notice that the pulpit was empty," he said as he put his glasses on, "that the confessional was silent; that the Christero Wars were raging all around. They cared nothing at all about reading Latin. Their vulgate was the language of the ceramic icons and paintings on the walls. The decorated wall filled with glyphs is their church, their bible. It had always been so."

He shook his head. But no matter how hard he shook, the confusion remained.

"They didn't need us." His voice broke as he spoke the phrase. "Neither side was necessary to the lives of the campesinos. So there was a war. What else is a government or a church to do when it is unwanted? There was a war . . . a war that no one here knows about."

Humberto had been the militant during the Christero Wars. He had hidden guns and preached rebellion when secular Mexico itself had revolted against church ownership of so much property, against years of smug Catholic dominion. It was Humberto who had hunted down the only schoolteacher in their village and killed him because his entertaining lessons had filled the classroom and had begun to extinguish the belief in the children's eyes.

He flexed his wrists and fingers and thought of the mummies in Guanajuato—and of his brother. His brother would be mummified by now . . . by now pieces of his hands and patches of his hair would be treasured artifacts in the reliquaries of obscure little *iglesias* and chapels all over Michoacán.

What insanity it had been! Villages hid priests in attics and armoires, while other pueblos hung them from magnolia trees on a Sunday in the *zócalo*. Humberto's innocent brother had never taken part in the resistance. Miguel Augustine had turned away from the skirts of common women to the perfect raiment of the Virgin and had never regretted it for a moment. He would never have condoned such horrid violence.

Beneath his threadbare sleeve, Humberto still has the initials VCR tattooed into the skin of his forearm. Against his wishes, he would live to an age when the letters meant videocassette recorder rather than Vivo Christo Rey.

Humberto, the expatriate landowner, had divided his newly purchased building in Stockton into three levels and sold the bottom level to two eccentric sisters, Perpetua and Felicity. The lowest floor of the Hotel Rose was transformed into the Rose Room Taxi-Dance Hall, while the second floor was informally renamed the Flip-Flop by the prostitutes who worked within. In truth, the upper floor had no name, but six women, all perpetually feigning ardor and teetering precariously on the cusp of middle age, had chosen the name one laughing evening because of the predominantly Filipino clientele. A flophouse for Flips. Humberto converted what had once been the attic into his own small home.

The women who worked at the Flip-Flop were women who dreamed in daylight, who have always had the same value, the same eternal price; all that has ever changed for them was the color of the hands that groped at them.

The six women were never the same people from year to year. They rotated in from the whore circuit that ran through Seattle, San Francisco, San Jose, and Los Angeles. All that was required of them was that they wear a particular kind of shoe when working. It was Humberto, the crazy man on the top floor, who required it. It was whispered in the hallways that he had a fetish for blue satin high-heel shoes.

The prostitutes that stopped at the Flip-Flop were no longer young enough to work the good rooms in the better hotels. They were preconvalescent, powder-heavy, dim-light-dependent women who had recently begun to dream desperately of families and of picket fences, and were becoming frightened of a mythical place called Machon . . . a place in fifth heaven where angels and virgins who had been corrupted were imprisoned.

According to whore legend, it was a place full of old, drooping blondes lounging in an endless faux-Victorian lobby modeled after one in Tijuana. All of them, while being dry-suckled by stubble-faced, grown men, have begun to imagine children pulling at the nub of their breasts, stretching their aureoles into the dark patches they had always mocked with dabs of nipple rouge.

Every West Coast prostitute had heard of Humberto's house, the house of ill repute that was owned by a priest. Those in the trade refer to it as the House of Blue Heels. All of the girls on the circuit considered the Flip-Flop the next best thing to getting out of the business. After all, there was a green cross over the door and a man of God on the roof, weren't there? Perhaps a trip to fifth heaven wasn't inevitable after all.

The Flip-Flop guaranteed work-weary Pinoys and braceros an iron bed and the company of a live woman for an hour or so. An iron bed with springs as squeaky as blackbirds or loud bickering crows. It was supremely important to hard-working fieldhands that their infrequent acts of hip thrusting be verified by noise . . . recurring, reassuring racket . . . memorable noise that flowed through walls and out into the streets and even to the Dead Pecker Bench, where old men removed their hats as a sign of deepest respect.

Humberto had discovered the sojourners during his flight from the Mexican government. He had learned of their needs when he, himself, had become a wanderer. Two failed businesses had refined that discovery into a pair of thriving enterprises.

"I give them everything they need," said Humberto as he stared out of the window.

"I give them the noisy gong and the clanging cymbal," he smiled, "though they have not love." There was amorous mumbling down below in one of the bedrooms. "I let them believe that they speak with the tongues of men and angels." The cash register at the front desk rang as the drawer was opened. "I let them deliver their bodies to be burned in the bedsheets." Outside in the park, the sun was setting and the moon was rising. "When the perfect comes, the imperfect will pass away." The old, arthritic men on the Dead Pecker Bench rose as one, and with painfully slow gestures, blessed the passing day.

Below the Flip-Flop, the Rose Room Taxi-Dance Hall moved at a slower pace, to a hugging two-step and to a revolving waltz with an occasional, polite gavotte. In 1958 it was a chapel to churchless men, a place for gentle communion and shell-eared confession in three-quarter time. A different kind of girl worked down there. Pure, retiring girls who sat in cool parlors reading letters from home, an earpiece of their spectacles between their teeth.

Its proprietors were two women who were well versed in heartache, harmony, and hagiography. Perpetua and Felicity del Santo demanded that their girls be from the finest families in downtown Stockton and Manteca and that they keep their clothing on at all times. There was even a strict dress code, typewritten and hanging in the parlor. There must be no cleavage visible, no heels over an inch high, and absolutely no contact below the waist. But, above all, no girl could ever come to work in blue shoes.

"The Flip-Flop is an abomination in the eyes of the Lord," Perpetua would say, rolling her eyes upward, toward the second floor. Her sister, Felicity, would cross herself at the very thought of the place.

"Come and meet my nimble beauties," Perpetua said to a new customer. "This radiant damsel is our Blandina. Blandina, come forward, my dear, and introduce yourself."

Blandina stepped forward with shyness glimmering in every gesture. She had astonishing hair that tumbled down in red rivulets to the small padded shoulders of a black velvet dress. Her deep eyes and her dress were of the same color. Blandina, with a deep curtsey, extended an ivory hand with long spatulate fingers. There were bandages on three of those fingers. Numerous small scars adorned her slender forearms and were evident on both of her knees.

"I am not careful when I move," said Blandina with a slow, cautious sentence. She spoke with a southern accent, a twang from Waycross, Georgia, but she always insisted that her deepest roots were in France.

"The long stem of a wineglass that is secure in your hands,

sir, is so very precarious in mine," she coos while pacing quickly through a dance step, her feet noiselessly crossing the floor. It is easy to see why men adore her.

"Being clumsy, I must cradle everything. It's so surprising that someone like me can dance at all. But then the music becomes my mind, captains my very spirit. When it plays, why all at once I have my marching orders. Then, as if by magic, grace and rhythm take command of me," she smiled.

Lucy came forward next, in a pink dress with a lace bodice. There was a deep red flower pinned to her breast. She had white gloves on that reached up to her pointed elbows. There was a black velvet choker around her swan's neck and a distant and detached look in her eyes. It was clear that she was listening to the noises from the Flip-Flop up above and that the sounds of those contracted ravishments disturbed her deeply. Her eyes softened only when the music of the Rose Room swelled up to cover the loveless complaints of the brothel.

"Only music and poor men can ever move me," she whispered shyly. "The Rose Room has them both."

Lucy confided to the other girls that she was still very much a virgin, that no man's fleshy knife would ever cut and pry rudely at her quick. Lucy was a dark-haired Italian girl who had worked at Arthur Murray studios across the country, but left when it became clear that there was a conspiracy of rich, fat men who wanted nothing more than to smash her feet and catch her eye. Now she worked as a waitress at the Cafe Venice in Lodi and moonlighted at the Rose Room.

"And this is dearest Agatha," said Felicity. "She came to us one night two years ago and has been here ever since."

Agatha, who was sitting at a small tea table, seemed distant and unhearing; her large luniform breasts rested on two plates and the fingers of both hands were crossed beneath her chin. Her dress was layered and white with a wide waist-belt of red flowers. It was said that she came to the Rose Room to escape an abusive suitor. Guadalupe "Cookie" Lopez, the madame from the Flip-Flop, had tried to recruit her, but Agatha had steadfastly refused, claiming that divine providence had sent her to the Rose Room.

"The rest of the girls are out on the dance floor," said Perpetua, touching Agatha's shoulder tenderly, then moving away.

"She's very sensitive," she explained. "Sometimes she has strange chest pains."

Perpetua led the way to the dance floor as she spoke. On the wall flanking the doorway to the dance floor were two photographs, one of Fayard and the other of Harold, the famous Nicholas brothers.

"I try to encourage the girls to practice as much as possible. Our clientele may or may not know the difference, but we here at the Rose Room certainly do."

She pushed open the door to the dance floor. A small four-piece band was playing "Begin the Beguine."

"This is Sarah. She dances as though she were once an angel. Spread sawdust on the floor and it will remain undisturbed as she moves across it. She giggles a lot, and sometimes very inappropriately. Sometimes I tell her that her laughing will get her into trouble."

Perpetua shook a finger at Sarah, who stopped dancing for a moment, her imaginary partner waiting patiently for her. Sarah smiled. Her husband had left her recently for another woman, some bank teller over in Lodi who could bear him children.

"I am a bit lonely, but I have my steps," said Sarah. "They cloister about me like my own doting children would if I had children. With my steps I fill my time with lavish leaps and swaying. I wade in music. I beget grace, if nothing else. My steps keep me company," said Sarah, beginning again to dance in the arms of no one.

"My name is Rosa," a young woman spoke while rising from one of the chairs that lined the walls of the dance floor. Rosa looked far too feeble to dance. Her hair was pulled back severely to reveal temples that were translucent and blue. Her fleshless wrists led to narrow fingers that seemed too frail for anything but protracted prayer. Her dress was a deep green and it rustled when she moved. The belt at her waist and the shoes at her feet were as black as coal.

"She sleeps here. She never leaves. She has a rich home but she refuses to go there. We even have to force her to eat," said Felicity. "But the men like to be around her. Everyone feels good around her, especially the Filipinos."

"I hurry to be alone, to sense my own vegetable compliance and to husk it slowly of its power over me," said Rosa quietly. No one seemed surprised by the thoughtful and solemn tenor of her speech. It seems she never spoke in any other way, though she danced with joyful, almost saturnalian grace.

Felicity then moved toward a stunning *mestiza*, a young woman with Irish hair and Mexican eyes.

"And this is Ruby. All those birds waiting up on the roof and in the trees outside are hers."

Ruby stepped forward. She was a girl who was still more comfortable with Spanish than English. *"Mucho gusto,"* she said with confidence. She was a woman who was sure of her beauty and its impact on men. Despite Perpetua's rules, she wore no shoes on her feet, and she loved to converse with anyone who wished to pass a few moments in polite conversation. Some worried that there was a note of desperation in her speech, as though she feared the lull, the silence, as though the very act of speech was an end in itself. She was a strong woman who could tolerate almost anything but would never allow anyone to tell her to be silent.

She had left Mexico as a young girl. She had worked as a waitress at Cesar's in Tijuana, then as a hostess at Señor Pico's in San Diego. Her best job had been at the now defunct Margarita O'Leary's School of Charm in Santa Monica. She had been a teacher's aide there, instructing all the little Chicanas in the art of conversation and table manners.

"All the men love her," said Perpetua, "especially that Teodoro. He spends every dime he has on her. He won't dance with anybody else. *Pobrecito.*"

"He pines for that woman," laughed Felicity.

Ruby did not seem amused. It hurt her lower back to dance with the strange little man. The huge soles of his corrective shoes had smashed her toes more than once. Ruby's attitude was not the same as the other girls. The other girls were certainly worthy of emulation, and perhaps someday she would emulate them, but not just yet. Maybe she would do so in thirty years, perhaps after six future husbands and countless lovers. Maybe someday she would be able to see beyond Teodoro's body. But tonight, as with every other Friday night, his fawning attentions would only offend her.

Ruby was seldom silent because she was born in quiet, raised in it, then condemned to it. She'd never known her true parents. It was rumored that she was the daughter of one of the nuns at the Carmelite convent at Pedernales, in her home state of Chihuahua. Ruby had spent much of her infancy in that convent. Once Ruby had overheard her *madre adoptiva*, her foster mother, referring to Ruby's true mother in disparaging tones. *"La monja Irlandesa,"* she had called her. The Irish nun.

Her foster mother was forever telling her how lucky she was that the nuns had not smothered her at birth.

"Those nuns are always getting pregnant. There must be a thousand children buried above ground, within the bricks of those shameful walls."

When she was just five years old, her foster mother had dressed her in a pretty dress and had taken her back to the convent. She had placed her into the foundling's wheel and spun it hard, until the child disappeared behind the walls . . . immured. Without a word, the woman turned and left the child to the silent barefoot nuns.

"I have five children of my own," she'd called out as she reached the street. "I have my own flesh and blood to feed."

Ruby realized sadly that the years she had spent with the nuns were devoid of any real memories. There was not even the single memory of a moment of recognition in the face of a nun who might've been her mother. Ruby had looked for it every day. She fantasized about it every day.

"This one is my mother. No, this one."

She had peered into all of their shaded eyes hoping for the smallest glint of recognition, a single word of solace. Hopelessly, she listened for an Irish brogue among women vowed to silence.

"For memories, you need words," she would say aloud. "You need to tell a thing and have it heard."

The convent consisted of four buildings, connected and forming a square with a rose garden in the small plaza that was created by their inner walls. There was a small chapel on the western side of the plaza and above its doorway was a large wooden arch on which was carved a single word: *Silencio.*

Her childhood had been muffled silent in those enclosed gardens. Each day was a series of hiding places, each walk a

movement away from hard walls where she imagined that children inside clawed and screamed for breath. There had been
no one to turn to for companionship. No one but the silent
people who abused themselves to repay the debt left in the wide
wake of the death of Christ, their perfect and untouchable
husband.

In her solitude, Ruby turned to the only creatures that had
access to her, the winged creatures above. At first she had been
angry at the birds for their effortless ability to fly away. But they
had freely chosen to stay with her and so she hovered beneath
them and soon came to love them.

They would fly off to unknown places only to return to share
the pieces of the far-flung world they carried in their beaks. They
brought wooden buttons from Zamora, blue thread from Janitzio, and pieces of blanket cloth from Cuernavaca. She soon
came to identify with birds more than with people.

Were it not for the swallows, the sparrows, *y las palomas*, Ruby
would have had no one. She passed all of her days at the convent
with her plumed friends, learning their language and their flight
patterns and their family histories. She even herded grubs and
beetles for their delight. In time, she came to pray for feathers
of her own. It was all she had ever asked of God, for feathers of
her own.

It was at this early age that Ruby first started stripping. She
would rip off her small dresses and stockings and stand naked
before God to demand a layer of feathers, a full complement of
primary and secondary coverts. She petitioned to become a
fledgling, and to molt into another life. The earthbound girl
prayed fervently for asportation, for aerodynamic lift.

"Feathers or nothing," she'd vowed.

"Feathers or not a single stitch."

It was her sole chastening admonishment to heaven.

Then one morning, the foundling's wheel, the rotating
dumbwaiter that had always been locked to her, stood open and
turning, the brightness of the town below beaming through
the cracks and carrying with it the sounds of children on their
way to school. Ruby, dizzy with disbelief, ran cautiously to the
wheel, then spun it wildly, diving through to the sidewalk on the
other side of the gate. Once free, she ran dashing through

the horse-drawn traffic to stand breathless and crying across the street from the convent.

Turning back, Ruby could see a single nun standing behind the wheel. She stood unmoving in the rose garden, her face hidden in the shadow of her habit. Had she been there when I escaped? she wondered. Ruby had waved at her to thank her, but the nun had only turned away. Was she Irish? Ruby would always wonder if that shadowed face had been the face of her mother. When she heard the unrestrained voices of the townspeople surrounding her, Ruby suddenly remembered that she had a voice of her own and raised it to the woman who had turned away.

"Mother!" she'd screamed, and would always imagine, thereafter, that there had been a halt, a small moment of hesitation in the steps that receded to lock the foundling's wheel.

"*Madre!*" she'd called out again, but the woman had gone away forever.

For the first time in her new life, Ruby heard music in the air, to her left and to her right, all around her as she stood enchanted on the sidewalk. There was a wedding going on in a small chapel on her left. People were talking, touching each other and laughing in a crowded church! She wondered if this jubilant sound was unholy? A hundred people had taken a solemn Saturday vow of noise and celebration.

She walked to the open doors of the chapel and peered in. The sight inside amazed her. An angelic woman adorned in an aura of white was dancing with man after adoring man. And each loving partner, in his turn, pinned money to the wedding gown. Ruby thought it was an indescribable, heavenly sight, a love fledgling receiving her plumage and nest. The waltz, framed in dahlias and roses, went on and on, building the future of the married couple.

After the cold, rueful silence of the convent, Ruby found the music and the profusion of words and the whirling, laughing faces exhilarating. She would never know that her own mother had once swooned at her own money dance at her own wedding, in a faraway time and place. And Ruby would never hear her plaintive voice, muted by a vow.

"*Tá brón orm, m'iníon.*" I am sorry, my daughter.

Ruby would never know that her mother's name had once

been Maura, that there was a hall closet in Dublin, Ireland, that still held a couple of her dresses in a trunk along with a few precious letters and photos. She could never know that Maura had come to Mexico with her new husband, an Irishman from New York, only to be abandoned in Matamoros in favor of a dark-eyed young *cantinera* who wore only a suggestion of a skirt when she served overflowing glasses of tequila, her breasts teasing like liquid at the brim of her bodice.

To get even with him, Maura had taken a Mexican lover, and when the Mexicano left her forever in a small hotel in San Miguel de Allende, she stayed on to work off their hotel bill. Then she delivered his child alone in the stifling solitude of room number 3 of the Hotel San Patricio. Maura had then carried the nameless child to a convent in the North, where she asked to be a novice, to marry God—a love that could not fail.

Ruby could never know that Maura once had hair as yellow as summer wheat that fell down to her thighs. She would never hear the lilting laughter that turned men's heads or the Gaelic songs sung during chores. She would never know that the green dress kept in the trunk, the one with the padded shoulders and the black piping, when out and aired proper and draped smooth on Maura's fecund hips and body, once had the tease and look of dance, of stripping the willow; it once had the look of a woman who could giggle and make small talk while tasting the bubbling progress of a stew made of cabbage and *ispín*.

"Hunger is the best sauce," Maura would say with a smile.

Ruby had promised herself that someday she would have a money dance. Someday, when she was sure that she was marrying the man she loved, she would have countless dollars like feathers pinned to her gown. Then Ruby turned north and began to walk, toward seven husbands, and toward cities whose names she could not then pronounce, Minneapolis and Tuskegee.

As she walked north, a flock of birds followed, chattering and swooping excitedly just above her head. They and their chirping generations to come would follow her for the rest of her life, diving to intercept raindrops, protecting her from mashers, warning her of danger. People who saw her walking below a living cloud would pause, then cross themselves solemnly when she passed by on her way toward America.

"*Slán leat,*" they would hear her whisper. It was a phrase that she had whispered since infancy and would whisper on her deathbed. It was what she murmured each night before falling asleep. She had no idea where she had learned the words or even what they meant. The words had been whispered into her pink ear at a time when her tiny lips had first puckered to suckle a blue-veined breast, to kiss soft allegiance to kindred flesh.

"*Slán leat.*"

Over time the words had become magical to her, almost holy, words that softened the silence and solitude of sleep. She would never know they were Gaelic words.

"Good-bye."

The carload of Pinoys parked in front of the dance hall. The men walked inside quietly, courteously filing through the front door of the Rose Room. Perpetua recognized them immediately as the three handsome Garcia brothers and Ted For Short. Perpetua smiled; she liked Filipinos. Their temperament was somewhere between the solemn Hindus and the raucous Mexicans, thought Perpetua. The Hindus were courteous to the point of paralysis in the presence of women, while the Mexicans were brash and forward in their stylized advances. The Pinoys were Latin, but with an Asian reserve. And the Pinoys always spent more than the Mexicans, who had obligations, families, and homes just across the border. After the Pinoys came in, two Hindus came shyly through the door after them.

"Do you gentlemen want dance lessons?" asked Perpetua. To put them at ease about the local ordinance against dancing, she emphasized the word lessons.

"Lessons? Yes!" nodded one of the Gudjaratis. "Yes, lessons, please, missy . . . lessons."

The girls were made up and seated in their padded chairs. The small band was warming up and the two matrons, Perpetua and Felicity, were busily greeting the men as they came in. Each man handed Felicity an amount of money and received, in return, a roll of tickets; each was good for a ten-minute dance lesson.

This was the last day of the asparagus season. Tomorrow the men would be elsewhere, in a hundred elsewheres: Seattle, Alaska, the bean fields in San Jose. It would be almost a full year before they would return again to the Rose Room.

Tonight they would buy a lot of tickets, mused Perpetua, especially that Teodoro Cabiri, whose heart ached for just one gentle word from Ruby, a single gesture of kindness that Teodoro's imagination could live on for the next ten months that Ruby would be lost to him.

Perpetua noticed, as she surveyed the dance floor, that one of the Pinoys waited alone, in silence, outside the Rose Room. He had not come in with the rest. She had never seen him before. He was thin and dark, but his hair was white and wild. A very distinctive-looking man, she thought. He looked gentle and contemplative.

"Are you coming in?" she asked Faustino.

"No, madam," he smiled wistfully at her. "I'm quite all right out here. I'll just watch the sun set and enjoy the music . . . and the birds."

"I'll keep him company, ma'am," said King Pete Claver, already at his post under the awning and flexing his arms beneath his jacket. Faustino had stepped back at the sight of the huge man, but quickly realized that he had nothing to fear.

The two men stood together watching a large truck as it pulled up to a street corner about a half-block from a tiny store. The sign above the store proclaimed it to be Morris Yee Sing Lam's general store. The men in the truck piled a stack of goods in the street, then left. The Teamsters would not deliver to the doorstep of a Chinese store.

Inside, the dancing had begun. The Garcia brothers had found Lucy, Agatha, and Sarah. Tony the leper had arrived with Jeanine and the two were moving smoothly about the room, Tony's pleated pant legs sticking to the petroleum jelly–soaked gauze that covered his legs beneath the tweed fabric. The two Hindus had matched up with Blandina and Rosa and were both repeating aloud the box step they had just learned.

"Step, one-two. Back, one-two."

They were calling the steps loudly enough that police officers in the next county could hear it.

"Such good lessons!" they exclaimed.

There was a swirl of kinetic calm as clasped fingers, arms, and feet synchronized with the music. Jaunty shoes flashed below the swaying thoughts of a dozen dreaming dancers. Pleated dresses opened in whirling turns and long necks craned in soft pretense. Shoulders touched shoulders and hands nestled softly in the smalls of backs. Languid napes met with sunburned necks in minor clinches while earrings swung softly from receptive ears.

Gloved hands were lightly lifted, and lowered eyes met with diminishing discomfort in the quiet interval between tunes. Music rose and evaporated once for each precious *fichera*. Medleys of coy overtures were abated, then reformed; ticket by ticket, measure by measure, the evening was spent, men and women moving in concert. For each ten-cent interlude, there was a moment of temporal alchemy.

Teodoro Teofilo Cabiri, staring upward at a fawning, awkward angle that hurt his short neck, was doing his best to sweep an impatient, exasperated Ruby off her feet. But Ruby was clearly unhappy with the situation. What did she need with the flattery of elves? The two of them were doing impossible and innovative steps as they crossed the room. In reality, Ruby was trying vainly to avoid being stepped on by his unwieldy prosthetic soles. Her bare feet were raw by the third dance.

"Play 'The Tennessee Waltz,' " she called out to the band. She hoped that a slow dance would save her poor toes and keep her from twisting an ankle.

For his part, Teodoro was elated that she had chosen such a romantic and intimate waltz. His heart swelled and fluttered with hope—the hope that perhaps Ruby would someday see beyond the crumpled container of his body to the bright, endless horizon of his spirit.

Teodoro began to sing softly—barely under his breath. The other Pinoys joined in. Though electronic reverb had not yet been invented, the singing Pinoys all seemed to sense that something important was missing.

I was dancin' with my darlin' to the Tennessee Waltz,
When an old friend I happened to see . . .

Teodoro resolved at that very moment that "The Tennessee Waltz" would always be their special song. And more than thirty long years from this night they would dance this way once again, but to a waltz that was all their own.

Humberto, looking downward because that was the only direction that he had ever looked, had seen the Filipinos arriving at the Rose Room. He had watched the Hindus park their car and walk timorously toward the front door. Then he saw the other men park their cars in front of the Rose Room.

These men were not there for dance lessons. They certainly did not have the gentility of dancers. They swaggered as one, feeding off one another's bravado; they grunted from a single throat. He knew these men, or men just like them. It was clear to him that these men were capable of doing irreversible acts. Although they wore no lavender epaulets, men exactly like these had celebrated his and his brother's deaths so many years before.

"Why is it that the easiest, most accessible emotion is always hate?" Even as he said it, he winced with the cut of the stropped and honed memory of the fledgling schoolteacher that he had assassinated in the name of the National League for the Defense of Religious Liberty. The young teacher had traveled to Spain for an education and had dutifully returned to his home in Michoacán to teach his own people. But he had instructed in more than just penmanship and subtraction. He taught Darwinism and told his malleable students shocking stories about the flight of Simon Magus and about the host of angels surrounding Muhammed. He had spoken to impressionable children about beings of light fluttering like dazed, drunken swallows above the crucifixion. The young man had even been so brash as to show paintings by Bosch and Chagall, to show the children other views—distorted views of the heavens!

The situation had become completely intolerable, Humberto thought at the time. Some action had become necessary . . . as necessary as his own execution just weeks later at the same pile of logs and before the same riddled, wooden silhouettes.

"My brother was innocent," he said aloud to the hateful men below. "He was killed because I was a killer. I dragged that educated boy from his classroom and shot him myself, right through the left lens of his spectacles because I was a believer without beliefs." He groaned deeply and shamelessly.

The thespian whores in the Flip-Flop and their sweating johns above them ceased their ardent calisthenics for a moment to listen to the man wailing upstairs. He usually spoke to himself in this fashion each evening, but on this night he was much louder, much more vehement.

"God help us all!" he moaned as he watched the men gather on the sidewalk in front of the Rose Room, then walk together toward the entrance, weapons upraised in each of their hands.

"I know your faces," he yelled out the window toward the street. "Hell is indexed and catalogued with faces like yours!"

From somewhere below, King appeared, with both of his hands raised in his familiar boxer's stance, the stance that had failed him so often. Nevertheless, he was confronting the entire group of men with courage and defiance, if not with skill.

One man stood directly in front of King, challenging him, when suddenly another man, out of view, struck the boxer savagely over the head with a metal pipe. King groaned sharply, then fell across the entrance to the Rose Room.

". . . eight, nine, ten, you're out," sighed Humberto, who then hummed a wordless cavatina as the men below quickly turned their attention to a thin man with long white hair, smashing him on the head and body several times before leaving him bleeding and unconscious on the sidewalk next to King Pete. The attackers kicked both bodies as they entered the Rose Room, one by one.

Humberto, above it all, drifted in and out of his own lifetimes as the men noisily shattered and smashed the beautiful Rose Room, shoving the protesting girls rudely to one side, then challenging the men inside to fight back.

"We own the cops!" they screamed below. "We own the town and we don't like niggers and monkeys dancing with our women! There's a law against it! There's a law, and we're here to enforce it."

It was the voice of Pietro Ditto. Humberto had heard that voice many times. He had once been a regular when a girl named Lilly had danced in the Rose Room. Pietro Ditto and his brother Simon were peasants who had become landowners during the war. They had a farm just outside of Stockton that was rumored to be little better than a minor serfdom. They treated their workers like slaves.

On the second floor, the prostitutes and their men scurried around their rooms to hide themselves from the violent cracking and splintering down below. From beneath the protection of a half-dozen beds, the soles of a dozen blue high-heel shoes peeked out tentatively, waiting for the pitched battle that must surely come.

But this time the Pinoys would not resist. The peaceful Hindus were forced into a closet, where they were savagely beaten, then locked in. The key was thrown away. Jeanine was pulled forcibly away from Tony. Pietro Ditto, who knew of Tony's malady, began beating the leper's legs with the pipe. Tony refused to scream even as his loose flesh fell away under the battering. Jeanine, seeing the pain in Tony's face, screamed for him. The Garcia brothers and Teodoro Teofilo Cabiri could only groan under the weight of anger and crushing humiliation. Their assailants were armed with pipes and machetes. They would resist on other days, suffer brutal arrests and face white judges on other days, but not on this evening, the last day of the asparagus season.

In one year, after a fallow time, when the verdant shoots of sparrow grass pushed upward once more through the flooded furrows, Pietro Ditto, who tonight had swung a fierce, threatening machete at gentle necks, would himself feel the fear of the alloyed edge, the senseless thrall of torque. A sneering Pietro Ditto could not know that he was only months, a season away from his own violent death, that the cruel bile in his bloodlines would catch the notice of heaven.

On this day, not only Faustino and King Pete would suffer, but also the Rose Room, its floral, papered skin ripped, its double-hung eyes shattered, its sconces and porcelain fixtures smashed unceremoniously, its stairwell rungs cruelly broken at the knees, and its gentle dancers horrified and shamed.

In his rooftop apartment, Humberto, a six-ounce bottle of pure iodine to his quivering lips, would attempt yet another small heresy. There was a skull and crossbones on the label. To Humberto, it was a symbol of hope.

"To *Señor Toral y Madre Conchita.*"

Another final toast to two real soldiers of the Christero Wars, an artist and a nun who had killed a well-guarded president at his banquet, not some poor, underpaid schoolteacher, bending at his desk.

"The gods are crazy in heaven, they laugh at our belief. They feed us diluted flan, one part love to nine parts grief."

He placed the mouth of the bottle to his tongue and let the bitterness drain. He heard car doors slamming down below and knew that the besotted thugs were leaving and that tomorrow he would order more poisons from the hardware store and a dozen rolls of faux-Persian, Victorian wallpaper.

Return to French Camp, 1959

A cloud obscured the moon. *Una nube cobró la cara de la luna.* Or was the moon merely turning away, shamefaced at what it saw? Did the moon look askance, lingering like a loyal lover who must now accept some new, previously well hidden flaw in its beloved? Did it darken and shed a brooding aura of airless tears or is the second full moon in a single month always so blue? Was it a beggar's moon—a teal-colored night for baneful acts that could not endure the light of day—or did a cloud obscure the moon?

Zeferino turned to see what his friends Ted For Short and Faustino had seen or heard just long seconds before. Now he knew why they had fallen silent, why the looks of sad remembrance on their faces had turned to a look of terror.

"It's the same bunch that wrecked the Rose Room last year," said Teodoro just under his breath, his voice trembling.

The group of men had begun the day as individuals. Then they had agreed to meet between the lime sacks and the manure pile. As each man had arrived at the appointed time and place, his single soul had joined the others to form a muddled amalgam, a mongrel mind. United by common impurities, they came around the packing shed just as the sky darkened. Moving as a practiced unit they heeled, then turned, a hesitant stampede that cast an enormous double shadow as they walked into the returning moonlight and into the darting light of Faustino's fire.

"I knew they would come here sooner or later," said Faustino with a trembling, weakened voice. He had tried to believe that it couldn't happen again, but in his heart he knew better. "I wish the boy weren't here. Why, in God's name, should he have to see this?"

Ted For Short nodded his grim agreement and nervously began to button his vest with one hand.

"They're the same men that put me and the security guard, King Pete Claver, in the hospital," explained a grim Faustino.

Faustino had learned the guard's name as they patiently waited together for treatment in the emergency room of San Joaquin General Hospital. They had both sat bleeding on the same bench in the crowded hospital lobby, watching people who had arrived long after them being treated before them.

"They almost killed you," said Teodoro, "and the Rose Room was shut down for repairs for almost two months."

The boy knew some of the men in the group and he saw that at least half of them were carrying machetes in their upraised hands. The rest had knives and one man, the leader, had a metal pole raised menacingly in the air. The boy recognized the man walking in front of the pack. It was Pietro Ditto, one of the twin landowners. He was there in his coveralls and his sun-bleached Sears workshirt.

"Take the boy away from here," Faustino said sternly to Ted For Short. "Get him away from here! They want more this time. More than just to see me bleeding on the sidewalk. Remember what happened to me down in Brawley."

Ted For Short pulled at the boy's shirt but could not move him. The thought of Brawley terrified the little man. Some local farmboys, backed up by their proud, laughing fathers, had set fire to Faustino's small silver house trailer. Before lighting the kerosene that they had spread around the trailer, they had first tied the door shut so that no one could escape. Teodoro and Faustino had barely gotten out of it alive. They had managed to crawl through an air vent at the top of the Airstream, but not before suffering second-degree burns on their hands and faces.

Faustino's car had been stolen that night and when it was finally located, the word *Queer* had been painted on the hood, the trunk, and every door. No garage or paint shop within miles of Brawley would repaint the car for him, so Faustino had been

forced to drive his car for weeks in that condition. The gentle
man had been hounded or beaten up at every stop sign and gas
station between Brawley and Lodi.

Finally, Teodoro and Faustino had been forced to paint the
car with an oil-based house paint. The brush strokes were still
visible on every surface of the vehicle. It had always offended
Faustino to know that the cruel words were still there on his car's
skin, languishing under a thin layer of paint.

The gang of heated men conferred among themselves, then
moved forward to within three yards of the fire.

"Come here, boy," said the man standing beside Pietro Ditto,
with a heavy accent that spoke of Ilocos Norte.

Zeferino did not comply. He was surprised that the gang of
men included one Filipino. It was Tacquio.

"I told you come here, boy," the man repeated, turning his
head to his left for the encouragement and approval of his boss,
Pietro Ditto.

Ted For Short had gathered his courage, then walked nervously over to the leader of the group.

"Mr. Ditto, we are just talking among ourselves, please leave
us alone. Mr. Ditto, I'm sure you know that we do good work for
our paycheck and we never make any trouble. Don't you remember us? Faustino and Ted For Short? We planted all those crowns
out there in your fields. He and I planted all ten thousand
crowns one by one. We put down lime and 5-10-10 fertilizer and
built those irrigation ditches over there. We spread gunnysacks
last year during the bad freeze. We've done good work for you,
haven't we? Please, leave us alone. Take your men and go."

Ted For Short stamped one of his tiny, tall shoes earnestly
into the dust as he spoke. "We are just talking," he implored
once again.

"This is not your business," barked the man in the coveralls
and sun-bleached Sears shirt. "We want the queer."

Tacquio suddenly pushed Ted For Short to the ground and a
second man rushed forward with his machete to keep him there,
the thin blade pressed angrily against the midget's neck. It was
the foreman who had married into the family.

"Did he touch you, boy?" the boss man asked while turning
toward Zeferino. There was a cold, leering grin on his face.

"Did he touch you down there?" He used his length of pipe to point toward his own crotch. He then ran the weapon up and down the zipper of his pants. "Did he touch you there as if by accident, then say 'oh, I'm sorry'?" he asked in a mocking, effeminate voice. "Did the queer offer to give you a massage? Did the queer offer to give you one of those sponge baths? Did his limp-wristed hand just happen to slip?"

The boss man leered demonically as he moved the pipe away from his pants, then grabbed his own genitals with his other hand. The men behind him were laughing with him.

"No, he did not," answered Zeferino indignantly. "He's my good friend. We were just talking about asparagus and about poetry."

"Poetry?" exclaimed the foreman derisively. "There's the proof! Poetry's for faggots and women."

"He is *bakla*," Tacquio muttered coldly as he pointed to Faustino. "He is a she and she wants to love a man. He is against children and every natural thing. Since she has been at this camp, the weather has gone bad and the shoots of grass are coming up small. The third cutting is going to be five hundred boxes short of last year. We've even had two full moons. It's a bad sign."

Others grunted in agreement. "It's a bad sign," one of them repeated.

It was the Malleus Maleficarum, twisted rationalizations of brutish persecution, still living in mortal mouths, five hundred years after the Inquisition.

The man in the fading Sears shirt moved forward into the firelight. "I didn't think you would come back after our little dance at the Rose Room last year," Ditto scowled at Faustino. "Maybe you need one more dance lesson."

"There ain't no skirts to hide behind out here," said the foreman, who was glaring at Ted For Short, "and no colored security guard to protect you."

Pietro Ditto laughed at the thought of an unconscious King Pete, then turned toward the boy.

"Come with me. Get away from that child-molesting queer," he demanded while extending his hand to the boy.

"I said come with me!"

A frightened Zeferino shook his head vehemently. The boss

man reached out to grab the boy by his arm but Zeferino extended his own arms and shoved at him with all of his strength.

The blow came almost invisibly, a backhand punch that the boy did not brace himself against. It sent him reeling into the open door of the Buick, where the boy's head struck the door edge violently. The boy stayed where he fell, dazed and lightheaded. The moon above was unobstructed now and the night seemed almost as bright as day.

A single, discrete shaft of moonlight had struck Pietro Ditto full in the face as he had hit the boy. At that moment Zeferino had seen the full depth of hate in the man's face. There had been hatred braided into every wrinkle of his cheeks and forehead and into every fold of skin. With the help of the clear pang of sullen moonlight, he had seen the satisfaction and effort in the man's face as his backhand landed full and hard. Then he saw Pietro Ditto lifting the pipe high above his own head and about to strike again. There was a strange, malevolent smile on the man's face.

"I'll teach your mother and her damned sisters that no woman . . . no goddamn skirt turns her back on me!"

The boy raised his arms to ward off the blow that never came. With a perception that seemed unclouded, yet detached and numb, the boy saw Faustino rising suddenly to full stature, his white hackles flared like licking flame about his face and down the swollen veins of his arched neck. He saw Pietro Ditto turning to meet him, a copper red and coal black rooster with neck feathers spreading, then standing on end. Tacquio quickly traded the machete in his hand for Pietro's pipe. Like a grim, silent cockfight, deadly spurs kicked out in furious, dusty flurries while worried, frozen onlookers laid down their mute bets.

The roosters parried and spun, their backs arched and bristling, their feet kicking up dust and scraping the earth with each thrust. They moved from the fire to the edge of the slough and back toward the blue Buick. When they neared the light of the fire once more, Zeferino saw that Faustino's shirt had been cut open and there was blood spreading on his chest. The boy saw the steel machetes flashing as inexorable sorrow clanged and licked ever closer to bristling nape, tufted comb, and skin.

There were violent outbursts of breath and frantic lunges

and retreats. Then all at once the two men froze in their tracks and were facing each other with only an arm's length between them, their half-moonlit and half-darkened faces sharing the same stunned look. It was clear that something mournful had happened. Something irreversible. The boy saw, on Pietro's neck, what he thought was a second tongue made of deep crimson, a tongue that grew longer as he watched. The red tongue reached down to taste Pietro Ditto's undershirt and to lap at his heaving belly.

Pietro dropped the machete from his hand, then lifted his shaking fingers to touch his wound. On his face, curiosity and horror had mixed to form a look of utter beguilement, as though some fearful mystery was finally, inevitably unfolding. The trembling index finger that probed his throat felt the warm air of exhaled breath where it should not have been. Pietro groaned, then dropped to his knees, then onto his back.

Ted For Short had gotten up slowly from the ground and had stood with the rest of the morose, disoriented men who were now cautiously circling the rich man with two grimaces. Only Faustino stood apart and aside, breathing heavily, his face seized by a look of tragic wonder. It was clear that the boss man would soon die. He was already staring out of himself, focusing on nothing, his left knee jerking sporadically in the darting firelight. The air that was leaving the dying man's lungs was confused now and unable to decide which opening to exit. His drying, dimming eyes, staring up at the crater Copernicus, were quietly drinking their last lumens.

In minutes, his twin brother's howl would be heard over the fields, discordant, pared of joy, awakening even the heedless termites sleeping beneath the bunkhouse floors. The cry would descend through the seeping soaked blood-vent just below his brother's ripped neck, to the sodden dominion of havoc where tendrils of shade were rising to claim their own. The cloven furies below would stand to applaud this grief, hail it with blue lips lined with white lime. They would raise a coal-and-pitch clamor for revenge in Simon Ditto's ear. Shaking shattered shankbones, they would sing their motley malediction. They would demand that all life be soured for all time, despoiled by the embrace of the irreversible oath of vendetta.

After the other men had run off in panic, Ted For Short and Faustino kicked dirt onto the fire. Both men were laughing sardonically, horribly. The boy had never seen grown men acting like that. There was such great pain in their laughter.

"A Pinoy homosexual and a midget," winced Ted For Short as sparks and embers from the dying fire flew into his brown face.

"A *bakla* and a hunchback and a little Mexican boy! God must be having some fun up there. He's grown tired of the usual leading men and decided to stick some extras into this tragedy. Who on earth is going to believe our side of the story? We've had it now. They're going to hang us. They're going to hunt us down and hang us in the packing shed."

The two men stood in silence for a moment. The full, unbeclouded countenance of the silver moon was a third face, hanging brightly in the charged air between them.

"God help us, we are so foolish," whispered Faustino into the moon's eager left ear.

"Help us," echoed Ted For Short into the luminescent right ear.

Neither man knew the full depth of it, but as they stood there, everything in their world changed once more. Zeferino anxiously watched the faces of his *tiyos* as panic and fear transformed into firm resolve, as helplessness was transmuted by moonlight into an unspoken plan of action.

All the knives and machetes had been discarded at the scene by their panicked owners. Each one in turn was thrown far out into the deep slough. There was a stern, hard look on Faustino's face as he tossed his own knife last into the dark water. Slowly, he walked back toward the Buick to finish putting his possessions back into his trunk. As he walked he watched the ripples from the drowning machetes and knives cross each other, then cross again; noding then compounding; liquid hands, one atop the other. The crossroads.

"You've got to disappear for a while," said Ted For Short, who was then suddenly stricken by the irony of the statement. "No one will believe people like us. No one will ever believe it was self-defense. You've got to go someplace you've never been, someplace the pickers and the bosses don't know. If they find you, they'll torture you before they kill you. You know that?"

Faustino nodded.

"Me, too," said Ted For Short, softly. He was suddenly distracted by the sheer uselessness of his own life. For a moment he thought about prayer, but shook his head. No book in the Bible could ever explain this. "Am I a hummingbird?" he said to no one. "I keep waving my arms at heaven and no one up there ever sees my signals. Do I move my arms too fast?"

He then turned to the boy.

"We've got to hide you somewhere. We've got to get you away from here. Go get your stuff, Zeferino, and don't forget to get your bag from under the bed. In an hour this camp will be crawling with police. The Dittos are important people."

The boy ran to the Quonset hut and down the long aisle to the back bunk. Everywhere outside the hut and within, harried men were hastily packing their belongings and pulling down their favorite pinup photographs of Tempest Storm, Lilly St. Cyr, and Candy Barr. The big boss had been knifed in the fields. Someone would be blamed. Someone with dark skin. Other workers would have to finish this harvest.

In the next Quonset the Mexicanos were leaving even faster than the Pinoys.

"*El amo está muerto, el patrón está muerto.*" The horrid news had already passed from bunk to bunk. "The big boss is dead. *El jefe está muerto.*"

By tomorrow they would be stooping in fields from Woodland to Sonoma. A frightened César Chávez had hastily grabbed a tall stack of handbills and was running wide-eyed to an old Plymouth pickup truck that had a cracked windshield and no reverse gear. He would have to change the weekly meeting place from Ripon to Gilroy. Pietro had finally gotten his due in the eyes of God and the angels, he thought as he ran. But in the eyes of the courts and the Ditto family, men would have to pay . . . and for many years to come.

The boy grabbed his pocketknife, his Yoo-Hoo badge, and his photograph. He put everything he owned into his cloth bag. Out by the slough, Faustino had begun to jack up the Buick to remove the cement blocks that had supported it for the past weeks. All that remained of his beautiful little Airstream trailer was the chrome hitch and ball beneath the back fender of his car. Infinite regret rose in his nose as he glanced now and then toward the dead man. No longer illuminated by the fire, the outline of the body was barely visible in the blue moonlight. As though following unseen, unheard orders to do so, Faustino walked over to Pietro's corpse and kneeled down beside it. The slough was still muted, and the thick, sickly-sweet smell of blood hung on the night air. Even the mosquitoes had been stunned into silence.

Faustino noticed sadly that the man's face had changed with death. It seemed petrified, as though even the marrow was turning to stone. Faustino then wondered if he had ever really seen the man's face. Had anyone? Pietro Ditto's face seemed calm, almost gentle. Had his life been a continual struggle against those kind expressions, a struggle that could not be continued in death?

"Somewhere inside him, something must be alive," Faustino whispered to no one. "Some small cell, some thing."

Death was real, tactile, and empirical. The Holocaust was real. The Trail of Tears was real. His burning Airstream trailer had been real. Cut the man's stomach open and you will find his last angry meal and the six glasses of whiskey that had fortified him into hateful action. In its eternal length, death was somehow more real than life.

"A man's life is instantaneous," he mused sadly, "less than the life of a tree. The death of a man is as everlasting as the death of a galaxy."

He looked for the last time at the body of the man he had just killed. The knee no longer moved. The blood at his throat had puddled and was beginning to thicken. The Japanese boy kneeling in the jungle was real. The poem on rice paper was his movable headstone.

Eighteen years had flown by and thousands of lonely miles and finally that World War II machete had fallen. Its pathetic spirit had crossed the Pacific with him, possessed him, shadowed his life for a second chance at a bared neck. Finally, in 1959, near the end of the asparagus season, it fell. It had cut his precious free will in two. Both men, the killer and the killed, had been scraped clean of aspiration by that flashing blade.

It suddenly occurred to Faustino that his life had been

haunted by blades, from that day in the Philippines so long ago to this terrible night. In that instant, as he stood immobilized by thought, he suddenly knew the form that his own death would take; he knew that every night for the remainder of his days he would touch his own throat and feel blood impending there.

He walked to his car and lovingly touched the volumes stacked in the trunk. "I don't deserve to own these books." He caressed them, especially one of them, the collected poetry of Constantine Cavafy. For a moment, he considered tossing them all into the slough right behind the machetes. Instead, he slammed the trunk shut. He did not have the strength for that sort of finality, the cold resolve needed to drown poems.

He would go to Chicago. He would disappear. He was expert at it. Like all sojourners, he had honed those skills to an imperceptible degree.

"I told your mother that I was taking you west to the water," Ted For Short had explained to Zeferino as he packed his own small bag of belongings.

"She's afraid that the Ditto family will blame her for Pietro's death, so she wants you to go with me. Your youngest brother's father is up there outside Livermore working in the Concannon vineyards. Your little brother Miguelito will be with him. I heard he has a job cleaning the wine casks during the off-season. It's hard work, Zeferino, but at least grapes grow up off the ground, and they make a lot of cool shade. They're easy to pick and you don't have to bend your back all day. And irrigating grapes is real easy, too. The vineyards are full of fat deer and spoiled rabbits that don't have to worry about threshers. It's called Camp Corregidor."

Ted For Short spoke in a manner that betrayed his fear as he loaded his precious Pontiac, then drove away from the camp. He did not even acknowledge Faustino when he drove by the brush-marked Buick. What was there to acknowledge? More pain? More wandering? In a year or maybe two they would meet up again in Chicago, at the train station. They would always have each other.

"Corregidor is just a one Quonset camp, but there's some year-round work in the cellars and the bottling plant. If you get year-round work you can live in one of the little kitchenette cottages at the trailer court. I used to live in cabin six. Look for my initials carved there on the picnic table. There's no toilet in any of the cabins but if you put a gallon jug behind the stove, you'll be all right. It's what I did. It's a lot better than a hundred-yard dash at two in the morning to take a leak. Of course, there's the communal toilets and showers. There's a little store in there that doesn't gouge people too bad, not like the Dittos' store. You could even go to school if you wanted to."

Ted For Short and Tony the leper had helped a flustered, whimpering Lilly and her fawning boyfriend hurriedly pack her belongings into the Oldsmobile. She had so many shoes and dresses to pack, and so much makeup! Her friend, Perfecto Lopez, had grumbled and cussed, resenting every man who lent her a hand, and with good reason. Perfecto was already history, thought Ted For Short. And Lovely Lilly runs away from history.

Rambling, hastily connected words were flying out of his shivering lips as Teodoro drove. He felt relieved by the absence of sirens and red lights on his way from the camp to the highway. He hoped that Faustino had gotten out before the police arrived and before Simon Ditto had time to organize a new mob.

Ted For Short's Pontiac was light yellow with green fender skirts and a plastic orange Indian head on the hood. There was a green sun visor mounted outside the car and above the windshield. Zeferino sat in the backseat while Ted For Short sat alone in the front. By necessity, the front seat had been shoved forward to mere inches from the dashboard. No one else could possibly sit in the front seat.

Ted For Short sat on a Los Angeles County phone book and had three custom-made pillows stuffed behind him and beneath him and both the brake pedal and accelerator pedal had huge wooden blocks strapped to them, using yards of black electrical tape. In the center of the dashboard was a four-inch plastic statue of Saint Christopher. Above the statue, a winged Raphael dangled from a string tied to the rearview mirror. It was one of the angels that had hung from the rafters above Teodoro's bunk. On the road, Ted For Short smoked like a chimney.

"Belair menthols. They'll stunt your growth," he laughed. "They taste better if you keep them in the refrigerator," he added as an afterthought. He was away from the camp and away from the dead body, and he was feeling a bit more courageous with every mile that passed beneath his wheels. He proudly adjusted the brightness of his courtesy and speedometer lights. He had personally installed green bulbs in all of the interior lights. He loved his car. It was all that he owned, and he could push in the cigarette lighter just by lifting his right knee.

Still, he promised himself as he drove that someday he would own a car that fit him, one that was made especially for someone of his particular physical attributes. He had always wondered if there was such a car to be found anywhere in this world.

When they came to Altamont Pass, Ted pulled the brim of his cap down tighter on his forehead and grabbed the wheel dramatically with both hands. This was a dangerous place to drive. Holding the wheel firmly with his left hand, he reached out to touch the plastic angel.

"Raphael," he implored, "guide us and Faustino safely through Altamont Pass." Then wordlessly, he asked that the boy in the backseat be given the gift of forgetfulness. Young Zefe must not grow up thinking that the whole world is crazy and cruel, thought Teodoro.

"This is a strange place," he said to the boy. "The winds are very strong up here. They blow my car around like it was a toy. There is such heavy fog and we are so far from the sea. Someday, when you are grown up and things are safe, come back up here. If you stop your car and get out and just stand, leaning straight into the wind, you will feel like you are snared in one of heaven's nets."

The car swerved violently just as he said it. Ted For Short fought the wheel, then changed cautiously to the slowest lane. There was a white guardrail at the edge of the right lane. Zeferino could see that the ravine behind the rail was a hundred feet deep.

Outside of the car were miles upon miles of rolling hills covered with fretting, brown weeds and rueful shafts of volunteer wheat that were perpetually bent low and davening in the chiding and unruly winds. It was the twin of the lunar landscape. Someday these same forlorn hills would be covered with windmills, dervishes of coiled wire, and white vanes. There would be spinning arms, catching the world's whims, from horizon to horizon.

Faustino, just miles behind the Pontiac, was passing through these same cold hills, his dark eyes filled with fear. Somehow he knew as he drove that someday barren, dry ridges like these would be his last mortal view of earth, that the headlights of his Buick could be illuminating the very ground that would one day catch his own spilled blood.

"We can stay at Camp Corregidor until your mother joins us," said Ted For Short. "She and her boyfriend have gone over to Placerville until the whole Ditto thing blows over."

Even as he said it, Ted For Short knew he was not staying at Corregidor, that a white man had been killed by brown men and that he and Faustino would have to run away and keep on running. In a country where it was against the law for dark men to be dancers, what would they do to killers? It might be decades before he could return again to the San Joaquin Valley . . . if ever.

Who would run ahead of the threshers? Who would keep the pink mice from drowning? Who would protect the rabbits? The boy would be safer if he were alone. A brown, hunch-backed midget was too easy to spot in a crowd. Ted For Short told himself that he would be saving the boy's life by leaving him. Surely, someone in the camp would shelter and feed him. What will happen to the boy? wondered Teodoro. Will we ever meet again?

We are running, he thought as he watched the hypnotic white lines of the highway disappearing beneath his hood ornament. All the sweating Mexican braceros and the Hindus are running. Lovely Lilly is running. Perfecto is running. Doesn't that make all of us good Americans? Isn't America running? Running from the downtown to the suburbs, and from there to those new tract houses, running from real neighborhood shops to those air-conditioned stores?

Americans run away from their old names, their old dialects, from extended families, from relationships. They run from languages, from people of color. The aggression of racism and the hatred against *bakla* are just more ways of running.

Ted For Short himself would run north, then south, from one unhappy job to the next. Finally he would find work with the fabulous Gonzalez Brothers Circus, based in El Paso, with winter quarters in Florida. While with the circus, he would rise from concessionaire and animal tender to become a headliner, his likeness painted on yards of canvas.

As *El Enanito Magico* he would thrill the crowds with breathtaking feats of magic and levitation and with his amazing prowess as a knife-thrower and fire-breather. In three years he would be promoted to the exalted post of head ringmaster. He would wear a tiny tuxedo and astonish children with the sheer size of his voice and the resonant depth of his imagination.

In each small town and in every enthralled audience, he would search for his heart's desire with one eye and for his own violent death with the other. He would look for the radiant face of Ruby and for the surreptitious, sequestered face of dark revenge.

The word would come to him on the road that a name from out of his past in the Philippines was hunting him in order to avenge his father's death. The word would come to him that Bambino Reyes, the hunter, had voluntarily relinquished his soul and was heartless.

"Americans run from culture and custom and from each other," Ted For Short said aloud, grinning madly as he descended from Altamont Pass into the fog-enshrouded Livermore Valley.

He turned on his high beams, but it made no difference. Not even the bright opaline moonlight could penetrate the fog.

"This entire place is homeless!" he cried as he passed Vasco Road. Seconds later his precious Pontiac was swallowed up by the pitch darkness of the valley floor.

The boy behind him stared out of the windows but the thick fog limited all visibility. He could see nothing at all; nothing was visible behind him or before him; the past was as obscure as the future.

"Then maybe"—Zeferino's small voice came from the lightless black of the rear seat—"maybe America is the place for you."

VIII

THE car careened through the fogbound streets of the West Portal District, moving out of the opaque darkness of Glen Park into the bright glare of the busy Mission District. Ignoring a stoplight, Stuart sped his treasured vehicle beneath an overpass where a stop sign caused only the slightest deceleration. Then he turned the Kosher Cruiser from Mission Street onto Cortland and headed up Bernal Heights toward Bayshore Boulevard.

As a single concession to traffic safety, Stuart dutifully used his turn signals whenever he made a turn or changed lanes, but all of the signal lights on his car had passed away years ago. Beneath the dashboard, the lonely, loyal flashing unit clicked and clicked, continuing to send its futile messages to the unhearing deceased. The single working headlight on the Kosher Cruiser had been skewed by a collision and illuminated little more than the trees and power lines above the street.

Zeferino sighed with relief as the car emerged from the dreary fog bank. He felt safer, though visibility did not seem to be essential to Stuart's driving. His investigator's driving methods did not appear to require landmarks, signposts, or even lane demarcations. Raising his eyes, the lawyer appreciated the waning moon shining overhead even more. Without it, the Kosher Cruiser was a blind cyclops.

"You know, Zef," said Stuart, suddenly breaking the silence, "I've always been proud of my Jewish culture, but I've never cared much for the religious side of it. I like the mysticism and the obscure writings, but that stuff is way out on the fringe. Lately, I've been having a strange feeling." Stuart tossed a halvah bar wrapper over his shoulder and into the darkness of the back-seat. "It's a sort of quivering or quaking and it's beginning to worry me." There was a hard tension in his jaws that meant that the worry had become an obsession.

"My friends have told me lately that they have noticed a vibra-tion on my skin, but it's not a generalized, nonspecific shaking. It seems to have a certain resonance and it's limited to a single physical plane. Maybe I've become anemic. Maybe I'm drinking too much. You haven't noticed it," he said with a hopeful note in his voice, "have you?"

"From the front of your head to the back," said Zeferino, who had recently begun to take note of the phenomenon. "You mumble, too, just under your breath. You've been doing it for months. There's an entire monologue going on around and be-tween your audible sentences."

"Oh, God!" exclaimed Stuart. He pulled the Kosher Cruiser to the side of the road as he passed Bonview Street. He turned off his headlight, then killed the engine, but it continued to run on for three or four minutes, spitting and bucking with emphysema.

"Listen, Zef, I've just got to stop for a minute. I'll get you to the jail by eight o'clock, I promise—but first I've got to tell you something."

The engine gave a final wheeze, then went silent.

"My *zaideh*, my grandfather, was not just a rabbi, he was a rab-binic shaman. Do you understand? He was way out there . . . at the absolute high end of the Talmudic scholars—he was a Char-lie Parker, a Miles Davis hovering menacingly at the edge of the stage; beyond measures, beyond keys; out there where music fuses with thought. Compared to him, everyone else was still learning the scales."

There was a tension in Stuart's voice that Zeferino had never heard before.

"By his final years, *Zaideh* had gone way past davening; each movement of his head had evolved into untold implications of things, each breath was an insinuation of other things—he just

vibrated imperceptibly, his lips moving one note ahead of the
beat. People who saw him knew they were witnessing a virtuoso
of prayer, weaving his shared learning and his shared pain into
the subtlest solo . . . a sonata for symbols."

"You're afraid that you're becoming your *zaideh*, aren't you?"
said Zeferino. "You think that it might be inevitable and you're
so afraid of it that you're making it come true—you've started
praying under your breath. Well, I've got news for you, hombre,
you will never be a rabbi—but you already knew that. What is the
fear behind your fear?"

"He was always ancient, Zef; even in my youngest memories
of him he had the eyes of age," said Stuart. "Maybe that's what
scares me. He smelled like Poland. He smelled like a combination of mothballs, tallow, and sausage. The liquids he drank and
the foods he tasted were from another world. His nostrils flared
to catch scents from another century, and he couldn't care less
about the paved streets and the electric lights of America. I can
still see his bristling nose hair and his skin like murky wax. But
most of all, I remember the feel of his shirts whenever he
hugged me; they were white shirts that had been starched yellow
over time. They were as yellow as gas lamps, yellow as curtains.
They felt as hard as parchment."

Stuart ran his fingers over his own shirt as he spoke. "They
were like curtains," whispered Stuart, "pulled across his body,
across his era."

"No," said Zeferino. "It's not old age that frightens you, Stuart. What frightens you is that you consider yourself a modern
man, a private investigator with three computers and a fax
machine, and all the while your own history is forcing its way to
the surface of your life—onto your lips and into the muscles of
your neck. It's there, between your sentences. You're worried
that it will overpower you." He turned to face Stuart. "Take it
from me, let it come. Something inside is telling you that clothing labels, professional sports, and pop music do not add up to a
culture. Just let it come."

After a moment of silence Stuart leaned into the backseat
and mixed himself an egg cream. He then restarted the Cruiser
and began driving, once again, toward the Hall of Justice. He
drank half of the egg cream as he drove but spilled the rest onto

the floor while making a hard right turn. The innocent, foaming drink was instantly abducted by the carpet.

"That street just ahead is Mrs. Cabiri's street," said Stuart in a low voice. He was still distracted by an image of his *zaideh*, but managed to return at least part of his attention to his work. "Have you met her yet?"

"No, not yet," answered Zeferino.

Stuart swerved the Kosher Cruiser violently to the left and up Anderson Street toward the top of Bernal Hill. Ruby and Ted For Short's home was a small bungalow at the crest of the hill where an access road wound its way to the peak. At dusk the dimensions of the house were impossible to discern. A light was on in two of the rooms, but the shades were drawn and only a soft, moving shadow could be seen behind them.

"She's home," said Stuart softly, "but we shouldn't bother her now. She goes to sleep early. You've got to go in there someday. There are a million places to sit and almost no furniture. I spent two hours with her yesterday and for most of that time I walked from room to room staring at the walls. Every room is a dressing room. The whole house is backstage, decorated with real props and true illusions."

Straining his eyes to see as the car pulled away, Zeferino spoke through the car window and into the night air. "Is the roof moving?"

Radiant Ruby in her home on Bernal Hill was once *una niña que estaba enojada con los pájaros*, a girl who was mad at birds and who envied their freedom. She was once a young woman who laughed at courtesies, was drawn to unkindness, who thought that hombres pulling at her skin was a sign of love, and she believed that inside her soft legs were *los huesos de la suerte*, the wishbones that men saved after every feast. These days men saw doves nestled in the perfumed clefts of her body.

"*Un hombre me robó el corazón*. One man stole my heart, whole and pumping," she says to anyone who will listen. "One man stole my heart whole, and yet I live on. Teodoro is not half a man, mind you, but a whole man. Don't make that mistake about him."

There is a pockmarked, rutted street in front of her home, a street whose organic undulations remind her of her homeland in Mexico. It was on this very street that the two entwined lovers first drove from the wedding to the wedding bed. They'd come laughing in the little pea green car, to the threshold of her home. Using his magical powers, Teodoro had lifted her into the front room. So many marriages and the only man to carry her over the threshold was a cherub.

Outside of her home, a tarp covers a small object in her driveway. It is his car. She cares for it and smiles at it affectionately. Their laughter is still trapped there, inside. It is a BMW Isetta, his one-cylinder, two-passenger, single-doored car that she keeps polished for his return. Above her head, on the roof of her home, her loyal flock of birds hovers like a windblown *chuppa*.

Inside Ruby's home, Teodoro's huge leather-covered trunk of special things waits for his return. Her own trunk is there right next to his. Each night she opens his trunk and lifts the sequined jacket up to the light, to stare at it. There are so many glints and sparkles that the jacket is almost impossible to really see. Yet she tries. There are small pockets sewn into the sleeves of the jacket. Within the pockets are coins, lengths of thread, a set of picklocks, and two decks of shaved playing cards.

Beneath the costumes, there are three silk hats and three pairs of matching tap shoes. She lifts a motheaten cloth bag and peers inside. There are his toy angels, their brightly painted costumes and hair rubbed away long ago by the anxious hands of a child. Faustino's angels are there, too.

There is a yellowed photograph in the bag. It is hidden beneath the plastic angels. It is a photograph of young Teodoro working in the kitchen of a restaurant in Manila. Above his head, on the kitchen wall, is a strange poster, a painting of three laughing hunchbacks seated at a table. Stapled to this photo is a tattered map of Venice. The angels, the map, and the photograph are Teodoro's most prized possessions.

Both trunks are filled with the props and costumes of a lifetime. Inside her own trunk are Ruby's costumes and her posters, one proclaiming her to be a "professional ornitho-ecdysiast who has performed before potentates, crown heads of state, and members of the Audubon Society."

Above Ruby's bed, there is a painting of *Los Voladores*, the flyers in Mexico. It is an ancient tradition that Ruby once loved to watch as a child. Four men, *voladores*, were tied to a high wooden pole, *el palo volador*. They launched themselves into the air and swung around and around, with arms outspread like eagles impaled on inverted crosses, until they reached the ground.

Each man circled the pole thirteen times. Thirteen rotations times four men is fifty-two, the magical span of years for both the Aztec and the Maya. In modern times, the *voladores* dove toward earth in honor of St. Francis of Assisi, but the true meaning was far more ancient . . . far more important.

The pole unified heaven and earth; the downward flight recalled the fall of man and his once lofty place in heaven. Its old name was *quecholli* and young Ruby loved to see the spectacle of it until the day she was told that a ceremony even more ancient than the flight of men preceded it.

First a deep hole was dug to accommodate the tall, limbless tree. Then a vibrant, copper-faced, living hen with darting eyes was placed into the hole, where she clucked and scratched quietly, peacefully until the shadow came from above and the heavy pole was so rudely lowered. The hen's blood was to be the lubricant for the spinning universe above. The cosmos would turn on the mire of feathers and blood and nascent eggs.

The poor hen in the hole began to fill Ruby's childhood sleep with pressing nightmares and stifling claustrophobia. She had owned the picture most of her life, but had never before hung it on the wall. She had recently begun to wonder if each belief on earth had an ancient hen beneath it.

Teodoro had put the painting up for her—the thick salve of pinfeathers and blood. For Ruby, the world of man would never be the same . . . in this, the final chapter of her life, she would be no one's lubricant.

"You know," said Zeferino as they turned onto Bryant Street, "you could always donate the Kosher Cruiser to the Jewish state." He looked around himself at the litter on the floor and the mold growing on the headliner. "It already looks like one of those archeological digs in the Holy Land."

"You're right," grinned Stuart. "I wouldn't want my family to say that I didn't give anything back. Besides, I could tell all those people who think I'm ruining my car that what I'm actually doing is planting artifacts for the tourists."

After they parked across from the jail, Stuart reached into his briefcase and pulled out some notes scrawled on a legal pad.

"I spoke to Miguel Govea this morning. He didn't give me much more than he gave the police inspector. He says that he never left his booth the night of the murder and that he was a witness to both the death of Bambino Reyes and the death of Humberto. When I told him that wasn't possible he just laughed in my face. I pressed him, but he refused to explain. When I asked him who killed Bambino Reyes, he would only say that Teodoro didn't do it. After that," shrugged Stuart, "he said I could stay awhile if I stopped asking my questions and had some coffee and Mexican breads."

"Did you read the message I left at your office?" asked Zeferino, who laughed to himself at the image of Stuart sharing the old man's food.

"Yes I did," answered Stuart, his eyes wide with amazement. "Before yesterday you had no recollection of having witnessed the death of this man Pietro Ditto?"

Zeferino shook his head, no.

"Do you think that the death of Bambino Reyes is somehow tied to that killing over thirty years ago?"

Zeferino glanced upward at the seventh floor of the gray building. He had brought a thermos of coffee for this interview and he intended to get some answers from his uncle, the protector of shipwrecked men.

"Let's go up and find out."

"By the way," continued Stuart as he and Zeferino exited the Cruiser, "Beatrice is not talking at all. She refuses to say a single word. Oh, I forgot to tell you, Miguel did say that a man named King Pete Claver talked to Bambino Reyes just a couple of days before a wedding at the Silver Cloud. I ran King Pete Claver's name through voter records and motor vehicle registration and I couldn't locate him."

"Go back to the Mission District and look for a yellow tamale cart on wheels," said Zeferino. "You can't miss it. The huge guy pushing the cart will be King Pete Claver." Stuart's eyes widened at the mention of food. "If you go after dark, he'll be up on the roof of Raphael's Silver Cloud, sleeping next to a silver tower.

Teodoro Cabiri," he added, "had his wedding at the Silver Cloud just days before Bambino's murder."

Inside the jail, the two men stood up as their diminutive client entered the interview room. Teodoro, once again, jumped from his heavy chains with a flourish, a lit cigarette clamped between his lips. As Ted For Short arranged himself in his chair, Stuart sat down but Zeferino stood, staring into his client's eyes.

Ted For Short was age, deformity, and difference, thought Zeferino . . . everything America fears. His daily intimacy with pain transmuted what little love he had experienced into a divine love complete with its own built-in opponent, its own great enemy. There were no moanings about the failings of powders and cosmetics here, no headlong rush to bob a nose or tighten a jowl. People like Ted For Short did not cry about cellulite or thinning hair.

What would the Book of Job mean to this world, wondered Zeferino, if the tortured man were never given reprieve or never made whole again? In the larger view, Ted For Short was more complete than so-called normal human beings. He clung to the container of the flesh with a power and intimacy that no narcissist or cover girl could understand. Yet he was joined to the contents within the container to a degree that would shame an ascetic.

He was the *quidam servulus*, the fool and the dwarf in the back of the triumphal chariot who reminds the conqueror, flushed with victory, of his own mortality, his own foolishness. He is the only man who can tell the truth to a king, who can ward off the jealousy of the gods, the man who spoke three insults for three honors.

"*Tre molestie,*" said Zeferino under his breath. He stared at his client's exterior for a moment, seeing for the first time what thirty years of running had done to him.

"What does Pietro Ditto's death have to do with the death of Bambino Reyes?" Zeferino asked with a hint of both impatience and excitement in his voice. "The newspapers say that Bambino Reyes had been moving from city to city for years," said Zeferino to an old man whose mind seemed elsewhere. "He's been chasing you, hasn't he, Teodoro? He's been hunting you all of these years. Was he Pietro's friend? Was he a paid assassin? Where is Faustino? What on earth made that huge hole in Bambino's gut?"

"Be patient, Zefe, I will tell you everything as promised," said Teodoro. "Are you angry with me, Zefe? Why are you so impatient?"

"Most of my clients never know what happened to them, and couldn't tell me if I asked. You are not telling me because you don't want to tell me. I don't judge my clients, Teodoro. I don't ask them to judge themselves. There are plenty of people out there who are willing to judge, whether they know what the evidence is or not. I just get impatient when a client who can help refuses to help."

Zeferino heard his own voice as he spoke; he heard the lawyer speaking when, beneath it all, it was the child who wished to be heard.

"It has been said, Teodoro, that a human being's first thought belongs to the devil and that the second thought belongs to God. Prosecutors are blessed with the right to ask the jury for that first thought; that first moment of repulsion upon hearing the charges or viewing the victim's wound; that first moment of judgment upon first seeing the skin color of the accused. Prejudice is so highly accessible.

"The defense attorney must ask for the second thought; for reason untainted by prejudice, and then, secretly, for the third thought: for reason tinged by a different quality; moderated by feeling for both the victim and the defendant . . . for the worlds beyond their lives, for all of us."

"The doctrine of mercy," said Stuart quietly, "agape." There were other words buzzing around that single word as he spoke it.

"Yes," said Zeferino, "though nobody knows it. The judgments and the punishments we mete out to our citizens are not so much a measure of their crimes as they are a measure of our own civility. In this world we arm everyone, even the chlidren; then we are stunned by what bullets can do. And what is our cure for all the killing? What punishment would a country choose that wipes out its indigenous people, assassinates its forests, murders its own diversity, tortures its rivers and lakes? Is there really a choice? Kill the killer, of course.

"The legal system that was once the dispassionate intermediary between hostile parties now asks those very parties what the punishment is to be!"

The room was silent. Zeferino realized that the other two men were looking at him, at the outrage now clear in his face.

"A defense lawyer," he began again, but with more calm, "has to cultivate within himself the ability to reverse the order of those thoughts. Only when the case is over may he, himself, indulge in first thoughts. By the time I sit down after giving my closing argument, Teodoro, I will believe that a reasonable doubt exists. I will believe that you are not guilty. Now can we get back to business? Start from wherever you want to start. We have time."

Ted For Short smiled, then cleared his throat. Stuart took out a notepad and pencil. The little man extended his right hand with his fingers spread. He pulled the sleeve of his shirt up to his elbows, then peeked over his shoulder as if to see what the deputy at post 8 was doing. Teodoro closed his hands and when he opened them again, there was a cigarette perched between each knuckle. One of them was lit and smoking.

"Did you know that your accent is completely gone, Zefe? When I first met you, you spoke English like a little *mojado*. Even after all of these years, I still have my accent. You know, you really have no choice but to represent me. All of this has been fated. Did you know that the man I killed was hunting you, too?"

Stuart suddenly sat upright in his chair, a startled look on his sleepy face. Zeferino said nothing and did not return his investigator's confused glances. Without waiting for an answer, the little man began.

"My life started before my birth. So did my death."

Stuart looked toward Teodoro, shrugged his shoulders, then placed the pad and pencil onto the table.

"Even before I descended into the first seconds of life, even before I was a small, tepid pool of encoded brine, I was a sojourner. I was a spirit who moved about between this earth and the next, waiting to re-enter life according to my so-called merits." Teodoro looked from Stuart to Zeferino.

"Well, I can only say that I must have been very cruel in my last life because God has certainly been cruel to me in most of this one. Look at me. What more could He do to me short of death? For me, the womb was an ambush."

Teodoro reached into the air with his right hand, then pulled down his shirt sleeve once again and rotated his wrist as if he were performing to an invisible audience. An Almond Joy candy bar suddenly appeared in his hand. He peeled back the wrapper and, with a smile, began to eat.

"As a sojourner, I think I must have drifted, airy and shapeless, out past Jupiter or Saturn, way out there where human prayers never resonate. We spirits were like wild animals out there; we knew that if you get too used to people you can't ever be free. But something happens to rob us of our weightless life.

"There's a combination out there, a sequence of numbers that is somehow known to algae and budding schoolboys; and when those numbers are lined up, all the tumblers fall. Some guy gives flowers or a box of candy or some girl gets stuck in the backseat of a Chevrolet and something happens; the tumblers click into alignment. A gold ring gets ceremoniously slipped onto a finger, or a forlorn whore forgets to douche in time and a bell goes off somewhere out there . . . a spirit's name gets called."

When the candy bar was gone, Teodoro smashed the wrapper into a small ball, then tossed it into the air between Zeferino and Stuart. The ball rose toward the ceiling, then vanished. A smiling Teodoro already had another cigarette between his lips.

"There is a corporeal conspiracy; the planet throbs with invention, fairly insisting on the spirit's leap into substance." He took the burning cigarette from his mouth, then replaced it, the lit end first—all the way until it disappeared behind his lips. He smiled mysteriously, then pushed his tongue out suddenly. The lit and smoking cigarette reappeared, reversed and perched at the tip of his tongue.

"Someday you just might catch my act," he grinned. "Now, where was I? Oh, yes!" he laughed. "We are called and we drop down through holes, edgeless apertures in the shell of the world, right into a waiting life. It's a beautiful thing to see: perfect, pure spirits dropping down past the seven heavens and down to the seven earths to spread out into flesh and be subjected, once again, to the arbiter of the length of life. Imagine it! A virginal free fall!

"I tell you, it's beautiful but scary. You could end up in the house of a rich man in Manila or begging in rags in some fetid ditch in Tondo. You could wind up in Chicago, on a nice tree-lined street where children and dogs run from lawn to lawn, dodging rain-bird sprinklers. Or you could land in Beirut, just seconds before an artillery round, and die while the helix is forming. I heard that some spirits are called into bodies that would never draw a breath of air. Then it's a short trip, you see? Fly down there and learn again the sorrowful meaning of time; stay a little bit while the disease so carefully navigates the vein, then leave just when the breath stops and the crying in the distance starts.

"It's actually good for the spirit. It gets a better assignment the next time, but it's still no fun. Though the priests try to tell the mortal people differently, no spirit has ever gladly left sadness behind. We can never forget the whimper of pain, and the stricken face of the crying mother never leaves you; there is always a residual sadness. The taste of her wasted milk coats your gums, from life to life, forever."

He ran his tongue solemnly over his teeth. He leaned toward his lawyer, looking suspiciously intense.

"I am going to tell you a secret," he said, looking both ways in the enclosed room, as though checking for eavesdroppers.

"Besides the spirits out there waiting to be reborn, there are these other beings, like ghostly overcoats that hang everywhere. I know they are essentially spirits, too, or perhaps they are a lowly kind of angel . . . I don't know anything more about their origin. The rabbis have names for them, but right now I can't recall what they are."

"The grigori," said Stuart in a monotone whisper, "or perhaps the nephillium, the issue of Cain and some fallen angels." The investigator was davening now, his brow trembling with concern.

"Yes," said Ted For Short, enthusiastically pointing at Stuart, "but, when you are a spirit, you can see them clearly. They hang everywhere, on street corners, in cafes, in bedroom closets. They are ancient parasitic forms that wait around like weightless greatcoats; they wait for humans to sling them upon their shoulders, to put them on and wear them until the day they die. Then the mantle hangs patiently near the deathbed, waiting for another.

"Right now there is a child out there somewhere destined to grow into manhood and be a prisoner and there's a child bound to wear a guard's uniform and brutalize that prisoner; one life haunts another. These people walk into these invisible suits you see and presto . . . there goes any real chance to be anything else.

"Every time, every era has its fools, its predators, its liars. Good, godlike, young children swaddle themselves in apathy and cruelty as naturally as night follows day. The same young man who could murder a helpless Jewish mother and her child in wartime Germany is out there on the streets right now, following another young mother as she leaves an automatic teller machine.

"A lot of people have tried to decide what it means to be human, what free will means. I'll tell you what it means. That's right. Me, Teodoro Teofilo Cabiri. I'll tell you."

He reached the fingers of one small hand into his own ear and struggled as though he had hooked something in there. He pulled out a small burning candle and gave it to an amused Stuart, who placed it carefully on the table edge near Ted For Short's cigarettes.

"Earwax," smiled Ted For Short, who simply could not restrain himself. After all, he had been an entertainer most of his adult life.

"To be human means to dodge those mantles. Freedom is the ability to see them. They're invisible, remember? Pure spirits diving down to a new life are often trapped in these mantles like moths in a web. Everywhere, there are foolish people who have traded their free-thinking souls for the warmth and comfort of the mantles. A mantle passed down to the man I killed and he wore it with comfort and conviction. He wore it for decades and tormented me and my friends for years. The mantles keep you in business, don't they, Mr. Lawyer and Mr. Investigator?"

"Yes," responded Zeferino, "but what I ask of those who sit in judgment is to turn from the grigori to the so-called better angels of their nature. I ask them to remove their mantles . . . for an hour, for a day."

Teodoro Cabiri grinned at his lawyer and wondered what happened to the small, sensitive boy after he drove him from French Camp and left him at that Quonset hut at Camp Corregidor. Then Teodoro returned to his story.

"Some Pinoys in the Islands believe that an angel comes to a newborn child and tells him not to whisper a word about the world that he has just come from, to keep the secret. Others say that children come from the womb with the ability to speak, but that a messenger angel seals the child's lips just when the little creature takes its very first breath of air. That way the child is forced to learn the confusing languages of men.

"I am told that we could not bear life if we recalled how glorious heaven was. That's why a child cries so hard when he first comes out, he has just a small memory of the beautiful world where he's been, and then all at once he sees the dreary world where he will die." He shook his head with disgust.

"Well, a confused, sinister angel must've come to me, because I remember so much of the other world and next to nothing at all about my childhood. Somewhere between Tondo and Stockton an angel must've descended and wiped out my recollections of the Islands. I once believed it was done to ready me for the beauty of America, this country, but now I know better. It was done to relieve my suffering."

Even as he spoke the words, he realized that the last seven years had given him something to remember and cherish. He rubbed the spot where his wedding ring belonged. The guards had taken it from him again.

"It turns out that my childhood memories are the descriptions that my *compadres* in the fields have given me, not my own, and I've built upon them over the years. I would ask some farmworker if he knew of my little village back home, and if he said yes, I would beg him to please describe it for me.

"Do you know Santo Paulo? I would ask every *manong* I ever met. Do you know Santo Paulo? Did you know my family? Of course, he did not, but then I would ask him about his own family. In a way, his family became mine . . . everyone's did. It has taken a long time to admit this to myself. Every man wants a history."

Teodoro spoke the last few sentences with his eyes closed. "In these real and counterfeit memories I always see my pretty mother, Angelica, crying over broken china plates; a very special one has shattered among all the rest and she cries for it, beyond consolation. She is on her knees, trying to piece it back together again. But it is clearly beyond repair. Slivers of ceramic have fallen through the floor and down into the animal pens. Pieces, like disheveled chromosomes, lost forever.

"I can see my father downcast over the death of his precious carabao, his water buffalo. His strong shoulders are quaking as he stares down at the huge lifeless body. I always wonder, does he cry for the cost of replacing it or does he cry for the years of labor it has given to him, the thousands of miles of perfect furrows that the faithful animal had learned to cut? I imagine . . . I remember that he is a man that never cries. And there I am . . . there I am, more broken than any serving dish and more dead than any carabao, and not a single tear ever falls for me."

Teodoro did not make eye contact as he spoke these words.

"They raised a pig for me, you see. In the Islands, it was our way that when a woman wants to have a child, a suckling pig is set aside by the parents. It is to be kept clean and fed only the best food. It is raised to be slaughtered, you see. It dies on the day of the child's birth. The blood of the pig is smeared over the clothing and the faces of every member of the immediate family, then the extended family. Finally, it is smeared upon the child, in celebration of his leaving the other world and his entry into this one. Then the pig's flesh is roasted and eaten when the child is named."

"The pig is a surrogate?" asked Zeferino, sipping coffee from a plastic cup.

"Yes, he is supposed to deflect bad luck from the child. Pigs have that power. But the little pig that my mother had chosen began to wither away with some disease and my father went crazy when he saw it. They had been arguing, you see, he and my mother. More than three children in a family was considered shameful in a time of famine and I was to be the fourth. He blamed my mother.

"This part of the story I know to be true. An old Pinoy janitor in Salt Lake City told me he'd heard stories of my father's madness. They were still talking about it years after I had left the village, about how his madness brought bad luck to the village, how his cruelty had wounded my mother. After a while, after all of his torments, she did not want me either. With all the evil there is in this world, that little pig had to defend me from my own flesh and blood, too. He was just given too much to do."

Teodoro ran his stubby fingers through his gray hair, then lit another cigarette, though his last one was still burning in the ashtray. His lawyer had not had a smoke since the last big earthquake, the one that cracked the Bay Bridge in two. But he was only a smoker who wasn't smoking and the smell of burning tobacco was pleasurable.

"Jesus, sometimes I almost believe I can see our home. The air in my throat is island air, so saturated you could almost drink it. There is wind in the walls—wet wind just short of hot rain—and animals shift and scrape beneath the elevated floor. Out on the water, far out on the water of our little bay there are bobbing dinghies, the sleepy tock-tock of painted hulls tapping painted hulls." He rapped his small fingers slowly on the table.

"I think I remember the monsters of that time, too: leaf molds bubbling under stems and beetles spreading their backs to raise wings and fly. I dimly recall the whole countryside mourning stalks of rice dying young with the blight; the raspy voices of the sickly reeds, unable to bend in the slightest prodding breeze. There was always the threat of hunger."

He said nothing for a moment, fingering his clothing. His jail clothing was red and black now, denoting highest security; his case was serious.

"Even when the poor little pig finally died, I lived on in a belly that barely swelled. You see, I never weighed down my mother's body—only her spirit. Her smile, her life sagged when her hips did not. They both prayed for a miscarriage but I stayed there inside of her, my poor ingredients vainly cooking within one of God's failed recipes. Finally, at his wits' end, my father bought the jar."

He closed his eyes again with the sadness of it. There must be stifled words somewhere in Tagalog or English to describe the closed-in feelings he experienced in his nightmares.

"It was a child's burial jar. He placed it right in front of the house for everyone . . . for heaven to see. My coffin, my urn. I should've been in it. All these years I should've been inside it. You see, I began as a weave of tangled genes, courting dust from the very moment of birth. But something always kept me alive. For most of my life . . . even when you knew me, Zefe, it seemed to me that some unkind thing let me live."

Zeferino looked into his client's face. In 1959, had he been too young to see Teodoro's pain? No, he decided to himself. Teodoro had never let him see it.

"Finally, they took me in my mother's belly to one of the psychic healers in Baguio for an abortion. It's not a short trip on foot, and they used up all their savings in an effort to get rid of me. The doctor there massaged my mother's stomach and placed smoking herbs on her. He prayed fervently at a small, flaming altar, then killed a hen by cutting its neck and letting it bleed onto my mother's flat womb. To this day, my spit tastes of chicken.

"Finally, the woman assistant announced joyfully to my parents that I was already beginning my trip back to God. I was pulling up my airy stakes and heading home. But a month after my parents returned from Baguio, my mother went into labor for five or ten minutes . . . and there I was.

"Shit, how can there be a God? God is supposed to be perfect, isn't he? And here I stand, living proof that He is a bungler." He lifted his arms, palms up as if to display himself.

"Either that or he threw my clay on the wheel and got tired of pugging and punching and took a cigarette break before getting back to the work. Now that would be all right with me; I certainly have no quarrel with a cigarette break, but in between those divine, blue puffs my lifetime came and went and I had to live my days out in this shape."

He stirred in his seat again and adjusted his unresponsive legs, moving the left foot by prodding it with his cane. Zeferino rose from his chair and moved to the window of the room.

"I'm not bitter," he smiled. "Look, I know you've got a lot of questions and I want to answer them, but I want to tell you the whole story. Bambino Reyes began dying a long, long time ago. Now be patient and sit down."

Ted For Short pointed with his cane toward the empty chair. Zeferino moved back toward the chair, then stopped.

"No, I can listen standing up. I've been sitting too long."

Teodoro lifted his cane each time he wished to make a point or punctuate a sentence with something more than a period. He stood and stretched. He tapped the cane twice on the cement floor. The two men moved away from the table and toward opposite sides of the tiny room. Each placed his back to the cold wall. Ted For Short's small hunchback forced him to stand at an angle, facing the door. Stuart remained seated, his pencil back in his hand and its lead tip circling endlessly in a corner of the yellow legal pad. He was mumbling again.

"My hunchback is my cargo, like the hold of the ship that so long ago brought me here. I carry my bile in there along with every song, every one-liner and misdirection move that I know. Sometimes it all just comes out. Loathing, lyrics, and legerdemain." He moved away from the wall and took his place at the table once again. "Can I have some of your coffee?"

The lawyer cleaned his empty cup with a napkin, then poured steaming coffee into it. He pushed the cup toward Ted For Short.

"Everyone has a special hidden hurt, a loss that they relive when alone, in the pause between breaths, then again in the smallest parts of those seconds." He took a swig of his coffee.

"I think about lost children, that's what I think about, Zefe. I think about the last time I saw you. Your Uncle Benny once told me something about you. Do you remember the duck and the rabbit?"

"Jesus!" said Zeferino, exhaling violently, then stepping suddenly out into the hallway where the line of dark cells stretched into the black distance. The deputy at post 5 was dozing over a newspaper. Zeferino remembered. Since going to Raphael's Silver Cloud, all of the memories had begun accruing in his soul.

Pinky and Peep-peep had been Zeferino's rabbit and duck, given to him by his Tia Juanita when he first came onto the migratory circuit. Juanita had realized that the boy would be alone in the fields; there would be no other children to play with. Only the Okies brought their children with them into the fields, and the Okies preferred to pick fruit in Oregon and Washington. Zeferino had raised the duck and the rabbit together, and the two had become inseparable, eating, sleeping, and exploring together. The two were a single constant in the boy's vagabond life.

One November evening at some forgotten labor camp the boy had gone into the Quonset hut for dinner to find that the fieldworkers were having a Thanksgiving banquet. On the table were three dressed turkeys, a duck, and a rabbit. For many of the farmworkers, it was their first attempt at an American holiday.

Just before the boy began to eat, he looked at the duck and the rabbit and grew suspicious. He dropped his knife and fork and ran outside to the animal pens. The pens were silent and empty; the gates had been left wide open. The white rabbit and the white duck were gone and there was new blood glistening on the eucalyptus stump where animals were slaughtered. The large killing cleaver was wet and embedded deep in the wood. They had killed and cooked his pets. The gentle creatures had been carried together to their deaths.

As only a child can do, he walked back into the Quonset screaming and cursing at grown men who sat dazed by the sheer ferocity of the boy's sorrow and anger. The men sat silently and said nothing in their own defense. They had no concept at all of the word *pet*. In their world everything was eaten.

The boy had run, wordless and blinded by tears, across the road to the winery, where he banged his hands and head against a tree to keep from hating. An hour later, he had walked slowly back to the camp, where he saw the thirty men from the Quonset hut surrounding a hole that had just been dug in the ground. The turkeys, basted, cooked, and stuffed, were buried steaming alongside the barbecued rabbit and the roasted duck. Thirty hungry, unfed men had surrounded a pit, staring down at their dinner, staring at their mistake, at their inability to understand America.

"I remember them," he said at last to Ted For Short. His voice broke as he repeated the words, "I remember them."

"You are human, Zefe . . . that's all," said Ted For Short in a soothing voice. "Like the rest of us, you are dust in love, divine mud."

Stuart Zikoren rose from his seat and lifted his leather brief-case from the table. It was time to leave these two men alone and he knew it. He looked toward his friend and said, "I'll go see if I can locate King Pete, Zef. A couple of tamales wouldn't hurt."

Zeferino was only barely aware of his leaving. He was still star-ing downward at his beloved pets. There was a pain in his stom-ach that he had not felt in years. A pain that went far beyond hunger.

"It's just a good thing that I'm not religious, I tell you, Zefe. If I believed in God, I surely would not want Him floating around in a mind as filthy and confused as mine. That's why I never go to church or pray. That way I do God a favor." He smiled, then lit a cigarette, then placed it on the lip of the ashtray without taking a second drag.

"It's almost impossible to be Filipino and not be either fanati-cally religious or a torch singer. God, my country is crazy." Teodoro shook his head at the thought of it all.

"My entire youth is clearly marked, you know, its sad begin-ning and its end. It began in Baguio and it ended in Baguio."

He reached for the cigarette that had died on the edge of the ashtray, then relit it with a flourish.

"Before I met Radiant Ruby," began Ted For Short, "my last good year on this earth was my seventh year. Sometimes it even seemed as though my parents might have cared for me, though I can't recall any acts of affection. I do know that all the other chil-dren were the same size as me until my seventh year, when all at once it seemed that everyone was passing me up, even the small-est girls. That was the year that my left shoulder began to twist upward and this hump was in its infancy.

"My father knew that his efforts to kill me in the womb were coming back to haunt him. Everyone in the village said they'd seen it coming, the wrath of God. My seventh year was the year that they took me up to Baguio for the second time. But before they did that they came up with a scheme to try and save the ex-pense of a second trip to the healers. Do you know about the Passion plays and the processions in the Philippines?"

"I know some Pinoys are maniacs," answered Zeferino. "They

are the craziest Catholics on the face of the earth, even crazier than the Mexicans."

Ted For Short nodded his agreement. Someone had once described the Philippines as a country that had spent three hundred years in a Spanish convent and fifty years in Hollywood. Oppressive, medieval Catholicism has made the Islands the only Christian country in all of Asia. And the partnership with America that the Islands experienced during World War II had left behind a poor, self-conscious nation that constantly compares itself to an exalted, mythological Yankee model. The Philippines have never had a father, only stepfathers: the absentee Philip II, the omnipresent Pope, and the forever-returning Douglas MacArthur.

"It was a great honor to be chosen as the boy who will re-enact the Passion of the Christ. Every year there was a competition to see whose village would have the most pious, realistic crucifixion. The village that won would re-enact the Passion at the provincial parade and would be noticed by God and be blessed with bounty and health in the coming year. It was another time, another world." He shook his head.

"Well, my father set about building a cross. He carried two driftwood logs up from the bay and strapped them together with leather thongs. You see, if I were miraculously cured of my small size while up there on the cross, the family would not have to go to the expense of a second trip to Baguio. It was a small cross, with a perch strapped to the base where I could place my feet. My mother tore one of her nicest dresses into strips for a loincloth and for the bindings at my hands and feet.

"The day of the local competition, there were five other crosses erected in the field next to the village church. My father dug a deep hole and put the vertical of the cross into it. Then I climbed up there and spread my arms so my mother could tie me down. One of the other boys had barbed wire wrapped around his wrists and I could see that my parents had noticed it, too. It was a nice touch and the cuts that the barbs were making in his arms would be worth a lot of points to the judges. Another boy had real goat's blood daubed at his side and on his brow. My mother had used red paint. We were worried about these other boys, but soon we stopped worrying altogether.

"The moment we saw him we knew that both worry and hope were pointless. As soon as we saw him coming, we knew the contest was lost. I knew that, once again, we would be making the frightful trip to the room in Baguio. Any possibility of being cured by a compassionate God while I was portraying His suffering Son had been wiped away forever by the pitiful, wonderful sight of Bambino Reyes, who, in the distance, was stumbling and staggering for the third time, struggling as he carried a huge cross on his back and toward the open field.

"I tell you he was shameless. He even had one of his sisters playing Veronica. She'd spent the whole night before painting a face on a towel. He had his relatives at every station, hamming up their parts like none others had in living memory. Of course, he won the local competition, hands down. Three of the judges on the day of the local competition had given Bambino a perfect ten for technical merit on the compulsories and a 9.8 for inspiration and originality. I, for one, couldn't see it.

"On the day of the grand procession, my family, which had fallen into a sullen, resigned silence, placed themselves along the processional route as they always had in the past. The padre came through the village first. I can still smell the incense. He was followed by the proud, unsmiling altar boys in their dark red and blazing white dress. I knew every one of them. They had all recently begun to torment me because of my stature.

"The boys were followed by the huge plaster figure of the blessed Virgin swaying on a flowered float. She was completely surrounded by hundreds of votive candles and photographs of those people in the village who prayed for divine intercession in their lives. On her plaster gown, the villagers had taped hundreds of dollar bills. My mother had placed a photograph of our family on the float. Next to it she had placed an individual picture of me.

"Finally, there was the crucifixion itself, hoisted aloft and carried on the shoulders of the strongest men."

Zeferino noticed that Ted For Short's voice had suddenly grown darker and deeper. It was not the sound of childish hatred or youthful desires that modulated his voice, but a life-long distillation of those things. It was clear to Zeferino that these ancient memories had been just as debilitating as Teodoro's twisted back and mismatched legs.

"There was Bambino Reyes up there, posturing, overacting, his elbows flapping as though they were thoroughly boneless. His head was bent down at an impossible angle; the bobby pins holding his crown of thorns in place were all too visible from where I stood. Was I the only one who saw it? The others were staring too. They must've seen it. But they only seemed to be staring in awe at the sight passing before them, the Passion.

"That Easter I saw no colors, heard no sounds. For me, there was only the sight of Bambino Reyes, his eyes rolled back into his head so that only the whites showed. I'd seen him scare the girls at school with that very same trick and there it was again, but this time it endeared him to the very highest vaults of heaven.

"How I despised him at that moment. The *mestizo* Italian boy had been chosen to portray perfection in the very year that my own imperfection had been so painfully discovered by everyone. When I think about it, I suppose nothing imperfect can be the Christ. It wasn't Bambino who beat me. It was God Himself. But it was also God who made the bearers stumble at the end of the procession and it was also God who caused Bambino to fall into the fire.

"What is it the Mexicans say? When God closes a door, he opens a window. Can you imagine how my guilty heart soared as the men struggled vainly to regain their balance? Like the foolish child that I was, I rejoiced as the coals seared his side. But when he called out from the flames to Jehovah, his Father, I knew all was lost, that Bambino had scored a Catholic touchdown. All processions in the future would attempt to reenact his fall into the flame. Burning children, years into the future, would practice crying out according to the Bambino Reyes legend."

Teodoro's hands were, once again, grabbing the edges of the table. The fingers and knuckles were almost white with exertion.

"When he was pulled burning from the flames, his side was scorched and bleeding and his smoking gut was stuffed with glittering charcoal. His wild face jerked about him to steal a look at his tormentors, his audience. He wept feverishly. I hated him. I despised him, even as it seemed, in my crippled soul, that a torrent of our iniquities was flying toward him, heaped upon him. I hated him, even as I ran home to stand before the mirror, hoping that Bambino's false piety, tempered by real pain, had somehow lengthened my body and smoothed my swelling back. As you can see, nothing had changed." He held both arms out as though presenting himself for inspection.

"Pain was just pain. My own foolishness was more apparent than ever. The sky was unmoved. The procession on that day so long ago still continues today, with as many leaders and as many followers as there ever were. I saw in the mirror that it would proceed without me.

"So, when the Easter season was over, my unhappy parents packed me up and we repeated the trip to Baguio that my mother and father had taken while I was still in the womb. It was a full retreat for the family. All the way up to Baguio my father said nothing at all, not a single word, not even to my mother or to strangers passing on the road. My mother said only that the doctor in Baguio would demand our life's savings to remove my hunched back and cure my shrunken, crippled body. I remember telling her that I would pay them back someday. I swore to God that I would. What a fool I was! I didn't belong in their world any more than I belong in this one."

Zeferino rose from the seat he had taken. He stretched his arms, then removed his glasses and began to rub his eyes. Teodoro could see that his lawyer was uneasy about something.

"My second trip to Baguio is a story for another day," said Teodoro.

Zeferino was only barely listening. The look on his lawyer's face told Ted For Short that Zefe's mind was elsewhere. Teodoro fell silent as once hidden memories migrated upward into Zeferino's consciousness, then drifted down as fluid from his eyes.

"You left me, Teodoro," he said. There was the voice of profound sadness, the voice of a small boy calling out from the midst of a man's body. "You left me at Camp Corregidor."

Three decades before, Ted For Short had hurriedly packed the boy Zeferino into his car, gathered the boy's few things together, then dropped him off at a work camp in the Livermore Valley. It was a little camp called Camp Corregidor that was made up of a single dark rusting Quonset hut that had the words TOJO WE'LL BE BACK proudly emblazoned on a hand-painted sign that could be seen from the main road.

As he backed out of the parking lot thirty years before, a
guilt-ridden Ted For Short had watched dolefully as the boy
walked slowly toward the tin Quonset hut across from the Concannon Winery. Did I abandon him there? wondered Teodoro.
His mother would be coming along soon, he'd told himself. Zefe
had brothers in the camps, brothers who had fathers. They
would take care of him. He had tried to convince himself for
years that he had done the right thing by leaving the boy there.

What kind of life would it have been for him to be circling
eternally in the migrant farmworker circuit, to be hunted by the
police and by the Ditto family? A migrant life on the run. The
thought had always made Teodoro laugh. A fugitive migrant.

A lacy curtain in the hut had moved aside tentatively as
the little boy walked away from the Pontiac, and the face of a
woman who was in the very last months of her youth had peered
out into the headlights of Ted For Short's retreating car. She
had the high cheekbones of a southern woman from Mindinao.
She was a picture bride. Teodoro had seen her black-and-white
photograph in one of the many catalogues that circulated
through the camps.

Which was sadder? Teodoro had wondered at the time.
Which was sadder, the boy whose childhood would never again
embrace a feeling of safety, or the poor woman, chosen by a
lonely *manong* from the pictures in a catalogue filled with the
faces of young, hopeful women?

The application forms in the catalogues always asked the
interested parties to list their first three choices of a potential
mate. Each photograph in the catalogue had a number beneath
it. If there was a match, an applicant would be asked to write a
letter of introduction. Both the woman behind the curtain and
her husband had probably exchanged numbered photos show-
ing themselves ten years younger. Other minds had composed
and other hands had probably written their glowing, poetic
correspondence. Both silently suspected that they were not the
other's first choice.

Finally, one sad and hopeful day, the woman behind the curtain had mailed herself off to the address she had memorized.
Number 37 was betrothed to number 91. Her face posted with
awkwardness, she had climbed nervously into the hold of a ship

for the long sea voyage, the steam whistle on the stacks wailing almost as loudly as her mother, who had been standing on the docks below and screaming her wonted womanly instructions.

"At first, you have to lie down whenever 91 wants you, and you have to smile when 91 undresses you. You have to make believe it's pleasurable. But after the first child comes, take your husband to the priest and make him use the rhythm method. That will cut down your responsibilities!"

At the same moment, thousands of miles away, number 91 had held his head in his hands as he stared at the picture on page 5. He was bringing number 37 to this miserable place. He had weighed the misery against his own loneliness until the two became confused and inseparable. His stomach had grown twisted with both anticipation and guilt. Then he would remind himself that she, herself, had placed the photograph into that catalogue. Nothing but the poverty of the Islands had forced her to do that. In all truth, it was America that she wanted to marry. He had looked around himself at the dreary Quonset hut that was his home. It was America that she would have.

Now number 37 cleaned a solitary Quonset hut and hung hand-sewn curtains to forget that she was marooned with a ship-wrecked stranger. A girl who once loved to dance, now she danced alone until a mirror trapped her image and she caught a glimpse of an imitation waltz. Now she cooked while visions of America were dissected by salesmen, squeezed onto a copper wire, fortified by banks of amplifiers and sent buzzing across empty space to the small black-and-white television in her cell. She'd had the very same view at home in the Philippines.

Now she daydreamed of the Islands as she stuffed lumpia wrappers with meat and corn and bean sprouts, then laid them one-by-one into the hot oil. Each lumpia protested, then sighed as it was eased into the heat. It was as close as she got to romance.

What had she expected when she moved the curtains aside to peer out into the headlights of Ted For Short's departing car? Did some part of her still expect to see the Sulu Sea? Did she pray that her family had frantically crossed oceans to come take her back? Did she expect to see her husband working late in the fields, sweating to support his small mail-order family?

What she did see was a small boy, walking in the parallel

beams of two headlights with a sackful of possessions in his arms. An unknown protector was leaving in his Pontiac. The red glow of a cigarette was all that could be seen of him in the darkened car. Another protector was waiting inside the metal building, not knowing that her cheerless life was about to be granted the boon of companionship. She would feed the boy and make a bed for him in one of the empty cubicles. That night, the boy would name the woman Gum. She would be known as Gum from that day forward. It was one of the few English phrases that she knew. Even her eleven grandchildren would call her Gum.

"You want gum?" she would say as the boy entered the Quonset. She echoed the American G.I.'s famous question as she offered him a choice between Blackjack and Clove.

Teodoro brought a pensive Zeferino back from Camp Corregidor with a question: "Do you remember the game we used to play when you were a boy . . . look into my ear?"

The lawyer smiled now. His sadness was gone. It was clear that he did remember. The midget leaned forward, placing his head on the table. The lawyer bent down and looked into Ted For Short's left ear. A light from within the little man's ear lit up the lawyer's eye as he peered in.

"Push your spirit fingers in there and spread my skull apart. Trephination is a trifle. Can you see the horizon in there, Zeferino? Do you see the huge light that can be everyone's life?"

"I see that you are in love," whispered the lawyer.

"I lost Ruby way back when we were in French Camp. Though I dreamed of her every day, I didn't see her again for almost twenty-five years. When I finally found Ruby again she was already lost beneath waves of men, their expectations, their problems. Like driftwood on the sea, she had bobbed under the keels of men for so long, men hard as teak, hard as manual labor. She had been caught in the toss of any man's net. You see, Ruby had forgotten who she was."

Teodoro's head was still on the table as he spoke. "I'll tell you something else, Zefe." Teodoro shut his eyes as he took a moment to mourn the loss of so many years. "Yes, yes," he hissed through clenched teeth, "that misbegotten boy who was nailed to the cross—Bambino Reyes has been hunting Faustino and me for all these years. He was Pietro Ditto's bastard son."

The prisoner lifted his head from the table. His eyes were swollen with emotion. Then the protector of shipwrecked men dropped his cane to the floor and hobbled unaided around the corner of the interview table. He reached up and pulled down on the shoulder of his lawyer's leather jacket.

"Yes, Zefe," he said, "I left you."

Zeferino turned slowly. He hesitated for a moment, then threw his arms around the little man. Sometimes it occurs that the work of the left hand and the work of the right hand are one and the same: to form an embrace. So it was that an embrace occurred in the jail on the seventh floor of the Hall of Justice, each man thinking to himself that heartbreak is certainly a childhood disease—and always just barely in remission. Ted For Short was crying now, his shoulders and short arms aching from the exertion of embracing a man while attempting with all of his power to hug a boy.

"I couldn't take you with me, Zefe. That would have been selfish and cruel of me. Look at me! Could I take care of a child who was already bigger than me? A man should teach a child how to get by in this crazy world. What on earth could I teach a growing boy?" He picked his cane up from the floor and walked back to his own chair. It was late and walking was a struggle for him.

"I had to lead Simon Ditto's people away from you. Faustino and I knew that all of our chances were better if we split up. And besides"—he wiped his eyes and looked directly into those of his lawyer—"I had gotten my portion in life, and I knew it. Though I have loved Radiant Ruby with all of my heart since the first day I saw her at the Rose Room in Stockton, I was always secretly happy that she had no use for me."

There was pain in his face once more. His eyes and skin bore unhappiness easily; the many muscles of his face were athletes trained in chagrin. Here, in this small demeanor, it was joy that took effort. Pleasure crept across this face in the same way that freed prisoners walk unbelieving from their cells.

"If she loved me . . . if, by some miracle, she could love me, I would be exposed for what I am—a cripple inside and out. Do you remember how it felt in those camps, Zefe? All those rich people driving by in their cars were from the real world and they were living out real lives. We would stand up from our dusty places between the furrows and see them seeing us. We all felt like we were just pretenders. Do you remember, Zefe?"

Zeferino inhaled deeply, then closed his eyes to remember his *tios* and *tiyos* in the prime of their lives, sweating away their days for a slave's wage. The images of his childhood came easily now and the fact pleased him. "Because of you and Faustino and so many others, Teodoro, I could never feel that way, not for a minute, not for an instant. I could never wish to trade places with those people driving by." He reached into one of the pockets of his jacket and said, "I would never trade my newly found memories for someone else's memories of a childhood in the suburbs." Zeferino held out his hand to show Teodoro what he had retrieved. It was a badge made from a Yoo-Hoo bottle cap.

"You kept it! You didn't hate me! Then things did turn out well," sighed Teodoro. Thirty years of guilt were there within that heavy sigh, collected together, then herded out along with a thousand nights of self-condemnation. "Perhaps leaving you that night was the right thing to do?"

Zeferino only smiled.

"I've never been very strong, Zefe. I knew that I was only pretending to belong in the same bed with Ruby. She has always been a woman that tall handsome men coveted. Out there"—he gestured with his head to some multitude of nameless places— "out there, on the run in city after city, I was safe from love even while I fled from Bambino's hateful vengeance. It's funny. I looked for both everywhere I went, and I don't know which caused me more fear, the possibility of her love or the reality of his hatred."

"That's all over now, Teodoro," said Zeferino. "I've seen the wedding photographs and I've read the vows. You had a beautiful ceremony. All of your friends came to the wedding."

"Yes," smiled Ted For Short. It was a smile only if a sublime tenderness could be embodied in a smile, and then only if a tremulous quiver in the breath and the down-turned edges of the mouth could be overlooked. If so, Teodoro smiled.

"Even Faustino came to see you take the plunge," said Zeferino.

Teodoro fell backward as though he had been brutally stabbed by what should have been a joyous statement of fact.

"There's something else, isn't there?" Zeferino asked, suddenly frozen with the realization that Teodoro had not been smiling after all. "Faustino's dead, isn't he?"

Without answering, Ted For Short jumped down from his chair and staggered out into the hallway. The tap-tap of his cane moved quickly away from the open door of the interview room. At the end of the hallway, he rapped on the deputy's window with his cane and cried out, "Post eight! Post eight!"

The deputy at post 8 frisked the little man, discarded a dozen contraband cigarettes and a candy bar, then escorted him beyond the iron bars and into the darkness of the main line. The suspect's lawyer had moved out of the interview room and was standing in the center of the long hall.

"Bambino Reyes finally found Faustino, didn't he?" called out Zeferino. "He found him here in San Francisco. Something brought you here—something brought all of you here."

Teodoro stopped with the deputy at a bay of bunks designated as the security cells. As the heavy cell door slid open, Ted For Short turned to watch as his lawyer signed out at the front desk, then left for the jail elevator. As he stepped into the blackness of the bay, beds that had been dark and dormant began to stir and faces that had been hidden to the guards all turned to see him as he hobbled to his bunk. Chilled hearts suddenly began to warm. There were whispers and rustling sounds in the dark as prisoner alerted prisoner.

"He's here," said someone who was waiting to go to trial to someone who was yet to be arraigned. "It's Ted For Short, he's back," said someone who deserved his long sentence to someone else who did not. "Is there going to be a show tonight, Ted?" It was the voice of a young man who would soon be sent to Pelican Bay, the maximum security prison up near the Oregon border. "Ted?" the young man said once more. The voice, emanating from a young life that was already over, sounded remarkably alive and hopeful.

"No late show tonight, fellas," said Ted For Short as the cell door slammed shut behind him. "The boys in the band want more money and my lovely assistant has called in sick." His voice sounded weary, distant, and wounded. One thing that all of the prisoners shared and respected was a man's privacy after a visit from his lawyer. Though each man was clearly disappointed that there would be no floor show tonight, no one would press the issue.

"I can't sing without my band behind me and my lovely assistant has gone home with all of my magical paraphernalia."

In the dark, heads turned away once more and blankets were pulled over eyes. Knees were pulled up to chests, fingers clasped the corners of blankets, and mouths moved to unfathomable rhythms. In the dark, grown men surrendered to sleep in postures learned in earliest infancy. Only the protector of shipwrecked men was awake and uncovered on his bunk. The tears had returned to his eyes and a newly baked loaf of bread was cooling on the pillow next to his ear.

Teodoro stared upward toward the ceiling of his lightless bay, his mind's eye burning with the brightness of his youth. In the blackness of the cell, the bunks around him had been transformed into the psychic doctor's office in Baguio, where his parents had taken him for a second and final visit. The doctor was a big man who had collected angels. There were exaltations of toy angels above Teodoro's head, bright Fiorentinos and Berninis swinging on lengths of string that were tied to the bamboo beams that held up a thatched ceiling.

Teodoro the child lay naked on a table that was covered with white paper. He looked to the left of the table, where a full-length mirror stood taunting his obvious deformities. He had quickly turned his gaze away from his reflection and to the doorway, where he saw a mirror of another kind.

A strange-looking boy had come into the room and was walking toward the operating table. Teodoro had never seen a face like the one that smiled at him in that moment so long ago. He had the large eyes of a hill tribesman and the smooth skin of a city dweller. Little Teodoro smiled as the boy first extended his hand, then told him his name.

"Hello, I am Faustino. My family brought me up here to Baguio because they think I am a *bakla*."

There was a tension in the boy's voice. Years later Ted For Short would realize that his friend's voice had always been balanced on the brink of verse.

"Are you *bakla*?" Teodoro had asked without really knowing

what the word meant. "I don't know if I am or if I am not," Faustino had smiled, "but my father seems to know and it makes him very angry."

Faustino had pretended to examine Teodoro's body for a moment, then asked, "What is it that your father fears?"

"He is afraid of everyone's opinion. Look at me." Teodoro had stood up and turned slowly in a full circle. He looked like a small brown question mark pivoting on its period. "I'm not growing. I don't know what I'm going to do."

"I know what I'm going to do," Faustino had answered. "I'm going to run away from home. I'm going to Manila to find work. Maybe I will go to America. Perhaps we can go together."

While their parents were negotiating with the psychic doctor over their respective medical bills, Teodoro and Faustino struck a gleeful bargain, then began pulling wooden and plastic angels down from the ceiling. The sound of their laughter went unheard by their parents, who were now involved in bouts of heated haggling with the surgeon. With tiny Teodoro on his shoulders, a jubilant Faustino danced from one end of the operating room to the other as his new friend liberated first Michael, then Gabriel, then over a dozen others, clutching them all to his breast. The two of them ran from that hospital room and out into the open air.

As he lay in his cell, Teodoro was overwhelmed by the feeling that something momentous had happened in that room so long ago; some inexplicable thing had transpired to change both of their destinies.

He could never have known that the gaze of world-spanning eyes had settled upon their faint and meager lives. Two boys who had been invisible to heaven were suddenly noticed in the very instant that they had succeeded in pulling it down—piece by piece—by snapping the dusty twine knots overhead. Somehow vast heaven had taken notice of their simple signal: there were imperfect, mortal boys down below tossing their despair toward the sun; there were human pups trailing a long banner of strings; there were drab brown boys below, clutching angelic spines and wholly festooned with hope.

IX

May 9, 1993

JUST days before his own death, he stood alone on the sidewalk and far from the misty shores of paradise. This man treaded where others walked and grappled with oratory when others only spoke words. He leeched cold air through his teeth when those around him merely breathed. He ciphered with delusions when others simply fooled themselves with wishes and frail human hopes. He saw sorcery when other men saw twilight. Where others went, Bambino Reyes trespassed.

He waited impatiently on the wet sidewalk, where chilled fog and foul, hot exhaust fumes mixed below his knees to turn the lowest air into a rolling, pale blue wraith. With darkened eyes, he looked around himself and realized cynically that the colors of his life had gone inexorably from the tincture and pigment of a glorious, brightly hued fresco to this deadening, wet tapestry of cinder-block grays and asphalt blacks, punctuated intermittently by the monotonous, infernal glare of stoplights. From St. Augustine to Thomas Hobbes in one lifetime, he thought.

The bus he had been waiting for pulled up and the door opened. The inside and the outside surfaces of the long articulated bus were covered with unintelligible scrawl in various languages and scripts. Exhaling compressed air, the kneeling bus genuflected obediently at the littered curbside. A bored driver rolled a wooden match from one side of his mouth to the other, while ignoring greetings and complaints alike. There was illicit cigarette smoke curling inside the bus; twenty people avoiding eye contact; the rude sound of a portable radio and the pungent smell of a woman who has recently eaten fish.

On the sidewalk behind him, he watched a small huddle of old people hugging each other. The sight of them mindlessly delaying the departure of the bus angered him, so he stared threateningly at them. Moving closer to them, he inspected their rituals with growing disdain. There were light brushes to the cheek, cloying touches that stayed too long, handshakes that sent probing fingers to seek out the failing features of the other's loosened knuckles. There were ardorless hugs followed by loud platonic kisses. The man who watched them with obvious abhorrence could already see the undertaker's glue in their eyes and the stitches set into their inner lips.

Two college students who had crowded in behind him to board the bus stepped back and stared at the strange and unsightly man. He was at least as old as the people he had been leering at. He was neither tall nor short in stature. His hair was black despite his age, and his face, though remarkably youthful, seemed nonetheless moribund and spoiling. His left eye was as lifeless as a moonscape and the flesh of his chest that was visible beneath his coat was like frozen waves of tallow. Long, long ago, he had been badly burned. Anyone with the power to see him clearly saw a hard life of harm and rags, a life outside of living. No harmonies came from this throat; his breath of life was counterpoint and gloom.

Bambino stepped toward the bus without realizing that a way was made for him wherever he went. He had stopped noticing it years ago. Some young, laughing children pushed past him to grab a seat in the bus before the old people could sit down.

He climbed onto the steps of the bus, using the sticky handrail on the door as an aid. He was slow now, maddeningly slow to the shoving, shuffling people behind him. His bus transfer was torn and wrinkled and had to be checked by an exasperated driver, who reached for it impatiently. The old man held it out to him between his index and second finger; the thumb of his right hand was missing, the edge of his palm was flat from his wrist to the tip of his yellowed index finger.

"I am here to bring clarity to your dreary world," he said to the bored bus driver. "I bring no light . . . no light at all, but I offer the kind of definition that only sharp shadows can bring. What is it that the prophet Ezekiel said? 'By the multitude of thy merchandise, they have filled the midst of thee with violence.' "

Waved back callously by the driver, he stood upright in the rear of the bus when he could easily have seated himself and relaxed under his large coat. Instead, he stood, intently watching the streets. Oblivious to the loud, raucous group of teenagers behind him, he stared through the stained, glass windows of the municipal bus.

"Hell is paved with faces," he muttered aloud.

A collector of faces, he was searching for certain features, peering into the crowds and into store windows, probing at the moving shapes of every small child for the unique, unforgettable face of a grown man. Once, as a boy, he had sought out that same face in a seething, passionate throng. Since that time so long ago, finding that face and the faces of two men he had never seen had become his life's work. He had always known that finding one meant finding the others.

As a child, he had once pretended perfection, and his motives for seeking that face had been just as imperfect then as they were now. Just days ago, in a stunning, blinding instant of disbelief, he had finally seen the face that he had sought out for so many years. There it was, peering out so innocently from an open doorway . . . that bantam face that he had once hated as a child, and now hated as a man.

"To be perceived is to exist. *Esse est percipi*," he whispered now as he relived that rare and delicious moment. He understood that his whisper was a blasphemy. As he repeated the phrase again, his taste buds flooded with venom.

"I see you."

Many years and many thousands of miles had passed between sightings of that face. Decades had passed and the search that had begun with such fury had gradually receded from the uppermost thought in his mind to somewhere in the shallowest subconscious; a reason for living had become life itself, as involuntary as breathing. It had gone from fits of heated frenzy and frigid bile to a mechanical, strategic darting of the eyes on back streets in Seattle, Portland, and Bakersfield.

To find the face, he had even stooped to become a lowly farm-worker. He had transformed himself into one of them, one of the Mexican braceros or the Filipino *manong*. He had become one of the brotherhood of sojourners that traverse the face of America.

"What does man gain by all the toil at which he toils under the sun?" The man who quoted Ecclesiastes had become invisible, languishing in countless, nameless, distressed hotels that were plumbed by corroded pipes and connected to the world of light by filthy windowpanes. He had lived in the Quonset hut camps and in the hovels that all of the labor contracts euphemistically called "accommodations."

He had even stayed in Manilatown at the once famous and now forgotten International Hotel at 848 Kearny Street. He had been there in 1977, masquerading concern and camaraderie as the old farmworkers were finally, forcibly driven out of their retirement home and into the cold streets of San Francisco. When the bullhorns were blaring outside and the sheriff's department was preparing to storm the building, he had huddled with the *manong* in the broken toilets and lightless hallways and over small, heatless hot plates as they devised a doomed strategy to keep their poor homes in the face of the powerful Four Seas Corporation.

He had been there, an imposter looking into all of their faces, poring surreptitiously over their mail and inquiring innocently about possible mutual acquaintances. He had slipped silently through a rear window just as the sledgehammers had begun to fall and minutes before all the old men were dragged into the street, their torn suitcases and pockets leaking letters and photographs with each resisting step.

To locate his prey, he had even established membership within the exclusive, secret order of ancient Pinoy and bracero hermits. It was not a purposeful secret, nor was it a true society. It was exclusive only because it was excluded. None of the old fieldworkers wished to become secular monks, not the Hindus or the Guatemalans or the Hondurans. They were just men who were tied together by their age, by their distance from their homelands and from the society around them.

"Bambino the Hermit."

The words burst from his lips along with drops of offending spittle.

"Did you know that my name is Bambino the Hermit?" he asked a pair of women who were sitting in the seats nearest him. The two women had done their best to ignore the strange man, but they finally gave up and left the bus for the privacy and safety of a taxi.

Like the other Pinoys and braceros, it was said that he had taken jobs away from the whites. Bending, cutting, stacking jobs in the burning sun that white people were just lined up to take. He laughed at the ridiculous thought. Once in a while a busload of whites would be brought out to the fields by the Unemployment Office. There they'd be when the bus drove off, wearing sunglasses, tennis shoes, and pressed slacks; young, unskilled gringos perched at the farthest edge of their consumer world. By the end of the day, only a few of them would be left. "Nigger work," they'd shout as they walked away and toward town. "Monkey work." None of them had ever returned for a second day in the fields.

"Animal work," he said out loud to no one in particular on the Geary Boulevard bus. America's unskilled white workers were always too overqualified for fieldwork and restaurant work. They wanted the skilled labor positions and the middle management positions that corporations were quietly exporting to Malaysia and Korea. Bambino laughed. When times get hard, no one will say a thing about the corporations; no one will dare utter the word *loyalty*.

"They'll turn on the immigrants," he smirked. There was a smug look on his face. He had done demeaning work out of choice. He was not like the other Pinoys who had come here before the war and just after. He had left the Philippines for a formal education and not for a life of anonymous stoop labor. And he was certainly not like those stupid Mexican fieldworkers who seemed to sing their way through everything, no matter how miserable. He shook his head. No one in the world sings about their country more than the Mexicans. They had a song for every state, district, and pathetic little village in their country. He hated Mexicans. For that matter, he hated Pinoys.

In time, his strange life's vocation of peering into faces, of sorting out hairlines and winnowing through facial characteristics, had led to a rather distressing habit. Distressing to others, not to himself. Without being aware of it, the old man had developed the practice of blurting out embarrassing descriptions when his practiced eye came to rest on a face or a head.

"Rhinoplasty!" he would scream out, unconsciously, upon seeing a young woman whose nose had the telltale, studied marks of architectural perfection.

"A hair weave and just a touch of scalp spray. I was almost convinced." He would raise his arm to point out an obviously embarrassed man who quickly exited the bus.

"A divot! Now that's a real divot! Vanity, saith the preacher. All is vanity."

Bambino had come to love his game of superficialities. He had always assumed that the men he hunted would attempt to disguise themselves in some way. Besides, it helped to break up the monotony of his endless search. There were no real rules of wig spotting, just a knack of seeing a change of texture, of watching light as it glints off a previously invisible border between patches of hair whose follicles of origin were on separate heads.

Wigs meant nothing to the daughters of Eve and Lilith, to womankind. Falls and pastiches have no psychological import among females. Every Woolworth's in America had extensive wig displays for women. Flips and bouffants of every color always lined the staircases between floors. But a wig on the skull of a man was quite another thing altogether. A man's wig is fitted in secret. For a man, a wig is a prosthetic device, a profundity, a restoration to wholeness.

A wig is more a window to a man's soul than even his eyes. Men can lie with their eyes; they can lie with their briefcases and with their statistics and calculations. But a wig is a sign that a man has come past the center of his life and when forced into a face-off with his own mortality, the man has blinked and backed down.

"Vanity. All is vanity!"

More and more people in the bus were staring at the odd man in the long coat. There was something very frightening in his aspect and in his heated, horrid monologues.

Only one man had ever punched him for spotting a toupee, for his fluency in the language of wigs. Bambino had always been protected by the same vanity that he assailed. Most men only wanted to exit the bus, their dignity and their personal fiction somewhat intact.

Bambino's absolute favorites were the bad wigs, those horrible bargain-basement perukes. He loved the wigs that sat on skulls like flashing neon announcements: I am a rug, I am a monument to skewed self-awareness. These were beautiful, polyester, nylon-backed, carpet-taped abominations. They were portable black holes that sucked in stares, stilled crowded elevators, and hushed noisy rooms. When he saw these ... out of deepest respect, Bambino said nothing aloud.

Finally, after he had inspected an endless multitude of hairlines and profiles, the miraculous had happened. After years of clumsy eavesdropping, years of following every rumor, every tip along the migratory labor circuit, he had seen one of the faces.

"I believe I saw him singing with a Korean band up at Fort Lewis, Washington," an old, gray Sikh from Yolo County had told Bambino. "He was telling jokes and singing standards at a USO club just off base. He had a small band and three back-up singers. I think there was even a dog act."

"I saw him when I was picking tobacco up in Canada," a Korean worker had said as he labored cutting squash in the next furrow. "He is a great magician. He did this trick with three glass balls that floated in the middle of the air; then he made a cocker spaniel disappear right in front of me. It was a damn good show."

"He was in Brawley last year," a blond prostitute recalled. "Then I saw him singing at a small club near the Salton Sea. Yes, I remember ... it was at a little Mexican bar called El Jorobado. He told the raunchiest jokes I'd ever heard, and believe me, I've heard them all. It was one hell of a show. I'd pay to see it again. Do you know where he's playing?"

The trail had even gone down into Texas. Someone had seen his prey working for a small Mexican circus that toured the Southwest and the Gulf states. But there were three Mexican circuses in the Southwest and no one who worked under the canvas tent would speak to Bambino. Their code of silence was as strong as that of the Mexican and Pinoy campesinos. Miraculously, after years of wig-watching in the wilderness, he had finally glimpsed the bantam face from this very bus while standing in this same spot across from the rear exit. He had glanced at him in that speeding instant when that hated face turned from peering into a donut shop to face the street. Bambino would never have seen him, but his attention had been seized by a man whose tonsure was covered by something resembling a sisal doormat. Just beyond the doormat, that hated face and that twisted body—aged by half a century—had resolved into focus.

With all his effort he had reached to grab the pullstop, but couldn't. It had been rush hour and the bus was jammed with anxious people and the bags and briefcases they carried. His way had been blocked by the armpits of tired workers who were in no mood to be shoved, in no temper to be pulled out of the weary, close-quartered anonymity that they expected when they paid for their tickets. Shoving his way forward, he had almost reached the cord, but he had finally been obstructed by a man with a half-crown implant of young hair, the rows of seedlings obvious to the old man's trained eye.

"Cabiri!" he had screamed in angry desperation as the face he had sought for so long disappeared into the white smoke far behind the bus.

"Cabiri . . ."

Since that momentous day he had ridden the same bus, every day, on every rotation that it made through the city, through matins and vespers. A frayed bus schedule had become his liturgy; the death of this man, his renewed vow of unremitting industry.

He stared out more carefully now, hoping for just one more glance at that face. He had come to know all the bus drivers on the Richmond line. He knew which ones were drinkers and which ones stopped at clubs on Geary and Fillmore and went inside for something stronger . . . their buses idling outside while the driver's heart was racing with cocaine.

He knew that the morning driver kept a girlfriend on Divisadero Street who would bring him a bag of fried chicken at noon. There she'd be, faithfully waiting at the bus stop in her housecoat and slippers. The brown bag that she held would be translucent with grease. The driver also had a pregnant wife in Oakland. Once when the wife rode along with her nervous husband, he drove past the Divisadero stop without even slowing down. There had been a dozen people waiting there for a ride.

"You passed your girlfriend," Bambino had said aloud while watching for the expression on the face of the driver's wife.

Every day, the same little black girl lay down on the large seat at the back of the bus and let the boys touch her under her skirt in exchange for money or drugs. She had seen every frieze, architrave, and cornice of this city with her panties down at her ankles. Just yesterday he had seen her drinking a root beer while a freshman boy was staring intently between her legs and probing her rudely with his unkempt finger.

Bambino knew what the kids were doing in the back of the bus, and he knew that most of the drivers were afraid to do anything about it. They looked the other way when children compared Colts to Walthers and bragged of drive-by shootings. He had seen sexual activities, drug use, and hundreds of handguns on the Geary bus alone.

The girl was in her usual spot again, today. When she got on the bus, Bambino had given her another glance of sanctimonious condemnation. He, himself, had seen the same posture of righteous disapproval so often that he had tried to imitate it. But the girl had seen right through the rebuke. Or had she? Was it a look of abhorrence that she saw growing upon the old man's rancor like a small malignant bud, or was it the recognition and the complicity of an accomplice that she saw there?

The disgust in her dark eyes seemed to mate with his own, calling upon him to drop the perfidious facade of piety and to hate in return, a deep, full measure of judgmental hate in return.

There was compliance. The man without a thumb heard the word *slut* leap from his deepest throat. It had squeezed out from behind the ancient posture, then popped from between his lips, lips that surely did not deserve to utter such an indictment. He sang the loathsome office once again.

"Slattern."

And the reclining girl smiled back at the victory; the turf was familiar after all. The sign and the countersign had been given. The strange, frightening old man without a thumb and with forearms covered with tattoos was no different from all the men and boys who gave her drugs in exchange for the menial right to ravage her privacy.

For a moment, the child, teasing ribonucleic acids to a soft boil, had been caught unawares in a remote recess of her own soul, a place in her heart that she would never again revisit. Without knowing it, for an instant, she had looked into the old man's eye and hoped for something different. Not pity, but perhaps understanding. But the moment had passed.

"You want some of this, asshole?" the girl sneered, coming back to herself and nodding angrily toward her own crotch.

"Probably how you lost your thumb!"

She was an apprentice prostitute. These circuits of Geary Boulevard were training runs for an old impulse in a new body. No hero, no friend, would ever come along in all the nights of her splayed and spreading life to heal her and cast out her demons.

Even the nice people on the bus were not nice. The old man smiled at the thought. *Nice* implies some affirmative, positive act. There was never, ever any such thing. Never, on six loops of the city and on seven days of the week. People who rode the bus wanted what the owners of automobiles wanted: a steel cocoon whose shape, age, and color defines the driver in society yet insulates him from it.

Bambino never saw the *manong* on the bus. They never rode on the bus. You had to walk to see them, and you had to look very carefully. They huddled together in parks and small hotels. People walked around them and through them like the old men were ghosts. Children stepped in front of them in theater lines, and cabbies never saw the *manong*'s hail. One of the men he was seeking now was unusual, the smallest big brother. Bambino Reyes would soon exact the fullest measure of vengeance from that man, and the impending feel of it made his skin flush with heat.

The tattooed old man with the missing thumb was completely blind in the left eye and suffered from a case of self-induced epilepsy that he himself had eventually come to believe in, so much so that, years ago, he began to take medication for the ailment. He fancied his infrequent seizures to be grand mal and nothing less.

This man who had labored in slaughterhouses in Phoenix and Seattle, and had long ago deluded himself into believing he could be a priest, had chosen murder as his true life's vow, his sacred obligation. After years in the church he had renounced his vows to embrace *sandugo*, vendetta.

"I've given enough to God," he would shout out to no one and everyone, "only to find myself so utterly forsaken. Listen to the paltry heartbeat that I was given," he would rave to faceless passengers. "Bitter pulse, bitter pulse."

He had not simply left the church; he had discarded it, abandoned it in every way possible. He had once believed that he loved the church above all things. But that belief had been replaced by a certainty. Now he was possessed of a black, stygian hatred that was so much more profound than his supposed love had ever been.

A man who has slaughtered animals has shown himself to be too cruel to honor the flesh of the Son. So Bambino Reyes had gloried in cruelty, working overtime at countless slaughterhouses up and down the coast, volunteering for double-time on the killing floor. The thing in him that once saw the innocent, bounding calf had been cut away and discarded. After numberless, endless killings, he saw only veal.

No one who suffers nervous fits can become a priest. A palsy in the hand or a sudden bout of epilepsy and the precious vial of transformed wine will fall. The Eucharist would be ruined. So Bambino had prayed for sudden seizures, cultivated the tremor and the dumb, fallen, tongue-biting stare.

No priest can deface with ink the body that is the sacred gift of God, and a thumb is needed to firmly grasp the frail wafer. As soon as the green tattoos had healed he had severed his own canonical thumb. The bloody digit had been unceremoniously dropped into a pocket of his coat on a drunken, rainy night in Seattle. There would be no turning back for Bambino Reyes.

His was a dismal, desperate mission that began so many years ago, so many worlds ago, in a small, unmapped village to the north of Manila, in the Easter season. The memory of it had the scent of ash, the scent of a mildewed leather trunk thrown open after years of neglect. The memory had the flash of fire colors, red and gold adorned in fretwork and filigree, flourishes and inlay, hand-tooling and brocade. It had the clanging sound of *kulintang*, of brass gongs; of wailing and joy, of faceless spectators lost in descant; village lives embellished by precious ritual and the warm promise of God-given furtherance.

The old man on the bus winced at the sudden, sharp pain in his wrists and in the soft flesh above his ankles. A young woman looking back angrily at the bus stop that she had just missed saw the eyes roll back into the head of the strange, demented old man in a long coat. When she looked closely at the inside lining of his long mantle, she saw the black handle and part of the bright blade of a sharpened machete. She grabbed the pullstop and tugged violently, then disappeared out of the rear door.

As a child, Bambino had been given the greatest honor a boy from his province can be given. He, out of hundreds of children in far-flung villages, had been chosen to play the Christ at the provincial reenactment of the crucifixion. Even more importantly, he had been chosen over pure-blooded Pinoy boys in his own village, children who had been altar boys far longer than he.

But, above all, he had been chosen over the sideshow freak Teodoro Cabiri, the man he had hunted from French Camp to Chicago and across Texas; from Placerville to Seattle and down to Brawley. Teodoro Cabiri, the face he had seen for a fleeting instant from this very bus. Teodoro Cabiri, friend and accomplice of the abomination Faustino. The two men who, with the help of a boy, had murdered Bambino's dear father in cold blood . . . so very long ago.

"Oh, Father, please punctuate this endless sentence, this vagabond sensibility that so wildly drifts between blunted stupor and astounding clarity."

Bambino Reyes began to repeat aloud the words he had once allegedly uttered from astride the wooden cross at the provincial reenactment of the Passion. As he raved, frightened people on the bus began to move away from him and toward the front or rear entrance. A young woman fearfully took a firmer grip on the handrail above her head. A balding man from the Pacific Stock Exchange imagined himself defending her should the crazy man do something untoward. In anticipation of possible heroic action, he removed his Montblanc from his breast pocket and placed it gingerly in his briefcase.

The village long ago had been stunned by the very same words, or so Bambino seemed to recall. The true words were gone now, their former shape lost in time, and the new words that he had chosen to replace them with had been polished smooth by a torrent of considerations and reconsiderations.

"The vision from this splintered rampart, the turbulence and tumult of symbol centered here in me, is more than I wish to bear."

The bus driver looked into his huge security mirror, then turned on the public address system.

"It's okay, folks, he does this every day."

Bambino ignored the taunts from below, the jeers and scowls of Roman soldiers dressed in Italian suits and carrying briefcases.

"This lamentation, this tangle of man's misdeeds, probes at the fulcrum where I am pinned." The old man spread his arms. "Here, where all of history—present, past, and future—pierces and penetrates me."

His adult mind was once again lost in the counterfeit memories of childhood, and it swooned from a torture both centuries and seconds old. He no longer knew which parts of his recollections were true, which were the sour ramblings of a misanthrope, and which were gleaned from scripture. He no longer cared. His sightless eye, on Geary Boulevard, stared down from the high intersection in the air, from his Golgotha of banyan and bamboo, to steal a furtive look at his tormentors and his lovers. There was a fury at his wrists where senseless metal entered, and a warm radiance at his fingertips.

"I, Bambino Reyes, was closer than centuries of emulators have ever been. As a mere child, I leapt to the forefront in that instant, passing paltry flagellants and maundering hermits and vain televangelists. I leapt beyond the bloody-kneed processions of penitents, the voiceless nuns tasting the floors of their empty cells. I went beyond repayment for His pain. I, Bambino Reyes, was His pain.

"Religion runs in my family, you see. My little village in the Philippines was the spiritual center for the famous Contracodgers. They were zealots who believed that the child Christ was more perfect than the adult. After all, who could tempt the child? Certainly not Satan, and not Mary's dark sister, Magdalene. It was His adult life that led to those rumors about an affair with the prostitute. It was a revelation that the Contracodgers understood to mean that age is, by definition, evil.

"So they mapped out antisenescent strategies and they attacked convalescent homes, tipping old people out of wheelchairs and pulling out saline drips. They spiked mounds of lime Jell-O with salt and callously ripped up quilted tea cozies. They smashed false teeth and brushed contact cement onto bedpans.

They raided and harassed all of the aged people of Luzon as cor-
ruptions of the original, youthful ideal.

"My mother's brothers belonged to the cult. Their first general, a toddler, was soon displaced by an infant who was born on
the same street that I was. It was a strange army. You were de-
moted in rank the older you got."

Bambino was silent for a moment that frightened those passengers that were unfortunate enough to stand or sit too close to
him. Even as the bus driver looked at the crazy old man through
his rearview mirror, the blood-crested child in Bambino's embellished memory was being carried high above the entire procession by the most important men of the village . . . including
his alcoholic uncle Emeterio, who was then a rank private in the
Contracodger army.

His mother, the sensual ruin down below, was said to have
cried out at the eternal scene. "Abiding, merciless wound!" she
was said to have sobbed, surprising even herself at how well she
remembered her lines.

"See it smoldering in this pulsing pyre of half-spirited flesh.
How the fruit of my womb is now so sadly tasseled with precious,
crimson fluids. Behold his viscous tears, all lost in the soil and
smoking sleet of God's sublime intentions."

Looking down from above, Bambino had seen that his
mother had written her lines on the back of her hands, and that
her falling tears had completely blurred the last two lines. His
mother had a confused yet satisfied look on her face. She had
joyfully forgotten her lines. There she was, enveloped in linen
and the dolorous aura of vinegar, her sexually transmitted dis-
eases and uncountable sins being washed away with each unut-
tered word.

"Such reserve!" the villagers would whisper to one another.
"Such restraint and marvelous understatement."

She had set an impossible mark that day for all future Virgin
Mary's. A perfect ten had appeared on all the judges' cards and
bonus points for congeniality were awarded.

"Did she die in Ephesus?" wondered Bambino aloud as the
bus accelerated down Geary. "Was she carried to Constantinople
to die basked in votive light, her womb smooth as God's skull?"

As he waned on his cross so long ago, and in a moment of

genius, the boy had suddenly mouthed words from an unknowable source: "Mother, the grave is a cold breast." He had been instructed to say the words: "Behold thy son."

His mother, and his grandmother the village grimalkin, and
all of his aunts had fainted dead away at this last sentence. The
phrase had not been written into the script. It had been a true,
extemporaneous miracle, or so Bambino recalled. On the route
to the small chapel, Bambino's entire extended family lay prostrate, pressed down by the sheer, unrehearsed holiness of it all.

His imagined utterances aside, the child Bambino Reyes was
actually nailed to his cross. He wasn't just tied up there with sisal
twine the way all the other boys had been in the past; they'd used
real nails on him. Galvanized, of course, but real nails. Sixteen-
penny spikes from the Manila Sears and Roebuck. While common box nails had been used at the village Passion, the villagers
were sparing no expense at the grand procession.

The local carpenter carried them from his shop and handed
them solemnly to Bambino's youngest uncle. His uncle's name
was José and he was considered the village simpleton. He was
dressed as a centurion guard, complete with a Roman helmet
fashioned from an inverted water bucket with a wide paintbrush
protruding at the top. The handle of the brush was pushed into a
hole that had been poked into the bottom of the bucket. The entire village had released an audible gasp, then held its collective
breath while the heartless hammer fell again and again. Tiyo José,
being severely cross-eyed, had missed the nails twice, hitting his
own thumb both times. An enduring tradition has since grown up
around this act of incompetence, the Black Thumb of Christ.

Marvelous things were promised to the little village with each
blow to the nail's head and to José's thumb. After all, lesser crucifixions in the past had brought great bounty. The entire village
could cash in. The fish would surely be fat and plentiful. The co-
pra would grow without cultivation. The Lord Jesus would look
with favor on the village and travel on its behalf to Bathala, the
sustainer of mankind, and petition him to keep Sitan, the great
evildoer, from the doors of the villagers.

There would be new wealth for all, maybe even a post office
or a septic tank. All prayers would quickly be answered. Reve-
lación Bautista would hit the provincial lottery. Incarnación

Begonia might lose her unsightly facial warts. Adoración Umali, a grown woman, might stop peeing in her bed. And perhaps the greatest boon of all: Bambino's mother, the sensual ruin, would finally test negative for gonorrhea.

There would be no barren mothers that year. No one would die of tertiary syphilis and children who had been lost to the big city would return, their drug habits gone, their sexual preferences all straightened out. But most important of all, Bambino's mother would be spared the tortures of Kasanaan, the fires of hell. Bambino's pious and posing mother had swooned as metal tied living tissue to wood, then fainted theatrically at the very sight of the fleshy drape. Other women from the village had rushed to her side to console her and to take their solemn places in the forming fresco of posturing, kneeling figures.

"It was foolishness," he said aloud to a new crowd of frightened people as the bus began another circuit of its route.

"What was done to me was insidious, hateful! Our hopes were built up so high."

Concepción Reyes had been treated for six kinds of syphilis and yet there she had been, playing the weeping Madonna to the very hilt. And that idiot, bastard fruit of her loins, Bambino, didn't even have a real name. His father had been an Italian merchant marine and disappeared out to sea when the boy was still suckling. Concepción had given birth to six more kids after that, all from different fathers. The only word that Concepción could remember from her spicy Italian episode was the name Bambino. It was not even her son's true name. Before he left, his father had called the child his little bambino.

"Bambino Reyes," he said his own name aloud. He had taken his mother's family name. Even as he spoke them, the sound of the words from his own mouth did not reach his ears. His Christian name was rumored to have been Pedro, Peter, but his mother would not verify it and he had always refused to use it. Bambino speculated that he had never been given a Christian name. He could not imagine his mother in a church, even for a baptism. She would have given him a name as a drunken afterthought or she would have renamed him to please a new man.

Years later, as if by providence, he had been given the name Brother Peter. But he had only tolerated that name while he was languishing in the monkhouse. Since that time of horrid self-deception, he had insisted upon Bambino . . . a name that was no name at all.

"Yes, I climbed that damned cross," he began to scream again and the bus driver considered pulling over.

"Sir, you're going to have to take a seat," he yelled over the intercom.

All those passengers who were seated on the bus quickly placed their coats or packages on the seat next to them to keep the madman from sitting there.

"I am a damned fool," he said, looking about himself and thoroughly confused now. He was no longer able to draw a clear line between reality and his memories. The people around him were coming and going. Bambino could not tell if they were passengers or a formal procession. Most of them ignored him and left him to his incomprehensible ramblings.

There was an ancient custom in the Islands, a custom that only the most warlike tribes followed. When a warrior or chieftain died, some tribes were known to have tied one of the dead man's slaves to the body of the deceased. A living slave was strapped beneath the body of a dead man to bear his weight, a breathing cushion to soften his voyage to the underworld. That poor slave was left that way, dying under dead weight and buried alive beneath his master.

"That is the true image of the Philippines, strapped beneath the Spanish, beneath the Americans, and even more . . . strapped, struggling and suffocating, below the church. No wonder I can't breathe. I was buried up there in the air, suffocated by the view from atop the skull."

The old man in the bus realized that he had been holding his breath as he thought again the same intolerable thoughts. He had been suffocating himself. He exhaled deeply, then began breathing once more, his lungs filling with air, then expelling it violently. People in the bus who had relaxed a bit moved away again as drafts of his foul breath reached them.

When the hard Centurions had hoisted Bambino up at last, the blood from his palms had run down his forearms and his naked neck had hung limp and flaccid. He was as magnificent as the child Teodoro Teofilo Cabiri, straddling his own poor cross at the village competition, must have been miserable.

Bambino, on the bus, smiled unknowingly at the thought. The collision of universes requires stark contrasts, blood splashes loud as thunder. His *mestizo* skin had once been so white, like no one else's in the village. The blood and the white skin were so perfect, so much like all the pictures of the Christ that he'd seen as a child. The very sight of it made all the boys in the village parade who aspired to be the Christ so completely hateful and so humiliated. Especially Teodoro Teofilo Cabiri.

On the day of the provincial procession, the entire village had rejoiced at the wondrous sight of the solemn parade as the ancient killing was being relived. There were fires everywhere along the route where the long vigil would be passed as night fell. One of the largest fires was built at a turn near the edge of town where the procession would have to carefully negotiate a set of steps that led down to the chapel.

The terrible thing happened at this turn. One of the two cross-bearers in the very front stumbled as they negotiated the tight turn. The cross teetered above the fire as the men in back struggled against the sudden shift in leverage. Bambino's eyes rolled forward and when he saw what was happening, he began to struggle against the nails in his hands and feet. It was instantaneously clear to everyone that the boy was headed into the flames.

"Father, Father," he'd screamed as he fell into the blazing fire. It had been another stroke of genius. It had been an accident, but an accident that would forever seal his fate. Simply by uttering those words, the smoking, scalded boy would win a trip to faraway California to study in a seminary. By uttering those words he would secure an honored place in the enduring lore of the village. He had unwittingly become a conduit for the very thoughts of Christ, burst forth in extremis.

The man on the bus could feel the scars on his chest and side where the searing embers had set a crazed seal. A stigmata, the villagers had called it. It was not punished flesh or the deep etchings of pitiless phosphors and slag, but a sign, the exalted kin of words.

"He was calling for a philandering Italian sailor!" the old man on the bus laughed aloud. "The villagers thought he . . . I was calling out for God, but he was really calling out for an

Italian womanizer who had sailed off to sea!" he screamed into the cold air that rushed in when the rear exit opened and
people hurriedly filed out, ". . . and the pain was indescribable."

He lowered his voice. The rear of the bus was empty now and
he was standing alone.

"No one felt for me. They felt for someone else. They didn't
treat my wound because they didn't want to erase a sign from
God. No one cared for me, they cared only for the symbol, the
drama, and prayed to some director on high, some omniscient
prompter in the wings.

"And then that cripple Teodoro came over to me as I suffered on the cross. I remember that he told me he was sorry that
it had happened, but I know he lied. I saw the joy in his eyes. I
despised him even then. You see, I was given a great gift when I
fell. I was vulcanized, hardened, given the power to see liars
everywhere I go."

He reached for his lips and pulled out a cigarette burned to
the nub hours ago. He hadn't felt the pain. There was no smoking allowed on the bus but no one ever dared say a thing to this
man who spoke to himself.

"He wasn't calling out to the heavens," he laughed aloud.
"The boy was swearing an oath to find his father, to find the merchant seaman who had called him his Bambino."

He was laughing now, still searching the sidewalks with his
one good eye. He could certainly use the other eye now, the eye
he had purposefully dowsed with drain cleaner one night in a
cheap motel in Barstow. It was the eye that a priest must have in
order to read the missal in the proper fashion.

"Someone had photographed the ceremony. Some ambitious priests in Santa Clara had shown the photographs to a fat
bishop from Manila; then an effeminate emissary had arrived at
my mother's hovel."

The holy man, hoping God would see him winnowing heroically through the human trash, had conferred politely, if not con-
descendingly, with Concepción Reyes, and the deal had been
made. Bambino would go off to America, to a place called Oregon.

He would pursue a contemplative life in the church. All of
the proper arrangements had been made in Manila; it would
cost the family nothing. Of course, Concepción Reyes would re-

ceive a small stipend, a modest sum . . . enough for some penicillin shots, a box of French ticklers, and some costume jewelry.

"Your father is from California," his mother had finally revealed to him on his last night in the Islands. "His family owns some small piece of land there; at least that's what the bastard told me before he skipped out on me. He said he wanted to acquire even more land. He told me that he would be a big landowner someday. Did you know he gave me the clap? No, no." She waved both of her hands in front of her face to cancel the last statement.

"That was Felipe's father, the Arab son of a bitch! Your father Pietro was pretty clean, for an Italian sailor. He only had herpes. Anyway, he hardly talked about himself. I guess he was afraid I'd come to America and sue him for child support. But, once when he was drunk, he told me that he had an identical twin brother back in the States. Though I don't remember much, I remember that your father's last name was Ditto."

Without his knowing it, the interior lights came on in the bus. The sun had gone down and the bus had emptied out. The coach was headed down Townsend toward the train terminal. Without being aware of it, Bambino had transferred to the 42 bus. After so many years of hunting, this unconscious activity was not unusual. The old man walked toward the front of the bus as it came to a stop on Fourth Street. The driver shut off the engine, rose from his seat, and walked out of the bus toward the train station, where he would sit for his fifteen-minute break, talking and drinking day-old coffee.

Bambino moved to the front seat and waited for the driver to return. Within a year of his prize-winning crucifixion, he had been sent to Troutvale, Oregon, a live-in high school that taught mathematics, Latin, and the eight beatitudes. The St. Francis Seminary was a converted mansion on the Sandy River; its three-car garage had been rebuilt into a chapel and its huge barn had become a gymnasium. Cold Oregon was a long way from his steaming jungle village, his paradise.

Bambino smiled when he recalled the long walks to the Colombia Gorge, then grimaced when he thought of all the young girls he had been explicitly told would never be his. Even dating had been forbidden. Coed activities and contact with all women and friends were simply not permitted. On one of those walks he had happened upon a group of teenage girls who were swimming in the nude. He had hidden himself to memorize their bodies and to hear their echoing laughter.

"At first, I considered all of it a small price to pay in order to find my father," he said to an empty bus. "I never wanted to go to class. I realized almost as soon as I got here that I was my mother's son. I soon discovered that a natural immunity to every possible sexually transmitted disease was my birthright.

"In the classrooms, there were no exalted thoughts springing from my mind, only lust thinly disguised as spiritual rapture. You know, over time, I had each one of those swimming girls. I wooed each of them with my seeming vulnerability; I dangled my naive innocence in front of them. I let each one of them have what they believed was forbidden. It worked every time. Each one of those innocent little girls cherished the guilt and the exhilaration of becoming the first to corrupt me."

Bambino cast his voice about the interior of the bus as though it were filled with eager listeners.

"Since then, I have never craved anything that wasn't forbidden. Time after time, in feigned fits of remorse, I discarded each one of them for her envious sister or for her shy friend.

"It was then that I knew that I was my father's son, too. I found myself to be lecherous and disloyal by nature. I ravished the girls in the chapel, in the new gymnasium, on the roof of the refectory while the whole school was busily eating its aspirations for dessert. In the confessional, I learned without surprise that my lips could form a lie with surpassing ease."

As a teenager Bambino had been sent to San Luis Rey College near Camp Pendleton in California, where he spent a year studying as a layperson. Later he had been sent to Mission San Miguel, near Paso Robles, where he had become a reluctant, moody novitiate, barely managing to hide his lechery beneath his robe. He had been renamed Frater Peter of the Order of Frateres Minorum.

"I had no high thoughts, no beings danced from their essences. None of Duns Scotus's forms revealed themselves to me. I gladly traded Occam's razor for this machete."

He felt beneath his coat for the long blade.

"I can see Spinoza's geometry in the blade, Bacon's power in the knowledge of my victims' names. And in these dark days when the general will is so meanspirited and weak, wouldn't Rousseau approve of me?"

Bambino laughed coldly at all the lost hours he had spent studying discourses long useless and dead.

"Poverty. I was born into abject poverty!" he laughed to himself as he thought again of his vows.

"Chastity. In this country it was illegal to consort with a Pinoy. Obedience? From the moment my mother placed me up on that cross, I have never exercised a moment's free will! Stability? I am as stable as a planet. But you must stand a universe away to see what a miracle of constancy I am."

He looked into the train station. The driver was laughing with a waitress and pouring himself another cup of coffee. It didn't matter. Here was just as good as anywhere else to look for Cabiri, to meditate upon a means of killing him.

"I'll torture him first," he said. "I'll have one scream for each day that I've hunted him. But before he dies, he will tell me where I can find that queer Faustino and the boy—the man—Zeferino."

Each day at terce the bus lines would stop running and Bambino would begin his search for a place to sleep. At sextus, Bambino would be asleep on a sagging cot in one of the cheap hotels in the Tenderloin or one of the homeless shelters in the south of Market area. At nones he would be back on the bus.

Only half of his life had changed since he had bolted from the monkhouse. He still lived in solitude and he was still a contemplative, but he had failed completely in the area of apostolacy, good acts. He had sworn another oath, an alternative vow more solemn than all the others. He had sworn an oath to kill three men. After all, vengeance was even more forbidden than lust.

Long ago he had traveled down every road in the state of California until he came to the dirt road leading into a place called French Camp. Somehow, he had stumbled upon his father's landholding. It had seemed like a true miracle had come to pass. There, at last, was his own family name emblazoned on a sign leading into an asparagus camp. Here, at long last, was the land of his forefather. Bambino had been filled with so much joy and anticipation in that moment. He had been ecstatic. Neither religion nor the supple bodies of young girls had ever given him such joy.

But he had arrived too late. His bloodline had been cruelly severed. His father had been savagely killed. Bambino would only be allowed to see a dim reflection of his dead father in the aging face of a twin brother, his uncle Simon Ditto.

Pietro Ditto had been ruthlessly murdered by a farmworker, a man with wild, white hair. Simon Ditto explained how poor Pietro had been killed for entertainment's sake, for the sheer joy of it.

"Faustino is the name of the one who sliced him. I should have known better than to hire that *finnochio*. I've sent many men after him, but none of those idiots could find him. No one seems to know where he's gone."

There had been two accomplices: one had a name from the distant past, Teodoro Cabiri, and the other was a boy. No one in the fields would give his full name. The boy's mother, Lilly, had remarried and disappeared. Her trail ended at a cafe in Portales, New Mexico. Simon Ditto's men had searched everywhere and asked their questions a thousand times to no avail. No one would divulge the boy's full name. Zeferino was the only name that Bambino knew.

"No!" Bambino had sworn angrily. "There were three accomplices. God had a hand in this. First, he mocked my dismal future by ruining my childish, paltry sacrifice, and now he ruins my entire past, my history. He made me a bastard twice over, then he robbed me of my inheritance."

"Find them. Kill them all," his newfound uncle had implored. "Don't worry about the money. I'll pay for everything. Kill them, and I'll see that you get your share of this." Simon Ditto swept his arm across the fields of French Camp.

The two men had walked together out to the dirt road by a slough where Pietro Ditto had died. They stood in the shade of the packing shed. Out in the fields, a machine was hacking mindlessly at the green asparagus spears. Each wounded spear, as it fell, dreamed of farmworkers' hands.

"I vow that the three men who did this will die by my hand. I shall give my life and my last breath to this task. I have never known who I am until this moment. I am relentless."

That day had been the beginning of years of searching,

seeking out enclaves of the oldest Pinoys, the sojourners, to ask them if they knew of men named Faustino and Cabiri. The boy would be grown up by now. Could he still be working in the fields? The other two men would know. Break Cabiri's misshapen knees and he will betray the others.

The old man, Simon Ditto, had sent a large stipend every month, just as promised, until the day he died. While in Chicago, Bambino had gotten word through the farmworker grapevine that there had been a will and that legitimate sons had taken everything, including the land.

Tired of waiting for the driver to finish his coffee break, Bambino climbed down the steps of the bus and walked to another that was idling on the Fourth Street side of the station. He had never taken this bus before, but it had passengers and seemed ready to go.

The bus would go down Fourth Street, then lumber down to the Third Street intersection, where it would make a right turn and a second right turn onto Seventeenth Street. As the bus crossed the drawbridge on Fourth Street, Bambino's breath left him, as though both of his lungs had suddenly collapsed. His breath returned as soon as the bus reached the asphalt roadway on the other side of the bridge. There was something about the green bridge that had filled him with frigid, uncontrollable waves of fear. Summoning all of his strength, Bambino pushed the strange feelings from his mind and began, once again, his search for his father's killers.

The shipyards were gone now from Third Street. One or two restaurant ships rocked lazily against their ropes where once huge tankers had berthed. The bus crossed Potrero and rolled down toward South Van Ness and the center of the Mission District. Bambino had never taken this particular route before, though he recognized the area.

There was a great concentration of transmission repair shops and auto parts stores in this area, he thought. Mexicans must live here. On the right side of the bus, just as it crossed South Van Ness, was the Rite Spot, a small restaurant and bar. There was an empty field beyond the restaurant where a rat scurried under a Cyclone fence. In the middle of the field was a small white tent. There were folding chairs, suitcases, and boxes arranged around the tent, indications that someone called the canvas structure home. A man wearing an Oakland Athletics hat was tending a fire that was burning just in front of the tent. Beyond the tent and behind a building was a gutted, canary yellow vehicle that looked like a New York taxicab.

Farther on there was a yellow tamale cart on the left-hand side of the street. Recently, Bambino's never-ending search had begun to take him into the Mission District, but from another direction. He had come to this area once or twice to eat lunch or dinner and to stare into passing faces. In fact, he had met the famous King of Tamales on two occasions and had spoken to him just yesterday. He had asked him the same questions that he had asked so many people before, in so many towns. Yesterday the tamale vendor had awkwardly hidden his huge, scarred face, as though he had secrets to protect.

Bambino had heard some gossip circulating in this neighborhood that the King of Tamales was a cuckold, that his new wife had left him for another man within minutes of the marriage ceremony. Rumor had it that the woman and her new lover had moved into a home that the King of Tamales himself had built with his own two hands. Bambino, ever the cynic, laughed heartily at the thought that such a delicious rumor could possibly be true.

With this information as leverage, Bambino had probed and prodded at the tamale vendor, but to no avail. Still, the huge man knew something. Bambino could taste evasion; he could smell a lie. The questions had made the big man break into a sweat and run off without even a proper word of farewell. But Bambino had seen right through him. The King of Tamales ran away like a mother bird luring a predator away from her nest. At that moment, Bambino had resolved to move his search from the area of Geary Street to the Mission District and the area south of Market.

There was a happy crowd gathering near a bar just past the tent and the empty field. Some laughing people were admiring a weird little car that was parked in front of the bar. Bambino had never seen an automobile like it. On the sidewalk behind the car was a tiny man with black hair and a cane and a strange gait, struggling to walk toward a local bar and café that had a dazzling neon sign on its roof.

For the second time tonight his hissing breath left him and he felt overcome with fear. Summoning all of his strength, he regained control of his reeling senses and, despite the sign, managed to focus his attention on the tiny man. The odd little man was dressed in a tasteless, blinding sequin suit, and he had an expensive wig on his head. Bambino Reyes was completely mesmerized by the sight of him.

The otherworldly sight of the tiny, grinning man limping beneath a repulsive neon sign shook Bambino's world to its foundation. For some reason unknown to him, the fantastic sign and the silver tower rising behind it seemed repellent, abhorrent. The very sight of the Mexican bar gave him a feeling akin to a profound car sickness. It was as though his stomach had been violently torn from his body, his diaphragm split open and his crop ripped out. Then, for just a single numbing instant, he saw what he thought was someone staring down at him, watching him carefully as his bus passed by.

For a moment, a shaking Bambino thought he saw a gray gargoyle moving about on the pillar on the roof of the building, a man built of myth and clay whose dark arm was pointing directly at him. When he looked again, the shadowy figure was gone. In his place was a naked woman, staring into a hand mirror.

Bambino's heart was racing as he sat stunned by the sight of the little man beneath the hideous sign. Could it be him after all these years, after all these decades? Could it be Teodoro Cabiri? He slumped into a seat and sat dazed for what he thought was a single moment; then he quickly rose to pull the stop cord. The bus had actually gone several miles past the bar, but it didn't matter.

He exited the bus and began running back down Seventeenth Street. He had seen him, and he would follow him. As he ran he caressed the machete beneath his mantle, feeling for the cruel edge. He felt closer to his father now than he had ever been. Soon he would know where all three murderers were. He exulted as he ran, glorying in the painful ache in his side and the knotted cramps in his aged legs. He laughed aloud at the wonderful pain. He had seen where his prey was going—and he knew the name of the bar.

Raphael's Silver Cloud Café.

X

The Mission District, May 12, 1993

WHEN Faustino rose from his bed on the morning of the last day of his life, there were seventeen syllables waning and waxing on his breath. Still reciting, he watched distractedly as the bathtub filled with steaming water; then he bathed alone in his small yellow bathroom. While calmly and carefully washing his neck he realized with some alarm that he had never bathed this way before; he had never in his long life filled a tub with hot water and lowered himself tenderly beneath the steaming surface.

Farmworkers always showered quickly and self-consciously in open stalls or took sponge baths out behind the Quonset huts. Tribes of migrant bachelors became almost monastic over time, childish and brutal in their nakedness. They never had the luxury of baths.

Slowly he lowered his head below the surface, letting the hot water cover his eyes and hair. Bathing was an act of leisure, he thought, an act of contemplation. He opened his eyes while underwater and realized that he was no longer in the world of air, that there was a turbid, prismatic curtain drawn across his body. It is an act of ritual, he concluded; then he sat up abruptly in the tub and began to shave. Without a mirror and without shaving cream he drew the razor up his gorge and over his windpipe to the cleft of his chin. Today he would have the skin and throat of a young man.

The rising sun had been rubbing at the glass panes all morning, so he rose after shaving and walked dripping to the window to let it in. As he dried himself with a towel, the rays of sunlight dove inside to paint a second window on the wall above the tub. Faustino's skin glowed white in the impossible light; his hairless legs and belly were fluorescent and edgeless and as warm as newly baked bread. Faustino turned his head to stare upward at the sun as though he had never seen it before. Perhaps he never had. For the first time in his living memory the sun was not being cruel to a farmworker.

"I'm sorry," he whispered through the window and across the sky and into dark space, "but we campesinos have always preferred the moon."

Faustino dressed quietly in his best work clothes and his new work shoes, then stopped at the mirror before leaving. It was a familiar face that he saw in the glass, a face so familiar that its specifics frightened him as he gazed carefully upon the aspects of a completed life. His hair was thick and silvery. The skin around his eyes and mouth was smooth and unwrinkled.

"Not enough laughter," he said aloud. He moved slowly to the door of his apartment and turned to survey his home. He laughed to himself when he realized that all of his worldly possessions could still fit into that old blue Buick that he had once owned. Without closing the door, he tossed the key to his room onto his bedspread, then walked out into the hallway of the hotel. He was going to have breakfast with his lover and with his good friends Raphael Viajero, King Pete, and Anatoly.

Teodoro would not be coming to breakfast this morning. His room just down the hall had been silent now for two days. Faustino smiled as he thought of the newlyweds up on Bernal Hill. As he passed Ted For Short's room he knocked, then opened the door. Like his own, it was a *manong*'s room: spare and efficient and eternally temporary. Most of Teodoro's things were already gone; they had been moved up to Ruby's house.

A sheaf of Faustino's poems lay fanned out on Teodoro's cot. The thin, dark-skinned man with wild, white hair picked up the pages and began to read silently to himself. No one but Ted For Short and Constantine had ever been allowed to read them. Over the years Faustino had drawn so much inspiration and sustenance from Constantine's exotic life and lovely poetry that he had begun to wonder if his own life was even worthy of expression. What was there to say about the life of a manual laborer?

Suddenly, he tossed the sheaves across the room and watched them as they separated in midair and alighted, stanzas askew, upon the stretched bedspread of the cot and on the windowsill. It was a common gesture of dissatisfaction. He had always taken more joy in revising his verses than he had in reading them.

Faustino sighed wearily and turned to his lover, who had seemingly appeared from nowhere and was standing behind him in the hallway. He was a handsome, older man in a white summer suit.

"Each word stirs," said the man in the summer suit. "Each word has its wake."

Faustino looked through the window in Teodoro's kitchen. In the distance was the towering skyline of the city. "Did you know that I've never been downtown? I've never put on a suit and tie to have dinner. I've always lived in the migrant camps or the low-rent district of every town that I've ever visited. All I ever saw of Chicago and Denver were the train stations. Sometimes I long for just a little bit of elegance. Constantine, tell me about Paris," said Faustino, who turned his back on his own poems. "Tell me about Paris while we're walking. *La rive gauche.* I want to hear again about the ramshackle Armenian hotel. Please. I'll never ask you again. I promise." Faustino gazed lovingly at the man standing on the faded hall carpet.

"Indulge me, dearest," he said to his silent friend while closing and locking the door to Teodoro's room. Without realizing it, he said an unmouthed farewell into the silent room.

"Constantine?"

It was clear that his friend was not yet ready to speak. The two men walked to the stairway and descended the two flights that ended at the lobby and the street entrance. Once through the entrance they turned right and walked down Seventeenth Street. They would be having breakfast at Los Jarritos, a small Mexican restaurant at Twentieth and South Van Ness.

"Now let's see," said Faustino impatiently. "It's a small three-story building next door to a boulangerie that is famous for its raisin-bread pigs, and it's directly across the circle from a tiny post office. When you walk to the post office you have walked halfway to the Seine and the Louvre is just a footbridge and two blocks away."

When Faustino closed his eyes he could almost see the walkway to the post office. There was an Algerian magazine vendor near the corner placing lead weights on his periodicals to keep them from blowing away. There were two young boys coughing in an alcove. They were far too young to be smoking. Whenever Faustino allowed himself to daydream, his intense desire for some other, more beautiful life would overcome him. In time he had taken on his lover's memories as his own. He had become a man with two bloodstreams and a single heart.

"Once you have passed the post office, you will see on the left a small bookstore with a painting of Jules Verne in the window. The proprietor's son has made a gondola out of matchsticks and glue. It's displayed in the window, floating in a hand-painted canal. Across from the bookstore is a coffee shop run by a Spaniard from San Sebastian." Faustino's eyes were closed now as he spoke. His grasp on Constantine's arm kept him safely on the sidewalk.

"There's a fat, lumpy chair near the entrance that he claims once belonged to Victor Hugo. He makes sandwiches filled with his famous *ropa vieja* and cold slivers of lime green avocado. Even at the *petite déjeuner* he serves *chipirones*, squid cooked in its own purple ink, a dab of butter, mushrooms, and shallots. I know . . . the French love it, but they don't dare ask what it is."

The man at his side smiled without looking at his friend. "You always seem to know more about my own past than I do," whispered Constantine. "Why is it you've never told me about yourself? In all the years that I've known you, you've never once told me about your family, about your past. I've asked you but you've never explained to me how it is that everyone you knew so long ago suddenly ended up in San Francisco at the same time."

Faustino said nothing for a moment. He considered the question, but as usual he preferred to think about a life that seemed far more romantic than his own. Slowly and inevitably, the sounds of the Mission District were replaced in Faustino's mind by the hush of a small hotel in Paris.

"In your room in the hotel, the plumbing is pitiful, the shower just dribbles, and the pipes clatter and bang whenever that lovely brute of an Australian guy upstairs goes to brush his teeth. There's only one lamp in the room, a converted gas lamp. You've been meaning to get a desk lamp but keep putting it off. Now years of low light have gone by and your eyesight has suffered. Every night at eleven sharp, the concierge, in an effort to save money, dims all the lights to near darkness. In that light, the dust is invisible and the threadbare couches seem new. The entire hotel seems magical."

"You still haven't answered my questions, Faustino," said Constantine. There was a hint of impatience in his voice.

"There is a Greek family"—Faustino continued as though Constantine had said nothing—"fresh from Belgium." His eyes were opened now. There was excitement in his voice. "They have opened an intimate, five-table restaurant in the small kitchen down below, and the foyer simply reeks of delicious meatballs and pungent avgolemono. And they have the most delicious house red in a water glass for just twenty cents."

It was Constantine who closed his eyes now. He had conceded to the force of the cherished memories. After all, they were his own.

"The Marcopulos family."

"I knew that, Constantine!" said Faustino, excitedly. "Yes, the Marcopulos family. Peter and Constance and their lovely daughter, Cynthia. Such kind people they are, they never skimp on their plates. You can have as much meat as you wish. And Cynthia always seems so happy. I remember her dancing a frantic hula right there in the hallway, the grass from her skirt flying everywhere. It is one of my fondest memories. It is so good to have countrymen nearby when one is so far from home. My . . . your room is on the *première étage* so the sound of demotic Greek can waft in through the ventilators along with the scent of garlic and roasting lamb."

Constantine nodded as he walked. He is a delicate-looking man, and impeccably dressed. He looks the way Faustino would have looked were it not for all those years of bending under the sun. He has a large, elegant nose, a set of small, round, tortoise-shell spectacles that age him a decade, and a head of hair that steadfastly refuses to lie down. There is no part in his hair, it is all pulled backward and flyaway. Constantine has three cowlicks that have always prevented any sort of successful hairdo. One of the whorls turns clockwise and the other two turn counter to that. Constantine believes it to be the result of having crossed the equator as a young child.

"Why not London, why not Alexandria? You know I prefer Alexandria?" he asked, peering over his glasses at Faustino.

"No . . . Paris. It must be Paris. I've never been. Oh, I know I've never been to London or Alexandria either, but somehow, never seeing Paris means so much more." Faustino fell silent for a moment. "Oh, I realize that these are your memories, and not mine. But when you speak of Paris, something inside of me comes alive."

The conversation between the two men created an eerie, atmospheric effect. Whenever they spoke, the world about them seemed to melt away into a backdrop of fused colors and edgeless objects, diffuse, steamy, and out of focus.

"Were you lonely in Paris?" asked Faustino, who had asked the same question so many times before.

"I will answer that question, Faustino, if you promise to answer my questions tonight," said a determined Constantine.

Faustino hesitated, then nodded. Constantine was surprised to see a look of resignation in his lover's eyes.

"I was lonely everywhere, and I felt every moment of it," said Constantine. "It is the curse of poetry to fall from a great height, if not a great distance . . . and never lose consciousness."

The two men looked at each other, acknowledging silently the bond between them. They turned left at South Van Ness and walked past a liquor store toward Twentieth Street.

"At least you have your poems," said Faustino, finally. "I have written so little that works. You've seen them; they're stilted and self-conscious. They're scraps of dreams about lives that I've never lived. Except for a few dear friends, my past has been so empty," sighed Faustino.

"Poems have their beginning in feelings like that," said Constantine. "I speak from experience."

Faustino fell silent for a time, then began to recite his favorite stanza from Cavafy's poem "Our Dearest White Youth."

It will seize us with its white hands,
and with a thin shroud drawn from its whiteness,
a snow-white shroud drawn from its whiteness,
it will cover us.

"Can life and death be the same color? Why did you choose white for your poem?" asked Faustino.

Constantine removed his bifocals, then ceremoniously brushed his suit with the back of his right hand. He did not make it a habit to discuss his poetry or its origins. He had never done it during his lifetime and did not intend to start now. He waited at a stoplight, then stepped out into the street, walking at a slight angle to the universe.

"E. M. Forster must have walked behind you just as I'm doing now," said Faustino as he stepped into the street. "He once wrote that he saw the angle in your walk, no matter how slight. I see it, Constantine. Poems come from people who are slightly skewed."

Constantine slowed to a stop, then turned his eyes downward to the sidewalk at his feet. "Have you ever been with a woman, Faustino?" he asked without looking up. It was a question that Faustino had promised to answer. They walked down South Van Ness for at least a half block before Faustino spoke.

"Just prostitutes," answered Faustino in a soft, self-conscious voice, "and only as a child . . . and I can't really say that I had any of them."

"You needn't apologize," smiled Constantine.

"I was a great failure with the prostitutes," continued Faustino, "even with those who had a deep and profound love for the discarded." He shook his head with the memory of the kindness of those women. His father had hired the women to re-educate his son in the proper ways of manhood. Only one had ever been impatient with him and that was only because she had children at home who were hungry and she needed to hurry back to care for them. All of them had understood the importance of their task. Homosexuals could not inherit under Filipino law, and in some provinces they punished homosexuality with the death penalty.

"How did you meet Teodoro?" asked Constantine.

"Oh, that was just after the prostitutes," answered Faustino. "I was still a hairless boy, not quite a man. It was up in Baguio. There's a whole community of healers gathered into this city north of Manila. They do X-rays without machines and perform surgery without incisions. My father took me to one of those healers."

"To remove your corruption?" asked Constantine.

"Yes, exactly," said Faustino, "to remove my corruption. Even after the women assured my father that I was a hopeless *bakla*, he kept trying to have me cured. He called every prostitute a failure and refused to pay any of them despite their heroic efforts. It was so humiliating. I wanted so badly to help those women get paid for their work, but it just wasn't in me. I can still hear that voice of his. 'Make a man out of him!' It was never in me."

Faustino suddenly walked at a slower pace, staring down at the wet sidewalk. "Then, in desperation, they decided to try one final measure. So they took me to the psychic doctor in Baguio. I remember that the nurse came in first. She was a pretty woman who had managed to hide the fact through overuse of makeup. I remember that she stared at me for a moment, then undressed me in the same unfeeling way that a butcher would dress a chicken.

"I squirmed under her rough and rude treatment, but my father told me not to complain, to stop fussing. 'If this cure does not work, there will be reason enough to complain from now until your death. Your life will be one long complaint.' My father had shoved those words through his teeth.

"I knew I had no friends there, so I just sat there, not helping the nurse undress me and not resisting. When they made me lie down on this papered table, I remember that I stared up at all of the angels that were hanging from the rafters and woven into the doctor's tapestries. There they were . . . all of them up there: Michael, Raphael, Uriel, Sariel, and hundreds more. Raguel the Friend and Remiel the Merciful flew together in one corner above a painting of Raziel of the secret regions. 'Protect me,' I asked them . . . I begged them.

"All I got for my fervent prayer was the good doctor. He was a rotund man in a white uniform who came into the room with a flourish, his hands dramatically upraised for the nurse to cleanse, and held up in the air as though each of his fingers was the philosopher's stone that would transform my misbegotten flesh.

"As the nurse swabbed his hands he kept praying aloud for the power to heal my deformities. The rotund doctor then placed a yellow sheet of stained construction paper on my chest. It had been soaked for three consecutive Sundays in holy water, or so the doctor claimed. He then put his right eye up against the paper and with his right middle finger and thumb made a snapping sound three times. Then he left the room for five or ten minutes, and when he returned he was smiling broadly and carrying three black, plastic sheets that he explained were the results of my telepathic X rays.

"Well, he rolled up a shade, then placed the sheets up against a window and triumphantly showed my father that he had located the exact cause of my problem. 'There's a malignant growth next to Faustino's heart,' he said. 'Its scientific name is *Cystus Abominus.*' "

Upon hearing the phrase Constantine suddenly broke into spasms of uncontrollable laughter, punctuated intermittently by failed efforts to apologize. Faustino patiently continued his story, but his lover's laughter had been a revelation. For the first time he saw the humor in this sad tale.

"Then the surgeon said, 'After we say a prayer to St. Martin de Porres, patron of male hairdressers, I will remove the offending cyst through psychic surgery.' A short prayer session was held; then the doctor lowered the lights in the room, ordered my father out into the waiting room, and promptly began my psychic surgery.

"He rubbed my body with alcohol; then he began probing in the region of my heart with his right hand, digging and spreading my flesh with his fingers. A pool of blood began to form on my chest. He did this for about ten minutes. I almost passed out from the pressure and pain.

"Then with great fanfare he called his nurse. She came over to the table with a small silver pan in her outstretched hands. The doctor dropped a bloody lump into the pan and ordered her to show it to my father. I could hear his shouts of glee out in the waiting room and filling the entire hospital. I'll never forget it. He came running in with the silver pan in his hand, the offending *Cystus Abominus* now trapped and harmless. The doctor washed away the blood on my chest and showed my father that the skin of my body had not been cut or torn in any way. The psychic surgery had been a rousing success.

" 'Let's test it out,' my frugal father demanded. 'I won't pay until it's tested.' So the doctor called his nurse in. Without asking her, he unbuttoned her blouse and pulled her brassiere down to expose her breasts."

Constantine daubed at his eyes with a handkerchief. His laughter had subsided to a controllable level.

" 'This visual stimulation treatment will cost you a bit more,' the doctor explained. 'I personally developed this unique procedure at the university.'

"My father ordered me to look at her large breasts while all six of their eyes were trained on the poor limp member between my legs.

" 'You see,' screamed the doctor, 'it jumped!'

" 'Nothing happened. I didn't see a thing,' my father said in a voice trapped somewhere between victory and hopelessness. 'Are you sure it moved?'

" 'Double the dosage!' shouted the doctor. The dutiful nurse ran to a nearby closet and returned wearing a blond wig, her breasts bouncing as she ran. 'Still nothing!' my father screamed. 'There was a deflection,' yelled the doctor, excitedly, 'a measurable deflection! You can't expect it to work right away! But I guarantee that he is no longer a *bakla*. Money-back guarantee! He will be a Pinoy stud.' The doctor raised both of his arms into the air, flexed his biceps while simultaneously making thrusting motions with his hips. The nurse demurely put her bosom away, then swayed to the front desk. 'Now pay my nurse at the checkout counter.'

"Well, my still-skeptical father paid the nurse and, along with a two-year verbal guarantee, he received a written prescription that required me to eat a dozen carrots a day and to visit two whorehouses a week for eight weeks and then to taper off after that as the miraculous cure gradually took hold.

"While my father was paying, I got down from the table, put on my shirt, pulled my pants up around my measurable deflection, then walked into the next operating room. It was then that

I first laid eyes on Teodoro. The doctor had inadvertently left the door open, and in that room I saw a small boy lying on a table just as I had been. His head was turned toward me, and when our pained eyes met, our lives were grafted together. His grief reached out and joined with my own. His sorrow felt and understood mine, and we had not even spoken a single word to each other. It seemed that his psychic operation had been just as successful as mine. The doctor had removed his hunchback and his small size." Faustino laughed sarcastically.

"There was a silver pan in his room that contained a *Cystus Diminutus*. It looked exactly like my cyst. I'm sure now that it was the same cyst, or whatever it was. It looked remarkably like a chicken gizzard. I knew when I saw the look on Teodoro's sad face that my case was no different from his, that nothing had changed. Our families were just a lot poorer, and Teodoro knew it, too.

"So we decided that very day that we would run away to Manila together. We decided to find work in Manila until we could both afford to go to America. Once we were in the States, we would send money home to our families and prove that we were good sons"—Faustino's voice broke—"despite our deficits.

"We exchanged addresses, and that was hard because neither of us lived on a street with a name. He lived in a village just to the north of mine, three houses from the well. We decided that he should come to my house and together we would go south to Manila. We picked a date and a time, but he never came and I did not have the courage to run away by myself."

Faustino and Constantine walked past a transmission repair shop and an antiques store. The Greek poet was no longer laughing.

"As a symbol of our new friendship we took down some of the toy angels that the doctor had hanging from his ceiling. I put Teodoro up on my shoulders and he pulled them down. I've had mine ever since," said Faustino. "I've taken them with me everywhere I've gone. Teodoro still has his." Faustino was silent for a moment, wondering for the first time why he had kept the toy angels for so many years.

"After the operation, a girl named Rosario came to live in our home and to minister to my deformity. She was not a prostitute.

I can never think of her that way. She was to be my father's final attempt to comply with the doctor's prescription. Oh, how she tried! And I grew to love her for trying, but not as a man loves a woman. That I could never do. I loved her as a brother loves a sister, even as she grew to despise my unresponsive male member. It mocked her. It tormented her. When my father threatened to sue her for malfeasance, I could no longer endure the pain I was causing her."

Faustino was crying now. A single tear streamed down his cheek.

"That final night I seeded her with my twisted sympathy, and with my tears. I penetrated her disappointment; I shoved and pulled rudely at her poor vocation until her laughter filled the room. I pricked and prodded her failings into cries of joy that soon re-echoed from my father's room. Then I rose to dress myself and I left my home forever. I remember that she smiled as I dressed, but not a full smile. She knew it had been out of love and not lust. But, at least, she would be paid her money. My father would grudgingly give her the money he owed her. At the very least she could believe that her beauty had done the impossible."

"She may have loved you a bit," said Constantine. "It happens, you know."

"She had a child, Constantine. Our child. One of my brothers found me here in the States and told me. I located her family when I went back for the war, but they would have nothing to do with me. They wouldn't let me see my son or his mother, not even a picture of them. They said she had married a real man and to leave them alone. Half of all the money I have sent home in the years since the war, I have sent to my son's family." Faustino ran his fingers through his long hair. "I have a son."

"Another thing that you've never told me!" said the poet.

"It is a painful thing, Constantine, to plant a seed out of pity. No other reason but pity. And the mother received the seed for money and pride. What would I say to my son? How could I explain to him who I am and why he was born? I've tried to find him since the war, but not very hard. Perhaps it's enough that I work my entire life for him. I am the buried asparagus crown, he is the harvest. I know in my mind that he's a grown man now, but I send the money anyway."

The two men were wordless for fifteen steps. The bus stop to their left was crowded with noisy schoolchildren and women with plastic shopping bags.

"How did you find Ted For Short after you ran away?" asked Constantine.

"It was an accident . . . a glorious accident! I was working as a messenger boy in Manila. It was the only job I could get. My older brothers got me the job. Thank goodness they didn't share my father's disgust for me. I was told to deliver a telegram to Hobie's House restaurant on Mabini Street, in Malate. What a crazy place it was, a Pinoy restaurant that specialized in Mexican food! When I went in to deliver the message, I got the shock of my life. All of the cooks and all of the busboys and waiters working the tables there were dwarfs and midgets! Every one of them! It was one of the requirements if you wanted to be employed there.

"I remember there was a help-wanted sign next to the entrance, advertising for a short-order cook. One of those waiters was my friend Teodoro. I spotted him standing under a large oil painting depicting the Ristorante Dei Tre Gobbi, in Venice.

"I have since learned that a job at the famous Restaurant of the Three Hunchbacks is the dream of every midget waiter. Midget waiters in Warsaw, Marseilles, and Dallas all share the same lofty dream, to someday travel to Venice and to wait on tables at the Ristorante Dei Tre Gobbi. What a sight he was, Constantine, standing there under a picture of three identical hunchbacks! The Jewel Song from *Faust* was playing in the background. Do you know it? *Ah, je ris de me voir!* I thought my eyes and ears had gone bad. I swooned at the sight and sound of him.

"When he saw me, he ran over and we embraced as long-lost brothers. We have been together, at least in spirit, ever since. We have certainly been in hiding together all these years. We endured the Pacific crossing together. Did I tell you that? American farmers and packing companies had passed out handbills in the Islands advertising for workers. Teodoro and I got one of those handbills in Manila and left to come here for work . . . to get rich."

Faustino laughed a sardonic, bitter laugh.

"What a miserable trip that was. We were jammed into wet holds with indentured Chinese and with peaceful Japanese who smelled the coming war. There were no beds down there and no lights at all. There was no separation of the men from the women. Worst of all there were no latrines. Can you imagine shy Japanese women having to use tin cans right in front of the men? It was horrible!

"The only things that kept us alive were my poems and Teodoro's singing. I started him on his career as an entertainer, you know. Did you know that? I first heard him singing in the darkest hold of the ship. I'll never forget it. He was hiding in a storage locker, trying to sing without being heard. He was singing 'God Bless America.' Like so many of us, he learned English with that song."

The song reverberated through the holds of the ship and through the thousands of chambered memories in Faustino's mind, all the hovels and huts he had lived in while laboring in this land blessed by God. All those perfect dreams of America were trapped there in that dark and dank hold, pure dreams that persisted despite the rancid cans of piss and the soft seasick wail of crying children. The vision of America, thought Faustino, is most perfect in an immigrant's closed eyes.

He and Teodoro had been taken directly to Alaska, to join the Alaskeros in the salmon-packing sheds. The bus driver had given each person a contract to sign as soon as they boarded. The packing companies called them covenants. They had been adhesion contracts requiring them to work through the winter, to buy their groceries at a certain store and none other, and to rent a cot in a shed, at a cost as yet undetermined. All those conditions in those contracts had added up to virtual slavery.

Both men, fresh from the tropics, had gotten pneumonia while sleeping in unheated, freezing barracks and had somehow survived the painful fits of sweat and shivering without benefit of medication or hospitalization. But the packing company had deemed their unexcused absence from work to be a material breech of contract and demanded that they work the remaining time of their covenant without compensation. A local judge had agreed with that interpretation of the law.

When the season ended, he and Teodoro left Alaska in the middle of the night, owing the company five hundred dollars each for lodging and for their meals at the company store. Faustino had refused to eat a bite of salmon since that time. Each time he had cut open a fish and found the ooze of living eggs, he had thought of his only son.

Though they had separated and joined up many times since Alaska, Faustino had always known where Ted For Short was, no matter how much time had passed. It was a simple matter of going back to Stockton, of rising in the earliest morning and walking to the park on El Dorado Street. The *viejitos*, the old ones on the Dead Pecker Bench, could be trusted to take a secret to their nearby graves. Faustino had learned long ago of Bambino's relationship to Pietro Ditto. The old men on the bench had told him. All of them had shaken their heads at Bambino Reyes's fierce confessions of unremitting hatred.

Six years ago, the old ones had told him on his last visit to the bench that Teodoro was alive and living in San Francisco. He had been there for almost a full year and wanted Faustino to come.

"If you don't go up north to Frisco, you can have that place," an old Mexicano had said while pointing to a spot on the bench. "Bambino knows that you and Teodoro are in California. If you come sit here with us, he'll have no reason to kill you. That would be *una cosa redundante* . . . it would be redundant."

Faustino had gone back to the railroad for a short time, but those days were over in this country. Something had changed. Now, it seemed that Teodoro felt secure enough to stay in one place for a full year. In the past he had moved at least once every four months. For the first time in years they would be in the same town together.

Perhaps the time had finally come to finish this horrid thing. Whatever the reason, both Teodoro and he had found rooms that had an unobstructed view of the rooftop of Raphael's Silver Cloud. Both had a clear view of the shining beings of light from their kitchenette windows. Both men, along with many others, had been inexplicably drawn to the twin beacons. He and Teodoro had been reunited beneath the light of the two angels. To his eternal amazement, Ruby had found her way to the bar, along with other names from the past—King Pete Claver and crazy Padre Humberto.

Suddenly Constantine's eyes widened as a realization unfolded in his mind.

"Bambino Reyes is here, isn't he?"

"Yes," said Faustino. "He's here in San Francisco. I've felt his presence for a week now. King Pete and Padre Humberto have seen him." The look of concern that had always invaded Faustino's face at the mention of Bambino Reyes had not appeared this morning. There was only a solemn, imploring look of curiosity as he asked, "What's it like? Please, Constantine, what is death like?"

Constantine seemed stricken by the question. Faustino had asked the same question countless times over the years, and Constantine had always steadfastly refused to answer it.

"White," said Constantine in calming, calibrated words, and suddenly referring to the stanza of "Our Dearest White Youth" that Faustino had recited, ". . . white is ineffable. It is a word beyond words, beyond furious invocations of light or oceanic tears. It is inhumanly pure. It is angelic. It is colorless, rapid beyond belief and druid slow."

"I've stopped running, Constantine. Thirty years is enough, don't you agree? My life is the best it has ever been. You came to me when I had no one, and you've stayed with me. My job at the wind farm is the best one I've ever had. I only wish I could have kept it longer. It's a long commute, but it's against traffic and the work isn't hard. The windmills inspire me. There is nothing more that I want." There was a moment of silence. "I stood in front of the mirror today, Constantine. I still couldn't see past the age in my eyes. What's it like?"

Constantine said nothing at first. Both men had stopped walking and were in the middle of the sidewalk. "What is the gender of flame?" Constantine asked rhetorically. "What is the weight of fire? The answer to the question that you ask cannot be given to a soul that still lives. Mortal words are too small. My own poetry is too small. Life that still clings to the clay can never understand the answer."

The lovers smiled at one another as something inexpressible passed between them. Then they stepped down from the curb on Twentieth Street and walked toward the front doors of the restaurant. Inside the restaurant were the smiling faces of Raphael, King, and Anatoly. Faustino was certain that they were still discussing Ted For Short and Ruby's wedding.

"I still can't believe there was a wedding at Raphael's Silver Cloud," Faustino said with a voice now utterly transformed by joy. "It was so amazing."

As he entered the front door, Faustino looked back at his friend. He knew that Constantine would not come inside. Constantine had begun to lag behind in the middle of the crosswalk. The closer Faustino came to the front door of Los Jarritos, the farther back the poet fell. The Greek poet would retrace their steps back to Faustino's small room and, grieved by separation, he would be waiting mutely there, between the covers of a book, for his lover to return.

Few outside would see Constantine walking home alone, his feet moving in meter, his thoughts in free verse. One or two sojourners would see him walk by as they pored over a pile of boxes and strewn garbage. A tall, unspoiled grigori, having disturbing flashbacks of third heaven, would see him clearly, would see poems in demotic Greek gathering together on his high forehead and would know that his white summer clothing smelled of Egypt.

Others, ungifted by otherworldly lyricism, would never have seen Constantine at all. They would only see an old white-haired Pinoy who habitually spoke out loud to himself, then listened patiently while no one answered. They would later swear to inquiring police officers that Faustino had walked to the restaurant alone.

After breakfast Faustino walked back to the Silver Cloud. His three friends were still at the restaurant, sitting silently at a table after an hour of several attempts both playful and serious to convince Faustino not to go to work. Raphael, King, and Anatoly had sat staring at their own cold food while Faustino had devoured a monumental breakfast of *huevos rancheros* with side orders of bacon and sausage.

As he walked up Seventeenth, he waved at Padre Humberto on the roof of the bar. The priest was scowling downward at him like a griffin. The air above the Silver Cloud had recently been thick with the old man's warnings and concerns. Humberto's voice had grown louder and louder with each passing day. He had pleaded with Faustino not to go to work, to stay in his room while that evil Bambino Reyes was skulking around outside. Queenie, by Humberto's side, was signaling desperately into her mirror for Faustino to turn around and go home.

"*Tengo una intriga, un ardid.* I have a scheme, Faustino," Padre Humberto cried. "I swear I do! He's here, you know. The fiend is here! I've seen him! I saw him again this very morning!"

Faustino knew that he was here, and close by. He had felt it, the oppressive fear, the presence of something foul. He had felt it in Chicago, in Salt Lake City, and in Los Angeles. He had felt it during Teodoro and Ruby's wedding. Bambino had been there outside, moving like a wolf on the perimeter, just beyond the light. And he felt it now, stronger than ever before, and for the first time in his life he didn't care. There was no fear in his face as he climbed into his car and headed down Folsom Street toward the freeway on-ramp, and there was no fear as he crossed the Bay Bridge and sank into history.

Once in the Altamont hills he drove down North Flynn Road and through quadrant after quadrant of white metal towers with huge spinning propellers at their peak. He knew each type by name. There were Whispers, Wind Barons, Bergey Windpowers, and ranks of Jacobs Wind Turbines. What had once been mile upon mile of forbidding, windswept hills was now a dairy farm with thousands of mechanical cows chewing the swift breezes for their cud. Faustino loved this job more than any job he had ever had. The yaw and chatter of the carbon and spruce blades was a soothing song to his ears.

Here there was no endless cutting and lifting. Here there was no burning, unrelenting sun. Here there were no haughty Amtrak passengers dropping their cigarette ashes on the carpet in first class and complaining vociferously about the small amount of gin in their martinis. At the wind farm he worked alone and he was paid by the hour. Up here he felt close to heaven.

He drove to quadrant 27, to a steep hill overlooking the freeway. The windmills in this area used generators and were scheduled to have their armatures inspected for glazing and to have their brushes changed, so he drove to the supply shack that monitored and serviced this particular grouping. There he checked the meter on each windmill. Given the present wind speed, outputs were well within tolerance.

Suddenly he heard it, the sound he had dreaded hearing for over thirty years—the sound of a footfall where none should have been. Then he saw a moving shadow skirting the ground behind him, moving with circuitous intention. Slowly, Faustino lifted his eyes to see the cruel face of a well-known stranger. Faustino had never seen this face before. He had only imagined it, once for every star in the skies, but he knew beyond any doubt who he was.

Without saying a word, Faustino fell to his knees. He dropped his head downward to see the soil, to expose the prepared neck, and his long white hair swirled and whipped about his brown face. The shadow moved behind Faustino and stood just to his left, a shadow knife uplifted, then lowered.

"What is it like, Constantine, this turning point?" whispered Faustino. Above his head, there was an endless torrent of words spewing brutishly from Bambino Reyes's lips, but Faustino heard none of them. "What is it like on the other side of the mirror, on the other side of the curtain? What is it like to die?" he said just before something ruined forever his ability to speak.

"It's like a threshold," said Constantine's sweet, disembodied voice.

Faustino answered in carefully chosen but unvoiced words.

At last the threshold.
Giving blessings, giving wounds.
Now it crosses me.

For the first time in his life, Faustino was completely at peace. Inexplicable things took place around him even as his mind sought to embrace its final images of this shore. Faustino would choose a single memory to take with him, to help see him through. With his last moment of life he resolved to recall every detail of the finery and festivity of the beautiful wedding at Raphael's Silver Cloud.

XI

Bᴇᴀᴛʀɪᴄᴇ the Changeling was standing at the entrance of Raphael's Silver Cloud, greeting wedding guests and ushering them inside with a kind word and a wave of the hand. There was a huge smile on her face and a look of vigilance in her eyes. Following Humberto's orders, it was also her job to stand guard at the threshold.

"Hello, Faustino," said Beatrice in a warm, lilting tone. She opened the front door for her friend, then giggled at some laughing people who were using a bar of soap to write ᴊᴜsᴛ ᴍᴀʀ-ʀɪᴇᴅ on the rear window of Teodoro's tiny car. A string of cans had already been tied to the rear fender.

Inside Raphael's Silver Cloud the dark dance floor was crowded with gyrating couples. Skirts were flying and heels were clicking and sliding on the wooden sawdust-covered floor. Pinoys and Mexicans were everywhere, dancing legally.

"Faustino!" someone cried out. It was Ted For Short, calling out from up on the stage. He was standing in front of the band and in the middle of a song medley. Anatoly was up on stage, humming and drumming away with his eyes closed. Singing in scat and forcefully kicking the floor tom, his lip movements were echoing his flying hands. Back home, in the old country, he'd spent many an endless childhood evening slapping the wooden tabletop in time with scratchy recordings of Gene Krupa and Buddy Rich.

His mother had saved some pin money and had purchased a tiny windup pygmy phone for him on his tenth birthday. It was a small tin box, painted green and decorated with black images of jumping, dancing Africans. When the lid was lifted, a miniature turntable and tone arm were revealed. It was through this small machine that Anatoly had first heard the faraway voice of America.

All he could afford back home in Bulgaria was a used bass tom. One of the first things he bought when he got to New York City was a full drum set. His floor tom and his rider were at least fifty years old. They had been purchased at a pawnshop in Queens. His rider cymbal was battered and discolored, but had a stunning smash and ring, a sound like all the dishes had been dropped in some celestial kitchen. It had been a gift from his loving wife.

A new tune began. Anatoly opened his eyes to get his emotional bearings, then quietly set the sticks down. With limp wrists, he spread out the soft metallic splash and tinge of rhythm with a fanned pair of brushes and a high hat and a slack, nodding head only loosely tied to his neck. It was difficult to believe that he was the same man who drove imaginary fares in a motorless taxicab everyday. The drums were always his true love. The cab paid the bills.

Barry Melton, a local musician, was standing to the right of the drummer and using a white flat-pick to flick a melody from his gloss-black Gibson GS. He was an old-time rock-and-roll guitarist who had played with the likes of Otis Spann and Bukka White. He could play anything on his Gibson. His large hands always moved with such seeming disinterest, such occasional ease—his fingers barely pressed the frets, yet the music flowed forth perfectly, effortlessly.

He had just finished the last few bars of "Caravan" and launched into the intro of "The Tennessee Waltz." Behind him, Anatoly set the brushes down and retrieved his drumsticks. There was a buzz of expectation in the room now. Dancing couples released one another and conversations died away. Tony, the ancient Pinoy leper, had brought an electric piano and was attempting to accompany Anatoly and Barry.

From the dark of stage-left a small figure moved back into

the white spotlight as applause rose up all around. The small figure wore a red-sequined waist jacket and black trousers. There was a satin cummerbund just visible behind the last button of his jacket. He wore four rings on each hand and a small earring in his left ear. His special shoes, one with a sole almost six inches thick, were fitted with taps at the heel and toe. His shoes were shined as only an old *manong* can shine shoes. It seemed as though a gleaming black puddle appeared wherever he placed a foot.

There was a wireless microphone in his left hand, and he held it like a teacup, his tiny pinkie finger extended. The long, thinning strands of hair that usually adorned his cranium had been replaced with a huge, glistening black wig. The wig shop in Beverly Hills had sprayed the toupee with Eterna-Gleem, a polyethylene coating that simulated a satiny layer of Dixie Peach pomade or Tres Flores Brilliantine. The cranial appliance had finger waves paralleled across the top, from the back to the front where it culminated in a waterfall that cast a shadow onto his forehead. Flanking these was a perfect ducktail, meeting at the back of the head, each tamed hair interleaved with its opposite.

The front of the stage flashed white for an instant as the shutter of a camera clicked down below. The bright light of the flash revealed for a millisecond the brown pancake makeup that had been patted onto Ted For Short's round face.

"Thank you, ladies and gentlemen and children of all ages, thank you."

He bowed as he transferred the mike to his right hand, then extended his left hand toward the back of the stage.

"Anatoly, ladies and gentlemen . . . and the Bear, Barry Melton, on guitar."

Applause rose up again.

"And a special guest on piano, an old friend. Let's give a big Silver Cloud welcome to Tony Espiritu."

Teodoro grinned at Tony the leper Espiritu, then at his wife, Jeanine, who was in the audience. Snapping his stubby fingers, Ted For Short caught up with the beat and began to sing the words of the beloved "Tennessee Waltz." His voice was resonant and deep—three times his size.

" '. . . when an old friend I happened to see . . .' thank you . . . Pee Wee King wrote this tune . . ."

Barry whispered "G" to Tony, who nodded thankfully.

Ted For Short reached behind his sideburn and pulled a lighted cigarette from inside his left ear.

"Did you know that Bob Hope and Johnny Cash both refuse to perform in the Philippines?" he said, exhaling into the spotlight.

"Yeah, in the Philippines there's no hope and no cash."

There was a quick rim shot from Anatoly. Teodoro took another long drag on his cigarette, then interrupted the laughter.

"Do you know what Mexican farmworkers have for breakfast? A cigarette and a piss."

There was knowing laughter everywhere in the room.

"Why is it that Sophocles and testicles don't rhyme? Testicleeze. That's something that really bothers me. Doesn't it bother you? What if a couple of balls wanted to get together and become a Greek philosopher?"

There was another rim shot and a smash at the cymbals.

"But honestly, folks, it's all venereal."

Behind him, the Bear kept up the melody of the waltz.

"Do you remember this, Ruby? Way back, a long time ago when my pompadour was real, we used to dance to this waltz at the old Rose Room in Stockton. Do you remember—down on El Dorado Street?"

Ruby, dressed in her seventh wedding dress, smiled with her eyes at the man on stage, and every eye in the room watched as the smile was joined by one that had formed on her lips. It was a smile that could be seen even through her lowered veil. It was clear to everybody present that she remembered very well. Someone brought a chair for her, and still smiling, she sat down just below the stage.

She was to be married on the same stage that she had danced upon for years. Tonight, the same musicians that had played her clothing off so many times would play her wedding march and her waltz. Tonight, she would blush when Teodoro reached up her dress for the garter, even though every man in this bar had seen her with every stitch of clothing off. Even those who talked or shot billiards during her striptease numbers would crane their necks to see Teodoro's hands climbing naughtily under her gown.

One of the stuffed white doves she used in her act was now clipped to her veil. The *paloma* was an old friend, one of the first to begin visiting her back at the convent in Pedernales. She had named it Poteh, after the dulcet balm of forgetfulness. She had taken his lifeless body to a taxidermist years ago. It had fallen to earth one sad day in Santa Monica. Ruby believed that it was the caress of Poteh's wings that kept her looking so young.

"Back then you wouldn't have anything to do with me," Ted For Short continued from the stage.

"Remember? You said that you wanted mister tall, dark, and handsome? Well, one out of three ain't bad."

Another rim shot.

He nodded toward the guitarist who had been in a holding pattern, and the four men converged at the same point in the first verse of the song.

I introduced him to my darlin'
and while they were dancin' . . .

Barry called out "C" to Tony, who nodded that he now understood the progression.

After watching his lifelong friend up there on stage, Faustino walked slowly and deliberately up to radiant Ruby, bowed to her in the elegant fashion he had learned while working in the dining car of the California Zephyr, and formally asked her to dance. Ruby rose gracefully and the two moved across the floor of the Silver Cloud with Ruby carefully holding her dress and train above the sweet-smelling sawdust that was strewn on the dance floor.

Over thirty years before, these two had almost danced in just this way, sensual, sexless, and rhythmic. Before the calligraphy of time had come to mark their burnished eyes, before the pared years of hiding had taken Teodoro and Faustino on their separate odysseys to the ends of the country and the earth, they had almost danced like this. But Faustino had chosen to stand, waiting outside the Rose Room, and Radiant Ruby had been preoccupied with avoiding Teodoro and his brutal shoes, so an act of friendship would have to wait three decades. They had been in two separate worlds back then.

As they moved to the music, the camera flashed again and once again—catching something new between them—framing the affection there.

They had almost danced together in 1958, in those calm moments before Ditto's men came shoving and grunting into the Rose Room to savage the furnishings and the paintings and the gentle men who waited with long strings of dance tickets in their hands. But neither Faustino nor Ruby thought of that night so long ago as they danced to the sound of Ted For Short's crooning. They simply wondered why happiness, the truth, costs so much . . . so very much. Did things have to take this long to be set right? Were they set right, even now?

"The two of you are finally together. Teodoro has always dreamed of this day."

"I was a fool," answered Ruby. "Worse than that, I was a fool for so very long." She sighed deeply. "All those husbands and no love."

They had been marriages timed with unwindable clocks, springs running downward from the tensile rhythm of infatuation through slowing boredom and finally to the pendulous stillness of dread. Ruby closed her eyes with the anger and the pain of the thought.

"I've run almost as far as you and Teodoro have. But Teodoro's not going to run anymore. I'm not going to let him. We've made a real home here. Stay with us, Faustino. There's lots of room at my house. Bring all of your books. Bring Constantine. Stay with us. We'll wait for that bastard Bambino together." She spoke with equal parts fervor and fear. Faustino only smiled.

They hugged each other as they danced—lives with six loud and loveless husbands followed the dancing lead of a life as a hunted, homosexual brown man who had killed a white landowner so many years before. It was a waltz between his archives of slain days and her hallowed gowns of threadbare hope. It was a slow dance in which her bodice of gauze and small vanities were held close by his sheaves of poetry that were daily dishonored by needless guilt. It was a waltz between cotton tunic and silk.

They danced long past the end of the song and no one stopped them. The band looked on and the crowd of well-wishers watched as they glided silently to the accompaniment of so many lost years. Raphael suddenly discovered that a mixed drink he was pouring had overflowed onto his fingers and down onto the floor.

When they finally stopped dancing, they realized that they had been on the floor alone and moving in silence. Both Ruby and Faustino seemed a bit embarrassed until all of their friends moved forward to touch them, to lay hands upon them.

Perpetua and Felicity were there. They were ancient women now, risen up from their wheelchairs for a last turn on the floor. The sisters were only months away from a quiet death in Carthage, Illinois. The saintly sisters would always long for the dance; they would always fear beasts and brutishness until all fear was gone. At the very end, each would suffer terrible, piercing pains to the throat and die embracing one another.

Lucy and Blandina and Rosa came forward to touch their old friends. It seemed that the effects of time had not visited these women. Lucy, the daughter of a wealthy merchant, would soon die blind and in abject poverty in Syracuse, New York. Blandina would meet her end while serving tables at a Lyon's restaurant in Frances, Washington. Rosa di Lima would spend the remainder of her days ministering to the needs of the poor and wretched of Stockton.

Sarah and Agatha moved in to lay their docile, soothing hands upon their old friends. Agatha would die of breast cancer on Sicily Island, Louisiana. Sarah, the youngest, would dye her hair even redder and move to Fairview, Kansas, where she would marry Eduardo Clancy, a Mexican Irishman.

Each of the taxi-dancers would remember the Rose Room with great fondness and would keep the civility of the dance sequestered in a safe, accessible place in their hearts. Each one would go to that place often in their daydreams, back to the applause and the sweep of nomadic laughter; to the trance and mystery of music and the timorous tremble of extended hands. They would see again the luminous jewelry, the diaphanous gown, the leap and plunge on hardwood and beneath a glittering chandelier. In their final days, each would spurn and tease, then give in coyly to the soft shades of death, the final eternizing shroud of music.

All of them leaned toward the center to join in the dance as a single, slow-moving unit, their hands outstretched to touch Ruby and Faustino. "The Tennessee Waltz" began again. They moved as dominions move, as a wheel moves, with spokes of reaching arms, a living hub of common memory.

Even King came forward, combed and sweating, but he wouldn't dance. He only pushed his huge bulk forward and whispered anxiously into Faustino's ear. Faustino nodded calmly and whispered to King Pete that he shouldn't worry so. When he released Ruby, the wedding party saw that Faustino had pinned a twenty-dollar bill to Ruby's dress. Ruby saw the bill and let out a small heartfelt cry of glee.

Everyone who loved Ruby knew about her escape from the convent at Pedernales. Ruby had told them all that she had seen beautiful Mexican weddings unfolding in the open air, weddings that always culminated in the joy and generosity of the money dance. They all knew that she had first seen the special dance the very day she had ridden the foundling's wheel to freedom. She had seen an extended family taking care of its own.

From that moment, marriage had become her avocation and lifelong hobby. She began attending the weddings of strangers in her travels across Mexico. The poorer the families had been, the more glorious the money dances had been—the more beautiful the bride in pesos and white.

Six weddings of her own and ... at last, a money dance! Ruby's face beamed as she moved from partner to partner and flashbulbs flooded the room in holy, time-suspending white. Thank God, thought Ruby, someone remembered to hire a photographer. Ruby saw her composing her shots, focusing and moving her camera as one partner after another came forward to dance.

The photographer was a sad-eyed, dark-haired woman. She had short hair and a sensitive Mediterranean look. Was she Jewish? Whoever she was, she smiled as she shot her photos. It was clear that she loved her work, that she coveted the moments she was forming in her lens, the long, white wedding dress covered with green bills. The pretty photographer smiled with anticipation at all the birds that had flown in through the skylight and perched chattering and chirping on the Ocumicho pottery above.

THE MONEY DANCE, the legend below the photograph would read.

The photographer had even captured the incredible variety that was spread over a long table at the back wall. There were huge bowls of *pancit*, adobo, *dininguan*, and *lechon* placed next to heaping trays of *carnitas y enchiladas de pollo* and a huge pile of *flautas* steaming beneath red-and-green sauce. There were flats of *bibinka*, plastic cups of *halo-halo*, and stacks of *pan dulce*. In a beautiful blue bowl at the corner of the table was a golden mound of filo dough filled with Bulgarian cheese and eggs. No one knew who had brought the *banitza*. THE FEAST.

"This has been my first true wedding," the effervescent bride had confided in a breathy, private whisper to each adoring dance partner.

"All those others were just practice sessions for this one."

Ted For Short stepped down from the stage after singing and tapping his way through a medley of sultry love songs. Up on stage, Tony the leper had taken up the microphone and was singing his theme song, "I Fall to Pieces." The photographer would call this photo THE FILIPINO JOHNNY RAY.

Ruby stopped to kiss a tired César Chávez, who had driven all night from Delano to attend the festivities. He was hoping, even as he danced, that another jar of motor honey and a can of stop-leak in the radiator would get him and his battered Plymouth Valiant back home. An ancient Mexican predilection for a belief in miracles had been carried over into the automotive age.

He smiled at his old friend Ruby. He had been present at two of her previous marriages. One wedding had been held down in El Centro and another in Turlock, and he happily agreed that this was truly her first wedding. It was true that all of the past ceremonies had been performed by legitimate priests and preachers, yet somehow only this exchange of vows would be dignified by deepest love.

"You looked tired, *viejo*," she said to him as they danced, "eat some food. *¿Ya comistes?* There's food from everywhere over there, even a dish from Bulgaria. All that crazy fasting you do is going to ruin your health. I know I'm wasting my time telling you anything, *querido*. I told you that same thing ten years ago, and you didn't listen to me then. But you've done enough, César. You should rest awhile."

César only smiled that smile of his. A smile that was somewhere between whimsy and strength of will, a smile that betrayed a spirit not meant for confrontation, but born into it.

"I have to go," he said in a way that externalized the necessity to leave.

He had to go. There were thousands waiting to hear him speak, thousands waiting to follow behind and walk beside him, and thousands more, hushed and desolate, waiting in line to see his wooden casket.

When they parted, the camera captured a look of profound fatigue lodged in César's eyes and the remains of a mischievous smile on his lips. On Ruby's lace shoulder he had carefully pinned a five-dollar bill wrapped around a UFW flyer . . . a farmworker's wad. The legend beneath this photograph would read BOYCOTT GRAPES.

At the end of the money dance, the floor began to clear for the bride and groom. It was a wedding in reverse. First the entertainment, then the reception, and finally the wedding ceremony itself. Radiant Ruby had planned it this way, as if to undo all of the other weddings.

"Ladies and gentlemen," said Barry, adjusting the microphone upward to his own height, "please clear the floor for the bride and groom's waltz."

Ted For Short and Ruby walked toward each other, embraced in the heat of the spotlight, then prepared to dance to a special waltz written just that morning by Barry himself. He had composed it especially for his two dear friends. Ruby, poised in green plumage and white lace and smiling beyond price, cleaved unto Teodoro, resplendent in red sequins and shining, coal black hair.

The music started as Barry began his song. A single spotlight shone down on the lovers, who were balanced on the shimmering, tugging edge of a note. Opposite feet moved together as they began in elegance what had once been illegal.

> *There are five-spots and ten-spots and glasses of wine. There are*
> *   twenties and hundreds, like leaves on the vine.*
> *Her wedding dress is smothered, but not one dollar falls, while*
> *   the band plays the sojourners' waltz.*
> *He swings her, he swoons her out there on the floor. He lifts her,*
> *   she's cooing and cries out for more.*
> *Their friends say behind them, love is true and not false. And*
> *   the band played the sojourners' waltz.*
> *There is darkness, then spotlights as shoes kiss the floor. There*
> *   are white gloves and cufflinks and champagne to pour.*
> *There is pancit and birria and there is crepe on the walls.*
> *   And the band played the sojourners' waltz.*

As the hypnotic dance spun on and on, others stepped from the darkness and joined in the timeless vertigo of the clockwise waltz, the graceful pageant of the luxurious poor.

Faustino, on seeing that other men were cutting in now on Teodoro's dance with Ruby, took the smiling groom aside on the dance floor and brought him to the *tamal* steamer, where King was nervously sampling his own goods. The sight of all the food at the back table had made him feel a little insecure about his own contribution, so he reassured himself with a taste of Annette's fingers. When he saw Ted For Short coming his way he quickly gulped down the pork tamale that had been nesting on his tongue.

"I seen him," said King, without greeting his friends.

"I seen him and I spoke with him. He asked if I knew you and Faustino. He said something about a third man who was once a boy. He asked so many questions that I got worried and confused. I know he's around here somewhere," said a shaken King Pete. "He asked where he could find you. He must've spotted you. I swear I didn't tell him nothing, but that man scared the dickens out of me. And you know I ain't scared of no man." King pounded one huge fist into a spread palm. The image of his meetings with the wicked man were still fresh in his muddled mind.

Two days before the wedding there had been a strange-looking man standing in the field near Raphael's Silver Cloud. King had seen the man before, hanging around the Mission District in the predawn hours before his tamales were delivered. He looked like a man who was very close to his own end. One of his eyes was already dead and there were quaking palsies beneath the slightest movement of his body.

At their first meeting, the strange man had tried to ask King something, but the presence of other customers had kept the stranger from pursuing the matter. King had immediately sized the man up as a lightweight, but there was something dangerous about him. He looked fearless and smelled like a slaughterhouse.

Both times they had spoken, the man had kept to the shadows, deliberately avoiding the light of the neon angels. It was on the second occasion that the questions were asked.

"I've ranged over this world, going here and there," he said. "I know a man who has been wronged when I see one. It had to be a woman, Mr. King. I can see it in your face. It had to be a woman. Is Queenie her name? Is she the hard stone in your shoe?"

"I gotta go," said King nervously.

"Just one thing," said the stranger. "I am looking for some men and I know you can help me. One is a thin, dark man with long white hair. He's a queer and his name is Faustino. The other is an ugly midget with a hunchback. His name is Cabiri. They're both Filipino. I caught a glimpse of the *bakla* some years ago in a train yard in Detroit, then again eight or nine years ago up in Chicago. The accursed midget's been everywhere, too many places to name. But they've both come back to California, where it all started. I spotted the dwarf just the other day, outside a donut shop on Geary Street. I know it was him. They're both old now, like me. Oh yes, there is a third man . . . a Mexican. He was a boy back then, but he is a man now. His first name is Zeferino."

When the stranger mentioned Faustino and Ted For Short, King quickly turned his startled face away so that his eyes would not betray his thoughts.

"The farmworker grapevine has always protected them. But if you can spot a lie, it's just as good as seeing the truth. Every now and again I'll catch wind of them. But I've had one advantage. One of them knew me back in the Islands, long ago, but neither of them knows what I look like as an old man. You might say I've changed," he smirked. "But they haven't. Once an abomination, always an abomination. They've always seemed to know when I was getting close, but now they're both here . . . and they're too old and tired to run anymore. You know this area like the back of your hand, Mr. King. Everybody says you're the man to talk to."

"Never seen or heard tell of neither one of them," said King, walking backward, slowly backpedaling away. "Don't know neither one of them from Adam," added King in a fearful voice.

"I think you're lying!" the stranger called after a disappearing King. "I know you're a damned liar. I've practiced lying so that I'll know a lie when I hear it. You're protecting murderers. They murdered my father!"

King abandoned his cart and ran, looking back at each street corner to see if the man was following him. Near Harrison Street he stopped to look up and down the dark pavement. He saw no one and breathed a heavy sigh of relief. All at once, out of nowhere a voice cried out, "She would still be with you if you had paid for her. You should have taken what you wanted. Everyone else did."

The old boxer ran into the yellow air of a streetlight. The stranger's voice had been like a torrent, like the voice of a crowd issuing and hissing from within a single throat. As he struggled to catch his breath, he decided against going home. He did not want to lead the diabolical man back to the Silver Cloud. His friends had to be warned, they had to be protected. The stranger could not be allowed to ruin Teodoro and Ruby's wedding plans.

Thoroughly frightened by the memory of that meeting, King Pete huddled in a corner of the crowded dance floor and covered up using his gloves and his elbows. He bobbed his head to the left and right, never making the same move twice in a row. He could just make out the crowd of faces around him at ringside, excited, contorted faces waiting for him to fall. A bell sounded frantically in the distance. A towel was thrown.

"He's not a man," said Teodoro to a despondent King Pete, whose mind had gone into a protective clinch. "Bambino Reyes was never even a child. He is only an unholy mantle of suffering and grief."

"He's out there right now," said Faustino, who was looking directly into Teodoro's eyes. "You know it, too, don't you?" Teodoro nodded. "But I can't run anymore," he added with calm resignation. "Not anymore. All that running is past for me."

"I have to get married," answered Teodoro with a smile. "And that's exactly what I'm going to do tonight. This is my life, you and Ruby and all of my friends—not that fiend and the fear he's given me all these years. Bambino Reyes has disrupted my life enough. Tomorrow—or the next day—after I have risen from my wedding bed, I will go find out where he is and we will do what's necessary to finally settle this thing."

He grabbed his friend's hand and squeezed it earnestly. His brave words could not hide his fear.

"Faustino, let me see him first!" he pleaded. "Promise me you'll let me see him first."

"I am going to work in the windmills tomorrow, and the day after that" was all that Faustino would say.

"I won't let you give up," said Ted For Short angrily. "I won't let you give up. We are friends for life, aren't we?"

Faustino nodded, smiling.

"Now somebody go find that crazy Mexican priest and let's get me married off."

"I'll go tell Beatrice what this man looks like," said an anxious King Pete. "That way he won't get past the front door."

Ancient Father Humberto, decrepit but still alive and refusing any offers of assistance, stepped forward to the front of the gathering. He held two Bibles in his hands, his brother's precious book and the one that Faustino had recently given to him without a word of explanation. It had simply appeared one day along with plates of food that Raphael had sent up one evening with the pulley and platform apparatus. It was a beautiful Bible in a hand-tooled, leather case.

Humberto wore black socks and black pants for the occasion. He wore no shoes at all. His upper body, pasty with age, was swathed in a used linen sheet that Raphael had purchased for him at the Salvation Army store. He had refused to wear shirts, choosing instead to dress in the manner of the ancient Greek and Egyptian hermits and anchorites.

He looked slowly about himself, at the extraordinary Ocumicho ceramics above his head, then at the feathered creatures that crowded and huddled above the wondrous icons. Humberto had never been inside the building. The Indians are still here, he thought, on seeing the sculptures for the first time ... and so am I. The devils are outside in the world, waiting there secretly, and far more vile and malevolent than anything depicted in these works in wood and clay.

The padre had just been told by Ted For Short that the wedding had to be hurried up a bit. Humberto had long ago learned about Bambino Reyes and his callous vow of vengeance. The news that the fiend was here in the Mission District had brought Humberto back to life. It had even lured him down from the high silver tower on the roof. He volunteered to do the wedding; he had happily agreed to descend because he had recently come to the startling realization that this fellow Bambino Reyes was his true vocation, his true holy work.

It had suddenly become clear to Humberto that Bambino Reyes was the sole purpose for which the tower and the spartan dwelling upon it had been built. There had been a blinding moment of insight one evening, when Humberto, prostrate on the roof of the Silver Cloud, had demanded of God to know why he, of all modern men, had been chosen to live in a tower in the sky. One of the angels had spoken to him then, in an unchronicled, private annunciation.

The tower had not been constructed to provide for interminable months of isolated contemplation and self-mutilation. The tower had not been erected in order to place two souls in closer proximity to heaven. It had been built for a strategic, far-reaching purpose. It was for Bambino. Among other reasons, Humberto had been kept alive for over sixty years past his first death so that he could man the watchtower that had been constructed to look out for Bambino Reyes.

"And I saw him!" Humberto had exclaimed to Queenie. "I saw him passing by in a bus." Both Humberto and Queenie had spotted him many times since then, hiding behind automobiles and peering through the broken windows of abandoned buildings across the street.

Queenie was not his disciple as he had once thought; she was his army, his personal platoon. Even Humberto admitted to himself that he was a failed stylite. He had sought out martyrdom, but had never been cut out for the ascetic life. He preferred Chesterfield Kings, strychnine, and erotic curiosa to prayer. His hopes for an easy sainthood had been completely dashed until he heard about Bambino's presence in San Francisco.

"I can help you kill the devil," he had announced to Ted For Short. "I possess a secret weapon. . . ."

He thought for a moment about his words.

". . . or it possesses me. It's the answer to your prayers, and to mine. I am part of a divine plan."

Though Humberto had made the offer many, many times in the last few days, neither Faustino nor Teodoro Cabiri had ever taken him seriously.

It's the price of insanity, thought Humberto, when he realized that Teodoro had not even considered his offer. Everyone thought he was crazy. Not even kindly Raphael seemed to believe him.

"I can kill the serpent," he'd told Queenie while she knelt praying in the shack up on the silver tower. She had been wearing blue satin high-heel shoes. At the very moment that Humberto had discovered the true purpose of the tower and of his second life, he had put down his tattered whip; then he had sent a note to Raphael imploring him to purchase the shoes, specifying the exact color and the size.

"Blue as lechery," he wrote with jubilation, "and size 9."

All those years of ingesting cyanide and arsenic and of smelling linger-creme had brought many strange ideas to life inside his cluttered, persistent mind. But all that the poisons had ever succeeded in killing was his case of congenital hopelessness.

"Deus ex machina," he had confided to Queenie in secret.

"God in a machine."

When Humberto's thoughts cleared to a reasonable degree, he realized, with some surprise, that he was in the midst of a wedding, and that everyone in the bar was waiting for him to begin the ceremony.

"Ladies and gentlemen, we are gathered here today to join in holy matrimony la señora Ruby De La Vida, whom we all know as Radiant Ruby, and Mr. Teodoro Teofilo Cabiri . . . Lover of God, Lover of God and protector of shipwrecked men . . . Ted For Short.

"We all know that this day has been a long time in coming, so if anyone has any kind of objection . . . he is not welcome here in our presence and our midst.

"First, before we proceed with this joyous celebration, I would like to thank brother Raphael for allowing us to use his beautiful bar for this magnificent wedding and for this splendid reception."

There was a general rousing applause. Only Faustino and King applauded tentatively. Faustino nervously watched the door. Beatrice had come inside to rejoin the company and to enjoy the ceremony. She stood with her back to the door, a huge plate of food in her hand. Faustino somehow knew that Bambino could not enter Raphael's Silver Cloud, but nevertheless felt the familiar power of his ominous spirit hovering outside in the dark and sullen streets.

"And I, personally, would like to thank him for the prolonged use of his roof," continued Humberto, "and for allowing us to build our silver watch tower and hermitage. This is a business day and he could have paying customers in here, but he has decided instead to honor his friends, his *compañeros y compañeras*. As most of you know, Raphael's Silver Cloud is a very special place; good people are drawn here. They are pulled here, like ambulances swooping to injuries, only to find that people are healed within these walls. The injuries are all out there." He nodded toward the street, toward the shadows where Bambino waited.

Faustino, who had surveyed the audience from his place between Ruby and Teodoro, stepped back and gestured to the bride and groom to move a little closer. Ted For Short, dressed in his best show clothes, was standing on a small wooden stool. His face was crowded with blissful expressions that vied with nervous anticipation for a resting place in the eyes, on the lips.

"Ruby."

At the sound of Ruby's name, the birds overhead shuffled, ruffling and twittering in acknowledgment.

Humberto turned to face her. Ruby stiffened as though she had never before stood in front of a preacher.

"Once she flew to abuse, threw herself at upright mistakes who walked in pants and promised canyons for a bed. Once she pecked and scratched in the shadow of men."

Ruby lowered her eyes beneath her veil.

"Ted For Short."

Humberto turned to face Teodoro.

"He was exhaled, a speck in the last breath of a dying family . . . he flew cutward, woundward into God's dumbfounding whirlwind. Faustino was with him in the Islands and on the boat. As children they were insulted together, first by the inscrutable will of God, then by every other living human being.

"Ruby and Teodoro." Humberto motioned them to stand even closer. Faustino, with his right leg, shoved the stool closer to Ruby.

"Each cut in their joining lips is fused over now. Sealed up by the sheer strength of will. Often, two wounds together will heal when one will not. For, contrary to popular opinion, it takes great willpower to love. Cleave each of you unto the other, closer than dying brothers, closer than colors on a palette. Cleave each of you unto the other, free now of chaff and dross, to covet the flower, the harbor, and the oil of a lover's brow. Each of you, be both wick and wax for the other, both illuminate and measure your own love."

Humberto lost his place again. For a moment he had drifted back to Morelia, but was stunned back to the here and now by the blinding intrusion of a flashbulb. The crazy priest then noticed one particular face at the back of the room. There was something familiar about that face. It was an old Indian face, framed by long black hair. Where on earth had he seen the face before?

"Now, before we hear their vows," Humberto began again, "I will repeat for you something that Queenie and I overheard last night when the two angels up on the roof were conversing. I will tell you one of their secret songs."

He extended an arm toward Faustino, who reached into his pocket, then gave something to Humberto. It was a diamond ring. Humberto held it up until a thin shaft of light caught it. It broke the light up into a thousand pieces that rested on faces and clothing and on the dark walls of the bar.

" 'There is a hearth in a ring,' they sing.

" 'There is a bonfire in the gleaming stone—all your mourning years aflame in the facets—a stay, a reprieve in your lifelong accrual of hurt amid acts of desperate normalcy.

" 'There is the blush of a last-time bride,' they sing, 'awash in a mane of veils, hair of sleet and rustling arpeggios of silk moving up candled aisles as bowing minstrels bend to their tremulous work. Her breasts are hoisted up for their last vault at that exalted height,' they harmonize.

" 'He is becoming heavy of hand,' they say, 'but never heavy-handed. There's a shiver in the legerdemain, but he is still *con la mano magica*.' "

Humberto shut his eyes to recall the words exactly.

" '*El pájaro mosca y la paloma,* the hummingbird and the dove. Together they will fly to the rhythm of the wedding vows, the soft ambush of words. They will truss themselves with sentences, suffer blows from a gentle assailant's arsenal of myriad, barbed desires. With prayers wreathing their skulls, it is joy that aches in their crying joints and weeping bones.' It's what the two angels said yesterday," said Humberto.

Humberto knew, as he surveyed the room, that he could never repeat everything that the angels had sung to him. By listening to their celestial gossip, Humberto learned that Jeanine would soon develop Tony the leper's noncontagious leprosy. He knew that they would both be buried in Lodi, their bodies swaddled in yards of white gauze and preserved in gallons of yellow petroleum jelly. He smiled at the thought that their only daughter would have perfect skin, as smooth as Chinese ceramic.

Humberto knew that Anatoly would die quietly in his Checker cab, his head resting softly on the horn. The doleful tones of Anatoly's muffled horn would be heard in Manhattan, where the headlight of every cab would be turned on for a full day. King Pete would carry the Gypsy from the Checker to the sidewalk, where an ambulance would take him away. All of Anatoly's things would be carefully placed into the tent and set afire. Next to his burning drum set and his blistering, smoking pygmy-phone there would be a photograph of his wife, the

Duchess, curling and dissolving in the spreading flame. No one in the Mission District would call the fire department.

The mad priest knew that the angels would effortlessly lift Queenie into the skies by the pliant leverage of her groin, then return her to earth in possession of a pristine vaginal vault growing into her hips. In time, she would return to King Pete and in their wedding bed, his gentle uppercuts would have her whimpering with joy; his soft roundhouses would stagger her and put her sweetly onto her back. She would return to King without her mirror; she would return possessing only dim reflections of her past life—a life in exile—a small, handheld universe in reverse.

While she waited at Stanford Medical Center, there would be a minor light-drenched annunciation in the dark hallway near the janitor's closet. She would be told by one of the twin angels that she and King would have a son; that their only child would have endless wind, a quick left jab and great footwork; he would be a contender.

Ruby cleared her throat. The old man returned from his visions. He nodded at the bride, indicating that it was time for the marriage vows.

"You can die from strangers," vowed Ruby, repeating Queenie's perfect words. When King heard them, he turned his attention from the food platform to the wedding ceremony. His wife's words were being used in the rites. It was almost as if she were actually present.

"You can live wedged between wishes, choose a life to live that belongs to someone else. You can live waiting for the shadow to fall from above. Or you can spin the wooden wheel and run birdbound and northbound. You can plunge your hands into all the words there are and pick only the best ones to say. I choose this waltz and this earthbound flight. I choose you, Teodoro. When everything is going good, I will be your partner, *tu compañera*. When everything goes bad, when everything breaks down, I will be your salve and full body cast. I choose myself by choosing you."

"I love you, Ruby, husk and cob. I love you meat and shell, ore and tailings. There is magic in this life," vowed Ted For Short. "It's not all lost to an ancient time of miracles. It's all ethereal once you get past the patter and the misdirection of His plan."

Teodoro Teofilo Cabiri then placed a gold ring onto the lovely finger of Ravishing Ruby.

"My God is a close-in magician," he continued as she placed a ring onto his finger. "You can stand right on top of his hands and not see what He's doing. My God is an absentminded old man, playing a trick on me, then forgetting over and over to let me in on it. And look—now I've been tricked again. He has given me love. All that I have ever learned in this life is how to watch God's other hand."

At vow's very end, there is a curving yearn in sideward glances, a swan's kiss as reaching muscle and rind stretch to place two sets of pursed lips at the same place in time and space at Raphael's Silver Cloud.

Beneath the turning shadow of a windmill, Faustino's precious memory of the wedding was perfect and immutable now, annealed by the heat and the cold of his own final breaths, tempered by a solemn act of will. Faustino relinquished his fear even as an endless torrent of words was spewing brutishly from Bambino's lips. There were crude questions being posed, but Faustino answered none of them. There was metal mocking the frailty of his skin, but Faustino was deaf to its taunts. He was too busy greeting the gentle Japanese boy who was kneeling at his side. The young soldier looked up from his newly written death poem and smiled warmly at Faustino. Then the two joined hands in that small clearing in the Philippine jungle.

Pietro Ditto, at Faustino's other side, stared silently upward from his place beside the fire and the green, torpid slough, his eyes drinking their last lumens. A nervous Constantine kept appearing here and there in his white summer suit, his hands wringing with concern as his lover approached the moment.

Then there was something unfelt yet terrible, something cold and mechanical that was drawn across living channels to spill the liquid and clot the breath with running streams of warmth. It was the third cutting.

Faustino's body lay there as the rejoicing killer marveled at his work, then left. And it lay there as nightfall arrived. His empty body lay there as his soul dove from failing cell to failing cell, then leaped out onto the breeze where the turning windmills tossed it skyward and toward the moon. Ensnared by unseen hands, his spirit was carried aloft in hourless time to a distance neither close nor far; then it was gently set down on a worn carpet in front of an aging and paint-ridden door. The spirit waited as unseen hands knocked.

"Come in," a voice called out from behind the door. "Come in," said Constantine Cavafy. There was youth and strength in both his voice and his face. On his forehead there were scores of poems yet to be written. The eyeglasses were gone now and his flyaway hair was as dark as a raven's. He had put his pencil down upon hearing the knock at his door. The poem hidden beneath a half-dozen hastily scribbled corrections was just becoming visible. He would entitle the poem "On Hearing of Love." He turned to watch as the door opened and the white light of the common hallway framed a thin, dark shape standing at the entry.

"Finally," sighed Constantine, who rose as he spoke and rushed over to meet the man. "We are finally of the same substance."

The two men embraced at last in his small rooms in the Armenian Hotel, the sounds of Paris receding into the distance with each touch of male hand upon male skin. They embraced long past propriety before one of them spoke again.

"You've seen them!" said Constantine, his voice rising with excitement. "You couldn't wait! You've been to the gardens and the cafes and you've seen them, haven't you?"

The two men walked hand in hand toward the bed just as the gaslights dimmed throughout the hotel.

"I saw Rilke," said the other man with a quiet yet profound sense of awe. Though the room was dark, he seemed to know where to turn and just where to place his feet to avoid piles of books and stacks of poetry.

"You know, don't you," said Constantine as the men removed their clothing, "you know that you can be anywhere that you love to be, touch any place where your memory resides. You can smoke as much as you want. You can be in a hundred places at once."

The other man smiled as he kicked off his shoes. He was already there at the water cooler at the end of a row of cucumbers, sharing the long dipper with all of the other sweating men. He was already laughing with his brothers on board the California Zephyr, eating cold ham and mustard and drinking from a bottle of purloined vodka as the train streaked through a sleeping Salt Lake City. He was behind the wheel of a beautiful new Buick and tugging a shiny Airstream trailer. He was dancing with a money-covered dove and lying naked with a poet in Paris, in the time between the wars.

After circling the earth for an unknowable time, some part of Faustino's spirit descended softly, settling upon Ruby's mind. He visited her days after his death, as she prepared for bed in her small home. Her new husband was in jail and so she must sleep alone. The omniscient spirit could see that there was a single pensive hollow beneath her hair where death's insistent finger probed, leaving sleep marks in the bright of day. But still, death could not yet enter.

Married half a dozen times before her marriage to Ted For Short, she sometimes cried because she could no longer remember her earlier husbands' faces. Each man had demanded that she destroy all remnants of her past life, so she had burned every letter and photograph she owned as an act of loyalty to her new husband.

"Each new man was like another stay on Ellis Island. Each one made me change my name." In her weaker moments, Ruby felt fractured and scattered, as though each separate man held discrete pieces of her image in their minds, shards of a shattered mirror, lost and irreconcilable. She had once been a collector of men, a woman who prized ephemera. But after so many men, she is finally in love.

"I have loved only one," she says now to no one. "Out of all of them I have loved only one." She turned her thoughts to her lover, the prisoner. In the last seven years, her entire world had changed. Raphael's Silver Cloud had changed it. Without knowing why, she had quit her job in Reno and come directly to the little bar with the huge neon sign. The love of her life and so many good friends had been waiting for her at Raphael's Silver Cloud. Ruby smiled at the thought; then the smile changed to sadness.

Their enemy, Bambino Reyes, had finally arrived in San

Francisco. Without saying it, everyone knew that he would come, sooner or later. Perhaps it had been on the very week of the wedding. Somehow Bambino had always been able to locate her husband, no matter where in the world he hid.

But Bambino Reyes had arrived at a time most propitious for his own cruel ends. His aging prey no longer ran. Only days ago, while stripping for the last time on stage at Raphael's Silver Cloud, she had been witness to two sacred acts; two deaths, years in coming, had finally come to pass. One death happened just outside Carmen's, the tiny Filipino restaurant on the Fourth Street drawbridge. Bambino Reyes's relentless hatred had at last been snuffed out. Everyone's prayers had been answered.

The second death had been *pobre padre* Humberto's. She could still see him dying on the sidewalk outside the bar, a bleeding and wingless old man. Her hand moved involuntarily to cover her eyes as she recalled his suffering. "The grave will be such a relief for him," she sighed.

A third death, just two days before these, made cold tears fill her eyes. A dear old friend had been murdered beneath the windmills in Altamont. She sobbed to herself as she recalled once again that death had come to claim dearest Faustino.

"Faustino," she whispered, a threnody that rose through her bird-covered roof. *"Esse angelos novimus ex fide,"* she said to comfort herself. After what she had witnessed, she knew now that there were still protectors here on this hard world.

"Esse angelos novimus ex fide."

She loved to repeat the Latin words over and over whenever sadness overcame her. It was a cherished phrase from Teodoro's days as a ringmaster for the Gonzalez Brothers Circus. Ted For Short had always begun his grand address to the expectant crowd with those words.

"There are those lucky few among us who know that angels exist simply because we believe in them! Tonight, let us all believe in everything that is fine and true! Let us believe in daring and heroism! And now, dear ladies and gentlemen and children of all ages, for your delectation, ascending to the very apex of the big top, the ultimate in dazzling, aerial artistry and breathtaking maneuvers in midair without benefit of a safety net—fresh from a triumphal tour of western Europe and the subcontinent, please welcome Norma, Maria, Susan, and Theresa, the Lovely Flying Lopez Sisters!"

Before sleeping, she pulled from the oven a small loaf of bread she had baked for her husband. She placed it on the window ledge for one of her protectors to spirit it away. Faustino's spirit watched as Ruby sensed his memory coming to rest on the skin of her face. She gazed about her own home . . . her tossed and cluttered home, then climbed into bed and gave in, becalmed, to dream of a street in Paris that she had never seen.

Across town at the city jail, Faustino's spirit descended onto Ted For Short's bunk just as the watch commander's clock reached midnight. In the security bay a bright overhead light suddenly snapped on, dimming every other light that burned in the Hall of Justice. Its beam began as a wide and diffuse spray of light, then slowly resolved downward to an intensely white three-foot spot of intimate illumination.

In the air above the bay, there were the sharp, electric sounds of readiness and the hum of anticipation as guitar strings were tuned, drum skins were tightened, and seemingly random chords warmed up the piano keys. There was the sharp buzz of a ground loop, then the piercing squeal of feedback and a voice offstage saying, "I'm not sure why, but I want to start this set with 'I Love Paris,' then we can go into that Jimmy Webb and Sammy Cahn stuff we used in Vegas."

There was a flurry at stage right as a soft drum roll began. Then all at once a hush moved through the audience when a small figure wearing a shining black wig and a sequined jacket stepped smartly into the beam of light.

Jail intercoms clicked on. Heads rose slowly from pillows, and from out of the darkness the drowsy voice of the young man who was being sent to Pelican Bay could be heard rousing his sleeping cellmates. "Wake up, it's showtime!"

The man in the spotlight had wrapped his jewel-encrusted fingers around a cordless microphone and, after undoing his bow tie, cleared his pipes with a stiff shot of bourbon. He lit a menthol cigarette, cued the band, then began singing his sweet songs to shipwrecked men.

XII

May 14, 1993

THE thin layers of oil-based paint that had once portrayed the angels' hair to be as red as Fiorentino's cherubs, and their mild skin to be as milky as Florentine marble, now blistered in the heat and peeled away before finally disappearing altogether in a pungent puff of black vapor. The angels' unseen souls, checking azimuth and inclination, set their course for a distant place where mountainous stones were not humbled into sand; where crawling infants were never flicked onto a path of lifelong grief; where nagging worries and rending woes were never woven into the weft to stain the fabric of a pleasing face.

Within the departing skirts and spreading wings of these beings of light, incandescent bulbs popped and went dim as the gasoline heat reached out greedily for fragile glass and glowing filament cores.

Of course, they felt nothing of the heat. They had never really invested in the low substance of the advertising sign. Even while the crazed priest and his one-woman army spread gasoline and tossed burning matches in the rising moonlight, one angel still pierced the other with the flashing red arrow and with its unseen, barbed essence. The cold, mechanical slam of the physical arrow merely masked its own pointed ideal.

Once the decision to leave had been made, the ethereal twins had conferred for a moment in subdued flickers of counterpoint; then they suddenly appeared before Queenie, having first arranged their substance to look as though they were made merely of flesh and blood. With sculpted hands, they lifted her from her feet. Then, after an unmeasurable time, neither long nor short, they placed her back upon the surface of the roof where she stood stunned and newly modest, her vestal breasts heaving above the growing heat in her womb. Without asking, Queenie knew that her guileless maidenhead had somehow been restored to her.

As they pulled away, the angelic twins had restoked Humberto's madness by touching his blistered forehead with the merest shadow of God's finger. They knew that the lunatic on the roof had finally acknowledged his true vocation and calling. The priest was now truly touched, his boiling mind enlightened by the rising fire.

Above Humberto's frantic face the angels were leaving. Like children at the cookie jar, their translucent cheeks were smeared with livid life, their chins dotted with crumbs of tragedy and smatterings of life's matter. They were packing their bags and speaking softly in billowing halos of chromatic harmony. They were leaving now, and each was swearing the other to a solemn vow of secrecy.

On the verge of their final task, they had worked their living furrows and had stayed until the harvest was in and tallied. They had tarried with mankind, and upon seeing that the pain of life itself is holy, that grief is the plate upon which joy is served, they endeavored to keep the secret from God. For He is bored now with songs and words. He is weary of lyrics that come too easily, melodies by the millions on the tip of His tongue.

So it is that all of God's shining, winged messengers, eternal migrant workers sent down on jobs to worlds where everything perishes, always return home laden and stricken with the grief and mystery of it, return hiding the knowledge that love and life are everywhere imperiled.

It is out of pity for God that they conspire to keep the truth from the true. For being all things to all things has taken its heavy toll. Lately She has no time to Herself and She has developed a growing fondness for those who are honorable without bothering Her.

The angels were on fire as they left; they were slowly pulling their skirts up and away from the rigid apparatus of welds and bolts that had so presumptuously sought to bind them. They had once been rank neophytes to the mundane riddle of this particular earth. Now they were seasoned sojourners who had seen the first clay castings of the primal garden.

Dismayed by the presence of a mortal emotion, the twin angels struggled against a tugging twinge of regret. Having seen Sirius from the backside, having rested on the Pleiades, how could this be? Wasn't this the world where a secret number of mortal days was cruelly dropped into the rocking cradle of each newborn child?

What should they tell their god of this task? Could they say that a dance hall filled with gentle saints had been savaged; that a mad, deathless priest, while in their keeping, had finally expired in ardor? Should they say that giants and rain dwarves still moved among men?

Could they tell the story of Raphael's Silver Cloud to a surly god who is afflicted with both amnesia and insomnia and is unable to recall that His own waking dreams are the fabric of life itself?

In a key two octaves above the spectrum of notions, their bloodless harmony as tight as Don and Phil Everly, the departing duet sang an aria of couplets devoid of lyrics. They sang No! Verses and unending refrains of No!

What lowly cherubim would dare attempt to explain grid coordinates, forward air controllers, and the arcane principles of field artillery? It was one thing to lift old Enoch into heaven; it was another thing altogether to place a pristine mound of Venus into the thighs of an old whore. It was best to say nothing about it to anyone, not even in jest. For who in the entire, wide celestial choir knew how to take a joke?

So it was that mild phantasms decided between themselves that they would return in their own good time and report in as usual that all the different and disparate worlds were one and harmonious. Then they would take their wonted place in the blinding glory of the chorus and forever keep secret the deeds they had done at Raphael's Silver Cloud.

Above the Mission District, they glided blithely past the listless lunar face; past the dour work camps where a platoon of childless bachelors quietly readied themselves for a Father's Day at school; past fields where dark-skinned creatures carefully pruned the earth's visage and lovingly wove the land's hair into perfect windrows.

They rose past a silent convent in Mexico where a young girl's winged prayers flew upward to harangue them as they soared by. The luminous duet levitated over Luzon while watching their own likenesses in plastic icons as they were being pulled down from a ceiling in a doctor's office in Baguio. As they left they calmly leafed through elegy after elegy until they came to the unspoken words of a boy who was lying by himself on a cot in a Quonset hut. It was these silent prayers for a reckoning of angels that would always catch their immaterial eyes.

Each would cast a backward glance as they lifted upward and away from the incendiary fresco of their complicity; at the scorching and smoke and at the spreading pile of icons in front of a small cantina. Their last sight of earth would soon be the green cross where a heavy drawbridge intersected a torpid slough. Their last sight of mankind would soon be the edge of the bay where the body of a wicked man bobbed like a dinghy on the incoming tide.

"*Esse angelus novimus ex fide,*" they would sing as they turned their faces away. They would return home and keep forever the secret of Raphael's Silver Cloud.

With his worn hands, Humberto and his naked trooper shoved the metal sign seven degrees this way and eleven degrees in that direction, until an inscrutable equilibrium was reached. There was an ineffable balance, a rightness in Humberto and Queenie's frenzied pushing and shoving at the heavy metal and glass sign. As he labored, the mad priest continued to preach to the streets below. When he was satisfied that the sign was pointed in the right direction, Humberto turned to his one-woman army.

"Can you see the signal?" Humberto asked excitedly. "Can you see the signal fire?"

Queenie, like Humberto, scanned the eastern horizon intently with her hand mirror. She, like Humberto, was earnestly looking for a sign. Now and again, she would turn her looking glass downward in order to gaze affectionately at a glow in her groin.

As the neon sign was being jostled and shoved, the angelic bowman hovering within it inquired of his partner, "When last you were in the Presence, what was it doing?"

"Speak up, *por favor*!" Humberto screamed as he worked feverishly now with his crescent wrench. "I want to hear the answer to that one myself."

"Speak up, please!" Queenie echoed.

Raphael had given the wrench to Humberto. It had been one of the last requests that Humberto and Queenie had sent down on the pulley and platform. With the tool, the old man had managed to loosen all of the large bolts that attached the base of the sign to two huge L-brackets that ran five or six feet down the face of the building that was the Silver Cloud. Of the eight bolts, six were removed completely. The other two were left hanging to keep the sign from plummeting to the street below. Four of the six guy wires had been cut.

"When you were last in the Presence, what was He doing?"

The other cherub, oblivious to the metal arrow, and sighing only at the subtle deftness and depth of immaterial penetration, at last answered the lover's question.

"Oh . . . the Presence was busily considering the image as traitor."

Queenie, mirror in hand, was visibly shaken by the response.

"And tossing the Urim and Thummim?" a shaking, sweating Humberto asked. With the help of Queenie, he jostled and shoved the sign a few more degrees before peering off again into the distance, his squinting eyes mere slits in his leathery face.

"Was there furious tossing of the Urim and Thummim?" Humberto asked once more, referring to the polished stones that the ancient high priests of the Hebrews had once cast to divine the hidden will of God.

"Oh, yes . . . cast the stones and one child is lost in the barrio," said the angel with the arching bow, in a breathless voice that was filled with the scent of Lebanon. "Toss again and one child is lost in the making."

Then the cherub with the glowing heart sang back an enraptured response.

"Still another child is lost in the sound of a cello."

At the same instant, just blocks away Ted For Short exited the bus at the Southern Pacific train terminal. He had decided against driving his little Isetta. He loved his tiny car more than any vehicle he had ever owned. The car fit him like a glove, and he couldn't bear the thought of some bestial, brute-driven tow truck dragging it down the street. If anything were to happen to him—if Bambino were to kill him—Ruby would care for it.

He walked down Fourth Street, across the railroad tracks and between the monstrous, gray pillars that held up the long free-way that loomed overhead in the night sky like a gigantic, twisted snake. The tons of concrete suspended unnaturally above his head were a dull yellow-orange in the light of sunset. The color reminded him of the first color television he had ever seen, back in French Camp.

After scanning the horizons to his left and his right, he limped his way cautiously onto the bridge. The light from the sign of the twin angels was just visible above the buildings to his right. Over-head, he saw the huge concrete counterweight and enormous, greased gears that operated together to raise the massive bridge whenever a tall-masted boat passed in the slough below.

Above the metal walkway there was a small elevated room that contained the controls for the drawbridge. Teodoro could barely see the soft flicker of candlelight inside the little room. All at once the dark face of Miguel Govea peered out at him as he hobbled nearer. A nervous Teodoro waved at the familiar face, who smiled and waved back confidently, almost enthusiastically and in sharp contrast to Teodoro's own growing dread.

Miguel was one of the most faithful patrons at Raphael's Sil-ver Cloud, and Ted For Short was sorry now that he had not got-ten to know him better. Teodoro had often seen him sitting in the bar, sitting as though he wished to be alone and as though he were anxiously waiting for someone who could appear at any moment. He had been in the audience many times when Teodoro had done his act, but they had never spoken to one an-other until the night of the wedding.

Teodoro smiled to himself. It had been worth the pain of a lifetime to be so happy for one night. What a night that had been! Just as the wedding was breaking up and Ted For Short and Radiant Ruby were preparing to drive home in the little Isetta, Miguel had sought out Father Humberto in the midst of the milling and jubilant crowd. The Indian had first embraced the crazed priest; then he had fallen to his knees and tearfully, desperately begged Humberto's forgiveness before God and the entire gathered assembly.

"*Santo Humberto, perdoname. Clemencia. Clemencia.* I have spent *mi vida,* my whole life, looking for you, señor, searching everywhere for you. *En nombre de Dios,* please grant forgiveness to my poor, worthless soul, *Santo Humberto.*"

A confused Humberto had lifted the man from his knees and asked him why on earth he needed his forgiveness.

"Who am I to forgive anyone under the sun?"

"I am so ashamed, padre. I have been ashamed since I was seventeen years old. *Madre de Dios,* how can I say this? How can I say this? Do I have the strength to speak these words that I've repeated to myself each night for twenty thousand nights?"

The Indian closed his eyes, inhaled deeply to regain his composure, then began to speak once more, using every ounce of his strength to form each word with his trembling lips.

"Padre, I was one of those foolish men who murdered you and your brother over sixty years ago. I held a heartless rifle in these accursed hands."

He lifted his hands to his contorted cheeks. *Lágrimas,* tears were streaming down his dark face.

"*Cobardía. Cobardía.* I was a coward. I closed my eyes and pulled the trigger and my eyes have not been open since that miserable instant. I was doomed to wander in search of you. God has cursed my whole life. Since that day I have swept floors and I have picked vegetables and fruit in the fields from Mazatlán to Modesto. I have followed every whisper and every rumor of your whereabouts.

"When I heard that you had come to *Norte America,* I knew that I would find you someday, because America is the place where the best things and the worst things always come. It is the place where you can starve within sight of food. I was sure that I would find you here. So I moved north, looking for a sign in every *pueblo y ciudad;* then I saw the light of the blessed angels. I know that I deserve nothing but your hatred, but I beg on my knees for your forgiveness."

Humberto had leaned solemnly toward the Indian's right ear and began to whisper softly.

" 'You must strike the heartstone and make it ring.' My brother used to say that phrase all the time. I think it was from an Indian song. 'Strike it blunt and full on—but strike it often. The human heartworm is nothing more than dreary certainty coursing through our lives. My death . . . my life has surprised me once again.' "

Humberto leaned back to stare into Miguel's eyes. "Is it from a Tarascan tune, my dear assassin?"

"Si, mi padre," answered a somber Miguel, who knew the song well. Every Tarascan knew "Corazon de Bronce."

"So many of us have found our destinies here in *El Norte*, Miguel. It is such a confusing, beautiful place, is it not? America has so many lovers, but cannot love itself."

Humberto shut his eyes. There it was again . . . the vision . . . the firing squad of Indian boys and the sights of their nervously aimed rifles moving maddeningly across his body. The second rifle from the left had been Miguel's. Even then his hair had been long.

"Did you happen to see her?" asked Humberto, his eyes still pressed shut. There was a new excitement in his voice that gave way to a tender caution. "Did you chance to see the woman in the doorway?"

A confused look had come over Miguel's tearful face as he heard the question. "Do you mean the beautiful woman with the bright blue shoes?" the Tarascan asked.

"Oh, my God!" exclaimed Humberto, suddenly gasping for breath. *"Ay, Dios mio!"*

The crazed priest had been overcome with joy at that moment. His tawdry life was not trapped in some poor parallel universe after all. His mad, desperate visions actually existed in another mind beside his own. Someone else had seen her. She was not just an insane delusion, a fantasy given reality by infinite repetition and an incurable chemical imbalance in the brain.

"I see that woman every single night of my life," sobbed Miguel. "She taunts my act of cowardice. She curses my stupidity.

Each night, just as I am dozing off, she lifts her palette of colors and condemns me to sleep in the depths of hell itself. She witnessed my cruel act on that hot day so long ago. I felt her staring right through my pathetic purple uniform. Her cold judgment was hotter than all of the sun's burning rays. Oh yes, *mi padre*, I still see her blue high-heel shoes every night. If a woman is wearing them on the street, I run far away from her. My poor heart almost stops whenever I pass a shoe store."

"I cleave unto them," countered an enraptured Humberto, who had thrown his shaking arms around his own executioner. Both men were sobbing uncontrollably now, their shoulders quaking.

"I cleave unto those shoes," whispered Humberto, who hugged his murderer the way he had hugged his own dying brother, over six decades before.

"*Como los angeles*, you and I are joined by a wound."

The wedding guests had surrounded the pair for a time, then had dispersed quietly through the front door of the Silver Cloud to wave good-bye to the departing newlyweds. On their way out, each one of the saintly dancers from the old Rose Room walked by the two men and gently laid their hands upon their heaving shoulders.

"Our cause is blessed," said a thankful, impassioned Humberto as each one passed. As the resplendent bride left with her smiling groom at her side, the plaintive, brash voice of Ray Charles had issued forth from Uriel's throat. *Ruby you're like a dream, not always what you seem.* . . . Behind the fanciful mask of her electronics, Uriel's face darkened from azure to indigo as the plaintive lyrics were wrung from her throat. The last of the revelers to leave swore the jukebox swayed from side to side in the manner of a sightless singer.

When the Silver Cloud was empty of well-wishers, the priest and the Tarascan were left alone with their common thread of memory. Above their heads, the flock of birds circled once, then flew up through the skylight. The silence within Raphael's Silver Cloud was suddenly palpable and profound.

"From one murderer to another, I forgive you," Humberto had whispered. "But there is one thing that you must do for me."

"Anything on earth," Miguel had answered.

"And beyond?" Humberto had smiled.

"*A sus órdenes.* Command me," said Miguel while snapping smartly to attention and saluting crisply.

"First," said Humberto, "*dígame*—tell me, did I flinch? Did I turn my frightened face away from the oncoming bullets?"

"Don't you remember?" said an incredulous, wide-eyed Miguel. "You faced the bullets like they meant nothing to you, as though you were an immortal."

Humberto had fallen to his knees upon hearing the words.

"The next morning, when we found that your grave was empty, some people went to hunt you down and some people went to begin their prayers with your name."

Humberto had fallen onto his face and had begun to drool a lifetime's supply of ingested venoms onto the wooden floor of the Silver Cloud. It would take Miguel and Raphael almost an hour to clean up all of the putrid toxins. Even as he had lain unconscious, it was clear to Miguel and Raphael that Humberto would die soon. He had purged himself of all of his life-preserving poisons.

Miguel watched from his control room as the tiny man limped to the metal grating of his bridge. In the years that he had worked as a span controller, he had seen many things on his bridge—bickering winos, failed suicides, and the heated arguments of freezing, homeless lovers—but never a pair of men such as the ones who were about to meet on this bizarre and miraculous night of the full moon.

As Ted For Short drew closer, Miguel nervously put down his coffee and watched him as he made his way over the bridge in the brown light of sunset. In the west, out over the ocean, the sun was just losing its fight with the moon for the full attention of the earth. Down below, Teodoro came to an abrupt stop on the bridge. He looked up at Miguel for some solace but the old Tarascan only signaled for him to move forward another few steps, then a little to the left. When Teodoro was in place and fearfully turning his eyes from one side of the bridge to the other, Miguel nodded.

"Don't move," he cautioned, but he was not at all sure that Ted For Short had heard him.

Above Raphael's Silver Cloud, the red arrow flashed again and again from one brilliant cherubim to the other. The metal-and-glass weapon of love had been maintained by King Pete Claver, who had gotten into the habit of climbing onto the roof just to hear his beloved Queenie pray or perhaps to catch a glimpse of her face reflected in her small mirror. It had been so long since he had seen her full countenance that a mere glimpse of her body would do, just a glance at her thigh or her long, dark-tipped breasts.

King had purchased a hog's bristle brush and a container of bearing grease and had periodically swabbed the aluminum track on which the metal arrow flew. He kept a screwdriver and a pair of pliers on the roof should any parts need tightening.

Once Raphael had even turned the sign off so that King could grease the hard rubber wheels that ran within the track. Even with the electricity off, the glow of the sign had not diminished and it had seemed to King that the arrow had stopped moving of its own accord, in order to facilitate the anointment.

As a final piece of upkeep, King had replaced the worn rubber bumper that was bolted to the end of the track. There was a matching bumper on the tip of the arrow. The flight of the arrow ended when the two bumpers met, precisely at the plumed rib cage of the second angel. The rubber had to be especially strong, as the slam of the arrow was surprisingly violent for such a delicate display.

So it had come to pass that King Pete became the lubricator of Theresa's rapture, the new embodiment of Tobias, and a newly recruited soldier in Humberto's own firing squad. Following Humberto's instructions to the letter, the huge black pugilist had filled his galvanized bucket with five gallons of coal tar and kerosene, and with Anatoly and Beatrice as companions, began the long walk toward the elevated freeway that stretched across the Mission District and the South of Market.

Because of a recent earthquake, the freeway had been closed for repairs. The surface of the elevated roadway was dotted with sleeping machines, arm-weary forklifts and cranes with stiff necks. The trio walked to Mariposa Street, then turned down Mississippi Street. At the corner of Division and Townsend streets, they climbed an exterior fire escape to the top of a large dormant warehouse. At the top of the warehouse they found the tall green tower that marked the halfway point between the Silver Cloud and the bridge near Carmen's Restaurant.

On his day off, Miguel had found the tower by walking along the high freeway until he stood on the straight line between the bar and the drawbridge. The only object on that line that was high enough to be visible from both places was a water tower perched atop an industrial warehouse.

It took Anatoly and King Pete almost forty minutes to make the climb to the very top of the building and the tower. Beatrice went up last. She had worn a dress and didn't want the men to see her pink panties as she ascended. At the top of the tower, King looked to his right, toward the bay and the Fourth Street Bridge. He then looked to his left and into the wind. The lights of Raphael's Silver Cloud were glowing there in the distance.

Though it had taken some time to walk to the tower using surface streets, the bar was remarkably close as the crow flies, no more than half a mile. King could see the angels clearly. He could see that they had been moved from their usual position. He could make out the form of Humberto, and more importantly, he could see his beloved wife, Queenie. For the first time in a very long time, he could see the form and figure of the woman he had married. She was stark naked and busily spreading gasoline on the roof. Oh, how the old fighter missed those big legs! His loins were burning as he watched her working. With some surprise and great concern, he noticed that her groin was glowing.

A distracted King followed his orders and dumped his five gallons of coal tar and kerosene onto the top of the tower, then sat down impatiently to wait with his Bulgarian and Tongan friends. All three watched the heavens as the top of the sun's head began to disappear below the horizon. Sunset was the appointed time for the all important signals. The moon above them was full and blue and seemed enormous. Beatrice the changeling reached up and pretended to caress the face of the man on the lunar surface.

"When you see the signal from Miguel," Humberto had explained to King Pete, "then you must give your own signal. We have to do it this way because the bridge is not visible from the roof of the Silver Cloud. Just make the signal fire and *los angelitos* will do the rest."

Anatoly, beside him, checked his pocket for the packs of matches he had placed there. Gypsies and fire had been fashioned by the creator at the very same instant of time. There was fire at the essence of Gypsy music and at the heart of Gypsy women. Gypsies lived by the fireside, and at death, all of their worldly possessions were given to the flames as a gift. Satisfied that the matchbook was dry and secure, he crossed his legs and began to hum a Bulgarian tune.

Beatrice sat down and arranged her dress around her knees so that the breeze would not lift it and the lascivious moon could not peek at her luscious legs. She looked upward demurely as the crater Tycho winked downward at her. Ignoring his overture, she turned her round face toward the Fourth Street Bridge and watched the horizon for a sign.

Humberto, shivering now from head to toe with the expectation of impending battle and of his own, imminent, second death, spewed his jilted lover's words into the evening air.

"Each morning when I am exhumed from my bedsheets, I come to see that my dark tossing sleep is a poor redundancy, that the shut door of my room is but a wooden lid lined with word-muffling silk."

Like the ancient baptist, he shouted his crazed words, pushing them out on tides of stale breath past his blue, cracked lips and out onto the rooftops below.

"In my next life, if I must have one, I want to come back as a blue satin high-heel shoe."

He preached at the top of his lungs to the earthlings below.

"El amor me ha astillado."

A lunate smile appeared on his lips whenever he spoke Spanish.

"Love has splintered me."

He had lived for two souls, in a life not good enough for one.

Now he was an earnest man in the moonlight who wished to end it all, to die a second and final time, a death more perfect than the first . . . and with infinitely better execution. An incurable disease, contracted at his first death, had rendered him immortal and doomed him to perish his whole life through in a hundred incompetent suicides. Now, at last, he could taste it. He had finally lived too long. There was a tincture of laudanum in his tongue's memory, the remains of an ancient remedy. All at once the old priest fell silent. The time was drawing near. He felt it on the shifting breeze. He had seen it in an angel's eye.

Earlier in the day, Humberto had sent King to seek out Bambino Reyes, the beast. King had been instructed to offer Bambino a meeting with Teodoro. The mad priest had purposefully chosen the precise time and the exact place of the rendezvous.

Down on Fourth Street, where the lazy green slough and the metal bridge formed a cross, a second man suddenly appeared, holding onto a handrail and creeping cautiously forward. He crouched down furtively behind a pylon, watching Teodoro carefully as he continued to move closer to the little man. The other man had somehow surprised a vigilant Miguel. Where had he been hiding? Carmen's Restaurant, on the other side of the slough, had been closed for hours, its front doors locked and bolted.

The second man darted out into the open with a strange stealth, as if he were hiding from someone who was completely aware of his presence. There was a stylized concealment in his walk, as though he had spent his whole life moving in imaginary shadows. He stood on the metal footpath and walked slowly, triumphantly toward Teodoro. All that remained concealed now was his hideous eagerness. Miguel would watch the two men from above, and he would listen to their words, but he would never thereafter fully divulge what he had heard and seen. Who in this world would ever understand him?

Who would believe that two men, who as children had once upon a time climbed separate towers on the same Golgotha, men who as children had once mimicked the Passion on parallel poles, would not even pause to exchange a single moment of charity, a solitary word of kindness? Who would believe that two men as close as these, as close as laceration and scar, as close as brow and thorn, would not even greet each other? Miguel understood very well. He had been as close to a man as trigger and wound, as close as lifelong guilt and the burning desire for forgiveness.

A lifetime had passed, and the two men stood face to face once again; their countenances were lit by the moonlight and by

the lamp overhead. After a moment of tense silence, the
stranger began to speak.

"Where did you dream that you would find your grave,
Teodoro?" said the taller man. "Did you dream that you would
find your death in your warm bed, or on the bottom shelf at the
supermarket, or at the deck rail of a cruise ship? Do you expire
peacefully in your reveries, or was I there each time you
breathed your last?" Bambino moved a step closer and bent
down to breathe his bile into Teodoro's face.

"Have you enjoyed your life underground? Dig enough
holes, Teodoro, and you will surely find your grave. Like all
things distasteful," said Bambino with a cold smile, "I am always
too punctual . . . no matter how late I may be, I am always early.
Unfashionably early, you might say. Oh, Teodoro, how I would
love, for just a single moment, to imagine what you have imagined of me. But as I am fearless, I cannot imagine your fear. You
do know that I am your death, don't you? How have you imagined your own death?"

"At first," answered Teodoro disdainfully, "I ran from you because I was afraid to die. Then somewhere out there on the road
I began to run because I was afraid that I would never really live.
I was afraid of dying alone. Now I know that I will die in Ruby's
arms."

"Then I will be the death of your lovely new wife," smiled
Bambino.

"I will kill you first," spat Teodoro. "She will have a death of
her own. She needs no help from you."

"Then we are not so different, are we?" laughed Bambino.
"You would seek revenge if I lifted a hand to hurt her."

"Some have discovered what is holy and what is not. That is
the difference between us," Teodoro said angrily. "You have
never made that discovery and you never will. You have never
loved, and someone who has never loved can never be hurt. To
be holy you must spend your time considering the gain and the
loss of love. I loved my fellow field-workers. I loved the asparagus
and the Gonzalez brothers. I have even loved looking at the
world from this low angle.

"Holiness would demand that you know your father for what
he truly was and yourself for what you have become. There's

nothing special about you, Bambino. The world is littered with men like you. Without hurt, there is no love. And without love, there is nothing holy.

"Why did you waste your fine education in the seminaries? All the years of solitude should have made you pious, Bambino. But piety without pity is barely a vowel. Don't you see? Our poor childhood crucifixions weren't hallowed, and they weren't hollow. They were only the price of admission to the lives that we all imagined we could have, and never could. You and I were hung up like posters before a parade by our parents and by a needy little village, nothing more. We were shelves, built to hold all of their desires.

"In our village the Bible was a wish book and you and I were the postage stamps on a hundred mail orders sent straight up to God. In the world of organized religion, we may have been a tawdry sideshow, but we did nothing wrong and nothing wrong was done to us. You are still living in the past, Bambino. You are more contorted and more twisted in spirit than I ever was in body and limb. In the last thirty years I have lived a life and you have lived on the scent of my life. Since that time you've given me so much more to be angry about."

Bambino did not wish to consider Teodoro's words. Those few words that had made their way into his ears had caused a sharp pain somewhere in the center of his chest. He dismissed the possibility that it was his heart that ached, that Teodoro's words had gone that deep inside and assailed his very core. Thirty years of hating could not be questioned now. The pain in his chest must have been an ulcer. Bambino had hundreds of them.

"What did you expect of me, Teodoro? Eyes of smoke? Did you think I would have lips of flint and that I would walk trailing a garland of weeds?" Bambino had gotten his second wind. "Did you expect to hear a waxen din from my teeth or the buzzing of flies? Did you anticipate hearing a tongue driven by craft and guile? In fact, I am none of those things. Don't you see me for what I am? I am your antidote, your salve. I, Bambino Reyes, who eagerly dabbles in rabble and cripples, am the sweet liniment for perversions such as you and your perverted friend Faustino.

"I was fooled for years by the sheer simplicity of it all, but I soon discovered who I really was. May I present myself?" He spread his arms and bent low in a mock show of servitude. "I am the issue of a stained trollop and the bastard son of an itinerant womanizer. Yet I hold even such menial bloodlines to be blameless. For it was religion that molested me as a child. It filled me with hope and visions of a sky filled with wisdom and concern. It won my confidence, then proceeded to abuse me in the dark." He placed his thumbless hand over his crotch.

"It touched me down there," he laughed. His face was twisted with mirth.

For the first time since they had met on the bridge, Teodoro could see the family resemblance between Bambino and Pietro. It was there in that obscene laughter, that sickly gaze. Both men had built their sad lives on twisted personal mythologies and distorted remembrances. There had been congenital insanity in the bloodline that Bambino had so desperately longed to claim. Years ago, word had come down from the migratory farmworker circuit that Simon Ditto had gone mad just before his death.

Still laughing, Bambino reached into one of his pants pockets and pulled out what looked like a used cigar. It was blackened with age and covered with the hair and lint of a filthy, unwashed pocket. Bambino turned it in his fingers, then let it drop to the deck of the bridge. Teodoro bent down to look at it carefully. It was a human thumb.

"That is all that is left of my faith," said Bambino. He held up his right hand to show an extended index finger that joined seamlessly to a palm. It was as though the finger of indictment was as long as his arm.

"It was faith that mauled me and drove me against my own nature. But I wasn't fooled for long. Not for long. Are you frightened of me?" he asked in a bemused tone.

Ted For Short did not answer. He was still staring in disbelief at the severed digit.

"Well, you really shouldn't be. You should be prepared by now, especially after all these years of running. Each small pain that you've ever experienced in your poor, unhappy life was merely an ambassador to this moment, a pale harbinger to this precise time and place."

With a flourish, he lifted the flap of his coat, then pulled out his long, shining machete. Teodoro stiffened at the sight of the sharpened knife and a cold chill ran down his curved back. The frigid gleam of the blade under the azure light of the moon was numbing and hypnotic. Deep in his entrails, an old fear gripped him once again. In a moment of stunned panic, Ted For Short began to fear that his job at the Silver Cloud and his marriage to Ruby had all been nothing more than just another farmworker's daydream; that all those years of running had been a horrible nightmare; that somehow he was still there—trapped in French Camp in the year 1959.

Teodoro could almost see the flooded asparagus fields and the tall water tower of the Dittos' farm in the distance. The enormous moon overhead seemed to be the very same one that was looming above the dark slough in French Camp three decades before. Faustino's hand-painted blue Buick was there, idling just to his right, and his cooking fire was smoking there by the end of the drawbridge.

All at once, Teodoro thought he saw those same mindless men who had once herded themselves around the packing shed. They moved from the shadows, wheeled and turned single-mindedly around Carmen's Restaurant and onto the metal bridge. For an eternal moment, the terrible hatred, the flashing blades, and the death of Pietro Ditto seemed only seconds old.

Bambino shifted the knife from his thumbless right hand to his tattooed left hand. As his narrowed eyes followed the blade, his face was possessed by a look of vile intimacy.

"It is only partly sated, Teodoro. It had a drink just the other day. Did you know that Faustino is dead?"

The cruel words readily found their way to Teodoro's ear, but were delayed on the way to his heart. They had been way-laid and assailed by a lifetime of memories. Bambino's words paid a heavy toll to reach their goal, but reach it they did, and Ted For Short knew that what he was hearing was true. The terrible thing he had feared for so many years had finally come to pass. Faustino had failed to come home from his job at the windmills and his small room at the hotel had stood empty and silent now for two full days.

Alarmed neighbors in Faustino's apartment building had begun complaining that a desperate, bespectacled man speaking Greek and French was gliding like a grief-stricken wraith through the hallways, knocking frantically on apartment doors and searching vainly for his dear lover and friend.

Constantine's sorrow had been so pervasive that two brothers, small black children living in the basement of Faustino's building, had awakened from a tossed and thrashing sleep to communicate with each other in a secret, new language. For a full day and a half, the two boys spoke to each other in demotic Greek, a dialect from the turn of the century. An ancient vegetable monger on the street who packed his broccoli in ice and dreamed daily of the noisy marketplace in Athens had heard the two boys and had dashed downstairs to marvel at their perfect tongues.

Faustino's co-workers at the wind farm had not seen him or heard from him in two days. Faustino had never been late before. Teodoro, King Pete, and Raphael had looked everywhere for their friend. They had called the highway patrol and all of the local hospitals. He was nowhere to be found, and a sudden coldness in Ted For Short's heart and King's dying liver had tried to tell them both that Faustino was dead. Neither man wanted to believe the warnings.

"He died on the wind farm," said a sneering Bambino. "He just kneeled down in a small, flat clearing between the windmills. He knew exactly who I was. I didn't have to say a word to him. It was almost as though he wanted to die."

One of Teodoro's knees buckled as he heard the terrible words. A sorrowful and bitter image pushed its sharp fingertips deep into the quick behind his brow. It heartlessly spread his skull wide open and leapt headlong into his hewn horizon. Ted For Short saw his beloved friend, dressed in his dusty khaki work clothes, his long white hair dipping like willow branches as his proud head bent forward. Faustino's long fingers were pulling at his own collar to clear an unobstructed path for the mindless blade. Two mismatched buttons fell into Faustino's lap as he tore at his own shirt.

Tears streamed down Teodoro's face as his soul witnessed the slide of the insensible blade through pulsing flesh. At the place where Faustino died, decrepit ingots of soft ambition and gentle hope would fall to the will of worms. Along with blood, a stream of unwritten iambic stanzas gushed forth in linked couplets from the open wound.

Ted For Short fell to both knees as a sacred, formal feeling came. Above his dying body, Faustino's unfettered soul had been caught up by the moving thrall of sleepless weather. It had spun in wheel after endless wheel until, at last, it was thrown free to frolic and play in magnetic fields.

There was something about the high wind farm that Faustino had dearly loved. On quiet nights in his hotel room, Faustino would often cook dinner for his friends Teodoro, Ruby, Raphael, King Pete, and Constantine. Sometimes even Anatoly would come for a meal. In a low, respectful voice, Faustino would describe his new place of work as he ladled food onto plates.

"Remember, Teodoro, when we slaved in the fields every day and the slightest gust made us all raise our sweating heads so hopefully? Perhaps it's a kind wind, we would say. Do you remember how we always prayed for wind and shade? Is death a cold gale, Teodoro? Is heaven a sweet norther that has come to dry our brows? I want to die up there with the windmills where long working arms move at heaven's whim."

Ted For Short lifted his head with a jerk. The vision had gone, vanished into the soil with Faustino's poetry. He wiped his eyes with his sleeves, then with the help of his cane, rose to his feet once more.

Bambino ran the same grooved skin over the blade again. This time the cut was deeper and blood began to run down his unwashed wrist and disappear into the sleeve of his filthy coat.

"I was there, outside, at your wedding," said Bambino. "Believe it or not, I was glad about your marriage. There is no irony in killing a man who doesn't care to live." He thought about the way in which that queer Faustino had surrendered. "There's almost no joy in it at all. I have waited so long for this moment. And now it will be doubly sweet. For the first time in all of the years that I've hunted you, you love your own life. When that huge black man came to me this morning and offered to arrange this meeting with you, I fell to my knees and wept with joy. It is one thing to kill a faggot and a gimpy old dwarf, but such sweet vengeance it is to kill a man who is still warm with the heat of his marriage bed."

"Do you want to know why your father was killed?" asked Teodoro.

"No," answered Bambino curtly. "I don't care to know. Did you spend many nights on the run wondering if a simple explanation would clear things up? Did you rehearse your feeble excuses in front of the water heater or the window shade? Did you search for the exact combination of syllables that would mollify me? The person who cared to know why Pietro died never existed. But I do have a question before I kill you. Actually, I have two questions.

"I am curious. There is a certain perfection that comes when a man can look back upon the entirety of his life, when he can stand at the time and place of his death and see the totality of his own days. There is only one point in life where nothing can be added. It can only happen once. After all this time and after all this misery, who is your God, Teodoro? Is He a different God than the one who let you climb up that paltry wooden cross? Who is your God?"

Teodoro stepped back upon hearing the surprising question. Miguel, up above, signaled earnestly for him to step forward again. The Tarascan had a paintbrush in his hand and had just painted a green cross on the side of the tower, below his window. Ted For Short complied with the signal, then inhaled deeply, unsure why he felt compelled to answer the question.

"My God does not grant wishes . . . just look at me. She doesn't hear prayers or I would not have been so alone for so much of my life. My God doesn't set things straight or you would have stopped hunting Faustino and me a long time ago. My God is just a holy thing. That's what my God is . . . holy—not religious or sacred—those are man-made things. She is holy. He is a fissure in the bending bones of my childhood. He is day's end in the hot fields, a dipper full of cold water on my head and running down my hunched back as I close my eyes and realize that now I can rest."

A strange feeling came over Teodoro as he answered the question. Bambino's query had so often been his own. He had asked himself this same question for years. Now, on the verge of his own death, Ted For Short had an answer.

"He is the stunned silence beneath the big top that sorrowful day when one of the lovely Lopez sisters fell screaming from the flying trapeze. My God is the sovereign loft at the very apex of the flyer's triple somersault, the sullen years of grief in her sister—the catcher's failing grip. He is the immeasurable instant when graceful flight transmutes into irreversible plummet. He is the awe and the empathy in the eyes of the crowd.

"My God is a living, working composer . . . and so He is virtually unknown. He is the crying of a neglected child, the tinkle of a solitary spoon stirring friendless coffee in a solitary cup. He is the ticket-buying audience, sent streetward happy by extreme sadness and by greasepaint and mirth."

"Who is your God?" asked Bambino disdainfully as he lifted his arm and raised the long, shining machete over his head. The answer had not been satisfactory. No answer would ever be. "Who is your God? Your friend Faustino gave no answer at all to that same question. He just fell to his knees and bowed his head. Then he started talking nonsense to people who weren't even there. I asked him just before I killed him: Do you think that your God will stop me? When has He ever interceded on your behalf? Do you know what he said?"

Teodoro did not answer; he only readied himself to jump out of the way of the upraised machete. Why on earth did he agree to place his trust in that crazy Humberto? How did he ever come to believe the fervent assurances of the old poison-swilling priest? Miguel, up above, was still smiling in his control room, his eyes never leaving the scene below. For some unknown reason it made Ted For Short feel calmer, despite his fears.

" 'There is no retribution here,' " Bambino mocked the whispered words of Faustino. " 'You are nothing to me. I am merely the third in a trinity of lacerations. Now . . . at last I can ask forgiveness of that young Japanese soldier. My God bends over me now, to harvest me and carry me away. I am the third cutting. See . . . I stain the buds.' "

"My God," said Ted For Short sadly.

"Just who is your destitute God? What God would claim a *bakla* and a twisted contortion such as you?" sneered Bambino.

"My God has arthritis," snapped Teodoro angrily as he once again wiped away his tears with the sleeve of his coat. "He bungled the job on me because of it. But He knows I'm here. I know that much, though I seem to forget it every day. Seven years ago, when I found my dearest Ruby once again, working at Raphael's Silver Cloud, I wanted to call her on the telephone to tell her that I was going to work there, too, as the house singer, magician-in-residence, and comedian. It took hours for me to work up the courage to call her. I waited outside a phone booth for four hours before I could even gather the strength to step inside and close the door behind me.

"So many people entered the booth, had their conversations, and left as I stood trying to talk myself into dropping the dime into the machine and dialing her number. You know, you can squeeze a coin in your clenched fist so hard that, pretty soon, you can't tell if it's even there anymore. Your very grasp on the coin has made you insensible to it. Your connection to it renders it gone. But that could never happen if you caught a firefly and held it in your hand. You would always feel its lust to take wing; its hunger for its own short life in the air, despite the grand designs of the one who holds it. That's what I am to my God."

Teodoro closed his right hand, then opened it again as Bambino moved a step closer, the machete upraised. In the palm of Teodoro's hand appeared a large, smooth stone, one of the many props that filled the pockets and hidden chambers of his clothing.

"People like me are the inflections in God's sentences, the punctuations. I am His relief from the monotony of perfection. I am His reminder that nothing is the same. It is the myth of sameness that diminishes us all in this world. The myth of sameness deprives us of our pride and our shame. It is the dogma of whiteness that has made us all so unhappy; our failure to see the many worlds in our world has left us all heartless and homeless."

Teodoro lifted the smooth stone and braced himself as Bambino moved even closer. He had promised to place his trust in Humberto, but time was growing short and there were always things that a magician could do to defend himself.

"'Am I a dog that thou comest to me with stones?'" leered Bambino, echoing the words of an ancient Philistine without hearing the irony.

It was clear to Teodoro that Bambino was not really listening to anything that he said. Suddenly, Ted For Short found himself smiling. Despite the upraised knife in his assailant's hand, Ted For Short was happier now than he had ever been in his entire life. Happier than on the day of his wedding, for even that glorious day had held the smallest bit of resentment for Bambino's persistent, unending hatred; it had held the faintest tinge of bitterness for what time and life on the run had done to them all. There was no such bitterness now.

"We are God's language in this country of worlds, God's own alphabet. How can we—without considering one another—ever hope to comprehend even the word that we are used in, much less the phrase or the entire book?"

For the first time in his life, Teodoro Teofilo Cabiri, the protector of shipwrecked men, was himself protected by a God who was his own, a God who would never completely overlook the botched clay in His collection of hand-thrown souls. Though he stood in death's very shadow, Ted For Short felt wholly enveloped, embraced by a sheltering spirit.

As the sun disappeared below the horizon, Bambino asked the second and final question to a smiling man who should have been frightened out of his wits.

"Who is Zeferino?" asked Bambino, who was clearly taken aback by the grin on the face of the little man. "Who is Zeferino?" he demanded as the moon took full control of the night sky. "Tell me, who was the boy that helped you and the faggot murder my father? Who was the boy that you spirited out of camp as my poor father lay bleeding to death? Tell me his full name and where he lives today and I will do you the great kindness of killing you quickly! Faustino refused to tell me, you know, and I laughed as his limbs went limp and he lingered. He protected the boy to the last. He would not answer my questions, so I bled him like a goat."

Bambino was smiling, or so he thought. The muscles that pulled up the edges of the mouth succeeded only in revealing a rabid lather and sickly gums.

"Now, who was the boy?" The machete in his hand was quaking with the tension that lies between rising exertion and diminishing restraint.

Miguel opened his moonlit window as Bambino moved forward. By the Tarascan's own reckoning, the assailant was standing just to the left of where he ought to be. The bridgeman reached behind his chair, then upended a trash can full of orange peels through his window. The peels fell down to the roadway, where an angry Bambino jumped to his right to avoid being pelted by the garbage. At precisely the same instant, Miguel activated the emergency lights of the bridge, which flashed alternately green then red and were visible for miles.

Bambino and Teodoro both looked up simultaneously to see the bridge alive and pulsating with flashing light to the brash baritone accompaniment of a loud foghorn. Teodoro's smile faded slowly from his lips and a look of awe gradually took its place. At the water tower, Beatrice saw Miguel's signal and nudged a sleeping Anatoly, who awakened abruptly. He had been snoozing in his idling taxicab, which was parked near Rockefeller Center. King Pete had already gone back to the Silver Cloud to catch a rare glimpse of his precious Queenie. But he had left the tower in capable hands.

"*Zapaly ogan!*" cried Anatoly in Bulgarian. "Light the fire!"

He then realized that the matches were in his own pocket. He opened the matchbook, struck a match, then lit the thick puddle of coal tar and kerosene just as he and Beatrice began their hasty descent down the ladder. Above their heads, the top of the tower was a blazing torch that could be seen in the next county.

"There it is!" screamed Queenie, who pointed excitedly into her mirror at the eastern horizon. "There's the signal!"

"Turn the angels another degree to the left. We just have to aim in the general direction," screamed Humberto as he nervously sighted down the surface of the sign, then shoved at it with all of his strength. As he did so, the arrow returned to its fully loaded position, then remained there, frozen with potential energy, the electric nock and the neon bowstring quivering with the strain. Next, Humberto hurriedly used the crescent wrench to remove the rubber bumper that restricted the flight of the arrow in its track. Now the throbbing machine was ready. Without knowing it and without feeling it, Humberto fervently caressed the glowing hair of the celestial bowman.

Down in the street below Humberto, King Pete was hollering and going crazy. He had called out over and over to his beloved wife, who had not even deigned to acknowledge her husband. Queenie had only stared into her mirror for a minute or two, then shrugged her shoulders as though she might once have known the frenzied man below. Out of curiosity, she watched him for a moment as he placed a galvanized bucket over his head and began running headlong into a nearby wall. The sharp, metallic sound of his collisions made her wince. Inside the bucket, coal tar, kerosene, and salty tears mixed to form a sorrowful brine.

The music of the band could be heard coming from inside Raphael's Silver Cloud. Radiant Ruby would be molting her feathers now for an eager, wide-eyed audience of men. Tonight she would dance mechanically and without much feeling for her art. Her heart and her thoughts were out there in the night, with the man who was her oldest lover and her newest husband. As she dipped a coy wing and turned on a rising thermal of men's expectations, she prayed silently for Teodoro and for Faustino, wherever he might be.

As she danced, she knew that the roof high above her head was now ablaze and that the beautiful neon angels had been transmuted from flickering neon advertisement to the awful, ignescent ardor of holy purpose and plan. In the distance the sound of fire alarms and sirens filled the streets of the Mission District.

She knew as she coyly unfeathered a breast in time with the beat that the blazing, trembling arrow had flown forward in its track and, finding no rubber restriction, had torn loose from its lowly costume of sparking wires and stretching springs and had arched skyward in dazzling flames—iron coiffed with an unearthly aura—past the glowing, giddy heart of the second cherubim and high above the Mission District . . . toward the Fourth Street Bridge.

In her mind's eye she saw the angels' poignant spear burning like a small, exploding sun as it sped onward to its living target; the twin angels mounted upon it in haute dressage and humming a dulcet tune of modest rage—an assuaging alloy of metallurgy and metaphysics, plummeting majestically to winnow out and smite down a blighted harvest.

"Ange passe," she whispered solemnly.

In time with the music, Ruby slowly spread her sensual retrices and curved coverts and whispered a devout prayer for the supreme accuracy of angelic artillery.

On the bridge, Bambino placed the cold tip of his thirsting machete against the pulsating skin of Teodoro's neck.

"Who was the boy? Who is the man?" he screamed. "Tell me or I'll start by removing those long, hideous ears of yours. I'll carve them away from your ugly, deformed skull like fungus from a rotting stump!"

The shadowy form on the roof of the Silver Cloud had bent intently to his task, then had retreated quickly as something on the roof exploded violently, sending a flaming arrow high into the air and out toward the East Bay. The violent blast from the explosion had knocked the man and his accomplice flat on their backs.

He had stood up slowly and watched, squinting with fascination as the apparition slashed across the evening sky, leaving in its wake a carpet of drifting embers as crimson red as Fra Angelico's vestments or Orozco's pit of fire.

"My ex-voto!" he had cried out as he watched the object rise. He had been joyous and had bounded across the roof, arms upraised in victory. His cries had wafted upward from his smoking rooftop censer, his pulpit and pyre and hermitage.

Those who saw the burning missile did not believe it and so they only stared upward in disbelief. Those who would have believed—who had waited the entirety of their lives to believe in just such a thing—were not looking at it when it passed overhead in the lowest heaven. Their numbed gazes had been averted by centuries of uncaring skies; their heads were bowed by the weight of inherited, inbred disappointments.

Those who would have believed did not join the legion of frantic calls flooding the switchboards at Mission Police Station and at the Hall of Justice.

Had they lifted their heads, just one or two of the believers as they moved here and there along the earth—had they raised their downcast eyes to see the glowing spear, spanning air, spraying hot rivulets of solder, they might have rejoiced with the rare mystery of it. They might have turned it over on their tongues and passed it on to their children; they might have embellished it a bit, lied about its height and power, given it the weight of myth and written it down.

Even those who failed to see did not fail to hear the loud, piercing voice of the madman on the rooftop. A voice that seemed to send the blazing specter on its way.

"*Para ti, mi hermano;* for you, my dear brother," he shouted. "For you . . . a victory for saints and for poor sinners like me! Even now the beast is clawing vainly at his mortal wound! At last I can answer your question. I can tell you in which faraway land I am to die."

Old Miguel, *El Tarasco,* watched transfixed, a mixture of fascination and fear on his face as the fearsome arrow arched upward in the night sky, then nosed downward toward his precious Fourth Street Bridge. Teodoro, unmindful now of the impatient machete pressing at his windpipe, turned to watch as the blinding apparition streaked downward toward him, its pathway cleared by harbingers and heraldry; a thousand blazing horns, a mad and tender madrigal in countless choirs, row upon row; as endless as the fields of the Central Valley. His eyes widened as it came on. The years fell away as it came, and once again he was in Baguio, staring upward tearfully at winged toys strung from the ceiling. Carelessly, he tossed the smooth stone to the ground as it came. God's will. Somehow, he was unafraid.

"What is that thing in the sky?" bellowed a shaking, confused Bambino. His voice was drowned out by an unheard noise, by the titanic rustle and the sudden flap of a dove's immense wings in a dark, untouchable rafter high overhead.

The green of the slough and the olive drab of the bridge were no longer evident as the loud and bewildering missile came hurtling on. The entire South of Market had glowed an eerie, otherworldly white as the smoking, spitting projectile passed overhead. Teodoro flinched twice as the sound barrier broke in two, cracking the mirrored windows of every high-rise building on Market Street.

It carelessly ripped the shivering air as it came; it slit the night sky wide open, and for a fleeting moment, the vaulting and airless alcoves of secret heaven shone through; the tall poles that held high the big top were revealed. It sundered molecules as it came on, and the severed, shaken air in its wide wake sang an ionized hymn.

"Ruby, my dearest Ruby!" cried out Ted For Short as the light came on. Teodoro tried to choose his new wife as his last vision of this world, but another vision intruded. All at once he could see the true faces of his father and his mother—not faces that he had chosen to be theirs, but their true faces. After all of these years he could see their eyes, lips, and mouths perfectly! "I love you," he said to two faces that were scowling at him as he hung from a bamboo cross. On his left were the other village boys who had been entered in the local competition. On his right was poor Bambino Reyes, small and half-white and vainly hoping for so much more in his life. But the nails in his body were causing him so much pain.

"I remember now!" cried Ted For Short as the entire China Basin turned fluorescent white. "I untied myself and climbed down, and I walked over to your cross and tried with all of my strength to pull the nails out! Don't you remember, Bambino?"

Bambino Reyes could say nothing. The man who could not imagine fear was seeing it now. His single eye was blinded by the white light, and his feeble, guttural voice was breaking with animal terror and drowned out by the oncoming din.

"I managed to pull one nail out, and your family almost beat me to death for doing it, for trying to stop your pain. Even my father helped them to beat me. I can see the anger in the faces of my parents, who wished I had never been born. I can see your desperate, hopeless mother, who saw you as a meal ticket. She is clawing at my hand and biting my fingers, trying to retrieve the nail."

The two men were invisible now, lost in a ghastly glare. Miguel could no longer see them. His control room was whitewashed with thundering beams and radiance, and he couldn't see that Bambino Reyes had moved another step forward and was not standing where he should be.

"Your mother hadn't seen what I saw in your face. No one else saw it. But I saw it. You were dying up there," screamed Ted For Short, "bleeding to death from the four nails. The hole they had dug for your cross was filling with your blood. You didn't want to live anymore. I saw that you had made up your mind to die—and I made them take you down."

"She saw it," said Bambino in a new voice. Beneath the hard tenor of the man was the tremulous alto of the boy. "Oh, my beloved mother saw it, all right. What a windfall my death would have been for her, a life of leisure and eternal consolation! She saw it, but it was you that I chose to despise."

Teodoro was silent now. The machete at his neck had pushed through his first layer of skin and was pinching his vocal cords. Though both men were nearly blinded now, Teodoro could see a new level of detachment, a new depth of coldness in Bambino's working eye, and prepared himself for the pain he knew was coming.

"We were pretending, just pretending!" Bambino screamed. "She pretended to be my mother. Our lousy little village back home pretended to be the Holy Land, and I pretended that a father far away cared whether I lived or died. To pretend is to lie!"

"To pretend," shouted Ted For Short the ringmaster, "is to believe!"

"Believe me," said Bambino with a numb and desolate tongue, "nothing in heaven or on earth can stop this death."

The machete began to slide slowly across Ted For Short's neck. Gripped by panic, Teodoro raised both of his arms and, with all of his strength, shoved at his assailant. A surprised Bambino staggered a single step backward and exhaled one final, explosive breath as the awesome blow from the celestial shaft slammed him with impossible force across the drawbridge and backward into the murky green water where his savage wound steamed and boiled. Glowing with the glory of perfect marksmanship, the metal arrow dove downward into the brackish silt and black mud, carrying with it Bambino's dark heart and leaving the lifeless husk to float sluggishly to the swelling and surging surface.

On the bridge, a stunned and confused Teodoro felt around his own small body for wounds or burns. Except for a thin line of blood at his throat, he found nothing, not a scratch or a cinder. He then bent down slowly to pick up Bambino's fallen machete. It had been dropped upon impact. Its sweat-soaked handle was still hot with Bambino's angry grip. A trail of smoke and a seething wash that climbed both shores was all that was left of Bambino's presence. The sound of the impact was still echoing from the tall buildings on Market Street, and the charged air above the bridge was pink with the settling mist of Bambino's banished blood.

Ted For Short then walked in slow, devout steps to the edge of the bridge and watched Bambino's smoldering, empty shell come bobbing back up to the surface. Up in the control tower, Miguel calmly turned off the emergency lights and the foghorn. He sighed with relief and reached for his little accordion. Miguel's old Mexican song would have new American verses.

At the same instant a half mile away, Radiant Ruby finished her final dance and hurried off the stage to the sound of rousing applause. White feathers flew into the air as she ran. Outside, King Pete Claver fell to the ground blissfully unconscious, his entire body buzzing with numbness. His eyes had swollen shut with the coal tar and the force of his self-inflicted blows, and his gray, throbbing liver had been mercilessly hooked. He had never figured out the southpaws.

Across town and caught in the rapture of an impending final rest, Father Humberto was about to die in a moving ambulance. He was pulling feverishly at a young doctor's white lapels and answering his dear brother's ancient question. Queenie, at his side, was flooding the floor of the ambulance with the heatless light of her renovated crotch.

Teodoro would remain standing there at the rail until a rookie police officer cautiously removed the machete from his hand.

"I did it," he would say quietly, to anyone who asked.

Zeferino and Stuart silently rode the elevator to the fourth floor of the Hall of Justice. They were on their way to Homicide Detail. Both were staring straight ahead as the elevator moved, though the investigator's head was moving imperceptibly.

"Tomorrow, I'm going to synagogue," said a pensive Stuart Guedenken, as the door of the elevator opened, "if I can remember where it is. I'm sorry to say that except for a wedding or two, I haven't been to synagogue since my bar mitzvah. You know, the guy that sang at my bar mitzvah was a midget. You don't think . . ."

The elevator door opened, but not before registering a metallic complaint. "I hope this elevator makes it," said Zeferino.

"In this life," responded Stuart, "you need some mazel."

At Homicide Detail the Inspector was seated at his desk with a paper cup in his hand. It was half filled with something alleged to be coffee. The cup was from Donut Heaven, and the illustration on its side depicted two small cherubs hovering gleefully over a mound of shining donuts. Seated around the Inspector's desk were Alfred Giannini, the Assistant District Attorney, and Dr. Boyd Stephens, the Chief Medical Examiner. When the defense attorney and the investigator walked in, everyone but the Inspector exchanged cordial handshakes.

"I hope we can take care of this case today," said Zeferino.

"I don't foresee any real problems," said the District Attorney, who was glaring at the Inspector, who was obviously unhappy with the situation. "Everyone present knows that you and I have had extensive discussions about this case. There are no secrets here. Everyone here knows my position. I have more than a reasonable doubt about the culpability of Mr. Cabiri, and I won't prosecute a case that I can't win.

"The Inspector has a different point of view, but I've explained to him that no jury of twelve citizens is going to convict that man. Now, out of respect for the investigating officers in this case, I brought the good doctor up here to explain to the Inspector just how substantial our proof problems are going to be at trial. Dr. Stephens has made it very clear in a memo to me—that I have provided to counsel—that if called upon to testify he could not say that the machete was the proximate cause of the injuries, nor could he say that a criminal agency was involved in the death."

Dr. Stephens nodded his complete concurrence with the District Attorney's statement. He had never been able to determine the exact cause of death. There had been no usable evidence of stippling or blunt trauma, no lacerations or contusions, no proof at all as to the exact nature of the trauma. In truth, all of those things had been present, but to a degree that the doctor had never before seen. As far as he was concerned, there was no case against Cabiri or anyone else, for that matter.

"To hell with it," said the Inspector, who tossed his cup of coffee into a nearby trash can. He then cursed and reached for a napkin. The coffee that spilled from his cup as he threw it had landed on his new boots. As he bent to clean his boots, the wig line at the back of his crown lifted to reveal a scalp livid with anger.

"I'm retiring in a couple of weeks anyway."

In the parking lot behind the Hall of Justice, Stuart strolled slowly around his beloved Kosher Cruiser, admiring and touching every new dent and defect. There were new growths on the armrests that looked remarkably like truffles, and a fairy ring of fungus had begun spreading out on the carpet in the rear storage area.

"They never left you, did they?" he said to a silent Zeferino. "Your Aunt Juanita was right all along. Your protectors have always been there with you. Always."

"*Mis angeles morenos,*" said Zeferino quietly, thinking of the group of people who had been drawn to Raphael's Silver Cloud and of all the men and women who had spent their youth bending in the fields and their old age dying slowly on the bench down on El Dorado Street. They had all been his parents. He had been standing on so many shoulders.

"*Mis angeles,*" he whispered again. "Let's go up to the jail and tell Teodoro."

Now he remembered all of it, every detail. The retreating headlights of Ted For Short's Pontiac had caused him to feel so lonely and abandoned. He had walked into the Quonset hut, and a strange woman there had given him Blackjack gum and prepared a plate of hot food especially for him. She had made a bed for him and she had even sung a bedtime song to push the overbearing darkness away from them both. It had been a simple Spanish lullaby about guardian angels. The woman that he called Gum could not speak Spanish but had memorized the words as a child.

Zeferino remembered that he could not explain to her what had happened at French Camp, the terrible accusations and the horrible killing and all the men who had run away from it. But the woman had already seen the fear in the boy's face. She had understood and had answered with a song. That same night he had dreamed that something or someone had been sent to save them all . . . Faustino, Teodoro . . . all of them.

That night he had dreamed that angels had flown out to the

fields and had run from furrow to furrow lifting fragile life above the waters. When he awoke the next morning, the sun was shining, the air smelled of coffee and was filled with a woman's humming, and all of his fear and much of his recollection of the horrible incident at French Camp had disappeared. The dream that had seemed so very real had vanished, too.

The guard at the seventh-floor jail brought Teodoro Cabiri to the interview room. There had been loud yelling and applause rising from every cell on both sides of the main line as the guard and the prisoner had strolled the length of the hallway. Somehow, the word that Teodoro's case would be dismissed had already gotten up to the prisoners.

This time there were no *esposas* and no ankle or waist chains, no full body search at the frontier. The little man was smiling broadly as he sat down in the interview room with his lawyer and his investigator. He was wearing the yellow clothing of a trustee. As the guard turned to leave, Teodoro stopped him by tugging at his sleeve. Cabiri then handed the officer a pair of slender aluminum humidors, each containing a single large cigar.

"They're Cuban," grinned Teodoro. "Fidel Castro himself keeps me supplied with them."

The guard smiled broadly, then left for his office. He then broke into loud laughter as he walked and tried to read the paper label on the humidor. He and another deputy had given the little man a thorough full body search that morning and found nothing. The deputy handed one of the humidors to another guard, who immediately bit off the end and lit a match.

"You know, these things are illegal." He smiled as he blew a smoke ring.

"The charges will be dropped tomorrow morning," said Zeferino as he shook his client's extended hand. In an instant the handshake became a hug. "The District Attorney and the Coroner agreed that both the corpus delicti problem and the proximate cause issue were insurmountable."

"Either one would have been enough," added Stuart. "It was that nayfish inspector who kept the charges alive."

"Do you mean to tell me," smiled Teodoro, "that I made all of those confessions for nothing?" He exhaled a long stream of smoke as he spoke. From nowhere a Cuban cigar had appeared

at the edge of his mouth. There was a look of mischief and devil-
try on his face.

"Do you really mean to say, Zeferino, that someone who
can sever the tender shoots from the asparagus crown without
hurting it . . . someone who has gutted a million pink salmon . . .
someone who was once an expert knife thrower, renowned
throughout the entire Eastern empire and the subcontinent for
his stupendous feats of accuracy—and, mind you—someone
who was also a colossal, world-renowned fire-breather with the
fabulous Gonzalez Brothers Circus—do you mean to say that
someone like that could not have sliced that evil Bambino Reyes
open in a flash, then burned him shut?"

Zeferino and Stuart stood staring at each other in awkward silence. Ted For Short's eyes were gleaming with mystery and glee
as he stared at his defense team. From behind his ear he produced another Cuban cigar. He then reached into his left sleeve
and pulled out a fireplace matchstick over a foot in length. It was
clearly longer than Teodoro's sleeve.

"Almost as long as a machete." He laughed a naughty urchin's
laugh. As he struck the match, he held its blazing tip an inch
from his lips. He took a deep breath, then exhaled a two-foot
torch of flame that licked out and lit the cigar. Then he handed
the smoking cigar to his lawyer. The room began to fill with
smoke. Teodoro closed his lips to douse the flames, then offered
a stogie to the investigator. Stuart shook his head. He didn't
smoke on the erev shabbat.

"What if all those years of running finally gave me the power
and the will to make a stand?" asked a smiling Teodoro. "Have
you considered the possibility, Zefe, that Faustino and I saved
you so that you could grow up and become a lawyer and perhaps
save one of us? What if the lights of Raphael's Silver Cloud drew
you and your shayner Yid investigator, just as they drew in all of
the others?

"Do you remember, long ago, that crooked man who came
out to the camps and sold us that plastic sheet to make our black-
and-white TV into a color television?"

Zeferino nodded.

"Do you remember standing on top of the long table and explaining to all the farmworkers that they had been cheated? Do

you remember what you did when he came back to the camp to try to sell the Hindus a color television?"

Zeferino smiled. He had picked up a handful of rocks and run the man out of French Camp, pelting him and his car and his sheets of cheap, multicolored plastic. The man had gone into Stockton and called the police. The police officers who came into French Camp an hour later had not seemed to care that the salesman was a thief.

"On that day," said Ted For Short, "you chose the side of the few against the many. On that day you began your trip to Raphael's Silver Cloud. On that day, over thirty years ago, you became my defense attorney."

Zeferino stared through the haze at his small client. For the first time he could see the advanced age of the man who looked so much like a child. What he saw saddened him. There it was, in his carriage and demeanor, a small, ominous darkness like a spot on an X ray.

"You are a free man," said Zeferino quietly as the three men settled into their chairs. He breathed deeply to clear his mind of the psychic X ray. He would leave such things to the quacks up in Baguio.

"No," answered Ted For Short in a soft and gentle voice, "it is you who are free. I want you to answer one question for me, Zeferino, my boy. Answer one question for your old *manong*; your old *tiyo*. You know how all of your old *tiyos* were very religious men, almost crazy religious?"

Zeferino nodded.

"When you leave your homeland like I did, you leave wondering who you will be in the new country. Everything that I was, was given to me by my Islands. Here in America I was nothing . . . less than nothing. What a surprise it was for me when I found out that people here deny their past. Each person here believes that he has succeeded on his own, without help from anyone. I asked myself, why is this? How is this possible? Everyone knows that even the strongest man rides on his grandmother's back. After years I realized the answer. If you don't share a past or a culture, you don't have to share your labor or your earnings or your future. Here, personal fulfillment has been transformed, *abracadabra*, into private fulfillment!

"An unwillingness to share slowly suffocates any feeling of community. That is why starving people scream and no one hears. That's why schools have no money. That is why America is so cruel to people of color who come with their proud cultures still wrapped around them like a halo.

"People who share will buy less," he said with a slow nod of the head. "Everyone knows that the market has no conscience, Zeferino, but what a shock it is to learn that America's conscience is the market! It is very bad now, with all this anti-immigrant hysteria and those fools who believe that three centuries of lies have been completely cured by three decades of affirmative action.

"But it was worse when your *tiyos* and I first got here. Back then, the newspapers and the radio did not care about us, so we were all tortured in private. All we had to keep us alive, to keep us going, was our religion.

"Here is my question for you, Zeferino Del Campo"—a smile crept across his face—"after all your education, after all this time, after all that you've seen and remembered, do you really believe in angels?"

Raphael Viajero sold the Silver Cloud Café on the very day that Ted For Short was released from jail. After saying good-bye to his friends at the hotel, Raphael walked out to the street, where he tried to buy lunch from the King and Queen of Tamales, but the happy couple would not let him pay for his meal.

"She's in a family way," King Pete had proudly announced. Queenie was smiling coyly by his side. Raphael had never noticed that her eyes were green.

On his way out of town he stopped for a long visit at Faustino's gravesite in Daly City. Then Raphael finally followed his own directions home.

As he drove his truck down Highway 5, he noticed that his terrible power to see death in metal did not follow him as he moved south, and he was glad to be rid of it. *En el futuro*, the power would return to him only when he drove in a direction away from home. He had taken down all of his ceramics and packed them carefully into the truck. He and King had carefully loaded the rebuilt sign of the angels. Though covered with mattresses, his dear friend Uriel played music from the moment the truck crossed the Bay Bridge until he parked in front of his wife's house.

Ocumicho would have music, whether or not it had electricity. And Ocumicho would have one other thing: the body of a true martyr for its small stone church. Raphael had claimed Humberto's body from the morgue and was returning it to Mexico. The old priest's desiccated body was in a child's coffin next to the sign of the angels.

Raphael would open a new bar in his hometown. He would call it *La Nube Plateada de Raphael*. Strange, wonderful things would begin to happen in Ocumicho as soon as the bar opened and the sign was turned on. Vagabonds and lollards and beguines would come into town to dance and dream, and Raphael would never again leave Mexico.

A coy Apollonia and a bashful Jesusita would step shyly from the darkness of their little wooden houses to welcome their family back home. Both women had already dreamed of Humberto's homecoming and had celebrated by building a huge new ceramic altar for the local church. People in nearby Tzintzúntzan, the place of the hummingbirds, were already singing songs about Padre Humberto. "El Artillero de Dios" was the most popular song. The artillery man of God.

The centerpiece of Apollonia y Jesusita's altar was made up of two angels embracing next to a small house atop a silver pillar. There was a blue, ceramic, high-heel shoe at the foot of the altar that would hold most of Humberto's earthly remains after the bones and extremities were claimed by other churches. A huge nail that was driven into one side of the altar would hold the holy crescent wrench and the holy hand mirror.

There would be relics enough for all of the small churches that dotted the countryside near Morelia. Humberto's fingers would rest in Janitzio and his left ankle in Tzintzúntzan. His hip bone would go to Uruápan. His skull would be given to the beautiful cathedral in Morelia where lovely cavatinas would forever echo through his ear holes and into the cavity where his thoughts once resonated.

Humberto's oversized, hollow clavicle would be placed in the same dry alcove where his brother's bones had been laid to rest long before. The two brothers' bleached bones would lie together in a box lined with soft silk where they would embrace forever.

Each year, at the anniversary of Humberto's first death, a strange old woman would place woven black flowers and a votive candle next to his dried clavicle and the bones of his saintly brother. When the latest petition for the commencement of canonization was sent to Rome bearing the name of Miguel Augustine, hers would be the first signature at the top of the first page. Beneath her mourning clothes and a black veil that was wholly impermeable to disbelief, she would wear eye makeup and there would be bright blue flats adorning her once lovely feet.

Beside Raphael in the front seat of the truck was Miguel Govea with his beautiful accordion. There was a serene smile of gratitude on his face as he played along with Uriel. What man on earth was as lucky as he? Who on earth had been given the privilege to put right such a terrible wrong? Over sixty years ago, as a callow boy, he had fired a bullet, then followed it on its path toward Humberto's body. He had arrived as an old man just before the bullet struck, and he had been granted forgiveness by a living breath that should never have been breathed. What man on earth was as lucky as he?

As Raphael and Miguel were passing through Bakersfield, Zeferino drove up to Bernal Hill and parked his car next to the little Isetta. In the light of day he noticed that the roof of the house was covered with hundreds of bickering, gossiping birds. He walked up to the front door and knocked. It was Ruby who answered the door and ushered him into the little house. She was dressed in white traveling clothes, and there were two suitcases standing in the hallway behind her.

"*Buenos dias*, Zefe," she said with a wide smile. She then gave in to an inner need and threw her arms around Zeferino. "Come in, sit down," she said after kissing his cheek.

Zeferino sat down next to the kitchen table. He looked around himself at the most amazing home that he had ever seen. It was a virtual museum of entertainment equipment and paraphernalia. There were gowns and dresses everywhere. There was an entire wall covered with circus posters and handbills. There were photographs of Radiant Ruby doing her act in lounges from Atlantic City to Portland.

There were faded photos of old men whom Zeferino had not seen in many, many years. There were all of his uncles, young and handsome and hopeful, all crowded together at a barbecue somewhere in the Imperial Valley. In the corner, by the couch, was a straitjacket covered with huge padlocks. Above it, hanging on a leather thong, was an old asparagus knife.

"Teodoro is putting on his outfit," said Ruby. "He calls it his world traveler suit." At that moment Ted For Short jumped into the room with arms spread and a shiny black cane in his left hand. He was dressed in a white suit and white, woven shoes. There was a lavender kerchief folded into his breast pocket, and he was wearing Faustino's cufflinks from the railroad. On his head was his top-dollar wig.

"What do you think, Zefe? The shoes are Puerto Rican. I think you wear these during hurricanes. I wanted just a hint of tawdriness, a touch of the shabby, that certain *je ne sais quoi* that all the girls just love." He winked at his wife, who laughed knowingly.

"You're due at the airport in thirty minutes," said a concerned Zeferino, who seemed entranced by Ted For Short's appearance. Once again, the old man looked immortal—like a child.

"We have to leave now."

Teodoro stepped forward and asked Zeferino to bend down. The taller man complied and the little man reached behind Zeferino's ear, then with a flourish presented a set of keys to his lawyer.

"On the refrigerator there's a note with everything you need to know. There's nothing to it, really. Just feed the cats. We have cases of cat food, but Buster and Snowball will eat anything. They prefer table scraps."

"Scraps?" laughed Ruby.

"Well, they eat what we eat," admitted Ted For Short. "They'll eat albacore and you can defrost a strip steak for them. Throw a five-pound bag of birdseed up on the roof every morning when you leave. Eat everything and anything, Zeferino, and don't worry about the dishes. But make sure you go through every drawer and trunk in the house . . . every one."

Zeferino laughed at the suggestion, but Ted For Short was insistent.

"Go through everything, all of my things and Ruby's." Ruby by his side nodded her firm agreement. "Go through the medicine cabinet. Look at every photograph and touch every memento and piece of clothing. Read every ledger and diary. Open all the trunks and rummage around. Drive my little car, too. The ignition key is on the ring. But watch out"—he winked—"the women just love that car. Soon"—he looked at his dear wife—"all of these things—everything here will be yours. Now, it's your turn, Zefe." He tapped his temple with his index finger, indicating that horizon where memories are stored. "You will keep us alive. Now, you will be our protector."

In accordance with Teodoro Cabiri's lifelong dream, the new husband and wife would fly to New York City and from there on to Rome. They would have their honeymoon in beautiful Venice. They would exit Santa Lucia train station through the huge front door that looked down upon the Grand Canal. They would turn left and walk, arm in arm, into the Cannaregio district, past Calle Carmelitani and Calle Cavalleti to the Lista di Spagna.

With the ancient street map of Venice in his trembling hands, Teodoro would lead Radiant Ruby straight to 148 Lista di Spagna, just a half block from Misericordia. The two lovers would pause solemnly at the entrance of a restaurant. Teodoro would pull out his precious yellowed photograph and compare it to the sign hanging above the doorway. His eyes would fill with exuberant tears.

Ted For Short would be royally welcomed into the Ristorante De Trei Gobbi as a long-lost brother. Radiant Ruby would shoot two rolls of pictures of Ted For Short standing beneath the original sign of the Three Hunchbacks. For a full week he would wait on tables and bus dishes at the restaurant he had dreamed of as a child.

Wearing a special, tiny apron, he would seat his dear wife at a checkered table in the piazza; then, with a white towel draped over his arm, he would serve her *saltimbocca* and *insalata di pomadoro* as she smiled beneath a blue umbrella that was covered with cooing white doves. At midnight they would toast dearest Faustino and dance in the piazza as a local string band played "The Sojourners' Waltz."

Eventually their little house near Bernal Hill would clutter even more with small items and keepsakes that would become weighted down with sentimentality and immovable with age. All of Faustino's precious possessions had been brought to the house, including dog-eared volumes of Constantine's poetry; Constantine himself would lounge about lazily in his white suits and brass spectacles, drinking retsina and composing poems that had been written and finished long, long ago.

The Greek poet would fill whole summer evenings with rambling talk of Alexandria and London and of his recent visits with Faustino in Paris. As Zeferino listened and a sleepy Teodoro lay nestled between Ruby's feathered breasts, he would describe every detail of Faustino's room in the Armenian hotel.

Ted For Short and Radiant Ruby would spend their final years above the soil saying words into the earth, planting syllables in the dust against the advent of a silent grave. Hand in hand and digging in the garden for the soft bones of gladiolus, the lovers would face old age together and finally conquer it.

With each new illness and each fluttering fibrillation of the chest, Teodoro would don his wig and sequins and step regally into the center ring. As loud as a ringmaster, he would introduce death as a good friend, as an old, well-rehearsed act that was always staged in front of a new audience.

On mumbling days when he would go halting and insensible, she would anxiously peer into his long ear for a cryptic message from down deep within. Like novice tightrope walkers nervously stalking balance beneath the big top, they would prop each other up when the dizzying spins of senility came stumbling around. In time, each would surrender fully to the other and their two enchanted hearts would dovetail perfectly.

Slowly they would have a sublime meeting of the minds and resolve to go gently mad. For both lovers knew that only the amorous insane can safely behold *la cara de Dios,* the face of God.

Beneath the tender and hallowed care of heavenly wings of feathered air, their cluttered and spliced souls would sigh harmoniously. In ever-dimming light, they would hug and babble endlessly of romance . . . and always of romance . . . and of a place where it was legal for brown men to dance.